The Hunter, the D

House by the Shore

Peter Groom

For the Family

Introduction.

The Mesolithic (Middle Stone Age), is an archaeological period between the Upper Palaeolithic (Old Stone Age) and the Neolithic (New Stone Age). Though dates are not definitive, the British Mesolithic is divided into Early and Late periods. The Early Mesolithic dates from about 11500 to 9500 years ago and the Late Mesolithic from about 9500 to 6300 years ago. Though the evidence for Mesolithic hunter/fisher/gatherers in the British Isles and Ireland is reasonably widespread, there is not a lot of it. Yet archaeologists have discovered such varied items as house structures, fish traps, flint tools, some human remains and cord. What archaeological artefacts we have demonstrate that Mesolithic people were highly specialised, with a range of skills that most people today have unfortunately lost. The end of the Ice Age was a time of major environmental change and with the melting of the ice sheets came the re-colonisation of large parts of the British landscape by a range of flora and fauna, including humans. Over time, the extensive wetlands, grassy scrub and heathlands would have become mature woodland, while in parts of the country extensive wetlands would have remained.

We know that throughout the Mesolithic sea levels rose, at times quite dramatically, causing tidal surges and coastal inundation. We also know that large animals such as aurochs, elk, wolf, wild boar, wild horses and bear, together with beaver and lynx shared this changing landscape with our Mesolithic ancestors. However, we are less sure about the day-to-day activities, the interactions, the social life, and the communities that existed. How did they make fire? How did they hunt? How did they fish? How did they understand the world around them? This book goes some way toward taking those few strands from the archaeological record and weaving them into a story, a story of a people and in particular of one man, living in a changing landscape where the people were a part of nature, rather than apart from nature.

Part One. The journey to the coast.

Chapter 1.

Silence… breathing slowly through my open mouth, I tried to control my breathing to slow it down, I was quite breathless from the effort of crawling softly and quietly so close; I was kneeling only some seven paces away. Now I was here I needed to shift my position from flat on the ground to upright, to get a clearer view. I moved my left leg and brought it slowly forward until my left foot was flat to the ground, then gently pushed myself up and lifted my chest, starting to bring my right leg forward so that I could kneel on it. I had lifted myself from the leaves and was now in position, kneeling on my right knee and shin, left foot to the floor, abdomen resting against my left thigh. Simultaneously three things happened. One, a damaged tendon in my right leg the result of too much kneeling on hard ground, made a loud crack. Two, the roebuck heard this and looked up. Three, the arrow struck home.

It was not a clean shot and the buck barked and ran into the blackthorn thicket, I admit that I cursed. Standing, I gathered my kit together and jogged after it. It was easy enough to follow the tracks and I noted the fresh droppings where the scared animal had crapped itself as it had paused for a second to decide which way to run. I paused at the shit pile myself, to gather some of the shit and to gather my thoughts, then heard it crashing through the scrub ahead to my left and noticed a blood splatter on the ground. I figured that it would not get far; the arrow must have wiggled into an artery as the animal had run off. That was the beauty of these multiple bladed arrows, they were easy to make and the combined cutting power that the small blades gave as they rocked up and down, sawing their way in to the animal, made them lethal as the animal ran. After some time spent scrambling through the thicket, I saw the buck lying on the ground; the arrow was sticking out of his neck, blood was pouring out of his mouth. It was in a lot of pain and was clearly terrified, panting, his tongue out, brown eyes rolling wildly. I could see that he wasn't going to run anymore so another arrow wasn't needed.

Diving onto his flanks, I pinned him to the ground clamping his mouth and nostrils shut while avoiding his small but sharp antlers. He fought strongly, but so did I, clinging on as hard as I could; as I held his mouth and nose shut he jerked in spasms, choking on his own blood, breath steaming from his mouth because of the chill of the morning, hot blood sneezing from his nose through my fingers and onto my face. In his eyes, I could see first the pain of the injury and the terror of what was happening to him give way to the realisation of what was about to come. He was panicking and as the light began to fade in his eyes, I sensed his understanding of his loss from the world and the loss of those experiences with which he had become familiar. Indeed, with which we were both familiar; the quietness of the green wood's in which he lived, the warmth of the sun on his soft back, the cool of the rain on his head, the pleasure of grazing in a sun bathed dew kissed glade of an early morning such as this. He fixed me with his eyes; I was the animal that was taking all those things away from him and I was going to be the last thing that he ever saw in his young life. There was no need for me to scare him anymore than I already had done, he gave in to me and in respect to him, I stroked his head, gently releasing my grip on his mouth and nose so that his last moments in the world were more of a shared experience, rather than me just throttling him to death.

The death of another animal was not something that could be taken lightly, my tribe firmly believed that it was always important that the hunter showed great respect to any animal that had died and given up its soul so that the hunter could live. I had lived by this guide all of my life and believed it to be wise and true. Softening my eyes and mouth as much as I could, my features were now as friendly as I could make them given the situation; I held his head… stroking it gently… easing his painful passing... until he could see nothing at all.

When I was sure that he was dead, I drew in a long deep breath then kicked back from his body and kneeled, head down, eyes shut. My right hand felt for the rawhide cord that was around my neck, drawing it up from beneath my buckskin shirt to reveal the antler deer head that I had carved when I was young, the totemic emblem of my tribe. I kissed it and thanked the dead animal in front of me for giving his life so that I might live. Now that I could get a closer look, I could see that it had been a lousy shot. I had been aiming for a lung shot because he had been facing me, the arrow was supposed to have hit him at the base of his long neck to penetrate the lungs and deflate them, he would find it difficult to run with collapsed lungs. Anyway, he was dead now and I could eat. Taking out a finger long blade of black chert I made an incision just on the belly, cutting his skin up toward his neck, I wanted to make sure that I had food for several days, so I needed everything. I started to remove the skin first, deciding to let the body cavity cool before I cut into it. I used the flat of the blade in my right hand while my left hand teased and peeled the skin away from the body membrane in one piece. I slowly rolled the carcass from left to right as I worked round the arse, legs and neck to make the skinning process easier and make sure that I didn't burst the body membrane yet. I had plenty of time before dark so there was no need to rush. Once the skin was cut away from the body, I placed it to one side and focussed on the meat. First, I needed to get the guts out; I punctured the body membrane over the lower gut cavity with another blade and, slicing up toward his chest, made as neat a cut as I could so that I could see all of his organs. I wasn't interested in the heart, some people are but I find it too fatty and it greases up my mouth which I don't like. Cutting through his windpipe and gullet, I folded my arms together inside his body and embraced everything so that I could draw it all out of the gut cavity and onto the floor behind me, a big pile of guts and organs. I kept the liver, I like liver, and I kept the kidneys as well but nothing else of the innards. Scrambling around on the floor I found a patch of moss, I took several handfuls and mopped out the gut cavity until it was fairly clean, there was no water nearby so this would have to do. It being summer I didn't want the meat to get fly blown so wherever possible I cleaned up. Several careful final cuts removed the bladder, so that now in front of me was a roe deer without its skin and without most of its vital organs; I thought about cutting off the lower legs to lighten the load but figured that they would be useful later on. Deciding that tonight I would just eat the kidneys and liver and that I would take the rest of the carcass with me, I folded the carcass up on itself. I pushed the arse end into the gut cavity as tight as I could and wrapped it up in its skin, tying the leg ends of skin together to make a neat bundle. With that done, I looked about me to try to work out where I was. I had followed the roe into this thicket; and I had lost my bearings. Backtracking, by following the deer tracks and blood that I had followed in, took me to the place where I had kneeled to take the shot. From here, I could see where I had crawled through the grass, it had taken a long time to crawl that distance to where the roe was grazing, but walking it took only 40 paces. I arrived at the tree. It was my habit that whenever I was hunting, the moment I spotted an animal to kill I would mark the nearest tree by sticking three long white swan feathers in the ground, equally spaced. This showed me where I had left the trail when I followed the animal. After the kill, I would mark the tree itself by breaking off three branches at eye level and sticking them in the ground evenly spaced in front of the tree, I would bind the tops together so it looked like a small tepee frame. At a future time, these branches sticking out of the ground would remind me that this was a decent hunting area the next time I came out here along this trail; but that would be some time ahead of me. There was no need to kill everything in an area; the idea was to take enough then move on. In this way there was always enough to go round, also we viewed it that everything had work to do, whether plant or animal, it had work to do. The grass fed the deer and the aurochs, the deer and aurochs fed us or the wolves, the swallows and bats ate the flies that plagued us in the summer. Jays planted the acorns that would grow into the oaks that would provide us with acorns as food or bark for tanning hides. Even the ants that wandered past me now had the task; it seemed, of tidying up the woodland floor, busily carrying items of food back to their nest and ridding the nest of any rubbish. Everything around us had a task, everything was linked to everything else and everything was equally important, nothing was more important than any other thing. We knew this and we respected this for this was the way that the Great Spirit had made things. We were all together, all things, together, all living things carrying life forward together, until we died and returned to the earth, for all our bodies, plants or animals, to be used again by the yet to be born. In this way our spirit moved from one body to another, from one plant to another, from one animal to another, forever, we knew this to be true, because we saw it, everyday.

Having now backtracked from the kill site to the original spot site as shown by the feathers, I knew that this was where I had wandered in. The swan feathers went back into my quiver, I broke off three branches and placed them in front of the tree and it now only took moments for me to locate my original tracks and set off back to my shelter. This was a temporary shelter; I used it now and again when I was passing this way. I often made a journey through the large marshes and meres of the Great Plain to this long sandstone ridge, once a year anyway, though this year I had a feeling that I may be a bit early. There had been four full moons since the long winter had ended, but out here on this ridge I wasn't sure whether it was mid or late summer and the weather wasn't helping, rain and cold one day, roasting the next. I fancied a trip to the mouth of the Great North River where the salmon would be collecting before they pushed up the rivers of the Great Plain. Though normally the salmon didn't run till the 5th or 6th full moon of the year after winter, anyway it was better to get there early and sit it out rather than miss the fishing; I had never fished for salmon in the Great North River and I didn't know what to expect.

My temporary home here was a simple rockshelter, a sandstone overhang on a long ridge that stood out on the Great Plain. It wasn't perfect and the water did run down through the sandstone at times, but it was fine for lying up for a few days and there was a good stream near to it which was always a bonus. When I was out on my own, I often took time to repair gear, collect resources, make up some medicine and let injuries heal, or simply relax. On your own you had to look after yourself, no one else would. There was still plenty of light left today and it was warm, but I needed to get a fire going, as I wanted to cook the liver and kidneys and melt some pine resin. I didn't need a fire for protection, there were no bears or wolves in these hills, these hills were not big enough and were surrounded by the marshland of the Great Plain. Over to the west, where the hills became much bigger and the valleys more wooded were bears and wolves and over to the east, my lands, there were a few wolves and a few bears but the bears seemed to stay up in the hills.

From within the cool still air of the shelter I took my fire kit, a bow drill set; the bow was hazel, the cord was a plaited rawhide cord, the hearth board and drill were willow and the bearing block was holly. A crushed holly leaf pushed into the recess to provide some lubrication for the top of the drill. Placing the ball of my left foot on the hearth board I twisted the drill into the cord and placed the flat end of the drill into the black hole in the hearth; finally I trapped the pointed end of the drill in the bearing block so it could not escape. I began to work the bow back and forward, the drill spinning, first one way then the other, a nice steady rhythm. Smoke soon started to rise from the hole in the hearth board, but also from the bearing block, a sign that the drill was wearing out and it would soon be time to make another, but I persisted. I had re-pointed the end of the drill that sat in the bearing block so many times that the drill was now quite short and stubby, but it was a great set and it worked every time so I favoured this one. The hearth itself had five notches and drill holes but there was room for another three or so, so it should last longer than the drill. As for the cord, I always had spare cord, whenever I had the time I made cord, I always needed cord.

Soon the hot black wood dust had formed a neat pile in the notch, it smouldered as the breeze caught it and I laid down the drill set and took a breather. Carefully removing the hearth so it didn't break up the hot pile of dust I let it sit on the piece of pine bark that I had lying beneath the hearth board, then transferred the now solid smouldering dust into a small tight bundle of tinder. A dry mouse nest and some small very thin strips of birch bark that I had placed into a small tube of birch bark, blowing gently at first the smouldering pile glowed brighter until it started to burn. The strips of birch bark started to curl in the heat and began to spit and produce that unmistakeable acrid smell. After a moment, the heat got so great that the tinder bundle set alight and I was thankful for the protection that the bark tube provided to my hands. I had already prepared the base of the fire; dry finger-thick sticks a forearm long lay parallel to each other, then thin sticks on top of these, interwoven like a bird nest. It was into this that I placed the tinder bundle, the breeze did the rest and I sat back and enjoyed the heat. Placing some bigger sticks on top I let the fire get going and sorted out my bed. I started by removing the dry bracken and placing it to one side, some of the thin pine branches had moved during the night, exposing a sharp stone that I hadn't noticed yesterday when I got to the shelter. I trotted across the slope and spent a while gathering some more soft green pine branches, plenty to make it comfy, I needed a good night's sleep. After last night's uncomfortable sleep and the hunt today, I was tired out so I needed to make this as comfortable as possible. Confident that I had enough material to make a deep bed I wandered back to the shelter. In an oak tree a squirrel chattered away at me, wafting its bushy red tail from side to side, I laughed at its bravery, so small yet so angry that I was nearby, "I will be away from here tomorrow little red man and then the trees are all yours".

Back at the rockshelter, I increased the size of the fire by placing six lengths of wood as long and as wide as my arm, so that their ends pointed into the fire in a pattern that resembled a snowflake that I had once seen, only for a moment. This type of fire allowed me to build up a good hot ash deposit in the middle, give me some heat and light, and I could manage the size of the fire by either pushing the logs into the fire or pulling them out. That done I returned to making the bed. I laid down the extra pine branches so that the stone was covered, I couldn't dig it out, it was too deep set, and with the shelter being so small I had little option of moving to either side of it and it was only for one more night after all. On top of the thin pine branches, I replaced the dry bracken, a nice mat of it. It looked so comfortable I could have lain down right there and then. The wind shifted, blowing smoke into the shelter, I coughed, I wasn't a fan of smoke and it hurt my eyes. My brother back at our camp smoked; mind you, most of my brothers smoked and so did some of my sisters. I did not join them in this activity and I would normally leave the house when they lit up, leaving them to it. With my fire done and bed made, all I needed now was food. With the weather set fair, I intended to travel tomorrow, so a good meal was needed. Taking my water bladder, a blade of chert and a small buckskin pouch I went foraging. I didn't need to travel far, that is why I had chosen this rockshelter in the first place. A few paces away were wood bittercress and hedge garlic so I collected a few leaves and put them in my pouch, which I tied on to my belt with one of the several rawhide thongs that hung from it. I wandered down to a clearing where red deer and aurochs often grazed. All their piss and shit had caused nettles to grow, so I broke off a couple of stems and with this range of greens walked down to the stream to fill my water bladder. At the stream, I used my thumbnails to strip some nice flat flexible lengths of bark from a young willow that had many branches and coiled them up then set about filling the bladder. I had become aware that this trusty water bladder was starting to lose water, particularly when I was moving, that is why I had taken the roe bladder just in case. I undid the willow bast cord from the mouth of the bladder and dipped it into the stream. Squeezing out any remaining water, I rinsed it out a couple of times to get rid of the rancid taste of the water. No matter how many times I washed it this old bladder always gave the water a bit of a piss taste, it was from a big red deer stag, so I guess it still had his scent. Part of me hoped that with each mouthful of water I would be taking in the strength of that stag, but in reality, I was probably just taking in bits of his piss. I filled it and sure enough, it immediately started to leak, nevertheless I took it back to the rockshelter. Settling down to eat as the sun started to drop, I first ate the greens; the bittercress and hedge garlic I ate raw, the nettles I waved back and forth through the smoke and heat of the fire till the leaves had wilted, this got rid of the stings and made them more edible. I had a flat stone slab near to the centre of the fire, which I had positioned between two of the logs so that it sat in the ashes. Spitting on it caused the rock to sizzle so I knew it would be hot enough to cook the liver and kidneys. I placed them on it and watched them flinch as though alive as they recoiled from the heat. The smell was immediate and delicious, turning them over with a small stick, I watched the blood run away onto the ashes, hissing and steaming. What would go well with this would be a black headed gull's egg, but eggs were now out of season unless you could find a woodpigeon, which seemed to nest all year round. I looked forward to egg season, spring and early summer, I would eat so many eggs during that time that I nearly made myself sick. As kids, we used to run around the place looking for the first eggs, trying to be the one who got the most. Of course, you had to be careful that you didn't rob all the eggs in the nests or there would be no birds and eggs next year. Not wanting to overdo them, the first smell of the cooking meat meant that they were done, I ate the liver and kidneys quickly, I was hungry and they tasted wonderful. Unfortunately the bladder was leaking at a fair old rate, so I drank all of the water from it deciding that it was better that it was in my bladder rather than letting it run out of this leaky one onto the ground, then having to go to the stream again. It still tasted of piss.

The light was beginning to fade so I pushed the logs into the centre of the fire and placed some small sticks on top to increase the amount of flame, I could work by this light.

Starting with the willow, I used my thumbnails to peel the soft outer bark away from the inner bast. It was these inner bast fibres that I wanted, they separated easily and I discarded the outer bark. As I did this, the soft outer bark collected under my thumbnails, if I didn't clean them out this would make my thumbnails throb later. I then split the bast lengthways into strips that were half as wide as my little finger, I now had lengths of bast that were thin enough yet strong enough to make some cord. By twisting and plying at the same time, I turned two of the thin lengths of bast into strong two-ply cord as long as my arm. It was a task I could do with my eyes shut, even so, I worked as quickly as possible before it got dark. The only trouble with this repetitive twisting action was that it caused the tendon in my right elbow to hurt, so when I had finished I flexed my arm, extending the fingers several times trying to ease it. Not having time to go to the stream to wash the new roe bladder I worked it dirty, needless to say, it stunk of piss. Never mind, I had eaten and if my hands got dirty now so be it. From another buckskin pouch on my belt I took out some of the pine resin I had collected last night, when I had first gathered the pine branches. I didn't need much for this task it was a bit of a makeshift job, I just wanted to seal it and I could sort it out properly when I was stationary for a while. There was no shortage of water in this low-lying landscape and I would be travelling along the riverbank for some of the way, but you never knew what was around the corner so it was always wise to carry some water. I blew into the roe bladder to shift the piss that was still inside and then looked for the biggest tube, which would be my mouthpiece. The other two tubes needed to be tied off with the new willow cord, so that they were totally closed. I did this though it was a fiddly slippery job, but this is where the resin came in, I had been warming it on the rock that I had used to cook the meat and it was now almost runny. To this I added a couple of pellets of the roe buck shit that I had collected earlier and a bit of charcoal from the fire, mixing them together till it was pliable. I then used a small stick to daub the mix over the cord and all round the two tied off tubes and pinched it between my right thumb and forefinger, the pine resin sticking to both. Rolling the remaining glue into a little ball, I let it cool and become stiff before placing it into my kit pouch, which already contained some spare deer sinew. When you were on the move as much as I was you always carried several pouches and made sure that they were topped up regularly with things that you might need, important things such as dry tinder, cord, spare bowstring, flint or chert blades, sinew and so on. With luck the glue would set overnight and hold the willow cord tight on the tubes and in the morning I would have a new water container. But I must remember to wash the thing well; I was getting a bit fed up of the taste of piss. The last thing to do before I turned in was to clean out the sludge of willow bark that was under my thumbnails, you should always look after your tools.

Settling back, I rolled my shoulders to ease the tension and aches. Down to my right, I watched the long stems of grasses begin to glow, a light green-yellow glow as the glow-worms began their night-time display.

I had slept well, very well in fact, but now I needed a crap and it was pouring down, last night I was convinced that the weather was set fair, but this summer it seemed all over the place. Mind, I often thought about how our time must be better than the time of ice, some of the elders told stories of ancient times when everything was icy and not many people lived here. I didn't know how long ago that was, but the stories were ancient and it was a tradition that each generation had to remember them and recite them… for some reason. Personally speaking, sitting in a smoke filled house listening to some old bloke witter on about ice was not for me, which in part explained why I spent so much time on my own. It's not that I didn't respect the elders, I did, who wouldn't? After all, they held all of the old skills in their hands and all of the old knowledge in their heads. It's just that after a while it gets repetitive, *'And the ice wall was as high as a man could see, and the animals that lived here were big and hairy, and it was freezing'* and so on, quite boring really. But then I suppose they did it so that we didn't forget who we were as a people, didn't forget where we came from, and made sure that we recognised that we were part of the land. Made us remember that the land and our tribe had emerged together from the time of the ice and that the land and our tribe had put those times behind us and together we had filled that empty, cold, time of ice, with life.

Looking for a good place to squat, I saw it under a big holly next to a blackthorn bush; it seemed as good as anywhere and at least I would have some cover from the rain. Leaving my trousers in the shelter; I didn't want to be wriggling out of them while it was chucking it down, I put on my boots, grabbed the moss that I had collected yesterday and legged it to the bush. Crashing through the thin branches to the centre, it was nice and dry under the holly so I stooped down, though not too low, in case I caught my arse on the brown leaves that had fallen last year. Lifting my shirt, I had a crap, checking my droppings for evidence of tapeworm. I couldn't see any, so the bracken root tea must have worked; I felt better knowing that I was worm free for a change. All of a sudden, I went crashing forwards to the ground my left hand reaching out to stop my fall, as a big ball of brown belted past me. The boar had come smashing through the holly not expecting to find a man with a bare arse having a shit, I was on my feet ready to escape, but the boar had buggered off down the hill and into the thicker woodland. I looked around for my moss which was scattered everywhere amongst the holly leaves; I didn't fancy wiping my arse on it now, what with the chance of a holly leaf in there so I decided to combine tasks. Going back up to the shelter and quickly grabbing the new water bladder, I legged it to the stream. The web of my left hand was sore and I noticed that I had a thorn in it probably from the blackthorn bush, perhaps from when I reached out as the boar rushed past me. At the stream I washed out the bladder, repeatedly filling it and squeezing it empty until I was satisfied that it was as good as it ever would be. That done I hitched up my shirt, gathered up a handful of damp moss from the stream edge and gave my arse a wipe.

The rain was easing as I got back to the shelter and it had saved me a job by putting the fire out, I took off my boots and put on my trousers and waist belt. My quiver was attached to a thin loop of rawhide that went under my left arm and over my head onto my right shoulder, then back down to the quiver. In this way, the quiver was at my waist on my left with the open end by my belly button facing to the right. As a right-handed hunter this set up suited me better. After attaching my pouches to my waist belt by tying their drawstrings around it, I put my boots back on. Placing my fire kit into a piece of buckskin I wrapped it carefully then put it into the biggest pouch. The fire bow had gone into my quiver, carefully so not to damage the arrow heads on the arrows that were already in there, and that was me. The last thing to do was to look around to check that I hadn't left anything, I had, my stone kit; this comprised roe antler, some small pieces of chert and quartz and two small stones that I used as hammers when I was making stone tools. All packed in dry grass so they didn't rattle when I was hunting and all held together in a reddish buckskin pouch, which was the same colour as the dry bracken. No wonder that I nearly left it. I wriggled to make sure that everything was secure and tight and with that picked up my deer bundle in my right hand and my bow in my left. In this way, should I need to quickly let off an arrow or two I could drop the deer from my right hand, reach into my quiver and as my right hand delivered the arrow to the bowstring the bow would already be in firing position.

I had a good journey, it had stopped raining shortly after I had left the rockshelter and I didn't need to shoot at anything that was big and scary, but the rain had made this wet landscape even wetter. I wasn't a fan of wet land, yes it was full of food and resources but it was also full of biting insects and it was wet. I had managed to stay above most of the wet land by following the line of the ridge which pointed north across the flat marshland of the Great Plain, across and on to the next ridge which I was now on. In the really wet areas I had stripped some larger pieces of bark from a willow tree and lashed them using cord from the willow bast to the soles of my boots as a bit of protection against the tough reed stems and water. The one low point had been where I had crossed a small river, I had stripped off and begun to wade across but found it was muddy and I could have got stuck. I had to cut a load of reed, which blunted two of my blades and sliced my right forefinger in a few places, the reed was so tough and I had to be careful or it would have cut my fingers to shreds. In the end I had bunched the reed together tying it with some willow bark lashings and made myself a small raft, onto this I placed my kit, a bit at a time and swam across like a frog, carefully pushing the raft in front of me with my left hand. It took a few crossings to get everything over but it was worth the effort to keep my kit dry, apart from the bloody great leech that stuck itself to my leg. Fortunately, it was sunny and warm so I sat on the bank watching the dragonflies and dried myself off. Other small rivers were easily crossed by hopping over a beaver dam or fording across the shallow water where old beaver dams had collapsed. The second sandstone ridge that I was now on was similar to the first, with lots of little rockshelters, good mixed woodland, plenty of streams for water. A sudden heavy rain shower forced me to hide beneath a group of hazel trees. Sitting beneath the dense cover of leaves the rain drummed on them, playing a tune that my mind started to follow. Clumps of wet moss clung to the rocks, trunks and branches, stems so thick with lichen that I could no longer see the bark. Wood sorrel and wood rush carpeted the floor, gnats danced over a water filled deer wallow, damp, humid, no breeze, a few tiny moths fluttering from branch to branch, otherwise calm, serene silence.

I had been walking for some time and though my feet were a bit sore from the constant wetting and rubbing I felt pretty good. I had thought about going barefoot as I walked, but one slice from those reed or sedge stems and it might become infected and I still had at least three days walk.

On my way across the wet land, I had spotted some birch trees that had tinder fungus growing on them. Two types, one that was black and hard that looked a bit like the hoof of the wild horses that I had once seen in the dry grassland far to the south of my lands when I was a child. The other looked like a great brown/black cinder, which had a yellowish base when I got it from the tree. I had a job removing the cinder one and ended up twatting it with a big stone, which broke the fungus in half. I knew that both were excellent for tinder and though I wouldn't use them now, I might need them later. I was also very pleased that the new water bladder had worked, but I hadn't yet got rid of the old one, I was hoping to mend it later. Drinking the last of my water I filled both bladders from a clear stream and wandered off to find the rockshelter. I hadn't been to this place this year so I was hoping that the sign I had left was still where I had left it the last time that I had come this way. It took me a while to find but there it was a big cherry tree with a round piece of bark removed at eye level, I knew that about fifty paces up the slope from here was the rockshelter. When I got there I was surprised to see that someone else had been here, there was already a bed made up, they had left dry sticks in the shelter, tinder fungus and a little basket made from rushes. There was nothing in the

16

basket, but I wondered if whoever it was who had used it might be back soon. I was unsure whether to stay, but I would only be here for one night and there was no evidence that they had been here last night, no fire and no ashes. Deciding to stay, I got a fire going and opened up the deer bundle, it was still alright but I needed to eat a lot or smoke it soon, otherwise it would go off. I decided to eat as much as I could manage then smoke the rest. Using a blade, I sat and cut thin strips from the meat of the deer until none was left. It took some time and when I was done, I stuck them on a pointed stick, which I held over the smoke and flames until it was cooked, it tasted great. I cooked it all in this way and ate as much as I physically could, packing the rest of the cooked meat tightly together before placing it back into the deer skin. Then I cut off the lower legs below the knees and hacked away at the base of the small antlers with a chert blade, resorting to a stone to bash them from the skull. I thought about taking the eyes and brain but decided against it, but I did take the length of tendon from the back of the neck. Throwing the rest of the body, which was just the bones, part of the neck and head, away from my shelter down the slope some 50 paces away, I returned to the fire. I made up the fire so that it would keep me warm then lay back in the flickering light of the shelter, burping and farting and listening to the badgers scrapping over the deer. I thought about my travels so far and the path that I had taken to get here today, by doing this it seemed to reinforce the things that I had done, seen or achieved, it made the landscape clearer in my mind, and it helped me to get to sleep that much easier.

This day dawned cool and clear and though there were a few high white clouds I could tell that it was going to get very hot. I set light to the base of the horse hoof fungus just enough for it to smoulder, then wrapped this in dock leaves and then burdock leaves before placing it in my spare pouch. I then collected some dry sticks to replace the ones that I had used and placed some of my tinder fungus in the rush basket, just to show my appreciation to whomever had been here before me, it was good manners. After making up the bed for them, I gathered my things and set off north along the dry sandstone ridge. It was dense woodland all along this ridge and it was often difficult to find a way through. Keeping my eye on the sun, on the occasions that I could see it through the dense canopy, I pressed on, making the most of any streams or springs that I could find rather than using my bladders, just in case I didn't make my next shelter. Finding an elk track I followed this for a way until it went down the slope to the east; I left it at that point and stayed on top of the ridge which was now getting wider and less defined. I slogged on for ages, it was roasting and I had to make frequent stops for water, flies pestered me all day.

The sun was still fairly high but I thought that I should have arrived at the shelter by now, so I was beginning to doubt my direction finding skills. It was time for a decision. The shelter might only be a short walk from here, but as I hadn't been this way since last year I had forgotten the pattern of the trees, so it might take a while to find it. Deciding to stay put, I would get a temporary shelter built, then eat, drink, sleep and set off at sunrise. A big old pine tree had fallen over and its shallow flat root plate was upright, intact and full of dry soil, the tree was solid and heavy so it was staying where it had fallen. I laid my gear down on the root side of the upright plate; this would be my rear wall, collecting as many branches from the floor as I could I propped them against the circular plate until I had a frame that protected me from both sides and above. On this frame I stacked lots of green bracken, built up in layers until it was a tight thatch with a gap for the door that was just wide enough to crawl through. For the floor I used loose twigs and more bracken, it was simple, quick and cosy. I was pleased that this morning I had planned for a possible makeshift shelter, glad that I had had the foresight to do this I now removed the still smouldering fungus from its wrapping of leaves and gently blew on it. After a short while the fungus started to glow and get hot, using the rest of the mouse nest that I was carrying as the tinder bundle, I quickly had a little fire going just outside the shelter.

The web of my left hand was still causing me a problem; in the light of the fire I could see that the thorn was still in there and the wound had started to go septic. Of all the thorn bushes that I regularly caught myself on blackthorn seemed to be the worst and this was no exception. The wound was sore, pink and was swelling; I needed to get the thorn out before it got any worse. I had what I needed with me; taking a lower leg bone from the deer, I smashed it several times between two stones that were lying under the tree roots, when I had made several small sharp splinters I selected the thinnest. By grinding one end against one of the pieces of sandstone that I had used to break the bone I made the bone splinter as sharp as I could. Heating the sharpest end in the ashes I stuck it into the webbing of my left hand at the base of the wound. It burnt my flesh and was as sore and painful as I could manage, but I continued to hold it there, pressing and pushing against the base of the thorn and trying to push it out of my hand until the thorn and the pus came out in a burst of stinking yellow. As soon as it was out, I sucked on the wound in an attempt to cool it down and clean it up, I threw the bone splinter away, I don't know why, perhaps I was angry that I had had to use it in the first place.

The little fire crackled away outside, the smoke was keeping the midges off me but was occasionally blowing in. The smoke aggravated my eyes, drying them, smoking them like the meat. I always stunk of wood smoke; my face, hands, beard, hair, even after a bath, and with so many tasks requiring fires and smoke, you just had to get used to smelling of it.

I ate more of the meat that I had smoked last night and drank some of my water. Eating more of the smoked meat caused my tooth to hurt. It was one of the two remaining big teeth in my upper left jaw. The rear one had fallen out last year, with a bit of help and the stinking pus and crap that ran out from underneath it explained why it had hurt so much. Abscesses were common enough, our teeth ground down quickly, chewing on bark, seeds, hides and so on, so toothache was usual, but I had been lucky for most of my life, until the abscess of last year. That bad tooth had seemed to set off the one next to it. I went to look for the bone splinter that I had just thrown away; I could use it as a toothpick, despite my best efforts I couldn't find it. Instead, I softened a tiny ball of pine resin on the edge of the fire and jammed it up between the two remaining big teeth, wedging it between them, hoping to stop any more food from becoming stuck in the gap. As I did this, there was a crack from one of them, so I sat there, with the pine resin gently trickling down my throat and a throbbing tooth. It wasn't long until I pulled out the resin and drank some water to rid my mouth of the taste of resin and blood.

After a while, the throbbing in the tooth lessened and I could begin to relax, I sat back and began thinking about the day, thinking about my travels, making a map of the landscape in my mind. Then I began thinking about this little warm shelter, how simple it was yet how warm it felt. I fell asleep in that cosy little place and slept like a bear in the winter.

I awoke to the noise of a woodpecker banging away on a nearby tree, this day was cool and clear like yesterday, a few small white clouds were high up against the pale blue sky and the sun was still low in the east. This morning the air smelled good, fresh and bountiful, it would be hot again I felt sure of that and I had a long walk ahead of me. I ate some more of the meat then chewed a few pine needles to freshen my mouth, a swill of water and I was off.

After only about 100 paces, I found my trademark ring bark sign, this time on an elm, the rockshelter was just to the right I felt good knowing that I was back on track and I pressed on, waiting for the view to appear.

Chapter 2.

Soon after, there it was; the tree cover ended suddenly on a large rock outcrop, and out in front of me was my destination. Rotating slowly on the spot, I took in the view while mentally mapping the landscape, trying to remember as much as I could. Being up high, meant that this was a perfect opportunity to imprint this picture, so that when I was back down on the flat it would be in my head, my mind map. When I was back down on the flat, as long as I could see this large rock outcrop, I could remember the view from the top and orientate myself in the flat landscape accordingly. To the south-west of where I stood was flat land then low hills leading to distant high hills. Behind me, to the south, the ridge that I was walking along and the now distant ridge of two days ago. To the south-east, the broad wet areas of the Great Plain and the sudden rise of my lands. To the east, the flat land of the Great Plain then low hills leading to high hills. To the north-east and north, the wide low lands of the Great North River. However, best of all, to the west and north-west was the estuary of the Great North River. It seemed that in this area two Great Rivers flowed out to the west, either side of a stub of land. I knew from speaking to travellers, that the Great West River flowed from the high hills that were far to the west and south-west of me, but I had never been there and it was difficult terrain. I knew the Great North River much better, as part of it, where it was very small, marked the northern edge of my tribal lands. Eating some greens while on the hoof, I picked the leaves of chickweed, dandelion, cleavers and the odd gorse flower, when I could find it; the fresh leaves, picked from plants that were sitting basking in the sun, were warm in my mouth. There were no early blackberries around; the main berry season would start some time later, probably a full moon or two. As I reached a grassy slope I noticed that it was covered in the feathery leaves of pignut, I thought about digging some up for later on, but it was still early in the day and I would rather get to the river and see what was there.

Standing on another bare area of rocks, the view west now opened up, fully revealing the estuary and distant sea; below me on my right, scrubby trees and marsh gave way to a reed fringed slowly flowing river which weaved its way into the Great North River not far ahead. I saw an elk feeding in the margins, the massive antlers waving as it shook its head, a marvellous animal. I had never killed an elk, they didn't seem to live in my lands, but looking at it now I could see why a hunter would want to kill it. The meat, the skin, the antler, the bone, the sinew, I could have a lot of food and resources in that one animal. Seeing it there, feeding quietly by itself on this clear beautiful morning I felt it was a kindred spirit. Wandering on its own through this rich landscape, in many respects just like me, I whispered to my fellow traveller, "good morning to you brother, may the Great Spirit guide and guard you,"

Time to move on; I started down the rocks and through the tough and scrappy knee high heather, glad that I had my boots on. Unfortunately, I arrived at the wrong point of the river. I should have taken more time up on the last lot of rocks to get my bearings rather than gawping at the elk, and now that I was down on the scrub marsh, I could not see. The problem here was that the reedbed was vast so it was difficult to work out where the actual river channel was. If the tide was low, my plan was to get to the edge of the Great North River and walk along the bank, but if the tide was high, then I was buggered. If it was high tide the river and the reedbed would just merge into one big wet area, so I just hoped that it was low tide when I got there.

Reeds, reeds and more fucking reeds; this was hopeless, I was getting nowhere fast and was really pissed off with myself for getting excited and rushing in here, I would have been better off staying out of the reeds, skirting round the scrub and at least keeping some height so that I could see where I was going. I put up two white storks that had been feeding nearby; bursting out of the reeds right in front of me I nearly fell over in shock. I was looking like a complete learner; ashamed of myself for not noticing them, some hunter I thought. I stopped where I was, I needed to concentrate, otherwise I could end up wandering round in this reedbed all day like a prize dickhead.

Sitting on my haunches I closed my eyes and listened; now that I wasn't crashing around like a knob, the reedbed started to settle down. The reeds brushed together in the wind, a gentle shushing shimmer of a sound. I concentrated, eyes still shut; a reed warbler chirruped away to my left, a grasshopper warbler creaked away to my right, wasps were chewing on the reed stems next to me. Then I heard what I was after, the stiff and rapid flapping of a flight of ducks circling, teal, they scooted round a couple of times, I didn't move a muscle. I listened to them as they moved fast and low overhead, hearing the wind through their feathers as they stalled and made a rapid landing to my right. I knew that they must have landed on open water because as I stood up I could still hear the skeesh of the water beneath their webbed feet. Now less like a knob and more like a cat, I was moving slowly and deliberately as I went toward the open water, aware that it might not be the river, it might just be a pool within the reedbed.

After 100 or so paces I was standing on the muddy south bank of the Great North River, it was low tide so I was in luck; the teal took off quickly and vanished away to my right, their fluting calls disappearing over the reeds. I thanked them for showing me the way and looked about me; it was warm already so I sat myself down on the bank. Removing my boots I looked at the sun which was still low, judging by the debris strewn along the banks of the river, the water level still seemed to be dropping and I reckoned that I had plenty of time before I needed to move. Lying back on the bank like a basking lizard, relaxing into the sense of the place, letting it encircle me, I fell asleep listening to the murmuring whispering reeds, the warblers answering and the occasional plopping of a fish.

I hadn't meant to fall asleep and I was well out of it when I heard a voice shouting, shaking myself awake I sat up to see two young men paddling a log-boat towards me. I waved at them to show that I was friendly and as they approached I smiled, I didn't want confrontation, this was probably their hunting area after all. They reached the bank, "Hi lads are you alright?" I couldn't think of anything else to say. It was clear that they were twins; both were strong and lean, with shoulder length dark brown hair that looked as though it had been cut around an upturned bowl. They wore only short buckskin skirts, split up each thigh so that they could sit cross-legged in the canoe. Both looked solid, dense and immovable, like rock or perhaps like the dense nuggets of orange-brown stone that we would sometimes find, washed down the streams of my tribal camp. These stones would stain the waters of the streams orange-brown and we could crush them and colour our skin, or our hides. Both lads were well tanned had big shoulders and strong broad chests from all the paddling, as they landed I noticed that they had sparkling blue eyes. Thankfully they smiled, "Do you want a lift? We are going down to the mouth of the Great North River, to look at the fishing." Well that suited me just fine; I accepted and shook them both by the hand before stepping into the back-end, behind the rear lad. Then the questions began, "Have you come far? What have you seen? Where are you going? What is your skill?" I answered politely without waffling on, but this last question got me. "What do you mean, what is my skill?" "What is your skill, what do you do?" I still wasn't sure what they meant, "I am a hunter," it was all I could think of; as far as I was concerned I didn't have any skills. "We are all hunters my friend, but what is it that you do when you are not hunting?" I thought about this for some time, "Fuck all." They laughed, "We make these, fire hollowed fixed transomed log-boats," they spoke and gestured to the boat with their paddles at the same time and I got the feeling that these two boys spent all day paddling up and down the river telling anyone that they met how clever they were with their effing skills. They were certainly spending most of this day telling me all about them, and as the reeds passed by and the river widened they carried on rattling. By now it was all that I could do to stay awake and as my head rocked around on my neck I nodded, "Very nice," it was all that I could muster. Why I was so miserable at this moment I didn't know, after all they were giving me a lift quite a long way down the river. They were doing all the work and they were friendly enough, apart from waffling on about how fire hollowed pine trunks produced better canoes than did birch bark or skin. The truth of the matter was that I wasn't really into canoes, they were a tool that got me from here to there, some people spent ages making them and even longer talking about them, which was not for me. Taking a handful of water from the river I splashed it into my face to try to wake myself up, I shook my head and looked at the boat, they were right it was nice. In fact it was very nice, "So how did you make this one?" "Haven't you been listening? First we find a big pine that has fallen, when we have decided on the length that we want, we set fires at each end of the trunk. We stop the fire spreading by constantly throwing water or covering it in wet plants where we don't want it to burn. When we have the right length we start to burn along the top, again using water and green wet plants to stop the spread, and we just keep going. Some people use stone tools or even beavers teeth, but we prefer this method, it is what our father and fathers always did." "How long does it take?" "A few days, it depends as much on the weather, as you know; whenever you use fire you need the right weather." I nodded it was true. Whenever we used fire, we were always watchful of the weather, particularly of the wind. "Do you make them for anybody?" "Yes." "Just log-boats?" "Yes." On my last trip I had met a man who made beautiful canoes, one was from birch bark another was made from elk skin. It sounded like a nice idea to cruise up and down the rivers of the Great Plain, and for me trekking through shitty wet landscapes was getting less enjoyable. I wondered whether if I traded a load of dried salmon I would be able to trade the elk skin man for a boat, of course that was if he was still there, he might have moved house. With that in mind, I asked, "Is there anyone around here that makes skin boats?" "Yes." "Where might that be?" "Hang on," suddenly after all their waffling it was now getting difficult to talk to them for some reason. "There is a woman who makes them near where we are going, but could you please be quiet as we need to focus." I was amused by this given that they had spent most of the journey going on about moveable transoms, fixed transoms, trim and weather helm and stuff that I had no idea what they were on about. Then up ahead I saw what they were both concentrating on, the river was very wide at this point and there appeared to be a wall of white water approaching us at some speed. "Is that normal?" my question was hopeful, I was hoping that the answer would be 'yes'…"No," came the answer from one, "Bollocks," was the answer from the other. Gripping the boat I checked that my gear was safe and handy should I need to grab it suddenly. There was a silence then a roar as the water hit us, we bucked around in the foaming rolling white water like a red deer in a neck snare, I wasn't happy. I had never experienced anything like this before, the boys paddled crazily, both leaning from side to side as the waves pushed past us, lifted us, dropped us and roared on up the river like a load of aggressive animals. Then it was quiet. "That's the beauty of a log-boat, plenty of beam, nice and heavy to ride out the waves." Sitting there with a wet arse and legs I was not convinced and I started to look to the shore for a place to land. "We will be alright now I think, it

25

was probably just the tide on the turn," the front lad said, I looked at the lad nearest to me, "Do you think?" "Yes, I think so, I will check." Dipping his hand in the water he took a swig, "Blah, salt, definitely turning, and coming in fast, look at that floating weed, we won't make much progress now, we will put in here somewhere and carry on tomorrow." Turning to me, the rear lad said, "Traveller you choose, the north or the south bank? We are in the middle of the river so either way is fine by us." I thought about it then chose; to be honest I was relieved, I was glad to get out and stretch my wet legs, we had been floating down the Great North River for a while now and I needed a crap. The lads offered to give me a lift the following day, but I told them that I would walk; I thanked them and gave them the bulk of the cooked deer meat, which they were thankful for, but I kept the lower legs, the antlers and the skin.

Gathering my thoughts, I took a drink; looking back down the Great North River I could see the sandstone ridge in the distance, we had come quite a way so far today, the lads had done well.

The landscape was changing; there was now the occasional patch of sand amongst the reeds and rafts of debris along the shore. Pressing on, I ate the last of the slivers of deer that I had cooked. I figured that I would find something to eat where I was going and it was normal to expect people to be along the rivers so I hoped that I would bump into someone with food already prepared, it would save me scrabbling round looking for something. Sometime later with the reedbed far behind me and the sun well on its way down in front of me, I topped a sand dune and saw the open sea just beyond me. The mouth of the Great North River was on my left, a rippling muddy rolling mass of river with the sea pushing back against it. Taking another drink from my bladder I smiled, pleased that I had managed to get all the way here, the Great Spirit had looked after me and here I was. Taking another drink, I walked down onto the beach. Removing my boots, I strolled on the warm sand, feeling it gently massage my toes, slightly tickling, very pleasant. It had been two years since I was last in the area, on that occasion I was on the south side of the river. I was planning on returning to the south side, but the wall of white water which had forced the lads to stop had presented me with the opportunity to see what was on this north side of the Great North River. When I was last on the south side, I had met a man who told me that the north side was better for fishing, so here I was with the chance to find out for myself. If I remembered correctly he told me to walk past the mouth of the Great North River till I met a small river coming in from the north; it was near here that I should set up camp and here that I should fish.

I walked on. The coast was mainly sand which extended as far as I could see, a large dune system went away to my right. Every now and then along the beach, shingle ridges broke through the sand and I hobbled over them onto the softer sand beyond. The shingle always seemed to lie behind rocky outcrops that jutted out into the sea; I noticed that the rocks were covered in shellfish. I liked the look of this place, lots of food and many resources, it looked promising. A cloud… clouds, of small greyish birds running away from me, lifting then dropping back to earth, all along the low tide mark, they seemed to be calling "Not, not." Taking no notice of their negativity, I moved on.

As I walked, shapes began to grow from the sand ahead of me; set back from the shore in the shelter of a large dune, was a skin-on-frame house, a big shelter was nearby. Drawing nearer, I could make out more features; drying racks set to face south, one of the racks was full of eels hanging lifeless over a gently smoking fire. Next to these was a small thatch-on-frame lean-to, under which a spiky scruffy brown dog slept, twitching and yipping in its dreams. Behind the house was another thatch-on-frame lean-to shelter, which protected a pile of well-ordered driftwood so that there was always dry wood for the fire. As for the house, it was cone shaped, about four paces across and was similar in shape to ours back home and easily big enough for three or four. I was now standing next to it, it was made of long poles pushed into the ground, these were tied together at the top, but where it differed from ours was that this frame was covered with skins that had been expertly stitched together with sinew. Our houses were thatched with plants such as bracken, unless you were an elder, elders got special houses. The house flap-door was positioned so that it faced south-east, making the most of the early morning light when it was open. Round the back of the house was the other lean-to shelter, this was the biggest of the shelters; at least four paces long, four paces wide, almost as tall as me and had thatch on the roof and on one side. Under the shelter were three skin-on-frame canoes, two were completed and one was under construction. I noticed that the side of the shelter that was covered was on the south, this would be to protect the canoe skins from the drying nature of the sun, particularly by the sea, where the wind, sun and salt spray could dry out anything, hence the drying racks. The main campfire was about six paces from the house; the fireplace was circular, about a pace across and edged by stones to contain the fire. In the hearth, lay several flat stones that I assumed were for cooking on, there were what appeared to be some small round cooking stones on the edge of the fire. Next to these but not in the ashes were a pair of green-twig tongues to lift these stones when they were hot, green wood was wet wood, it didn't set alight as you lifted the heating stones out. I guessed that these small stones were for making quick hot drinks or soups; they were on the edge of the fire in the ashes so they were always hot. Finally, a pile of dry kindling and sticks was to the left. I liked the set up; the main campfire was beneath a simply made lean-to. At the front, were two long branches about as thick as my wrist that had been pushed into the sand about two paces apart, a pace each side of the centre of the fire. These upright poles were about as high as me, perhaps a bit taller? The upright poles forked at the top; a pole went between these two forks to support the roof at the front. The entire lean-to roof was held up on this supporting pole, from which long thin poles of willow sloped down to the ground; their ends pushed into the sand about three paces to the rear of the fireplace. These willow poles were still green and must have been collected recently to reduce the chances of catching fire. On top of these poles, lengths of reed stems were placed lengthways to help fill in the gaps, finally a light covering of sand for insulation, though much of the sand had blown off in places. The lean-to was an effective place to cook and work, and even if it pissed it down, you knew that your main fireplace and wood would be reasonably dry and that you could get a fire going soonish. On a wet, cold, windy day, that was all you needed to know. Overall, it was a good, well-organised set up; whoever stayed here was obviously efficient and organised, particularly judging by the number of skins that were here on the house and the canoes.

It was always likely to happen, the dog woke up and there I was, barefoot, feet unprotected. I hopped around shouting as the damned thing moved in for another go. There was a whistle and the dog immediately stopped and ran to the whistler. The whistler jogged toward me and I waved and smiled, trying to show that I was friendly and not at all angry that the dog had just mauled my left foot. You cannot do much hunting when your foot is knackered, so I was not happy. The whistler's right shoulder went under my left, and I was helped into the canoe shelter where I sat down on a large beaver hide. I was given a drink of water from a wooden bowl, which might have been the dogs, then whistler jogged back to the house. Collecting another wooden bowl, whistler jogged down to the sea, filled it with seawater then walked back to me slowly so as not to spill it. Carrying the bowl and stirring the water with a finger, she showed me the contents, "A handful of crushed burdock root, in some seawater for the salt, this mix will clean and heal you. I always have some in store, I am always cutting my feet on sharp shells, so whenever I find any burdock I dig up the root… and of course it is good to eat." I let her get on with it without saying anything and looked at her feet, which were hidden inside some kind of twined grass slip-ons. My foot was sore so I wasn't thinking about food at the moment; she asked me what I was doing here. "What are you doing here?" "I am here for the fishing, I am going to camp by a small river that runs into this bay, it is further west from here so I have been told." She nodded, "Yes it is further west and it is good fishing there, I go there myself." She emptied some water from a bladder and continued with the questions. "Where are you from?" I waved, "Over there, several days walk, I live in the hills over there away in the distance, I don't' think that you can see them from here." She nodded and bathed my foot with water and the crushed burdock, I smiled and thanked her, she seemed nice enough. I explained how the wall of white water and the changing tide had caused us to stop and that I had made the decision to land on the north side rather than the south side of the Great North River, so here I was. "Yes ... so here you are," she said flatly, not sounding thrilled about it.

I was not sure how long I had been asleep, but the sun was falling fast, there was no woman and no dog, I got up and hobbled out of the canoe shelter. They were outside, the dog was chewing on some dried up seaweed and she had just made up the main campfire. She was now wearing a long sleeved buckskin top; I guessed that I was going to be sleeping next to the main campfire under the lean-to shelter, she gestured to a red deer skin lying on the ground, I was right.

She must have eaten earlier because there was no food and as the sun set she said goodnight, and drew the flap of skin across the door. I could hear the occasional chattering croaks from the natterjacks at the back of the dunes, otherwise nothing. It had been a long day, a very long day indeed. Reflecting upon the day's events, it hadn't ended as I had expected, I built up the fire even more then snuggled down under the deer skin, it was a clear night so it was likely to be cool.

Chapter 3.

I awoke to find the dog pissing on my legs, I tried kicking him away but he bared his teeth and growled so I left him to it. I was already stinking anyway, so I reckoned dog piss wouldn't make that much difference. It was early but it was already a cracking day, a clear blue sky from east to west and north to south. I sat up in the warmth and looked closer at the set up. The drying racks, house, shelters and general layout meant that she must stay here most of the time. There was a sense of permanence about the place but what was odd was that she appeared to be on her own, apart from the pissing dog. To the rear of the canoe shelter, about 40 paces away, was a stream that had a good flow on it, it came through a small gap in the dunes through which I could see that there was scrub woodland of willow and alder only 60 or 70 paces away. This scrub seemed to extend some way along the stream into the dune system itself and I recalled that the landscape was similar on the south side of the Great North River. Looking south across the mouth of the Great North River I followed the line of coast of that stub of land, and in the distance I made out the mouth of the Great West River. Across that, I could see a coastline of high hills. Following that distant coast further to the west, I could see even taller mountains that were making white clouds. Looking out to the open sea, a pod of dolphins were working their way around the bay, I dare say that they were here for the salmon, as I was. I checked my kit, the hide was beginning to fester and I needed to sort it out before it became maggot ridden. Finding a thumb thick stick from the woodpile and a couple of sharp edged stones, I lay the hide on the sand hair side down and kneeled on the bottom edge. Working quickly with the stick, I scraped away as much of the flesh and membrane as I could, then used handfuls of sand and the stones to grind away any finer remnants. It wasn't brilliant but it would do, I washed it in the sea and stuck it back into the canoe shelter where it could dry slowly, I wanted the hair on it because it would work as a light cover for me at night or whenever.

As the tide was in, I decided that it was time for a wash. Stripping, I collected a black chert blade from my blade pouch, black chert seemed to produce sharper blades than brown chert and for this task, I needed as sharp a blade as possible. Wandering down to the water's edge where the tide lapped gently against the shore, I looked about me. She had chosen a great place for her camp, the shape of the dunes here meant that not only was she sheltered from the predominant westerly and south-westerly winds, but she was also sheltered from the full force of the tide, a good choice, smart woman I thought. The water felt lovely, cool but not cold; knee deep in the shallows, I could feel warm spots as it heated up under the strong sun. I bent over in the calmest bit so that I could just about see my face reflected and started to cut away at my long hair, pieces came off as I carefully sliced through it at shoulder length, then a wave would ripple the surface and I would wait until it flattened out again before I continued. I felt the length; it was about level with my shoulders now, so that would do. Next, I started on my beard, with even more care, slicing pieces off; I was pleased with myself for doing such a good job. "Hey, hello." She startled me and I turned to face her as she walked from her house, I noticed that she was fully clothed; wearing a long sleeved buckskin shirt and a long buckskin skirt with slits on both sides that ran from just above her knees to the bottom of the skirt. She also wore long skin boots that looked like the skin used on the house. I answered, "Hiya, nice day." As she neared me she started to giggle, soon she was standing there on the dry sand only a few paces away, bending forward with her hands on her knees laughing uncontrollably, she could barely speak "You... you... look like the dog... here let me do it." Wading ashore, I somewhat ruefully gave her the blade, "Thanks." "No problem... you look really stupid," "Thanks," I replied again, somewhat miffed, "It's no problem." She moved behind me and began to work on my hair; she was mostly silent throughout, apart from humming occasionally, I contented myself by watching the sand flies that were climbing over my toes. "Done, go look in the water, see." Paddling out to knee depth, I looked, as far as I could tell it was now disastrously short. White parts of my neck and head where my hair had once covered them stood out against the tanned parts. "I look like a young boy," I objected, "You look like a nice man, I can see your eyes now, come back here and I will do your beard." She continued in the same vein, skilfully cutting my beard until it was fairly neat and short, and every now and again abusing me with things like, "You seem to have a small cock, is that normal where you are from?" What do you say to that? *'The water isn't very warm, or,*

32

yes we all have small cocks, or, no I am celebrated amongst my tribe for having the smallest, or, this is actually massive.' I just stood there blushing and took it; after all she was waving a sharp chert blade around my neck. Her insults continued, "You smell very bad, stay there," she jogged up the shore and disappeared into her house, returning almost immediately with a handful of a plant that had pink flowers and stiff fleshy leaves. "Rub it between your hands with a bit of sand and add a bit of water, use it to clean your stinky body, the sand will rub the grime off you." "What is it? I don't recognise it, I don't think we have this where I live, we tend to use chickweed." She shrugged her shoulders, "I haven't named it yet, I only found it in the spring, when I was walking out over to the marsh, it tastes horrible and it took me a while to work out what it could be used for, there was not much of it, just one little patch." Wading back out to where the water was thigh deep, I did as she said and was surprised at the results, a slick formed on my skin that made me feel clean and smooth, making sure that I gave my knackers and arse crack a real good clean. The soap worked and it even got rid of the pine resin stains on my finger and thumb, which were still black after several days, but it did make my cock sting. I had developed thrush while I was travelling and I put that down to being warm and frequently wet and not cleaning under my foreskin regularly. When I had finished, she told me that it was time for us to go and find some food so that we could break fast. I nodded, sunk into the shallows to swill off the last of the soap then stood and waded ashore where I wiped the bulk of the water from my body, jumped up and down a bit, smoothed down my new short hair which was spiking up, and sat down on my shirt. "What are you doing now?" looking up, I answered, "Just using my thumb nails to pick my toe nails while they are soft from the water, they are getting long." She nodded, "Oh, be quick though, we haven't got all day." When I had done, I stood and put on my trousers to cover my 'small cock.' My left foot was still a bit sore where the shit hound had bit me so I put on my boots to keep the sand out of the wound, but I left off the shirt, as it was great to feel the sun on my back. I went over to the shelter to pick up my bow, "You won't need that," I nodded and followed her. We walked past the camp and up to the top of the biggest dune where she stopped. We were facing north-east; she waved her hand at all we could see. "That is the Great Marsh; it is full of

33

streams, small rivers, scrub woodland, open water, reedbed and small dry islands, and in places it is very boggy, so it can be dangerous, but if you stick with me you will be safe, as long as you don't get yourself bitten again." I wasn't sure whether she was being rude or was trying to be funny. "What is the other side of the Great Marsh, to the north?" She followed my gaze, "Another Great River, then more hills, another Great River then more hills, and then the Great Bay, it is a huge bay that eats into the land as though a great whale has taken a chunk from it. The Great Bay gets full of water very quickly and empties very quickly, to leave a vast flat place of mud and sand and in places the sand will give way and you sink and if you are unlucky… you die. Anyway, many rivers pour into the Great Bay, there are many fish, shellfish and birds… it is very rich indeed, and then on the north side of the Great Bay are mountains with many lakes and many, many rivers, great and small." I was impressed, it sounded good, "I take it that you have been there?" Turning to me in surprise, she spoke as though I was a dickhead who was already supposed to know, "I am from the mountains... it is my tribal home. *We* are *the people*, *the people* who live in the lakes and mountains... but since I have stayed here I have become *the one who lives by the sea*." Stopping for a moment, she looked at the far horizon, "But I suppose that I am still part of *the people*." I took this in; I was part of *the people*, only my people were *the people of the woods and hills*. At least that is what we called ourselves, I dare say that other 'people' had different names for us.

I continued with my questioning, "Right, well… how many days walk is that?" Shrugging her shoulders she shook her head and curled her lower lip to think, a nice lip but chapped and dry from the salt filled winds. "I don't know, we came by water, by canoe, the coast is very beautiful, a wide flat coast with dunes, reeds and marshes, grasslands, heathlands and dense woodlands in places, and it is all very rich in resources." Now I curled my lower lip and nodded in acknowledgement as she continued. "We travelled over many days, from spring to late summer, four full moons I think; close in, the sea is shallow, we saw turtle, basking shark, dolphin, porpoise and seal ... and killer whales which were stacking up to feed on the huge shoals of salmon and sea trout that swim along the coast." "It sounds amazing," I said, "It was amazing, and at night we would pull our canoes up on a beach somewhere and prop them up sideways on the paddles to use them as shelters, we would then collect driftwood and get a fire going. As we paddled our way along the coast, we would run a hook and line out from the back of the canoe and catch fish, so fresh fish would be our evening meal with whatever fruit or greens we could find. It was beautiful... really beautiful." She had tears in her eyes and her lips were beginning to tremble, "It was a really beautiful time for me." As her eyes watered, it dawned on me that the key words in this tale were 'we' and 'was', I asked her what had happened. "We were only together for a short while; he was also from my tribal lands. We had grown up together, learnt to fish, to hunt, to paddle a canoe, done everything together, so it was only natural that we would be together as partners." She stopped and sat herself down on the warm dry sand; I sat down near to her, not too close as I didn't want to invade her space while she was feeling upset. It was obvious that she needed to be grounded before she continued, taking her time to speak. "We had decided that we wanted to see what was south of the Great Bay, we both wondered what lay in the land of the sun, the sun always seemed to be in the south, no matter how far south we travelled, so we set off in our canoes and worked our way south. Eventually we arrived here and it seemed like a good place to camp. There was shelter from winds, plenty of freshwater, plenty of driftwood and fresh green wood, many resources just over the dunes and in the scrub woodland, and we had the sea and the Great River, the Great North River as you would know it, so we decided to stay." Turning to face me, she wiped the tears from her watery blue eyes with her strong-bronzed fingers and sniffed before continuing. "Anyway, we needed new skins to repair the canoes; they were drying in the sun and wind and had begun to crack. Well you see over there to the south, in the bay," I followed her right hand as she pointed to a low island in the distance. "Well, that is a seal colony, so we went out to hunt two, he saw a huge bull seal, at least three paces long and he decided to go for that. He thrust the harpoon into its lower back, near the feet, but for some reason the harpoon head didn't detach, the strong rawhide cord was hanging in a loop and he wasn't able to get out of the way when the seal turned." I could just about picture the scene, although I had never used a harpoon and I had never seen a seal up close. Though I had used spears when we were on a wolf hunt, but they were really for self-defence in case the wolf ran at you. I made an observation, "I suppose that he didn't want to let go of the shaft in case the head did suddenly detach as it should, then you could both hang on to the cord and let the seal tire itself at a safe distance." She nodded. "Exactly... exactly, normally a seal would dive into the sea with the harpoon head still attached to its body and you can drop the shaft on the ground and just hang on to the cord until it tires and drowns, then you pull it back in. But he was reluctant to let go of the shaft, because if the seal dived in and he let go it would take the shaft, the cord and the harpoon head, it would take some time to make all of that again." I nodded, you had to get all the things in the first place before you could make anything and that could take a while, particularly if you had just moved into an area and had yet to find where everything was. "Well it was all so quick; if you can imagine a great big heavy seal rolling around barking and snorting and my man hanging on to the shaft of the harpoon, the loose loop of cord wrapped around his right foot, he tripped and went over on his ankle with a crack. While he was lying on the wet sand, the seal was rolling and thrashing its head and back feet. The cord looped round his wrists... the seal rolled on top of him and bit him in the neck, a deep wound... then it launched itself into the sea... dragging him shouting and bleeding beneath the waves." "Shit," I said. "Too damn right... it was shit. I just stood there on my own, utterly useless, blank, horrified, waiting for him to reappear. Surrounded by many, many barking seals all racing past me, the ground rumbling as they thrashed into the waves and into the deeper water, then silence... just heads bobbing up and down looking at me, while I looked at the red slick on the water and the bubbles." Not sure what to say, I tried my best. "That is dreadful, dreadful... so what did you do then?" Her chest lifted as she took a deep breath before continuing. "Well, I sat there on the bloody wet sand for a while and let the shock wash over me, and then I am afraid I just broke down like a nutter and ran back and forward along the beach shouting and screaming for him, just in case he had somehow escaped." Wiping yet more tears from her eyes and sniffling, she continued with her story, though I felt uneasy, uneasy that she was telling me this considering I had only just met her. "When I was worn out, I dropped to the floor and cried my heart out, swearing and shouting, beating the sand, throwing stones at any seals that popped up... pointless... stupid really. Then I just stayed there all night, shivering by the rocks because I did not know what else to do. Up to that moment he had been a major part of my life since childhood and we had always made decisions together, so I really didn't know what to do." As she said this I looked around at the set up, the way it was so organised suggested to me that she knew exactly what to do, unless he had set everything up, I asked her. "So did he, did you, set all this up?" We both shuffled round in the sand to face the camp, she nodded to each feature as she talked. "Both of us set up the house and the canoe shelter, and the fireplace of course, but I have added things here and there... and of course I have to repair things regularly. Oh, and most of the fishing gear I have made... and one of the canoes... and all my clothes. I suppose that the taste, the feel and the presence of him is gradually leaving the camp. And with every full moon that comes and goes... I suppose that I feel more at home and less lonely." Pausing, she shivered as if from the cold, "Anyway, you didn't let me finish my story; the next day I left his canoe on the island, just in case he had survived and wanted to paddle back to me... and I came back here, decided to stay and started to think for myself. Just because I was on my own didn't make this a bad place, and I wanted to be near him." I smiled at her, "Was that recently?" She shook her head. "No, last summer, I have spent a winter here on my own and it was good. I had dried or smoked plenty of meat, fish and shellfish, I had many fresh duck and geese from the marsh, in the scrub there were always fresh greens, even in winter and I had made sure in the autumn that I had dried enough mushrooms, berries and leaves, so I had a comfortable winter." "You weren't lonely during the winter?" She shook her head again, "No, I had the dog; I had the seals during the day, though at first I thought they were mocking me, but I got to like them, and at night the eider ducks cooed to me with their soft calls. Then of course, I had the stars, the moon, and sometimes the green and yellow lights that shimmer across the night sky... I wasn't lonely." She smiled at me, and I believed her.

Chapter 4.

We were now well into the Great Marsh and surrounded by the reedbed, she was in front of me moving stealthily but deliberately, always looking, always listening and the dog was doing exactly the same. I could now see why she was wearing the long sleeved shirt and long skirt, because as I walked the tall reeds brushed against my upper body, cutting and scraping my bare skin. It struck me that she could have at least told me that they were this tall and unpleasant but then I suppose she assumed that I would know this, me being a hunter and all. She bent down and picked up some shit, "Red deer, good, I thought they were moving in, there are some areas of the marsh that seem to be drying out, so the grass and heather are growing more in those parts and the deer are moving in to graze." We moved on, it was magnificent, reeds as far as I could see to the east, while in front of us was open water, edged by lush grassland and scrubby alder and willow. To the west was more reed, then heathland, then big dunes, all that I could hear about me was bird noise; whistles, quacks, songs, and I wished that I had brought my bow with me.

Stopping suddenly on the bank of the open water, she leaned down to pick up a length of finger thick, plaited willow cord that was wrapped around a stake; she started to draw the cord toward her and from out of the water came a fish trap. I watched her as she lifted the thing out onto the platform on which we stood. It was a large cone with a smaller cone inside which acted as the gaping mouth into the larger cone. It was obviously effective as it was full of eels. I looked at how it was built; about as long as the span from my left hand to my right hand with my arms held out to my sides. As wide at its mouth as a forearm is long and made from thin withy's of alder, which were held together using a tight paired weave at hand width spacing. It was a well-made tool and I was impressed. I could also understand why her fingers were so strong, weaving these rods this tight would test your fingers and I wasn't sure that I could do it. "I have met in two days, three skilled people, two made fire hollowed log-boats and it seems that you make everything." She smiled, "Don't you have any skills?" I shook my head, "None that I can think of." She was generous and tried to help me out, "You must have some skills." I thought for a while, watching as she unwound the withy at the top of the trap and poured the eels into a wide wicker basket that was next to her. Quickly placing the lid of the basket back on, she fastened it by pushing two bone toggles, one at the front one at the back, up through two corresponding small holes in the lid; each toggle was attached to the body of the basket using a small length of willow cord. Meanwhile I was still thinking. "I suppose that I must have some skills, after all, I can make shelters, make fire, I can navigate across the landscape by night or day, I can find water, I can make all the tools I need and all my hunting gear. I make my own clothes, I can track, I can hunt, I can feed myself and I know what to eat and what not to eat. I know where to be at what time of year, to get the fish and the berries and the birds and the eggs and." She interrupted my skills list. "They aren't skills, they are life, everyone does those things everyday as part of living, skills are something different. This fish trap and basket making is not a skill, the canoes are skills, because I am the only one in the area who makes skin-on-frame canoes. This platform that we stand on isn't a skill, it is a necessity, I put down brushwood like this so that I can stand here easily and set my traps and work my traps without sinking into the peaty wet shit of the marsh. In the spring I made a brushwood track over there," she waved to the east, "That is there so that I can get through the wetter reedbed to where I have a small canoe tied to a stake. When I want to fish for pike I go along the track, get into my canoe and go and set lines, or I spear them in the early summer when they are spawning in the reed margins." At this point, I didn't really know what to say, it seemed that I was right first time, I didn't have any skills at all, so I said nothing. I just watched her as she baited up the trap with what appeared to be a piece of festering fish. Then with the trap in her left hand and a large stone in her right, she threw out the stone, as the stone flew through the air it drew out a short length of cord that was attached to the trap, she was swinging out the trap at the same time. The stone hit the water, the line tightened, the trap sunk into the depths and the plaited cord snaked out after it, she finished by tying off the loose end round the stake. She might not think that it was a skill, but from where I was standing it looked very skilful.

"All this brushwood that you used for the platform, the track and the traps, where did you get it from?" She pointed to the scrub, you see the scrub," I nodded, "Beavers, there is a beaver lawn there, they must have been here for years, there is so much scrubby coppice regrowth, I just go in and collect it from there." "Do you use a tool to collect so much stuff?" "I do take a large blade, but normally I don't need it, my hands are strong and I can break off the thin branches at the base easily enough. You would probably have to use a blade, because you have no skills. Anyway, lets break fast." She turned and walked away from me back to the camp; considering that we had only recently met, I was already finding her aggravating.

After we had broken our night-time fast with fresh eel, sorrel, roast burdock root and some kind of shellfish, I helped her to sort out the rest of the eels. Slicing them lengthways, we then removed their heads and guts, putting these in a wood bowl full of water to keep the flies off, they would be used for bait, we hung their bodies over an alder log fire. The smoking rack looked odd, bathed in sunlight with several long fish hanging in the smoke, some still wriggling. "Do these things ever die?" I asked. "Eventually, they are strong willed, they are strong animals." They might well be strong willed animals but it wasn't doing them any favours, their strong will was just prolonging their suffering. I lowered the rack to put them nearer to the heat and smoke so that they might die quicker, I don't think that it made a scrap of difference to them but it made me feel better. I looked at her, she was busying herself making something, another skill no doubt, I just moped around feeling skill less, then it dawned on me, I hadn't any plans for tonight and I needed to get myself organised. I put on my shirt and gathered my gear together, "Hey skilled woman, I am off... thank you for giving me shelter, for giving me water and food and for showing me your land. It is very beautiful here, but I have travelled here because I was told that it was very good for fishing and that is what I intend to do. So I must move on now along the coast to the west and look for the little river where the fish collect so that I can set up my camp and organise myself and be ready for when they come." She looked up from whatever it was that she was doing, "Ok." And that was that, nothing else, just 'ok.' Feeling miffed, I wandered past her house, past the windbreak under which the dog was lying and growling at me, on past the canoe shelter, skipped over the stream and lastly past the pile of shells and bones which was her rubbish tip. I stood on top of the big dune that sheltered her camp; I needed the best viewpoint to plan my trek. I took one last look at her down there working, wondering whether I would ever see her again, after all, my reason for being here was to camp by the small river and fish, not to spend time with this skilled woman. Firm in my conviction I turned from the camp and looked westwards along the shore; the sea on my left, the dune system and Great Marsh on my right. The dune system stretched into the distance along the shoreline, away beyond the small river that cut through the dunes and across the sandy beach, only about 400 paces away, "Bollocks," I said.

I walked the 384 paces and sat down on the sandy bank of the small river. So, this was my destination then, just over the dune from the woman. She certainly had got a strange sense of humour, she knew full well that this was where I had intended to set up camp and fish, she knew full well it was just over the dune yet she still let me pack up all my gear, make my leaving speech and set off, very funny.

I threw a few stones and shells into the water, then whatever else was at hand; feeling like a kid with no mates who realises that he has been stupid. Just as I was running out of things to throw I heard shouting, she was standing on top of the dune. I couldn't hear her so I stood up and started walking toward her until I could, my left hand cupped to my left ear. "Hey, food is ready, there is plenty for both of us, but if you don't hurry the dog gets it." She was waving, dog at her side growling, she turned and disappeared down the dune, I walked slowly back to her camp, head down, sulking. She was kneeling by the fire and cooking something, "Did you find the river then?" "Funnily enough I did, thank you; I don't know if you are aware of this but it is just over that dune." I used my right hand to demonstrate the rise and fall of the dune, then repeated myself to emphasise my point. "Just up and over that dune... just there." "Oh, really," she passed me some flat grey thing that looked suspiciously like aurochs shit, on to it she scooped out some mush of crushed small red berries. I took a mouthful, it was alright,

41

the berries were a bit sharp and dry but the two flavours worked, the grey thing was warm because she had baked it on a flat stone next to the fire. "This is nice, but what is it that I am actually eating?" "The grey flat cake is made from reedmace roots, I simply pound the roots with a bit of water until it produces a greyish gloop, then I leave that in the sun till the mixture thickens then I make a drop scone by scooping portions onto a heated flat stone, they cook easily on the hot slab." I was mildly impressed, "And the small red berry?" "You don't recognise it? It is cranberry, there is a lot of it growing in the bog, though most of them are not ripe yet, I was lucky to find those few." She smiled at me again, though this time it was a proper smile and as she did so she played with her hair, good signs, I smiled back, while the Shitbag hound sat growling.

In between mouthfuls of food she started. "I was thinking, you came here to fish at the small river, but as you know it is only just up and over the dune and it is too exposed to camp by the river. Besides, other people may move in to fish as well, so you don't want to be camping in their traditional fishing grounds do you?" I shook my head, I didn't want to do that, they would tell by my accent that I wasn't local, so me fishing there might cause a problem and if I insulted them by camping at their traditional fishing site they might just kick my head in. "So where do you suggest that I go?" Looking around the camp, she pointed to the canoe shelter; you can stay in there, make it comfortable for yourself, it seems silly for you to have to make up another shelter, just use that." Nodding, I thanked her and ate my cake and jam.

Asking her about the little river, I took a swig of water from a wooden bowl as she explained. "I call it the Alt," it was a descriptive word which summed it up perfectly, "I can see why you call it that, I noticed that its banks are steep where it flows through the dunes… what is it like, upriver?" Looking up from her work she smiled, "It is very pretty, very pretty indeed. We took the canoes upriver when we first came here. Beyond the dunes, its steep banks become reed fringed and grassy and then it becomes marshy scrub woodland, mainly willow and alder, with hazel, oak, pine and birch in the dry patches. The water there is slow flowing and not very deep, about as deep as my waist," she held her right hand against her waist to show me, even though she was kneeling, then continued. "Then it opens out and becomes many channels which link many pools and lakes, all within the Great Marsh and reedbed. The river then swings to the southeast, towards its headwater." While she was describing the river, I had drawn a map in my head; I now checked its accuracy. "So basically it flows from the southeast towards the northwest then turns south through the dunes and pops out just there," I pointed over the dune, "Correct, it is a very rich place, a very rich little river." I was curious, "Do you go in there often? I would like to see it." Switching position she looked at me, "Feel free, but it is hard work dragging the canoe up and over the dune and on to the river." "Then why not paddle round?" It seemed an obvious thing to do. She shook her head, "The outflow is very shallow and fast, it runs over a shingle bar where it empties into the sea so you cannot paddle up into the river mouth at low tide because of this shingle bar. At high tide the sea pushes in hard at the little mouth and where it meets the shingle bar it gets very choppy, very slidey, the canoe slips all over the place and the undertow is very dangerous... and there is a lot of drag. I have not been in there since I have been on my own, I didn't want to risk it... but now that you are here we could carry a canoe over the dune and drop it in where the trees begin, it is fairly sheltered there." I didn't really understand the bit about the river and the sea being slidey, but she had just flashed me another smile, so I returned it.

Chapter 5.

I hadn't slept well last night, this unwanted short haircut of mine had exposed the skin of my neck for probably the first time since I was a kid, the result was that it was now red raw from the sun and wind. Judging by the lack of clouds in the sky and the stillness of the air this morning, my neck was going to be cooked some more. I was over by the little stream getting a handful of mud, which I wiped around my neck for protection, then wandered back, stretching and yawning.

She was just finishing off a basket that she was making from rushes; she had started it last night, before I went to bed. Big rushes, bigger than the ones that grew around my way; she had called them club rush, they grew around the lake margin. We didn't have any lake margins around my way, we didn't have any lakes, they were out on the Great Plain. Around my way we had fast shallow rivers and streams and the occasional shallow pool, but mainly trees, and more trees, that is why I liked to move down to the coast once in a while, I liked the change of scenery and the new experiences. Like this now; I watched her fingers as she twined the weave stems around the warp stems of the basket, quickly and rhythmically, humming to herself and feeding in new weavers effortlessly. She hadn't seen me; I got dressed in the canoe shelter and wiped the sand off me. I wandered out, "Morning, nice basket." She looked up smiling, "Morning, thanks…did you sleep?" Yawning and stretching I nodded for some reason, "Fine, though I will make a better bed later, I didn't collect enough of that marram grass last night so the bed was a bit thin, I also cut myself, and it is sharp stuff."

"Did you clean the cut?" I shook my head, "Well, I sucked it for a while," "Go wash it in the sea, the salt will help, and you can have another deer hide tonight." I did as I was told then wandered back to top up the fire, just to make sure that it didn't go out. She looked up from her work, "When I finish this I will make the break fast, will you collect fire wood?" Nodding, I went along the beach; it was not a difficult task as there was plenty of driftwood lying around and I made several journeys. One piece of softwood was almost as long as me, I thought at first that it was pine, but it might not have been. It was well worn, without bark and was rounded at both ends from its time in the sea. I picked it up, slinging it over my right shoulder; it was riddled with small holes less than a little finger wide. As it went on my shoulder, stinking water ran from out of these holes, all over my shoulder and top and causing me to gag at the awful smell that now coated my shoulder, it smelled of sick.

All along the shore was a scattering of things that I had not seen before; one thing in particular caught my eye. Back at camp, I sorted out the wood, breaking what I could into small kindling, then separating small, medium and large pieces and placing them on the pile as she had organised it. After making sure that the cover of the pile was completely covering the woodpile, I joined her by the fire. She looked up, "You smell of sick, what have you been up to?" I explained about the stinking water running from the holes in the wood all over my shoulder, she laughed. "Sometimes, strange wood washes up on the shore, it looks like no tree that I have seen, and the holes that you talk about are made by little worms, or sometimes shellfish that bore into the wood. I think that the sick smell is from water that surrounds their dead bodies". "Great, that explains the rank smell."

As it was a warm day, she had different gear on; simple plaited rawhide sandals, a short apron type buckskin skirt, which had a flap at the front and back for maximum mobility, but which still hid everything. Up top was a sleeveless buckskin shirt that was dyed green, on her head she wore a hat made from rushes, which was open on the top so that her head stuck out and her ponytail hung down her back, the hat had an extended lip at the front, I was intrigued. "What's the long bit for?" "This?" she pointed towards the lip of the hat, I nodded, "It keeps the sun out of my eyes." "Do I need one?" "It would be useful… it looks as though you need it for your neck, you are burnt, you must have weak skin… is that why you have a small cock?" I didn't give her a reply I just stared into the distance feeling pissed off with her crap sense of humour, she realised that she had pissed me off, "We will make one for you, when we are at the boat." "Great," I said, flatly.

As she stirred the porridge, I passed her the thing, "Any idea what this is?" Taking it in her left hand she turned it dextrously between her fingers, "It is a scale from a sturgeon, they spawn in all the Great Rivers, I have seen them swim beneath my canoe, they are 3 or 4 paces long and look very old." "Have you killed them?" "No, too big to take on my own, they come into the shallows sometimes and they wash up dead, I have used the scales as scrapers and even tried a smaller one as an arrow head, but I have never eaten them." We ate the warm porridge, made from the crushed seeds of wood millet and flavoured with meadowsweet flowers, both plants grew along the damp scrub by the stream. The porridge stuck to the fire hollowed bowls and fire hollowed spoons. "Did you make these as well?" Smiling and nodding modestly she answered, "Yes, it is a nice thing to do, to burn and scrape, then burn and scrape, it passes the time in the evenings, and I enjoy it. But you have to watch what you are doing; you see that one over there that the dog is by." She pointed to half a bowl that was leaning against her house. The dog was lying half in it, chewing a tree root and I could see that the bowl had almost burnt away. "That was one where I couldn't put the fire out." Looking at it I wondered how the Nugget Twins managed to control the fires in their fire-hollowed log-boats so well. I took another spoonful, "You are very clever and very skilled... I am impressed by you." "Thanks," was all she said.

I didn't need to take any kit with me, so I undid the string from my bow in order to give the bow a rest and placed it back in the shade of the canoe shelter. We walked to the platform; because we had walked this way only the other day most of the tall reeds were still lying flat, which was why she didn't need her long sleeves and boots, and neither did I, so I was red hot in my long sleeved shirt and trousers. I watched her lift and check the eel traps which were empty, she then laid them on the platform and picked up a serrated scallop shell from among her assorted fishing gear. She told me that she had cut the serrations along the edge using a chert blade; it quickly sawed through the leaves of the reedmace, she collected leaves that were dead or dying as these were less fleshy, until she had 20 of them, all just shorter than a forearm in length. Under instruction, I started folding all 20 in half, 10 would weave east-west and 10 would weave north-south. I started by making a corner, by fitting two together in the fold. With each newly added folded stem east-west and north-south, I alternated the weave under and over, until all 20 leaves had been used. She called it a cross weave, and who was I to argue.

The last bit was beyond me so she took it off me to finish it, or we would never have gone fishing. Beginning with the inside weavers that faced east, she weaved each one under and over towards the outside edge, until it tapered. She now did the same with the weavers that faced north; it now resembled a new moon. When she was satisfied, she tied the two thin ends together and stuck it on my head; of course, she had made this last bit look easy. "Not bad," she said, "Your hat is deliberately open on top, this bit at the front is just to keep the sun out of your eyes out on the water." I held up my hands in submission, "Whatever you say, I am learning all the time." "Right lets go, oh and leave your boots on the platform, they may get slippy in the canoe with all the fish slime." She was right, my buckskin boots might get wet and slippy and I didn't want that to happen; also because they were made from the neck part of a deer they were thicker than normal boots and might be uncomfortable as I messed about in this canoe.

To say that I was excited was an understatement; I was loving it. Pike fishing was new to me, I had never even seen a pike so I didn't know what to expect, the only fish that we saw round my way were sea trout and salmon when they ran up to spawn, and there were also trout, chub, dace, minnows, bullhead, stone loach and brook lampreys. Yet here I was now, all tooled up with my new hat with extended lip, sitting in the back of a small skin-on-frame canoe as she began to paddle and we nosed away from the brushwood platform out onto the lake. Turning slightly to face me she spoke softly and quietly, "About two full moons ago, the pike were spawning right in close to the bank along this edge, and I could fish for them using a leister, but now they are out of the margins so we will use lines." Fine by me, when I fished back home I used lines made from all sorts of things, hooks made from the nose bones of deer, as well as bow and arrows, and scoop nets on the trout and salmon when they were on their spawning redds. I didn't know what a leister was but I wanted to learn new things so that I would become a complete hunter. After a while, she placed the paddle softly by her side so as not to send a noise through the water, "We are here." Picking up a coil of strong willow bast cord she passed it to me. It was 3-ply and nearly as thick as my little finger, I unrolled it and guessed that it was about ten paces long, just before the last section started a small stone had been tied into the main line. The last section which was as long as my arm was a thinner 2-ply length, on the end of which was a bone toggle similar to the ones that fastened the lid of her eel basket. Looking from above, the toggle was like a tiny canoe in shape; as long as my forefinger, thin and sharp at one end, the middle was as wide as my little finger, it then became thin and sharp at the other end. She had the same set up; I watched her push the head of one of the eels over the toggle so that it was completely covered, with that, she swung out the eel and let out the line, it splashed into the water, she passed me an eel head so that I could do the same. Both lines sank gently into the water as the weight of the small stones took them down, the ripples gradually disappearing to leave a flat clear surface.

We drifted slowly in the heat of the morning to the sound of warblers chittering and chattering amongst the warm waving reeds; swallows brushed the water as they swooped and caught flies, a huge marsh harrier flew low overhead, I was familiar with these birds as they were on the marshlands of the Great Plain. The sun beat down, the wind dropped altogether and I was thankful for my new hat with the extended lip, it was a beautiful time. The water was so clear that I could see shoals of fish shifting from the shade cast by the drifting boat, a black cloud moving over them. A drop of water fell from the edge of the canoe onto the surface of the lake with a ting and in my head, a soft, lovely tune was playing, I felt so relaxed that I fell asleep.

It was fortunate that I had tied the line to my left wrist as otherwise, it would have been lost over board and she wouldn't have been happy with me. I awoke to find my left arm under the canoe and being dragged down, I started to pull back. "Go easy and don't yank it, just a steady pull." Nodding, I pulled the line steadily with my right hand, holding it with my left, the fish was not giving up so easily and the line slipped out again. "That is alright, keep doing that but don't let go, keep it tight at all times." The lightweight canoe started to follow the fish around the lake, I noticed that while I was hanging on, she pulled in her line, turned to face me and cleared the area between us, then stared into the water, concentrating on the line as we were towed around for what seemed like a long time. She must have thought that it was a long time as well, "This is getting boring." She was lying back in the canoe now, letting her right hand trail in the water, as I hung on to whatever it was that was dragging us around the lake. Trying to make light of the situation, I joked, "Well we are seeing a lot of the lake." "I have seen this part of the lake three times now," she said, "Just drag it in, I am hungry and the tide will be out by now, I want to collect some cockles. My idea was that we came pike fishing, had lunch then went cockling at low tide, at this rate we will still be here in the dark." I must admit that by now I was fed up too, so I answered abruptly, "Well instead of lying there on your back pissing me off, what do you suggest?" She sat up, "Well, you have three options; one, you pull it in and risk the line snapping, two, you cut the line and we go home, three, you dive in after it." Options two and three didn't exactly appeal so I went for it and just started hauling, hand over hand until there was this green and gold thrashing thing coming right at me. As it closed on me, I saw big yellow eyes and big teeth, it looked pissed off. Given the circumstances and bearing in mind that I had never seen one of these things before, I think that I handled myself fairly well. "What the fuck, what is it? It's fucking massive!" I shouted, as it reared up from the water and splashed across the surface on its tail towards me and my extended left hand to which the line was attached. 'Bat', 'bat', 'bat', she hit it three times right on the head between the eyes with a stone mace, it hung limp in the water as blood started to run from its gills, my arm suddenly taking its weight. "Right, if you have quite finished playing with your fish, I would like to get back now," she picked up the paddle and started back to the platform.

When we were once more on the brushwood platform she kneeled down to retrieve the hook from the mouth of the pike, it was far too deep to retrieve so instead she gutted the pike. Sawing up along the belly from its tail to its head with her shell saw and feeling through its gut until she could find the hook. After she had burst the gut wall to get at the toggle and slipping the toggle from out of the end loop in the line, she pulled the hook-less line back out of the mouth of the fish. She used its guts to bait the eel traps and threw both traps back into the water. "This toggle hook," she waved it under my nose, "I use big bait because it covers the whole hook, so the fish eats it all, it gorges itself on the bait and when we pull the line the toggle swings out and jams in its gut, holding tight like the toggles on my eel basket lid." I nodded, fascinated at what I was learning.

To the right of the stakes to which the traps were tied was another stake to which was attached another willow line, she drew this in carefully and another pike came in although this one had no fight in it. She had set the line last night and it looked dead, it was only about the length of my forearm, unlike my fish, which was almost as long as my leg. The gorge hook had jammed across the gills of the small pike and it had bled to death. As she wrestled the gorge hook from its mouth she commented, "We were lucky that another pike didn't eat this with all the blood in the water attracting them." Taking the wet willow lines, she coiled them loosely before placing them at the base of a clump of reedmace so that they were shaded from the drying sun. "If I think on, I will have to collect some more willow bast from the scrub along the little stream, your fish damaged the line with its teeth, see." Looking at its huge jaws, full of sharp teeth as long as my thumbnail, I could see why.

Back at the camp, she gutted the smaller fish, giving the guts to the dog, he was still sitting at the shelter minding his own business, he seemed to have accepted me, well, he hadn't bit me or pissed on me so far today. Taking the large pike over to a drying rack, she hung it so that the inside of the fish faced south, facing the sun and wind, the moisture of its flesh began to dry almost immediately.

While we had been fishing, one of my unguarded boots that had been on the platform had developed a hole in the side. I didn't recognise the teeth marks and neither did she, but some animal had obviously decided that it was food and had begun to chew on it. I was moaning about this and blaming the dog, but she said that the dog never came into the marsh unless she asked him to, fair enough but I wouldn't put it past it. Throwing the boot down by my shelter, I decided that I would repair it later.

While she was occupied, washing herself in the mouth of the stream and collecting firewood from the shore, I split open the smaller pike so that it was splayed out in front of me. I had left the skin on the pike and now began preparing it by running my forefinger along the backbone and working outwards along the bones. Working the flesh from the bones on both sides of the fish until I could peel out the backbone and most of the large bones in one go, though I noticed that there were many small bones in the flesh. After rinsing the flesh in the fresh water of the little stream, I started to sharpen four small green willow branches that I had collected in the scrub along its edges. With the fish lying opened out in front of me I inserted a piece of willow through the inside extreme left side of the pike, I then fed it back out through the extreme right side, so that it came out through the inside of the fish. I repeated this half way down the fillet and again at the bottom so that the skewers were shielded by the splayed-out flesh. The fourth branch was slightly longer than the other three and I inserted it through the flesh at the top, went under the first crosspiece, over the second and under the third and back through the flesh. I then pushed this stick into the sand next to the fire and angled the meat of the splayed-out fish towards the heat and smoke. Pleased with my work I went back to the stream to wash all the slime from my hands, throwing the skeleton of the fish onto her shell tip.

Returning with an armful of wood she stacked it carefully on the woodpile, then checked the cover and placed a couple of stones on top, to make sure that it didn't blow off the next time we had strong winds. She then took two smoking logs from the fire and carried them over to the small hearth beneath the rack on which the big pike hung. Adding a few smaller twigs of alder to the logs, she quickly got a little fire going. Straight away, the smoke drove the flies from the flesh of the pike. Joining me by the fire, she sat down cross-legged and proceeded to twist her freshly washed long dark hair into a ball on top of her head, where she pinned it with what looked like a long thin bone from a bird, perhaps a heron or bittern, I wasn't sure. I looked at her shell necklace; the cord made from a fine 2-ply willow bast cord that hung around her tanned golden neck. Needless to say, her conversation about my fishing talent wasn't exactly flattering. "It is a great shame that you took so long to catch that fish, the tide is coming in and the full moon last night means that we will have very low tides for only two more days. We need to collect as many shellfish as we can, then I will show you how to preserve them." I just sat there taking it, I didn't want a row.

We both sat facing the fire and the sea beyond, our backs to the windbreak. She had different gear on this evening, a knee-length buckskin skirt, on which she had drawn circles of red, yellow, brown and black, obviously mixtures of blood, ochre and charcoal, it was very effective. Her long sleeved shirt was coloured with yellow ochre and on it were stitched small round pieces of dried and polished fish skin as decoration, they caught the setting sun and the flames of the fire as she moved. It was a good look; it suited her.

We ate and said nothing while she filed her toe nails with a piece of pumice that she had collected from the high tide line, then out of nowhere. "You know all about me, you know where I am from, you know how I got here, you see how I live and you know I am alone. Yet all I know about you is that you are here for the fishing and have come from over there somewhere." She waved her hand to the south-east; I followed her hand and looked into the distance. Although she was making an attempt at conversation I wasn't really in the mood to talk to her, I was still feeling pissed off with her. I couldn't understand why she had to make comments that made me feel small, there was only two of us here so what was there to gain from it? "So are you going to tell me?" Somewhat reluctantly, I began to tell her my story. "It is not far away, you can just about see it from the high dune, the long grey hills lying north to south far away in the distance, high land rising suddenly from the east of the Great Plain. Seven or eight day's walk that's all, it would be quicker but the ground is wet and there are lots of lakes, rivers, pools and streams which slow you down." She looked to the south-east, "I have never been into the Great Plain, I have travelled into the mouths of both of these Great Rivers but I return here." I looked about the camp, "I can see why, it is a good place, you have a good camp here, good resources, well placed, it was a good decision to stay here." She smiled, "Thank you," she took a mouthful of pike followed by a sip of nettle tea and wiped a drop from the corner of her mouth. "Have you got anybody?" Surprised by the question I shook my head, "No... no woman for me." "A man?" "No, no man either." She nodded, "Why?" "I did have a partner, but she died in childbirth... in spring, two years ago." Not sure if she wanted to know anymore I stopped, but she looked inquisitive and seemed to invite me to continue, I did. "Outside the house that morning the cuckoo was calling... it was just after sunrise and mist was rolling across the camp like slow milky water, mixing with the wood smoke... the tops of the houses were sticking out above, like little islands. All the old women were inside with her; fresh whitethorn blossom draped all over the place." She interrupted, "Whitethorn?" "Hawthorn ... anyway, in the house there was warm water in big wooden bowls which was infused with the leaves of chamomile and meadowsweet and she was drinking a tea of bistort leaves to help with the birth. I was sitting on the edge of the camp, crouching underneath an oak and hoping that my child would grow as big and old as this tree. I remember hearing the cuckoo some distance away and watching swallows belt around the camp, their eager mouths open and gaping, grabbing at the flies that filled the air. I was always glad to see the swallows when they came home to us, we all were they brought the spring with them. They returned to our camp every year, to have their young; born here, from here, local like us, birds of the spring and summer. Then when ready, they would leave home with their young, leaving us in the autumn, travelling south, down the valley, chasing the sun and taking the warm weather and the long days of summer with them. I remember that there was a red squirrel scampering around the branches above me, it looked busy and I wondered if it had young, like I was about to have. I wandered if it was the mother or father, and if this was the first time that it had had young, like my partner and me. Other than the call of the cuckoo, it was silent, peaceful. The beautiful smell of the woods in late spring drifted about me, as the woods awoke to the New Year. It was a beautiful morning spring to come into the world... the mist was clearing and the sun filled the glade with a warm golden light which dappled the gentle curls of smoke that rose from our houses. I remember thinking at that moment, that the Great Spirit knew so much joy to create all of this beauty... all of this joy, but it seemed that as soon as I had thought this, the wailing started. I found in that moment, that the Great Spirit also knows such pain, and I saw some of that pain that morning. I ran to the house, the old women were wailing and waving their arms up and down, apparently the baby was the wrong way round and had been strangled by the cord ... and she... she had died through pain and loss of blood... I left the old women to it and went off in a rage of tears and cursing... it was shit."

During the time that I had recounted the story my head had dropped and it now bowed toward my chest, telling this tale had hurt me and I was embarrassed. "That is very sad," she said, looking up I saw that she too had tears in her eyes. Smiling, I shrugged my shoulders, "Ah well, it is life, it is death." She was quiet for a moment then spoke, "It is a shame that you have no kids, no one to pass on to." I wasn't sure what she meant by this and asked her to explain. "Well, we are alive, we have kids, we die, they live, they have kids, they die, and their kids have kids and so on. Each of us in our turn carries life forward to the next generation, until we die. When we have kids, we have passed life into them, we have done our work, and we can die, like the salmon. After spawning the salmon dies, its work is done." I looked at her, of course, it was what I believed too, but I didn't acknowledge this and questioned her. "So you believe that's what we are here for then, just to carry life on from one generation to another?" She nodded, "Yes, that is what all things do; plants spread seed, all animals and fish make young, and so do we." "Hah, all except me," I added bleakly. "So if you have no kids, what are you doing while you are on the earth then?" Not sure how to respond to her question I shook my head, "I suppose that if I am not carrying life onto the next generation... I suppose that I am... I suppose that I am just passing through." She looked thoughtfully at me while still eating. "You are just passing through, not leaving anything behind you, well that sounds sad to me." Shrugging again, I didn't know what to say, "It might well be sad, but there's not much that I can do about it." Taking a sip of tea she carefully placed the bowl down onto the sand, "Yes, but you might meet someone... you might, and you might have kids with them... you just might." "Who knows?" I said, I wasn't too happy about this and I couldn't let it lie. "But there are different circumstances that affect people, look at me for example, my partner died in childbirth, so are you saying that unless I have kids there is little point in my life, me just passing through?" She waved her hands in front of her, "Of course not, no of course not." "Well what are you saying?" leaning forward she seemed to wrestle for an answer. "I am saying that... well, if you... if you don't have kids then perhaps you are not fulfilling your purpose in life. Surely it is normal to have children and continue the life of us." She was pointing to her chest for emphasis, she continued. "If we all stopped having children, we would die out, it is that simple. Just think if deer stopped having young or fish stopped having young, or plants stopped having seeds, they would all die out, and we would die out as a result." I thought that she

54

had finished, but she carried on, "And who will look after you when you are old?" I shook my head, "I have no idea, but my tribe tend to look after each other, I am sure that someone will look after me." For a moment, I thought of Beautiful Eyes back at camp, I felt sure that she would look after me. "But will you feel less of a man for not having children? Will you feel less fulfilled?" All these sudden questions were doing my head in and I answered abruptly, "Fuck knows, I don't fucking know, I am not a Shaman, I can't see into the future, can we change the subject please?"

After a while of silence we continued to talk about more pleasant things, it was interesting to hear her thoughts and it made me think of a comment that she had made days before. "Remember what you said about the sun the other day… you said 'it seems that the sun is always in the south'. Well, when I was a boy, I went with my family for many many days and many many moons, very far south, walking almost every day, and even though we walked all that way to the south, the sun was still in the south. I think that the sun and heat is in the south and the cold is in the north, and that's it."

Chapter 6.

It was already warm by the time that I had woken and wandered down to the sea to freshen myself up. A clear blue sky, a clear blue sea, the hazy outlines of the mountains across the bay to the south-west shook gently. I was naked in the surf when she greeted me. "Hiya… be careful of the undertow." Turning towards her I waved and asked what the undertow was, I remembered that she had mentioned it the other day, as I turned and lifted one of my feet, I found out. The sand slipped quickly from beneath me and I was pulled over as if by unseen hands, at the same time, a wave dumped its load of water on me and I went under. I hadn't much air in my lungs because I had just shouted out my question, so I was caught unawares. The next wave lifted me up off my feet and dropped me on the sand with a slap, as the trough passed over me I was able to stick my head above the water and gulp in some air. Only for another wave crest to lift me up and off my feet again, pushing me over, under and down head first into the sand. In a slow river or a pool, I would have been alright. Normally I was a reasonable swimmer, but not in these conditions and I was having great difficulty staying orientated in all the noisy white froth. Suddenly, an even bigger, very heavy wave smashed down on my head and I was held flat, under the water, hitting my face on sand then gravel. Things were worsening and I would be swept out or drown if I couldn't think of something soon. Then, through the froth, a hand tried to grab what was left of my hair but missed and managed to grab my neck, then another grabbed under my arm and suddenly I was bumping into her strong thighs as she hauled me shoreward's. When the water was waist deep she let me stand, stumbling along beside her, spluttering and choking on the salt water which now seemed to be in every hole in my body. "Hiya… be careful of the undertow," she said, as calm as you like.

While she sat and prepared a hot drink and food I sat shaking, a bit from the cold and a bit from the physical beating and lack of air that I had just experienced, my head was still spinning. Today, when I had recovered, she was taking me salmon fishing and shellfish collecting.

The plan was to fish at high tide in the river Alt when the salmon would be moving from the sea over the shingle bar and into the little river, then at low tide this afternoon we would collect shellfish. Getting the kit together, she went to the canoe shelter to get the smallest canoe. "Will we need it?" I asked. Shrugging her shoulders she replied, "Well, if we catch fish it is easier to bring them back in this and if we want to go upriver it would be useful, what do you think?" "Ok, you know best," she dragged out the smallest canoe from under the shelter, it moved easily across the dry sand due to its light weight; into this she put two strange spear things and a mobile hurdle. The mobile hurdle was just that; a willow hurdle as big as a splayed out roe deer skin with a strong plaited rawhide handle on the back. It was an open weave so that water could go through it easily but fish couldn't, I measured the square gaps in the weave which were about as wide as three fingers. Picking up one of the fish spears I examined it; a straight hazel shaft about as long as the distance from my feet to my shoulders, then three separate serrated edges as the head. I looked at my half-open right hand and folded the little finger and thumb together so that they touched, then extended the middle three fingers and opened them as wide apart as I could. My hand now resembled the size and shape of the fish spear, without the serrated edge. "What's this thing then?" "It is a leister… a fish spear; you stab the fish with it… I use them for the pike when they spawn in the margins, I think I told you." I couldn't remember what she had told me, I thought that she had said that she speared them… whatever; I didn't want to argue over spear points. I had recovered enough from my morning water dunking to help her drag and carry the canoe up, over the dune, and on to the little river. She was right, where it met the sea the river was full of curling white waves, bucking, prancing and braying at the shingle, fighting to get up, over, and into the river. "You see," she pointed, "You wouldn't wish to paddle through all those white horses would you," I saw what she meant, the name fitted the waves perfectly, though the seals that were bobbing up and down amongst the white raging heads seemed to have no problem.

Three huge birds that had been sitting on the bank took off as we approached, they had white heads and tails and large yellow bills, "Fish eagles," she said. "They collect here at this time of the year to catch the salmon; they are beautiful birds aren't they." "They are magnificent, I don't think that I have seen them before, I think that they are bigger and much lighter coloured than our eagles, we have eagles near us in the hills, but I am sure that these are bigger." She was nodding, "Yes, in my land, in the mountains and lakes we have both types and there are many of these fish eagles, they live along the coast and along the lakes, so our young men and women make hides in which to sit. On top of the hide, they tie down parts of a dead animal. The eagles land on the top of the hide and have to stay put to feed on the meat because it is held fast. Then the person in the hide beneath reaches up through a gap in the branches to grab as many tail feathers as they can from the eagle. The more feathers you grab the braver you are. But some people have had their wrists and hands ripped apart because they were not quick enough to pull their hand back through the gap." "Sounds like a great idea, I am glad that my tribe doesn't do things like that, I think I will leave the tail feathers on the eagle, looking at the size of them it is probably a much safer option."

Arriving at the riverbank, I sat myself down on a dry patch of saltmarsh grass and sea plantain to take my boots off while she talked me through the plan. "You get into the water well upstream of the shingle bar and white horses, then find the channel by feeling for it with your feet. If you are not careful, those water horses will rear up and grab you, dragging you under and away." I was looking at them; they seemed to slide sideways, drop backwards then drive forwards again, while all around them the water raged. "Where I am from we have them on some of our big lakes, water horses, they will appear from out of nowhere, the lake can be flat and calm, and then suddenly, whoosh, they roll up the shingle and grab you. We have lost small children to the water horses, you must be careful, always keep an eye open for them, or they will drown you, for sure." She must have seen that I was frowning, "Just stay at the edge of the channel and hold the hurdle so that the base of it is just touching the bed of the river and the edge of it is against this side of the channel. It will be hard work because the water will be trying to push you over and rip the hurdle from you, but you must stay as still as you can and check that the channel is not moving. Oh and you had better have no trousers on." I looked at the raging water as I removed my trousers, I was thinking about what had happened to me already this morning and I wondered if this was a joke, "And what are you doing while I am in there?" Picking up the leister she said, "I will be standing on the bank using this." Still none the wiser I sought clarification, "What does that mean exactly? I am going to be standing in a raging river with a bloody hurdle that is going to be pulling me towards the sea due to the weight of water against it and you are going to be standing on the bank with that thing." "Yes, what is your problem?" I shook my head, "My problem is that I have already nearly drowned once today and I would sooner not do it again, and how does me standing in the fastest part of the river and you standing on the bank catch fish?" Dropping to her knees in the sand, she drew a diagram of what would happen. "This is the river, this is the channel, this is you here on the edge of the channel and this is me on the bank." It was a pretty good picture as far as these things go; about one pace wide and two paces long and everything was on there, so you could be in no doubt what was what. Both banks of the river, the white horses, the shingle bar and the channel, her on the bank complete with leister and tits, and me in the river with a hurdle and a small cock. I had to ask, "Why have you put tits and a cock on the people?" She laughed, "So that you know who is who of course." "Right, of course, daft of me to ask… but what is the fucking hurdle for?" I was getting pissed off with all this. She replied as abruptly, "Hey, don't get tetchy with me, just fucking listen and stop whining. The salmon come over the bar through the white water of the horses, they surge into the channel because it is the deepest part of the river, they follow the edge of the channel up across the rest of the beach, go upstream into the dunes where the river deepens and then they are away. If we do not catch them here then it is much more difficult to catch them further upstream." She still hadn't answered my question, "So what is the hurdle for?" "I hadn't finished speaking; the fish swim up the edge of the channel and because the water is raging here they cannot see far ahead, so they bump into the hurdle. You will feel that bump and you will say 'now' as soon as you feel it. As you say 'now' I strike into the water making sure that I don't spear your feet, so keep them well back from the hurdle, have you got that?" "Yup, I have got that," it sounded like a stupid idea to me and I couldn't help thinking that this was just a piss take, but I took hold of the hurdle and stepped in carefully. The freezing water nearly took my breath away as my feet felt for the channel amongst the fast moving sand and gravel. "Use the hurdle to rest on, if you have it in front of you and lean against it you shouldn't fall over and it will protect your feet in case I misjudge with the spear." Finding the channel I stepped, well, fell down into it. It was just under waist deep and the water was pushing against my arse, my bollocks felt as though a big fish with very cold teeth was nibbling at them. "This is bloody freezing," she, of course, was laughing, "Your cock will be tiny in that water, you will look like me down there." "Yeah, very funny, shall we get on because I don't want to be spending any more time in here than I need to." Leaning against the hurdle to stop myself from falling over, I let my feet do the work of checking on the channel edge as bits fell away under the weight and speed of the water. I moved the hurdle so that it touched the very edge of the channel so that any salmon that were running couldn't sneak up around the hurdle itself, 'bump,' the hurdle was knocked by something but I was too slow to respond. My mind was trying to work out what was happening beneath the surface of this raging water when some unseen thing bumped the hurdle again. "Yes, now, now," I shouted but I was still too slow and the leister caught nothing. "You must say it as soon as you feel it, just say yes or something, something quick and fast so that I can respond immediately, or the fish will turn back and go before I get near it." I nodded, "Alright, alright, I need to concentrate and to feel the presence of the fish, I will get it right." Head down I shut my eyes and felt the water, the cold water, the constant tremble of the hurdle as it resisted the current, the crumble of sand at the edge of the channel against my left foot and the bed moving against my feet. Familiarising myself with the feel of it all, so that as soon as something changed I would know. "Yes," I said short and sharp, she plunged the leister just downstream about a forearm length from the hurdle, and the shaft immediately quivered and shook as the salmon was speared. "Wow, look at that thing," I was amazed, she hit it on the head with a stone so that it wouldn't wriggle back into the river, then prized open the two outer serrated spears and pulled the fish from the middle spear. The fish was about as long as my arm, a bright solid bar of silver. It looked as though it had been made from the water, it had all the colours of the sea; grey, blue, silver, with green tints on its black eye and some strange little things that hung onto its back, she called them sea lice. The salmon that we got up in the river at my camp tended to be less silver, they had a bit of brown or pink on them, some had long upturned lower jaws and we never saw the lice, perhaps they fell off in the rivers.

We carried on fishing like this until ten salmon and three sea trout lay, silver on the sand, deciding that was enough she said that we should return to the camp and clean them. Lifting the hurdle from the base of the river, I was enthused by the activity and the result. "That was brilliant, absolutely brilliant," she turned to look at where my left foot was about to step, "Be careful there, the sand is soft and it may collapse, use the hurdle to prop you up." Too late, over I went, falling down the edge of the channel flat on my arse into the river with just the top of my head sticking out. This time she left me to it, she obviously thought that I was capable of getting myself out, or she didn't want to get wet. Struggling with the hurdle, I fought my way back out of the water and sat on the warm sand. The fish lay there pock marked with flies, a stunning sight, "That was great," I laughed, "I never thought that it would work, but it was great." She was smiling and was looking as happy as I had seen anyone in a long while. I sat there smiling back, knowing that I was as happy as I had been in a long while. "Do you fancy going for a walk tomorrow?" "Certainly, where to and what for?" I asked. "I thought that it would be nice to show you my tribal land, that's all." Thinking about this I answered, "That's some fucking walk." Shaking her head, she added, "No, you can see it by walking to the next Great River, to the north of here. It is about a half-day's walk. I think that you will like it." I shrugged my shoulders, "Yes, sounds good."

Using the canoe to carry everything back was difficult at times, it was heavy with the fish in it, so where the sand was dry, clean and free of stone or wood we dragged it rather than carried it. Wasting no time, we sliced open the bellies of the fish, pulling out the guts and keeping the roe when we had a hen fish. We cut around the neck on both sides of the head so that we could open out the fish for smoking. Lifting a larger fish rack from over by the house, we carried it to the main campfire, standing it so that the legs straddled the fire and making sure that the rack was positioned under the edge of the roof of the shelter to keep it dry. Draping the fish over the poles, she then placed a load of alder sticks on the fire and left the fire to get on with it. The guts went into a seal hide bucket that was half-full of seawater; she would use them later for the eel traps. After we had cleaned the sand from the canoe, checked it for damage and put it back under the cover, we ate a quick lunch of some of the smoked sea trout, fresh and oily; it was perfect eaten with the leaves of orache, collected fresh from the shore.

Low tide found us way out on the wet sand where it became gravel then larger stone, she told me that this was as low as it ever got and that tonight it would be as high as it could get. I knew that the full moon affected the tide, I had seen that for myself years ago, but I didn't realise that the new moon did the same. It was important for her to keep a check on both the full moon and the new moon; it was how she planned her time and her tasks here. She was using a long red deer antler tine to riddle through the wet sand to find cockles. When she found one she placed it into a collecting basket that was weaved from rushes, the basket hung on a raw hide belt over her left shoulder so that the mouth of the basket faced her right hand, eager to swallow the shellfish. I had a go and found that though they were plentiful in places they were nonexistent in others. Walking easterly to where one of the rocky outcrops extended out into the bay, we found many more shellfish. She gave me a lesson in identifying them; limpets that looked like her house and stuck tight to the rocks, dark grey winkles that looked like a type of snail, white dog whelks which, when I turned them over to look at where they came out of their shell, looked like a dead man's eye. I found an empty colourful shell, she called it a topshell, pink and grey with a shiny sheen to it where it was broken. I smashed the limpets from the rocks using a stone, while she prized them off using the point of the antler tine. The highlight for her were the tiny yellow periwinkles of which she only took the empty shells, I collected whatever she told me to as she told me what they were. As I collected, she told me to take only the bigger shellfish, there was no point taking the small ones, they didn't have enough meat on them and it meant that there would be shellfish here next year and the year after. We sat for a while feeding on seaweed fresh from the rocks, she seemed to enjoy it but I wasn't keen, it was chewy, salty and had a quality that I couldn't compare with anything that I had ever eaten before. She took some for later, though I was not sure how she could make it any more palatable. As we were sitting there, an otter was floating on its back in the gentle waves, not far out; it seemed unaware of our presence. Regularly diving into the shallow water, it first rolled onto its front, then disappeared head first beneath the surface, its long tail being the last thing to vanish. Shortly after it would re-surface and lie on its back chewing on what looked like either crabs or flatfish, I couldn't make out which. Away to our left, three curlews probed around the edge of the rocks, where the seaweed flopped onto the sand. While one of them seemed content to look for small things to eat, two were catching the little green shore crabs. It looked like hard work and I was surprised how much time went into the juggling of the crab in the long thin curved bill. She told me that they were trying to snap off the legs of the crab until it was small enough to swallow in one go. One of the birds had several attempts at swallowing but dropped the angry crab only to quickly pick it up and start juggling again. When it had got rid of enough of the legs and despite the crab hanging on to the bill with its one remaining pincer, the curlew swallowed it. The large lump in the bird's neck took a while to go, I hadn't a clue how long the crab would take to die in the birds gut, but the bird looked pleased with itself.

In amongst the rocks right down at very low water, she began pushing the long antler tine into crevices under the seaweed, not sure what she was up to, I watched closely. To my surprise, something grabbed on to it. At first I thought that she was playing games, pretending that there was something on the other end, until out came a red brown crab as big as my hand, with massive claws. "Fuck me, that's a big bugger alright." She carried on and found another two; both of them were nearly as big as the span of my two hands. To make them let go of the stick and to prevent them from grabbing our fingers, she quickly smashed their claws with a stone, so that they were broken and useless. The crabs went into her collecting basket, and she placed damp seaweed on each one. "Why do you do that?" "It calms them down, being in the dark and damp, and it stops them fighting and climbing out." I shook my head, "I wouldn't have thought that they could fight, you have just smashed their claws." She smiled at me, "That won't stop them trying." The last thing was to collect a few little green shore crabs before we started to walk back to the camp, as the sea started to move back in.

Once back, she gave me a cookery lesson. She let me try all the shellfish; raw at first, breaking the shells of the winkles and dog whelks by hitting them with a small stone, the dogwhelk had the toughest shells. Everything tasted pretty much the same to me apart from the dogwhelk, which had a strong meaty aftertaste. As for the limpets, she scooped out the meaty little animal with her fingernails, threw aside the black shit sack and put the meat in her mouth. I did the same, but noticed that the little animal inside was looking at me, waving its little antlers or whatever they were, which almost put me off. The limpets were very chewy and she laughed as I sat there trying to swallow them. Then she cooked some very simply in the ashes at the edge of the fire, again I thought that the dogwhelk had a strong aftertaste and the limpets were still very chewy. She placed the seaweed that she had collected earlier on the edge of the fire to dry and become crisp, it made it much more palatable than when we ate it raw. As for the small green shore crabs, she smashed those poor little buggers up while they were still alive, and put all their pieces, shell and all into a large wooden bowl filled with hot water. She continued to add hot stones to this so that it was on a rolling boil, and when she was happy that it had cooked, she drained it into our eating bowls by pouring the soup through a small tightly woven basket, which collected all the bits.

The large red brown crabs were chucked alive into the deeper ashes at the centre of the fire, where they jumped and whistled as the air heated up under their shells and came out as steam; she turned them over with a stick after a while so that both sides cooked. The shore crab soup was the tastiest of all of the methods, and I had quite a lot of that, but the final method would take longer. She wandered off to the stream and came back with a handful of thin green twigs of willow and alder, about as long as her arm. Passing me half of them she said, "Make a simple weaved rack for the shellfish." I did, the task was made easier because she was also making one so I could watch and learn. When both of them were finished, she placed them across the poles of the drying rack so that the racks were just above the smoke. "This will do two things; it will smoke and dry the shellfish so that I can use them much later, many days later. Also when the limpets are very, very dry, I can crush them between rocks and make flour from them, I can use the flour to thicken hot soups and stews." She looked up at me, and then added, "In the cold and dark of a winter's night." She shivered for effect, and smiled to herself.

All in all we had had a busy day and I was knackered, so it was understandable that I fell asleep by the fire in the warmth of the sun; lying on my right side and dozing I occasionally half opened my left eye so that I could watch her as she worked. She had tidied up all the shells from the cooking and these were now on her rubbish tip, it was quite a sight; bones of fish, seal, bird, shells of crab, winkle, limpet, whelk and any other crap that she didn't want next to her house. Even though I was half asleep through my half open eye I noticed that she would look at me every now and again; I don't think that she caught me looking, but I couldn't work out what her expression was.

When I eventually woke, she was winding sinew around the base of one of the tines on the leister that she had been using in the river, wetting it in her mouth then wrapping it tight. It would tighten even more as it dried and even though it would be used in the water again at some point, the sinew would hold long enough and would not slacken because she was then coating it in fat then sand.

We were beneath a sky that was pale blue in the west and dark blue, almost black in the east. Wispy clouds, as pink as the flesh of the salmon that we had smoked earlier in the day, moved slowly eastwards across a silver sliver of a moon that hung low in the west. She pointed, "You see, remember what I said earlier about the moon and the tides, when it is full and when it is a sliver that is when the tides are biggest and lowest... I don't know why, but it is." Looking from east to west, I enjoyed the view. "Well whatever the reason, it is beautiful, perhaps the reason is simple, perhaps the Great Spirit did it so that we would all know when and where to be, just like today."

I moved behind where she was sitting, I hadn't noticed it before, but now I saw that she had a tattoo on the back of her left shoulder. I had none myself; apart from the camouflage paint that I put on when I went hunting I was art free. Looking closer I could just make out that it was a dolphin, though the ink was fading. "Nice dolphin, but the ink is fading, do you want me to re-colour it?" Squinting at it over her shoulder, she gave me the impression that she had forgotten that she had it, "Oh… yes, er, no…thanks. My partner drew it from the ink of a large brown sea slug that we found in a rock pool on a very low tide. He spiked my skin using dry Marram and sharp pieces of flint, it was quite painful actually." I laughed, "I can imagine, did you return the pleasure?" Looking up from her work she answered, "Yes, I drew a seal on him, a seal, how about that?" Shuffling around the fire, I felt a bit crap; it hadn't been my aim to remind her of her lost man. "I am sorry, I didn't mean to," holding up her right hand she stopped me. "No need to apologise, you were not to know… that is why I am letting it fade, it will go in time, I am sure."

Chapter 7.

She woke me early, at sunrise. "Come on... the walk, come on, let's go." To be honest I had forgotten about the plan, and I was yawning and rubbing the sleep from my eyes as we set off along the coast. "How far is it again?" She was ahead of me and had a noticeable spring in her step; she turned and answered, "About a half a day, perhaps less." Shitbag was toddling along at the water's edge, sniffing and pissing on everything, chewing on seaweed and crab shells and any other rubbish that he could find.

We had started in a north-westerly direction, crossing the Alt at low tide, wading through at the shingle bar then onwards, the dunes on our right and the flat sea on our left. After a short while, we rounded a broad sandy point and started to walk northerly along a broad strand of beach. The sea was a long way out to the west, revealing mudflats as far as my eyes could see, with so many birds wading, feeding and flying that I stood rooted to the spot, mouth agape. "Wow." "I told you I thought you would like it, see." With this, she turned to her right, waving her outstretched arms towards the huge sand dunes that ran on our right and disappeared to the north into the distance. "Fuck me, that is some sight, they are massive." "Yes, they go all the way up to the next Great River which we are walking towards, and they go that way into the Great Marsh." She was pointing to the east with both arms, she was clearly enjoying sharing this stunning coastline with me, and I felt flattered and humbled.

We walked along the warm dry sand, both of us had our boots hung over our shoulders, the sand felt sensuous to my bare feet, the sun beat down and warmed the gentle breeze that carried us on our way. She was wearing a short wrap around buckskin skirt and a short-sleeved buckskin shirt on top, a necklace of small bone beads hung around her neck, her hair hung loose around her shoulders, occasionally lifted by the breeze. I was wearing my trousers and had tied the arms of my shirt around my waist so that I could feel the sun on my back.

Some of the dunes had great chunks scooped from them; she said that this was where the winter storms had ripped them apart, tearing the sand from the marram grass and leaving their roots exposed, hanging in great tresses, like giant cobwebs. I could also make out trees just behind some of the dunes; she reckoned that the woods were already there before the dunes, and that the dunes were moving in to the woodland, swamping it out. I asked her why this was happening; she told me that she believed that the sea was getting higher, closer to the land. Apparently, the elders of her tribe had noticed this over the course of their long lives.

Walking over a small rocky outcrop on the edge of the dune, she pointed out a collection of shells. "That is lobster, and that is sea urchin; here are fish bones and pieces of crab." She explained that it was the rubbish tip of an otter. "It is very similar to your rubbish tip," I said, "Yes, but without the seal." "And the dog shit," I added. In a muddy patch further along the shoreline we noticed fresh footprints of red deer, aurochs, and one I didn't recognise. "It is crane, a big bird, a very big bird." She held her right hand to her thigh to demonstrate its height, had a re-think and moved it up to her waist." "A very big bird," I noted. "Yes, they come from the reedbeds in the Great Marsh and feed out on the saltmarsh grasses and plants, over there." Looking to where she was pointing, I noticed occasional patches of vegetation, some large some small, in amongst the many flowing creeks and pools out on the mudflats.

We stopped for a snack of dried fish that she was carrying in her hide bag; with the fish, we ate raw glasswort and drank water from my new bladder. All three of us sitting in the sand, even Shitbag seemed happy which surprised me. I went to stroke his head, but decided not to when he curled his lip and started to growl. Out on the mudflat the sun was making the mud look shiny, the heat haze distorted the birds that were standing and feeding. It looked as though they had no legs, and that they were standing still but floating. Far out, on one of the patches of vegetation, we could just make out a red deer grazing, it too looked odd. Its neck was long and wobbling, and its legs seemed much too short. Moved to speak, I did, "It is stunning here, beautiful, absolutely beautiful." She smiled, "Thank you, I am glad that you like it."

A while later we arrived at a point in the coast where the dunes curved away to the east. The vast expanse of mudflat had now given way to a huge saltmarsh and we were surrounded by a mix of grasses; short grey looking scrubby willow, vetches, and a range of plants that I had not heard of before. "That little pink fleshy one is sea milkwort, that little pink spiky one is thrift, the one with heart shaped leaves is scurvy grass, that low growing one is sea spurrey, that one is sea purslane, that is seablite, and that beautiful purple plant is sea lavender." She continued like this as we walked, I loved it. I always enjoyed learning new things; she had a use for every one of these plants; either for food, for drinks, for healing, for cleaning, for keeping insects away, for whatever. For me to be with someone who knew so much about the coast was wonderful. In my previous visits to the coast to the south of here, I had muddled along, making do where I could. However, here, with her, it was... fantastic and I tried to remember everything that she told me, every detail. Life was so much easier being with someone who was able to open the door to that natural knowledge.

She told me that we were now sitting on the south bank of a Great River that came from the long chain of hills that we could see over to our right. Apparently, this long chain went way north past her homeland and seemed to carry on well to the south of here. I wondered if this was the same chain that my tribal lands were in, way to the south. If we looked north from the Big Step, all we could see was a long chain of hills. She thought that it might be and that it would be amazing if our two tribal lands were actually connected in this way, it struck me that not only would it be amazing, it would be lovely.

As the sun began to drop, the distant heat haze disappeared and the air became clear and cool. "Look... it is there... my homeland." She was pointing north and jumping up and down like an excited girl. Nutter, I thought, as my eyes followed the direction of her hands, across the marsh, across the wide estuary, across the flat expanse of saltmarsh on the other side, to the distant hills that were now showing grey. From their peaks, a plume of white cloud trailed away to the east, she carried on bouncing, "There it is, I can see it."

Sitting on the sand watching the distant white plume, the sky darkened behind us as the black of the night gently moved the sun away. "Sorry about the bouncing back then, I got carried away," she said apologetically. We sat in silence as the light left the earth, leaving behind a cherry coloured sky. It was now high tide, and the Great Estuary became quiet, the sounds of the birds ceasing as they settled to roost for the night. With the shimmering silver sea before us, we watched the huge sunset paint the land pink, red and yellow, painting the distant hills of her homeland. Two small porpoise moved slowly across the mouth before us, both took three breaths before disappearing beneath the waves. She began to talk, and in keeping with the surrounding quietness, she talked quietly, not whispering, just speaking quietly. She was talking about her tribal lands and her life there, occasionally nodding toward those distant hills, while I just sat and listened. But her quiet talking had a surprising effect on me. It was as though her clear, softly spoken words were stroking my ears and hair. I could almost feel her words running down my body and my spine tingled, it was soothing, gentle, calming. I became aroused but made no attempt to reveal this to her. Instead, I let the crackle of the fire and her soft words cloak me in warmth and comfort, as the dark enclosed us and the night became cold.

Chapter 8.

Rain threatened, low grey mist covered everything as we set off into the Great Marsh to check on the eel traps and gorge hooks. I felt low and grey myself, it had been a strange couple of days up at the estuary of the other Great River. We seemed to have been getting on so well, wandering around in the marsh and the dunes, I had been gaining new knowledge and skills and she seemed to be enjoying herself. Then, all of a sudden she isn't talking to me, everything that I do is wrong, 'Blah, blah, blah'. The fact that it had been a big tide and a full moon made me think that she was bleeding, that always seemed a safe bet. Anyway, after two days she had had enough, so we packed up and returned to camp, with not a fucking word all the way back, I just walked along quietly and soaked in the scenery. And, I did see another amazing sight, which she missed because she was so far ahead of me. Fish were throwing themselves on the beach right in front of me. I couldn't work out why until I saw that a pod of dolphins were in close, hammering them. I picked up one of the fish and showed it to her, when I had caught up with her, she said, "It's a herring," and chucked it to the dog, before disappearing into her house for the rest of the day.

Anyway, she was here now, leading us, the dog was with us because she had asked him to come to keep her company, obviously preferring him to me; he was quietly working his way through a patch of butterbur, reeds and reedmace. She didn't take him into the canoe so he lay there occasionally snapping at dragonflies that were daft enough to go near the scruffy Shitbag. Both the lines with gorge hooks had caught small pike, but one had been half eaten by another larger pike so instead of us taking the bits that remained, the head and gills went into an eel trap as bait. We had set the traps three days ago and both were full, eels really did fascinate me and I sat looking at them as they wriggled and writhed inside the wicker basket, opening and closing their mouths, slime dripping from them and onto the platform.

Back at camp, we stuffed some of the freshly gutted eels with water mint then wrapped them in the large leaves of butterbur and placed them at the edge of the fire in the warm ashes. They steamed away gently, the scent of mint rising occasionally and mixing with the smoke. The pike was clamp grilled over the embers of the fire; first she made a weaved grill from green willow onto which she placed some mint leaves, the gutted pike was opened out and placed with its insides down onto the mint. Another weaved grill was placed over the pike and the two were tied together using some willow bast, clamping the pike tightly so it could be turned regularly. The heat, the smoke and the mint produced a fine tasting meat and apart from the fact that it was still very bony, it was chunky, dry and good to eat.

The grey mist of the morning had rolled away, producing a blue sky with a few wispy white clouds and a warm day. Sitting topless in the sun I basked in the heat that fell upon my body, she was wearing the same short-sleeved shirt and short skirt that she had worn when we had been away up the coast. She was sitting cross-legged, despite the fact that she still wasn't talking to me, as the fire smoked gently, the warm breeze fanning the wood, the eels cooking in their leaves and the dog lying there grumbling, growling and wriggling in the sand, legs up in the air, I drew in a long slow breath of contentment.

From out of nowhere, she started to talk for the first time today; "It's funny isn't it?" Bringing my gaze back from the horizon, where the sea seemed to wash against the distant mountains to the south-west, I answered, "What's funny?" She shifted in the sand; she was sewing one of her skirts using a fine bone needle and thin strands of sinew, so her eyes stayed focussed on her work. "Well, how things turn out, you don't know what will happen; you just roll along with it all and find out what happens." I wasn't really sure what she was on about and I didn't want to start rambling on about something that I didn't understand, so I just nodded and confirmed her words, "Hmm." She continued, "For example, sometimes you might want to do something or go somewhere but the Great Spirit wants you to choose a different path. You may not realise it at the time but it may turn out to be the better path after all. Look at you for instance, you were going to go to the south side of the Great River but the wall of white water made you choose and you chose to come to the north side, where I am… you came to me. If the wall of white water hadn't made you choose, you would be somewhere over there," she nodded across the bay to the south-east, "We might never have met." I wasn't sure whether she meant that it was a good thing or bad thing that we might never have met, judging by the fact that this was the first time she had talked to me in two days. Besides, I was hungry waiting for the main food to cook, so I went and collected some nettles that were growing near to where she called her 'woman's area.' Translated into man-speak this meant the place just to the east of the camp where she had a crap and a pee, though if she was desperate for the latter she would often just drop to the floor wherever she was, except in the camp.

Rinsing the nettles in the sea so that the leaves picked up some of the salty water, I then made my way back to the fire, where I held the nettles close to the embers and watched the leaves wilt. When limp I moved them nearer to the heat of the centre of the fire and watched the leaves begin to dry and curl up. When they were nice and crisp I removed them from the heat and we ate the crisp salted leaves, a simple yet decent enough snack for us while waiting for the main course.

The flat smooth stones at the edge of the fire needed to be hot enough to cook the flatbreads, so she had made sure that they had been covered with embers and hot ashes for some time. Now she scraped the ashes from the rocks using a stick and spat on the rock surface to make sure it was hot, it sizzled immediately. Next, she spooned out some seal fat from one of her wooden bowls and placed it onto the hot stone, it fizzed, spat, and crackled as it spread out, melting and covering the stone. Then she took the spoon and poured out some of a reedmace root flour and water mix, only a spoonful of the thick mix, just enough to spread it over the hot stone, to do this she used the back of the spoon. When it was cooked on one side, she lifted it with a flattened wedge of a stick and flipped it over to do the other side. When this side was cooked, she lifted it off and placed it on a bark plate. The flatbreads cooked quickly, wafting their smell toward me with my hand, "They smell delicious." "Thanks, don't you cook these back home?" Shaking my head I replied, "Don't know, they probably do but I suppose that I have forgotten about such things." She looked as though she had accepted my reason, and cocking her head to the right she smiled and continued in her gentle task; pouring, spreading, cooking, turning, cooking, lifting, pouring and so on. The real reason that I had 'forgotten about such things,' was that my partner would do her 'drop-cakes' as she called them, in exactly the same manner. The spoon that she used to use was one that I had made for her. It had taken me an age to make; first, I had taken a nice ash branch about two fingers thick, I had snapped it from the tree, and then snapped it again into about my forearm's length. With a piece of flint I had scraped off the bark and began to pare the branch down. Any rough bits were sanded off, where I was from, there was no shortage of rough gritty sandstone, so you just sat there sanding until it was smooth. As for the bowl of the spoon, the stick had got a nice bend in it at the bottom which was where I repeatedly scraped and burnt, scraping with my flint and burning out a piece with a small ember, once it was roughed out it was back to the sanding. I finished it off with some melted beeswax, it was the dog's bollocks and she had loved it. Seeing this woman here doing this reminded me of my partner, it was a bittersweet experience. I snapped out of it when she handed one over, smothered in seal fat, it tasted smashing. After we had eaten, I wandered off on my own, not wanting to dwell in the strange atmosphere that seemed to be surrounding us. From the highest dune I could make out the long grey hills of my homeland, I couldn't see the hills that were nearest to my home camp, but the ones to the north were there. I wondered about returning, for some reason, sitting down there with this woman was making me think of home. I didn't understand my emotions, I wasn't even sure if I liked her, but what I did like was that she was teaching me things and that I felt better for knowing those things. Nevertheless, she was pissing me off despite teaching me skills that I valued, so I needed some time on my own, to work out which was the most important.

The sun was on its way down when I returned to her camp, I had spent time mooching around in the dunes, watching the birds, looking at little bright green lizards, watching little black wingless bees crawl around the sand, in and out of burrows. I found the rotting body of a porpoise, half covered in sand, what lay above the sand was covered in flies, its smell was strong and not like any other smell I knew. A raven had led me to it, it had taken off as I neared the edge of the dune where the body lay, it was natural for me to walk over to see what the raven had been feeding on. She was silent, still sitting by the fire and still working. I had decided that I would stay, at least for another couple of days to pick her brains and then I would fuck off back into the Great Plain, to where I knew, to where I could be on my own.

I was keen to know more about her beliefs and her stories so I asked her a few questions and she began to open up. We chatted about all sorts of things, and though I thought that some of them were stupid, I didn't tell her that. "When the Great Spirit created flint and chert, it was dropped all over the world, but some bits shattered and dug deep into people's hearts and eyes. This meant that those people could only feel harsh things and see the world in a bad way." I nodded, "Sounds possible," I lied. She continued with another, "When the Great Spirit sent away the ice and created everything, the first thing that was created was water all over the world as the ice melted. The next thing was reeds, sedge, and rush, and then grasses, then the Great Spirit created the animals that grazed on these plants. Then the Great Spirit said, *'The animals need shelter from the heat of the sun,'* so the Great Spirit created the trees; from the singing aspen or the beautiful birch to the mighty oak and lime. Then the Great Spirit said *'What I need now is an animal that can make things, and talk, and sing about the world and all its glory. An animal that can see how beautiful the world is and make sure that it stays that way.'* That is why we had the gift of speech so that we could always pass on these words." That story did sound possible, so I wasn't lying when I told her so. "Anyway, what about you and your stories? It is your turn, now you tell me one." For a moment, I thought about telling her our ice story, but it was a story that bored me silly so I told her another very brief one instead. "Well we have one, because we live in the woods, you know, the usual kind of thing; a young boy meets a wolf, wolf eats boy, wolf falls asleep, hunter finds sleeping wolf, hunter kills and cuts open the wolf, out pops boy, hunter skins the wolf, they celebrate. Boy says, *'I will never go into the woods on my own when my mother tells me not to'.*" She nodded, "Yes that story is as old as the world, but in my tribe it is a girl who is told not to go into the woods on her own." Tending the fire, she riddled it with a stick before placing it into the flames, I listened to it crackle as the fire caught hold. "Oh yes, I know of an old story, I think it is a very old story. Three women were sitting near to the coast, to the north of here; near to the Great

River that we walked to, anyway they were sitting at the back of the dunes by a stream." Pausing, she shut her eyes as she struggled to remember the story, it wasn't her story, she had been told this story by someone else, so the story was less real to her and less well remembered. "That's it, they were sitting by the stream and I think that they were making leister points, barbed heads for fishing leisters, like the one that you used, or was it harpoons? Anyway, they were sitting there minding their own business and mounting the barbs onto shafts of wood, when all of a sudden a bull elk strode into their camp. They were just sitting by the stream with no shelter and this thing came towards them." "What did they do?" I interrupted. "Well, I was about to tell you... well they stood and fought bravely. Sticking the points into the legs of the great beast, it was the biggest bull ever... that anyone had ever seen, but they fought it off and one of them hit it with an axe and they drove it away and it limped off into the scrub." When I was sure that she had finished I asked, "What happened to it?" "I don't know, I think it must have gone off and died, I don't know, I think some of the barbs broke off in its legs, but I am not sure, like I said, it is a very old story." She had seemed excited by the telling of this tale, I wondered if the reason for this was that she wished that she had been able to fight off the seal that had killed her partner. Perhaps she had told the story of the three women, so that she could relive the moment that her partner died and in some way find an alternative ending. I wasn't sure, but I felt that I needed to say something at least, "Big animals elk, big animals."

She went to a drying rack and returned with a smoked eel, she sat peeling the skin and nibbling the flesh, then passed it to me and I did the same.

We sat quietly in this way, passing the fish between us until all that remained was a leathery tail, which Shitbag happily ate, before I suddenly piped up. I don't know why I needed to talk about my partner, perhaps I was after sympathy, I don't know, but I found myself talking before I could think. "When my partner died, one of the elder women tried to console me by saying that life moved in odd fucking ways and that we just had to fucking follow. She said that the Great Spirit had all these fucking shit tasks for us to perform, and that in some way I would be a better fucking person, and in time, my life would be so much fucking better. I just sat there thinking what a load of shit these elders talk; they are supposed to be wise, bollocks, just bollocks." Looking at me, she made an observation, "She swore a lot did she, this elder?" Although I think she had intended this as a joke, I did not take it as one; instead, I threw another branch onto the fire and farted.

Time passed in silence then letting out a deep sigh she cast her head around, as if looking for something to talk about, she found something. "I know, how about a joke?" "Go on then," given her sense of humour I was interested to find out what her joke was. Shuffling round to face me, she patted the sand with both hands as if to demand my attention. "Right, alright, this is my joke. When the Great Spirit created us, she created a woman first, and the first woman had three tits. But the first woman found that three tits were uncomfortable, so she asked the Great Spirit to help. The Great Spirit agreed with the woman, removed the middle tit, and threw it into the bushes at once. After some time, this first woman noticed that the other animals were pairing up and making lives together. Therefore, the woman asked the Great Spirit if it could be possible for the Great Spirit to create a mate for the woman. The Great Spirit looked around at all the other animals, all was quiet as she thought about this request, then answered, *'I can see that you need a partner in life so I will agree to this request, now go and find me that useless tit in the bushes'*." As she sat laughing I smiled politely and looked up at the darkening sky, she was also looking up. "You see those small clouds that look like the wispy seeds of hares-foot grass." I knew what she meant, but we just called it hares-foot, it grew on the high moors near to my tribal camp, especially a year or so after a fire. "I want to lengthen this shelter, make more of a windbreak, I think that tomorrow will be a fine day and that it will be fine for a while" I wasn't going to argue, I was confident in her forecast.

Chapter 9.

I was dozing, feeling the gentle breeze against me; it was sneaking around the shelter carrying a few sand grains that it blew into my face, I listened to the birds. Oystercatchers were making a constant racket down on the shore, gulls were circling above me, yelping down the wind, terns were screeching as they fluttered along the edge of the lapping waves, looking for small fish. Dead stems of marram rustled behind me, a bumblebee stopped for a breather in my shelter, before wandering off over the dunes. I was lying in the shelter of the windbreak that we had made several days ago. We had extended it some way so that it joined onto the right side of the shelter that covered the main campfire. Made from willow and alder from the scrub in the Great Marsh, the branches were about as thick as my fingers and as tall as me. We had stuck the main rods upright in the sand in a curved shape like a new moon, we then weaved the thinner ones in and out, a bit like the fish hurdle but this was a tighter weave to keep out the wind. On and through this frame we weaved handfuls of marram grass roots, great long lengths that we ripped from the dune edge easily, we then kicked up sand all around the base of the windbreak; it was nice and strong. It had taken all day working as fast as we could and we were fortunate that the bulk of the weavers came from the re-growth in the beaver coppice, where there were plenty of nice straight branches all about the same size. That saved us a heck of a lot of time messing about looking for good material. As she said to me when I started looking, "Trees seldom grow straight." She was right; so it was a good thing that the beavers were managing the scrub.

The new windbreak was effective; it was as long as both of us lying end to end, and the curve meant that it gave some protection from the north, north-west, west and south-west winds. We were already fairly protected from those directions by the dunes, but as autumn approached, it was good to be prepared. When the bad weather came and then the winter, she wouldn't bother with this outside fire, instead staying inside and relying on the house fire. By the winter a range of dried and smoked food such as mushrooms, greens, meat, fish, limpets and mussels would be inside hanging from the poles. In two large burnt out wood bowls was the dried limpet powder which she would add to hot water to make a hearty stock, not forgetting her seal fat, she would be well stocked with supplies for her second winter alone. I got the fire going and put some water into the large wood bowl, when the small boiling stones that were in the ashes were hot enough I lifted them with the two green sticks that acted as fire tongs and then placed them into the bowl of water. When it was good and hot I dropped in some leaves of water mint and let it steep. She joined me, she looked tired, "You alright?" I asked, "Yes, I was working most of the night, I am tired and I bashed my thumb." She stuck her right thumb in her mouth to suck it. "What were you doing?" She didn't answer and instead sat down next to me in the windbreak warming her hands by the fire, before speaking. "Well I don't know about you, but I think autumn is not far away, it feels cooler this morning and the sun rose over that hill in the south-east, that is my mark for autumn and spring." My eyes followed her outstretched left hand to where she was pointing. Placing another dry branch on the fire I agreed with her then asked her again, "So what were you doing all night?" She sighed, then yawned, "I was making long pieces of cord from rawhide and from willow bast and bark." I was puzzled, "Why?" "I attach one end to the top of my house poles and peg the other end into the sand using stakes. I use plant fibre and animal fibre to spread the loading, because the hide cord expands and loosens in the rain when it is wet but plant fibre cord swells and tightens in the wet, and of course, when it is dry the plant cord loosens but the hide cord tightens. So whatever the conditions, as long as I have 5 plant ropes and 4 hide ropes at least some of the ropes are tight and holding down the house in the winter winds, so I am well covered." "So you have alternate ropes on each of the poles?" She nodded whilst taking a sip of tea, "That's right, that's good tea... yes it seemed to work last year and it was really windy, at times. As good as it is here, it is really windy in the winter. One night last year, I was in bed listening to the wind rattle my house so much that I was convinced that the Great Spirit was trying to get in to take me there and then. I don't mind admitting that it was very frightening, I was scared, really scared, I lay there curled up with the dog, shivering crying and praying. I didn't want to be taken away by the Great Spirit; I didn't want to be dragged away into the dark, not like that... not lying there all on my own." She looked into the fire for a moment before taking another sip of tea. She had never let me see this vulnerability before, this glimpse into her self, I thought of her there in the dark of a ferocious night, exposed, frightened and on her own. This image upset me and I felt quite choked up and turned away from her, wiping a tear from my eye, unsure if she had noticed. She wasn't vulnerable for long, "Well, come on, are you up to this then?"

We didn't break fast; she had told me last night that hunters were at their best when they were slightly hungry, when they needed the food. They were more in tune, more aware and more focussed, she swore by it, though I wasn't too sure because right now I was fucking starving. "Yes, I am ready, let's go." Today she was taking me seal hunting.

We carried the canoe to the water. In it was a shaft of hazel as long as me with a harpoon head on one end, a length of strong seal hide cord attached the harpoon head to the shaft. The kit also included two vicious looking alder clubs as long and as thick as my arm, which we had made very simply by snapping suitable branches from the trees in the scrub by both of us hanging from them at the same time. We then ground the handle end smooth, first against the barnacles on the rocks and then by using the dry rough skins of several dead dogfish that had washed up along the shore. That was it for the hunting kit. We had a bladder of water each and some dried beaver meat, I hadn't seen her kill a beaver so I had no idea just how old this meat was but it was well smoked so it would be fine. She also took two more full bladders of water with her; I thought that we already had enough, so I didn't ask her why she was taking so much in case she thought that I didn't know why she was taking them. The fact was I didn't know why she was taking them, but I didn't want her to know that. As for personal gear, I was wearing everything that I had; trousers, shirt and an over jacket, but no boots, she was wearing the same. Nothing out of the ordinary really, but we had rubbed eel skins all over the buckskins to mask the scent of land animals. "Ok?" she asked, "Ok," I confirmed, then we were off, pushing out gently into the waves of the bay of the two Great Rivers and off to the sand banks and small rocky islands where the seals would be starting to gather before the autumn. It was tiring paddling on one side all the time, she paddled on the right while I paddled on the left, so I was beginning to feel a twist developing in my back and was about to ask if we could swap over but she beat me to it. "Let's swap now, otherwise you might twist your back and get a spasm, we don't want you out of action before we even get there." I answered as manfully as I could, "Ok, I was fine like that, but you know best."

It seemed ages to get there, the sun had moved a fair way across the sky, the heat of the day and the effort of the paddling was doing nothing for me but generate an awful combined stench of eel, buckskin and sweat, what's more when we did arrive the place looked pretty bleak. It was a low island of sand and mud with a large area of rocks in the middle, great. As we paddled past, I guessed that it was about 500 paces long, possibly more and possibly 300 wide. Seals were in the water, on the sand, on the rocks, it was packed with seals.

As we slipped ashore on a nice flat sandy bit many of them barked and yelped and wriggled into the water, while others just rolled onto their sides moving their tails up and down as though they were waving at us, like they didn't give a shit, I was amazed. "What now?" I was keen, "We wait till sunrise." "Sunrise? But sunset will be ages away and sunrise is tomorrow, do we have to wait that long?" "Shut up!" I shut up, "Seals are very skittish, but they are also very nosy, we will stay here not doing much so that they will get used to us and accept that we are not a threat. Under cover of darkness we will move downwind of them but very close to them and in the morning, as soon as we can see, we will strike. Until then just keep your voice to a minimum, if you need a piss or a shit do it in the sea so we are not leaving our scent wafting around anymore than we have to, any questions?" I had just one, "Can I eat something?"

No fire allowed, we had dragged the canoe well up the beach and turned it over on to its side propping it up with both paddles so that it was a simple shelter. We both sat cross-legged in its lee as the wind blew across the island, me chewing on my dry beaver meat and swigging water to help swallow it and she with her eyes closed, rubbing her temples and whispering something. About 20 paces away was a rotting skin-on-frame canoe. Through the skin, the frame was exposed in places, falling away like flesh from a skeleton. The rotting corpse of a once animated craft, obviously her man hadn't needed it after all. Although she never mentioned it, I saw her look at it occasionally while we sat there, perhaps with longing, perhaps not.

The sun dropped into the sea and was put out for the night; she chose the closing dark to once more tell me of the plan. After three times I thought I knew it off by heart, but of course, she had lost her partner when seal hunting so she was probably just being safe. "As soon as it is light enough to see, we go in downwind of them, moving low and slow up the wind toward the rocks. If they hear us we can forget it, if they smell us we can forget it, and if they see us then we are bad hunters and we should give up and just eat plants." I laughed quietly at this joke, feeling confident in her and confident that I could get within striking distance of a seal, I just wasn't sure about this harpoon thing, particularly as her man had died doing it. "Is there any other way of killing them?" She thought for a while before speaking, "Well, as a tribe we had several ways. We used harpoons like this one," she nodded toward where it lay on the floor, "We used spears, we even used drop holes." "What's a drop hole?" She demonstrated by digging a small hole in the sand, "Where the seals stay regularly and where the sand is firm, we would dig holes while they were out at sea. Long enough for a seal and as deep as my arm pits, we would cover the hole with thin sticks and seaweed. The seals would return home and if we were lucky, some would drop into the holes; we could then come and kill them whenever we wanted. Also, we would often skin them there and just bring back the skin and blubber. But tomorrow we will take the whole seal back, we will use everything." She then took time to go through the plan again and when she was finally happy that I was clear on it, we slept, both of us tucked under the canoe shelter.

Fortunately, it was a warm night, because a persistent rain had found its way round the back of the shelter and when she woke me, I was quite damp. Tapping me on the shoulder she had the harpoon in her hand, "It's time to go," she whispered, "Bring the clubs." It was still dark so we took our time and moved steadily upwind toward the rocks, she was aiming for these because the seals here had further to go to reach the safety of the water and they had to wriggle over stones that would slow them down, it made sense. When we were about 20 paces away from some sleeping seals, I watched her select an animal. I could see her weighing up the advantages and disadvantages of each one; too big, too small, not in the right place, too near another one. When she was certain, she turned to me and nodded, and that was that. She was up and running at one animal that was asleep on its own, I was keeping pace with her. Holding the shaft in both hands she shoved the harpoon head into its lower back near the tail, with maximum force, the shaft nearly breaking, it was almost personal. The seal went crazy and started bucking, screaming, yelping and writhing around, trying to shake off the pain that had woken it. By now, she had backed away, the harpoon head had done what it was supposed to do and had detached from the shaft and she was now hanging on to the cord as the seal started to move toward the water. "Hit it, hit it," she shouted, so I did; belting the crap out of it, repeatedly hitting it on the head with the solid alder club until the club broke. While I was doing this, the bleeding animal was dragging her along as it moved toward the water. She was scrambling and trying to throw her weight back onto her arse, leaning back and digging her heels into the rocks and sand. Barefoot, trying to get as low as she could to the ground, trying to increase the pull against the seal, bashing her toes badly but still hanging on. It was chaos all around us; seals were awaking to find this going on and they were making as much noise as they could, I suppose they were trying to wake the others. It soon worked and they were all going mental. They were bursting into the water, great splashes everywhere as they hit it full on, jumping in, bouncing in, and getting in however they could to be safe from these attackers. Roaring past us, bellowing and yelping, the air full of noise and confusion and all this time she was tugging and yanking on the cord, sitting on her arse in the sand, heels dug in, but still getting dragged toward the water. She was sweating, straining, muscles bulging and all the time shouting, "Hit it, hit it, on the nose, hit it on the nose for fucks sake." Grabbing the other club I repeatedly walloped it over the top of the nose, just by the eyes until there was a loud crack and the animal stopped wriggling. "Thank fuck," she said, letting go the cord and throwing her arms over her head and lying flat on her back in the sand. The animal lay there with blood spraying from its nose as it still breathed. "Will it escape?" I was worried that all our efforts would be in vain if it perked up and legged it into the sea. "No, we should be fine, you broke its skull or something, I heard it crack."

Running her hands over her head and through her hair, she could tell that I was concerned. "Listen, if you want to make sure, just hit it again." I did so, repeatedly. If anyone had seen us it must have been a strange scene; she was lying on her back in the sand relaxing and catching her breath and I was standing there belting the crap out of this seal. Eventually I sank to my knees in the sand, knackered. The seal didn't look too good; in fact it looked as though it had fallen out of the sky and landed on its head. Its eyes were closed; no blood was spraying from its nostrils because it was starting to clot. Mush and blood ran from the hole in its skull slowly into the sand, I gave it the once over, I knew that it was dead now and I felt better. "That was a tussle alright, you did well to hang on, and they are bloody big animals." "Well if you had hit it on its head like I said, it wouldn't have been such a tussle." I was confused, "I thought I was hitting it on the head," shaking her head she corrected me, "You were hitting it on the back of the head, where it is just muscle and blubber, you were just pissing it off. Sometimes, even if you hit it on the top of the head it only stuns it and it wakes up when you are half way through gutting it, anyway, no matter, you did it eventually, so, well done." I think she was warming toward me.

Both of us now got on to the right hand side of the thick round grey body that was mottled with dark spots, we kneeled down and rolled it over so that its head faced down the slope of the beach. Propping its tail up on top of a small flat rock she told me to collect several more that lay around us, then as I lifted the tail she would slide a rock under it, then another, then another, we repeated this several times till the tail was about as high as my knee from the ground. In this way, its head was well below the tail and the slope helped even more. She jogged down to the canoe and brought back the two bladders of water that had the least water in them, passing me one she told me to drink as much as I could. She did the same then poured the rest over her head to cool herself down and wash the sand from her hair. I could now see why we had brought this much fresh water, as there was none on the island. As I watched her tip the rest of the water over her head, I saw that there was another reason why she had brought the two extra bladders. Sticking a blade into the animal's neck just behind and in line with its ears, she started to bleed it into the bladders. When one bladder was full, she swapped to the other while I tied the opening tight shut. When both bladders were full, she cupped her hands to the wound and filled them, taking a swig of the hot blood, she did it again then held her hands under my chin, I took a sip. As ever with fresh blood, it was hot and salty but where it differed was that I was sure that it tasted of fish, but I might have imagined it and at least it didn't taste of piss. I stacked the two full bladders in the shade of the canoe; we would have to make sure that the bladders were airtight as we travelled back. The motion of the canoe would keep the blood moving and this would help to slow down the clotting.

We walked down to the canoe to get more water for a drink; the next job would be thirsty work. As she knew the island well, she knew that at high tide the water came fairly close to where our dead seal was, she was going to use this. We sat chatting for a while watching the tide rise, it came in quickly on this coast, mainly because it was shallow, so when the time was right, we launched the canoe from our temporary camp and paddled round to the rocks on which the dead seal was lying. We could get as close as 30 paces away; we pulled the canoe out so it was safe and walked to the seal.

Less blood in the animal made it a bit lighter, not much, just a bit and because we had killed the seal on the top of the slope, we were now able to roll it down the slope towards the canoe. It was beginning to stiffen; she explained that this was good because it didn't sink into the sand like a recently killed seal would, with all its floppy blubber. I could also see why she had been so careful about choosing a particular size of seal. Of course, I would have gone for the biggest, but then we wouldn't have been able to shift it, she was a smart woman. Even so, this smaller seal took some shifting and on reaching the canoe, we drank the water readily. The last job to do was to load up, launch the canoe in shallow water then tie off the seal to the canoe. While I sat at the back of the canoe, she stood in the knee-deep water and used a sharp bone awl to make a hole through its lips and another through the soft edge of its flippers. She then threaded the rawhide cord that was on the harpoon, through these holes, from the front and back of the canoe, so that it floated alongside as we paddled steadily back to camp.

The journey back felt good, rewarding, yet another new experience, and as we paddled along rhythmically, we talked. We talked about all sorts of things, the sea, the land, men, women, friends, loved ones. We talked about our childhoods and our homelands, we talked about a whole range of things, and after we had exhausted our conversation, we sang songs. Little songs, big songs, ones that we both knew, ones that she knew, ones that I knew, even some that we made up as we went along. For a while we were followed and surrounded by dolphins, small ones with yellow and white flashes on their black shiny bodies, I had never seen anything like it, their busy chattering echoed around the canoe and filled it like a box of sound, it was amazing, beautiful, and I realised that I was enjoying this coastal life with her, a lot.

Chapter10.

The waves were strong as we approached the shore so we hammered in as fast as we could and beached the canoe in the shallows. Jumping out together, we grabbed the canoe and the cord that attached it to the seal, her at the front, me at the back, both of us running hard up the beach using the waves to push us as far as we could get. Lungs bursting with the effort, the weight of the seal tugging against us as the waves tried to pull it back to its home in the sea, the wet sand shifting under our feet causing us to stumble forward through the surf. Pushing, lifting, carrying, heaving, pulling, breathless, then ... dry sand. We sank to our knees on the warm dry sand, wet, hot, starving, both of us shaking with the effort, gasping for air, lungs hurting, covered in sand and absolutely fucking knackered, but we looked at each other and sat laughing, probably in relief. When she had finished gulping in air and in between laughing, she laid out her plan. "Right, get that fire going, I will go and collect wood for the store, then we will have a good feed to make up for the lack of a proper meal yesterday. Oh ... and well done, you had not been on the sea before, you did well." With that, she stood, brushed the sand from her knees and walked off happily along the strand line looking for wood. Meanwhile, I selected a short solid stick from the woodpile then used the remaining alder club to knock the stick into the sand; when I was certain that it was firm, I tied off the canoe. After seeing the fight and tussle that the seal had put her through, even though it had only taken a short while, I didn't want it to get washed away. Kneeling down next to the seal I took a good look at it, after all, I had never seen one close up. It was big, longer than I was and wider. It had a long nose and many whiskers, many more than the dog; a flat head, which I had given it, and a lovely skin, with very tight close hairs all over it. Grey and patterned with white and black blotches, the legs were short and weird, claws on the end, like feet, like hands, not unlike mine. The more I lay there next to it, the more similar to me it looked. Disturbing the flies that had clustered on the mush of its head, I opened its eyelids and stared into the dark brown eyes, I held its hands again, very like mine, five fingers, then looking at its feet I could see that it had five toes; "What the fuck?"

"Hey what happened to the fire?" I shook myself from my mild panic and waved her over; dropping the wood, she jogged over, "What's up?" "What is this?" She looked at me as though I was even more stupid than usual. "It is a seal, you killed it earlier, remember?" Getting to my knees, I grabbed its hand, "Yes I know it's a seal, but what is it? Look at it, it looks like a man, it has hands and feet, 5 fingers, 5 toes, look." Placing her left hand on my right shoulder, she kneeled down beside me and talked me through it, "Yes ... my tribal totem is the seal, and we have tales of seal men and seal women, tales of seals coming ashore and spending time on the land. You have seen them here looking at us when we are on the beach; they are just out there floating around watching. Sometimes I have sat and played my flute to them, I don't know what they make of it but they have never complained." Thinking about this, it led me to an obvious question, "So they are not men and we are alright to eat them?" Nodding, she confirmed that it was alright to eat them, "Last night I sat praying to the Great Spirit and to my tribal totem that we would have a safe hunt, we did. When we have used what we can from this animal, we will place the bones on the pile with the shells and fish bones, so that in death it can be with things that it is familiar. Come now, get the fire going and I will make a stew, we will eat well tonight."

We did eat well and then we sat together next to the fire, under the roof and given additional shelter by the new windbreak, talking about what we would do tomorrow. As we talked, the clouds cleared to reveal the stars; a cool wind picked out an opening between my shirt and trousers so I fidgeted to close the gap. She noticed, "Yes it is getting cooler at night, the fire is most welcome on a night like this." Standing, she wandered over to her house and came back with two lights made from the heads of reedmace. She had made these a while ago, by dipping the swelling seed heads in seal fat several times so that the fat soaked in to the soft thick heads. When she lit them in the flames of the fire they burnt well, and she pushed one into the sand on either side of us, it was a nice touch. She sat back down then turned to me, "Are you warm enough in your shelter with the canoes? You have no fire there, or are you staying here under this shelter by the fire?" "I will stay here thanks; the deer skin is fine as a blanket, I am fine for now at least, thank you anyway." Poking a stick into the ashes, I asked her a question that had been building within me since I had lain next to the seal. "I am sorry to ask you this, but as seals look so much like men, could it be that if we die in the sea, we come back as seals?" I wasn't sure that I should have asked this question, because if the answer was yes, then could it be that we had killed her partner? Taking her time to answer, she replied; "That depends upon what you believe doesn't it." "And what do you believe?" I was interested in what she thought. "Well, my tribe believe that when you die, your body returns to the earth and your spirit joins the Great Spirit and you move through everything, you are in everything, you are everywhere and you will be for always. You are not conscious of this as a person or a spirit, but you are part of the Great Spirit that is in all things. When something is born, part of the Great Spirit enters the body, be it tree, fish, bird, man or seal, and when it dies that part returns to the Great Spirit, but it takes to the Great Spirit all of the life, knowledge and experiences of that body. In this way the Great Spirit grows wiser and all living things share that inner knowledge and that is how we learn and remember." Shuffling onto her left leg she turned to me, "The trouble is that some people have forgotten that we all have that inner knowledge and they do not respect the Great Spirit or the world that they live in, instead they kill and take too much, just so they can trade for fermented drinks." Sighing, I thought about what she had said, "That is pretty much the same as my tribe. It is amazing that even though our tribes are many days apart they share a belief. It makes me think that this belief must be very old, when we were all one tribe perhaps... perhaps when the great ice wall was over much of the land all those years ago." She smiled at me, the golden flames flickering and lighting her face, her watery blue eyes twinkled. Returning her smile I turned about me and looked skyward to the many other twinkling stars. To the north-east was the shoulder of the Great Hunter, I pointed him out. "What do you call that?" looking at the few stars that I was pointing at she shrugged her shoulders and shook her head, I took this opportunity to teach her something for a change. "We call him the Great Hunter, it is the sign that we are coming into autumn. When he is up full, he has shoulders, legs and a belt of three stars, from which a long quiver hangs; to his left he extends his arm and holds a bow. He is important to us

89

because he reminds us that autumn is coming and we need to hunt deer and dry the meat." "Ah, I know the stars you talk of; to my tribe she is the Great Collector. Like yours, she has shoulders and legs but her right shoulder is a red pearl from a giant river mussel and her belt is made from the mother of pearl that you find in the coiled topshell, like the one that you found. The quiver that you see is to us a pouch full of pearls and brightly coloured shells such as the yellow periwinkles. She is important to us because she reminds us to collect shellfish and fish and preserve them for winter." I found this interesting and sought her thoughts on the moon, "So how does your tribe explain the moon and what it does and why it does it?" "No, you go first, I want a wee, talk loud so I can hear you," she disappeared out of sight just behind the house, the dog following; presumably he thought it was bedtime. Instead of talking, I placed some sticks on the fire, I wanted to get as warm as I could before I tucked in for the night, I had lied about being alright, I was cold last night and was thankful when the sun had come in the morning. Sitting as close to the heat of the fire as I could stand, I moved back when she and the dog returned. "Go on, the moon, explain," she insisted. "Alright, well the moon was of course put there by the Great Spirit," she interrupted, "As was everything," "Yes, as was everything," I continued. "Anyway, the moon is there because the Great Spirit wanted us to be able to mark time through each season. As the sun moves across the land, rising and falling in different places, the sun shows us the start and end of each season, but the moon divides those seasons. Every night the moon is different; we make sure that we note each change and we plan our movements so we know when and where to be; we plan our hunts, we plan our feasts and we even plan our breeding on it. Of course we take note of where the sun is but it makes slow changes as it moves across the hills, moving further east and west at sunrise and sunset as it gets to the summer, but the moon gives us daily changes. And on a clear moonlit night we can move quite a way into a new hunting ground." Throughout my explanation, she had been listening attentively, holding her arms around her knees, which she had pulled into her chest to keep warm. She was interested in what I was saying and looked almost excited. It dawned on me that she probably didn't spend much time, if any, talking to people and that this evening, sitting by a warm fire under a clear starlit sky after a hard two days, was actually enjoyable for her. She was happy with my company and was happy to sit here talking to me, despite the obvious fact that she was cold. This realisation made me feel important and I experienced the sudden, almost overwhelming gratification of her friendship.

Now it was her turn to explain the moon, as I settled down to listen. "Well, like you, we think that the moon was put there by the Great Spirit so that we can mark time through the seasons. But for us the moon is very important because it tells us what the tides will be; I think, though I can't be sure because my counting isn't good, but I think that when there is a new moon after about 15 days there is a full moon, then about 15 days later there is a new moon again." "That sounds about right," I added, she continued, "As you know, the big tides mean that the sea will be at its very highest and at its very lowest; at these very high tides they are good for fishing and the very low tides are best for collecting shellfish, because more of the shore is revealed. We get even bigger tides in the late summer, and that is when the salmon and sea trout run the small river and the seals sit greedily at the entrance, waiting to catch them. They are much better at it than us and sometimes they scare the fish away. When the very low tides occur I can find things that I wouldn't normally find in the rock pools, way out there." She gestured into the night, "I once found a very strange thing in a rock pool, on a very low tide, it felt a bit like the slug type thing that we get the ink from, but it kept changing its colour and it had several arms. It was most strange, then, as I picked it up, it made ink all over my hands, so I threw it back in the water and it was off. Another time I collected huge whelks from the sand; that was a very low tide that day." She smiled at me again while rocking back and forth on her bum; she was really feeling the cold tonight. "So that is my explanation, the moon tells me the tides, it is very important to me... oh, and my bleeding usually follows the moon cycle, I don't know why but it does, about thirty days. Perhaps it is because I spend all my time by the water, by the sea, by the tides, so that the moon seems to have some influence over me, I don't know, it's just a thought." She smiled and rocked again. I just sat there shaking my head in amazement, yet again, I was fascinated by what she had told me, I needed to say something, "It is fascinating how the same people can see the world in different ways, and it is important to them both." We smiled at each other, saying nothing, there was nothing more to say. Instead, we watched stars shoot overhead, sometimes two or three at a time. While in the sea, were strange yellow and green patches of light, where the waves lapped or the surf topped.

Later, lying under my red deer hide in the campfire shelter, I watched her as she squatted by the hearth; she rolled the larger logs from the centre of the fire. She did this so that they would not burn away completely during the night but would still keep me warm as they smouldered in the ashes, not quite going out, we could then start the fire quickly in the morning. Looking over her left shoulder, she threw a glance toward me, but with the light of the fire in her eyes she could not see me wave goodnight. I watched as she walked across the sand back to her home, just in case she looked at me again, but I was disappointed. The flickering yellow light from the fire gently lighting her as she walked, golden, flickering, tongues of light. Licking her figure, licking her limbs... all golden, and for a moment, I thought of her as a golden woman... my Golden Woman.

Chapter 11.

We had work to do; this seal needed butchering and the day was already warm just after dawn so we couldn't hang around or the flies would beat us to it. She was wearing a knee length skirt made from weaved stems of reedmace, instead of the usual brain tanned buckskin. "It is expendable and my buckskin isn't." Watching as she began to skin the seal using a sharp half moon shaped chert blade that allowed her to rock it back and forth as she cut, she was quick. She cut a line straight from its throat down its belly to its feet, "Nice blade, where did you get the chert from?" I always admired decent tools. Nodding towards the south she said, "Over on the far river, the one you call the Great West River, it is on its south banks, in a few places. She cut around its neck, inserted a flat piece of wood that she must have shaped by bone chisels and stone and began peeling away the skin. The way that she cut it meant that what she called the blubber, which was attached to the skin, came away with the skin, revealing the meat of the animal beneath. It was unfamiliar and unlike skinning deer or boar. "Seal skin is stronger than deer and more flexible, that is why it is good for covering canoe frames, because it will take beaching on sand or shingle, happily," she explained as she worked. Where it wouldn't come away in one go she carefully sliced and cut with a thinner finger length chert blade, I watched her eyes flit across the body, following her fingers as she worked. "Shit!" she cut her left forefinger; placing the finger in her mouth she sucked the wound clean then turned to me and smiled, "I slipped," "I noticed," I replied. She continued in her work; cutting, twisting and snapping her way through the tendons of the arms and legs until a large blubber covered skin lay in front of us. It was as wide as it was long, so she cut it in half lengthways to get two skins. Flies were already gathering on the warm meat so she needed to cut it up and get it out of the sun quickly. The skin looked very strange, the hands and feet were still attached, she turned to these and cut the skin around them so that two hands and two feet sat on the sand. I couldn't help myself, I picked them up and looked at them closely, very similar to mine apart from the claws. I dropped them to the floor, the dog immediately stole one and made off to the rubbish pile, he seemed pleased with himself, chewing a seals foot and sitting in the heat of the sun on a pile of stinking fish and shell remains.

She asked me to clean all of the blubber and any other crap from one of the pieces of skin then cut the blubber into fist-sized chunks, I was glad to do it. I had done many skins before but never a seal; but I guessed it would be the same procedure. "No frame needed later?" she shook her head, "Just do a quick job, I want that skin to line the pit, it doesn't matter too much if it still has some blubber on it." She smiled at me again and left me to it. As she only wanted a quick job on one of them I took the longest blade that I had, about the length of my thumb, and got slicing.

While I was cleaning the skin and cutting the blubber into chunks, she was using a seals shoulder blade to dig a pit in the sand two paces from the fire. The pit was just under two paces long, just less than a pace wide and about a forearm's length deep; she lined it with one of the prepared seal skins, fur side down so that it acted as a large make-shift bowl. Into this, she tipped some of the blubber chunks that I had cut. Now she used two sticks of green willow to lift fist-sized rocks that she had been heating in the fire and dropped them among the blubber chunks. With each hot stone, the blubber squirmed and hissed and some pieces immediately began to produce oil, I was amazed, I had never seen this before. We used hot rocks all the time back in my lands for a variety of things; to heat water, to heat food, to heat water and cook food in it, to make heat when we were in our steam tent or as smoke free heaters when someone had a chest problem. However, I could not recall seeing hot rocks used for this. She began to pound the heated blubber with a long smooth stone in each hand, I was fascinated as the soft fatty blubber began to melt and produce oil. She began to scoop the oil into bladders and wood bowls, whatever was at hand. "What do you use this oil for?" I asked, she stopped what she was doing and explained, "I will store some of the oil in the bladder from this seal. What I don't use for lighting I will use to cook with or as a spread on flatbreads like we had the other day, in fact I eat it with anything, greens, fish, deer meat, anything, it is good, strong but good, it gives you energy when it is cold." Endearingly she shivered to emphasize the word 'cold.' "But I will also use this liquid oil that I am making now to

94

re-proof my house, some of the skins on the south side are drying," she nodded toward the canoe shelter, "And I will re-proof the canoes with it and possibly my boots, it is very useful stuff and worth all the effort." She pointed toward the other half of the skin that was now covered in flies, "And that skin, I will use to finish the third canoe, you can use it for anything, see." Taking a drop from the edge of the pit on her right forefinger, she ran it over her lips, rubbed them together then smiled, "Good lip protection." She changed the subject, "Just drop in another couple of hot stones will you?" Doing as I was told, I watched intently. "Will you collect some greens while I slice up some of the meat for us?" "Pleasure," I said and it was. I was back fairly quickly, I had been collecting along the shoreline and in the dunes, I had gathered some leaves of sea beet, seablite and sea radish and pulled up some silverweed which lifted easily from the loose sand at the back of the dune. I had also topped up our water bladder in the stream while I was at it.

Not content with doing all the pounding, she was also managing to do the cooking; slicing strips of the seal meat and laying them on flat rocks next to the fire where they gently sizzled. It smelled good; I had never eaten seal before so I was looking forward to trying it. Brushing the sand from the mix of greens that I had collected, I passed her some of the silverweed; she took them and thanked me, then crunched into the raw roots. This was another new one for me; she told me that you could also steam it over the fire then dry it and save it for use over winter if you wanted to. Or, when the roots were dried you could grind them up and use them as flour for cakes or porridge, but it grew all over the back of the dunes and there was no shortage of it so you could always pick it fresh. Trying it raw I didn't much care for it so I ate mine roasted in the ashes, it had a nutty flavour, I passed her some more together with the mixed greens. We ate the meat as soon as it was ready, and as soon as there was space on the hot rocks she would cut several more strips and lay them out to cook and then resume pounding. It was all very natural and relaxed; I was in the presence of a very skilled person, this Golden Woman made everything look very easy. I felt extremely comfortable being here with her, and I reflected on all the things that I had learned, all the things that she had taught me. "What else do you eat from the seal?" she stopped and wiped a bead of sweat from her nose,

"Everything really, the liver is strong flavoured, the kidneys the same. If you dry the liver until it is hard, you can smash it up into a powder for later use, you can then add it to hot water for stock, I will use the blood that we collected in the bladders to thicken soups or make blood cakes. You can even eat the eyes if you like, my partner used to eat the eyes because he thought it helped him see under water ... perhaps it did." She looked around the camp for inspiration, "Oh yes and you can cut the skin into thin strips for rope and cord and if you plait it, it is very strong." "A very useful animal then," I noted, she smiled, "Yes, a very beautiful and very useful animal."

She began to sing a song, her song; everyone in her tribe had his or her own song. She had made it and it helped to make her what she was.

Here I am, in my house by the shore
The seals, the birds, the dog and me
I don't think I could want for more
My house, my life, here by the sea

The Great Marsh gives me all I need
It is a great and fertile land
It gives me all that I need to feed
As does the sea, as does the sand

Here I will stay with all that floats
And though I am without a man
I will stay here with my dog and boats
And live by doing just what I can

Personally, I didn't think much of it, so I hoped that she didn't ask me what I thought of it. Anyway, she shouldn't care or need to know what I thought of it, it was her song, it was part of her. It was hers to sing, hers alone.

"What is your song?" I shook my head, "I haven't got one." "You must have, everyone has a song, mine has changed, I first had one when I was a child, but now I have made my new song. It will change, when I need to change it."

As I sat there in the sun leaning on my right hand and enjoying the moment the dog yakked up the contents of its stomach, a slimy black mess that stunk like nothing on earth. Why, when there was all of this beach Shitbag had to do it over my hand, I had no idea. I shook the stinking mess from my right hand with some success, only for the dog to start to eat it up again. The scuzzy thing was struggling to eat its own pukey, slimy, stinking mess while both pleasure and trial played across his shitty muzzle. My guts couldn't put up with this and I legged it over to the back of the canoe shelter where I stood retching at both the image of the dog in my mind and also the stench from the slime that was all over my right hand. Of course, Golden Woman just sat there laughing, "Good dog," she said, as it sat wagging its tail, "Good dog."

Despite the fact that I had now washed my hand several times, both in the stream and the sea, it still smelled disgusting, and although I was aware of this, every now and again I would sniff it, just to make sure, funnily enough it hadn't got any less disgusting. Shaking the last drops of seawater from my hand, I walked back to the fire. I wanted to know more about how she would re-proof the house, "Come on, let me show you." Getting a wooden bowl she scooped up some of the freshly made hot seal oil and trotted over to the south side of her house, "Here, just wait for the sun to come out from behind that cloud," we waited; I could see that the oil was already setting around the edge of the bowl where it was cooling. As the sun came out she started, "Right, check that it is not too hot and dip your fingers in so that they are coated, then wipe it on to the skin in the areas where it seems to be the driest. It is always best to do this when it is hot or at least warm because it goes further when it is nice and warm, here, have a go." Holding out the bowl to me I took it off her, "Thanks," dipping the fingers of my right hand into the oil I began to smear it across a dry area of skin, it spread easily in the heat of the sun, helped by the fact that the skin itself was already warm. I was just thinking how easy it was when the sun went in and very quickly I could feel the oil start to thicken, first on my fingers then on the skin until all I was doing was wiping blobs of the stuff on and it wasn't spreading at all. "See what I mean about the sun," she said almost gleefully, "Hmm," I replied as I looked at my fingers, which were now covered in a thick greasy stinking layer of fat. "Leave it for now, we will make the oil and do this either later today or tomorrow."

The sun shone, the dog wandered around doing what dogs do; sniffing, pissing, licking his bollocks and chewing on any old crap he could find. We just sat there together; me removing and cutting the blubber from the other skin, occasionally sniffing my hand which now smelled of all sorts of things and her working systematically, heating and pounding the blubber into oil. The sea had shushed its way out some time ago and it was now shushing its way back in again, ever so gently on the sand, almost creeping up on us. A small flock of terns worked their way along the edge of the water, dropping into the shallows to grab small fish before flying on. Little grey wading birds legged it back and forth as the waves lapped in and out; chasing the waves out, then chasing them back in. She caught me whistling, "You sound happy." I thought about it for a moment before answering. "I suppose I am." "Good," she said and continued with her work. It was a beautifully quiet afternoon, only occasionally would we break the silence and chat about something, or I would ask her a question, but mostly we were silent and had the contented air of a couple who were sharing a task, knowing that they were doing something positive together… for each other.

After food, she was taking a break from the blubber pounding by doing something else. I was watching her skilled fingers working the spiky stalks of marram, I sat quietly, engrossed at the speed at which she was making the little coiled basket. Although I was familiar with such things, I had not seen marram grass used to make a basket before. "I suppose it's a bit like using rushes is it?" She paused and looked up at me. "Not really, if you look at this," she held a piece. "It isn't a tube like a rush, it is spiky like a rush but it is actually a long flat leaf curled tight in on itself." She demonstrated by unfolding the grass until it was a long thin flat leaf, when she let go it rolled back in on itself and became again that thin spiky thing. "Oh, right, I see, but it's a bit like a rush... spiky and that." "Well it is spiky, but rushes are a spongy tube." I could see that this wasn't going anywhere so I gave up and just watched her work. Working quickly, she popped the awl behind her right ear, where it stayed until she needed to open up the fibres of the basket so that she could push new grass stalks into the hole and continue coiling. As I watched her tuck the awl back behind her right ear, I noticed that she had ear lobes. Most of the women in my tribe didn't have ear lobes, I think that was the same for the men, but I wasn't sure and I hadn't looked too closely. I was fascinated by her ear lobes, so much so that I became oblivious to anything else. She was now waffling on about stuff that I wasn't really listening to, and anyway I was back to feeling pissed off about being treated like some numb-nut who didn't know anything, as far as I was concerned it still looked similar to a rush. Because of my crabbiness, I missed her question so she repeated it. "Hey, I said are you feeling pissed off because you know so little of my world?" Cheeky bitch, I thought, now she is a mind reader, she didn't let me give my answer, she provided her own. "It's just that this place is so different from your world in the hills and woods, you spend all your times in woods with big trees, in the hills, along little rivers. Almost every plant must be different to what I have here, every fish, bird, everything, so it isn't surprising that you don't know anything." I think that this was her way of being nice, "Er, thanks, I suppose you are right. I suppose that if you came with me to my lands you wouldn't have a clue either." She looked at me and shook her head, "I wouldn't go that far mate, I might not know some of the things but I would be alright." There she was again, making me feel as small and worthless as a piece of vole shit. Reconciling myself to the fact that I was lower down the food chain than the dog, the various other birds, fish, animals and plants that lived with her in her world, I shut up and watched her work.

I had to hand it her, she was very good. I noticed that the awl she was using was not a pointed piece of deer leg bone like what we used back home, but a jaw of something. At the risk of being made to feel like a dick head again, I asked her, "What are using as your awl?" "This?" She held it out in her left hand so that I could gain a better look, "It's the lower jaw from a gannet skull; it's strong, but very fine, perfect for using fine fibres like this grass." "Nice, it's a useful tool, what is a gannet? What do gannets taste like?" "It's a bird and I didn't kill it, I have never eaten gannet, they don't nest near here anyway, they might be over on the far rocky coast to the south-west of here, where you can see the mountains." I followed her gaze and looked toward the mountains that sat behind the distant dunes of the coast to the south-west, magnificent scenery I thought. She continued, "They sometimes move around the bay here between the two Great Rivers, they are marvellous to watch as they hunt." I was intrigued, "I don't think that I have ever seen them, describe them please." Stopping what she was doing she looked skywards, as if for inspiration, she continued to look at the sky as she talked. "How do you describe something so beautiful?" She paused, "Picture, if you can a bright blue sky that stretches out over the sea as far and as wide and as high as you can ever imagine. Now onto that picture, draw jet-black thunderclouds that are building on the left horizon into huge giants that begin to spread across that bright blue sky. I want you to see that contrast of colours." I had my eyes shut, picturing the scene, I nodded, she continued. "Up to the right, very high, something moves, almost imperceptible at first, drifting across the bright blue sky like distant thistledown, you almost miss them until they cross that bright blue and are now in front of the huge jet-black thunderclouds, their whiteness is emphasised by the dark of the clouds. The jet-black of the cloud, the bright blue of the sky and the red fire of the sun now conspire to light these birds. As they come nearer, you see white, black, possibly even a glimpse of yellow as they cut through the sky, all arriving together to gather over one spot of the sea. Then, as if held by some sort of death wish, they stall their flight and plummet head first into the water, sometimes from very high up. Suddenly, lightning erupts from the thunderclouds, striking the water, again, again and again, but you realise that it is not just the lightning that is striking the water, but so are the birds. The birds stab the water like many spears or arrows and as they hit the waves, white plumes of water fire skywards where the birds enter, like whales blowing out water. Then, there is a scatter of waves as the birds reappear on the surface with silver, quivering fish in their mouths. These great white birds then run across the waves until they are fast enough to escape the grasp of the water, then they embrace the air on their huge wings and once again fly up to rejoin their kin. All of them cutting the sky with their dagger beaks and dagger wings, up amongst the bright blue sky and the jet-black thunderclouds, once more like distant thistledown." She paused and looked at me. "Does that give you some idea?" "Yes, yes I think it does… thanks, and if I ever see such a glorious sight I will know that those lightning birds are gannets."

A short while later she had finished the little basket, I asked her what it was for, as it wasn't much bigger than a cupped hand. "Here, come and see," she stood and walked to her house, I followed her, noticing for the first time that to the left, just outside the entrance, was a long branch of willow pushed into the ground. It was straight up to shoulder height then curved downwards for about the length of my arm. Along the curve of the branch hung strings of shells of all shapes, sizes and colours, they softly clunked and rattled against each other in the breeze as the curved branch gently rocked. From right at the end of the curve were attached five lengths of what looked like tightly spun fish gut, about the length of my forearm, very thin, weighted down with a large leg bone so that they all hung taught. These gut strings had the effect of producing a range of low sounds as the wind moved across them, plucking them with unseen fingers. It was pretty and effective, though in my opinion it could have benefitted from having some type of sound box, to make the sounds louder.

Opening the door flap, she waved me in, pushing her long coat aside as she entered. This long coat would be for bad weather and heavy rain. It hung there ready for use, and when it had been used, it would drip-dry right by the door. All her boots were also here by the door, ready for use. This was the first time that I had been inside her home and letting my eyes adjust from the brightness outside to the dim light within took a while. The sealskins that she had used for its construction seemed thicker than those of red deer, but that might have been the way that she had prepared them. Save for the small hole at the top through which the nine poles poked, her house was totally sealed. Large stones on the outside held down the bottom of the skins so that the skirt of the house was flat to the ground, thus the wind was kept out and no sand or crap could blow in. When she had her fire going in here I would think that it would be very cosy. The fire itself was out, she had a small round central hearth of about a forearms width, and from where

101

I stood with my back to the still open flap it all looked very organised, but why wouldn't it be? Everything about her was organised. She sat herself down on the far side of the hearth and gestured for me to sit; I sat down opposite her with my back to the door. Her layout was similar to our houses back home, but where it differed was in many of the materials that she had used. For a start, the entire house floor was covered with closely packed reed stems at least two fingers deep for insulation, whereas we tended to use bracken and grass. A gap full of sand two hands width circled the hearthstones to prevent fire spreading from the hearth into the reed. On top of the reeds were mats of weaved reedmace, which provided a softer base to sit on than would just the reed stems. To my left, the area nearest to the door, was the food preparation area so as to maximise the early morning light, particularly with the flap door open. This area had a rawhide mat on top of the reedmace mat, upon which were two bladders full of fresh water and a flat stone as big as a man's chest for grinding on. There were also several round stones of different sizes for grinding and two flat stones which were both as long as my foot on all four edges, these were for cooking on. To her right, was a work area, again this had a rawhide mat on top of the reedmace. I could see a fire burned bowl as large as a head, perhaps larger, it was full of seal fat, which had hardened like a paste. Next to this green rushes, that had been split in half lengthways to reveal their inner spongy middle, were soaking in another bowl which had liquid seal oil; these simple wicks would be used as lights. A large scallop shell, into which she had nicked out serrations along the edge, lay on the mat, similar to the handy scallop shell saw that she had used in the Great Marsh. A large container, which she said was the stomach of a seal was full of seal oil, this was partially liquid because she kept it close but not too close to the fire. In a head sized rush basket were pieces of chert and flint, a small flint pebble which she was using as a blade core for tiny blades and pieces of worked bone and three hammer stones for knapping. There were also some small pieces of sandstone, worn smooth by their use as hide polishers for her buckskins. Still in the work area was a collection of wood for the fire. Next to this were several thumb pots made from clay from the bed of the stream, which had been hardened in the ashes of the fire. These contained liquid seal oil and were used with the rush wicks to produce light. Immediately to my right was a storage area; a bow and quiver were propped up against a house pole away from the heat of the fire together with the harpoon and both leisters. Various tinder's were crammed in a little fine willow basket which hung, as did her bow drill kit, from one of the house poles to keep it all off the floor to avoid any chance of moisture getting in. Another, fine little willow basket held several pieces of yellow and red ochre, this was for her artwork. Onto the walls of the house, she had used these to draw pictures of seals and dolphins, the moon and the sun, they were quite effective and as the light changed during the time that we sat there talking, they appeared to move slightly, like autumn leaves, particularly when the wind ruffled the skins of the house. Finally, behind her to her left was the sleeping area. Here, on top of the reedmace mat was a big red deer skin with the hair left on, the hair was obviously on the upside so that she could lie upon it. Her pillow was of soft brain tanned buckskin stuffed with swan and goose feathers then sewn tight. She slept with the pillow close to the bow and quiver, so that if she needed them in a hurry they were nearby. Several beaver pelts sewn together provided the warm over blanket. I noticed that above her bed was a dangling thing. Made from air dried, hard, shiny fish skins; she had cut them into small fish shapes. Connected to each other by thin willow cord, they gently swung, rotated, and looked rather pretty. Among the fish shapes were two very strange looking things. Reaching up to point I asked, "What are these? They look like tiny horses with fish tails." "I know, they came from the sea, they were lying dead on the sand so I dried them. I can only think that they are the young ones, I suppose that the bigger ones make the white horses of the tides… perhaps." I was fascinated by them, "And what do you call them?" she shrugged, "I just call them seahorses, I can't think of a better name." Resting on the bed was a flute made from the leg bone of a bird, she told me it was from a swan. "Do you play well?" "That is a matter of opinion," she said. Picking it up she shook her head to shift her long dark hair behind her back and cleared her throat, shifting into a cross-legged position she began playing beautifully. The tune that she played reminded me a bit of the song of the robin that nested in my house, well, in the thatch of my house. He or she, they looked the same to me, would chirrup away for ages. By the time that she finished I felt quite relaxed, "Thank you, you can play very well in my opinion, very well indeed." She smiled and placed the flute back upon the bed, "I have plenty of time to practice, having no one to talk to or be with gives me a lot of time to fill." I said nothing but I nodded, then remembered why I had been invited into her home in the first place. "So what did you make the marram basket for then?" "Oh, these," scooping up a handful of beautiful little pink and cream coloured shells which I had never seen before, she raised them to me, "Cowries, I don't normally find them here but a big storm back in the spring threw them up and I collected all these. I wanted to display them and I have been meaning to do it for ages, so I made my basket; I might make them into a necklace but I need to make a fine flint drill first, and I haven't got round to that yet."

I was just settling into this cosy abode when she decided that it was time for me to go, so thanking her again, I returned outside to the fire and began preparing the main evening meal.

While I did this, she was collecting dry sticks of alder about a finger thick; she wanted a quick fire and wanted alder, as it was the best for smoking the seal meat to preserve it for winter food. I left the food preparation and joined her in the fuel collection, busily collecting the branches from the scrub floor. Before long, we both had arms full of timber, which we took back to the camp; the dog was trotting along behind me carrying the biggest stick of all and on two occasions, he nearly legged me up. I left her to arrange the smoking of thin strips of seal meat, the liver, kidneys and tongue, she carried over a few lit sticks from the main fire where I was cooking and lit her pile of alder sticks beneath the rack. I had been building up the main fire to get a deep bed of embers; I had done this by using smaller thin stuff at first to get the fire going then I had placed very dry branches that were as wide as my wrist and as long as my forearm on top and had left these to burn down. The white ash that had formed on the embers would retain the heat for a long time and that suited the chunk of seal meat that I wanted to cook slowly. Next to the fire I scraped out a hollow in the sand and used a stick to drag some of the embers into it, I then placed the chunk of meat onto these embers along with several big roots of sea kale then pushed the remainder of the embers on top of the meat so that it was covered. Then scattering some of the sand back onto the embers I checked that it was pretty much sealed, I wasn't sure whether it would work in this sand but it was worth a try.

"I tell you what, while the meat is cooking why don't we go and get some berries from the back of the dunes?" I was happy with that suggestion, "Sure, why not, it will be a while in the pit."

I had seen these berries ripening over the time that I had been here; it seemed that there were only two bushes of this thorny plant in the area and the berries were a lovely colour. Like an intense orange sun, but they were on the spiniest branches that I had ever seen, so it was going to be interesting watching how she collected these.

Of course, while I was getting scratched to bits and stuck on spikes she was casually collecting the juice. We were squeezing the soft berries while they were still on the branches so that their juice ran into a hide bag, suspended from a hoop made of a thin branch of hazel, which kept the mouth of the bag open. When it was nearly full she said, "That is enough, good job... let's sit down over there," she gestured with her head toward a small dune. Both of us had bare arms, yet while hers were brown and clean, mine were brown and red, streaked with my own blood, long thorns still sticking out of my skin. Sitting next to her on the warm sand I began picking out these spikes and spat on my wounds, she was picking out the worst bits of twigs and crap that were floating on the juice. "Phew, it is warm today," I nodded in agreement as she drank the juice from the bag, which had become flexible as the juice re-wetted the dry hide. "Hmm, lovely," wiping her lips with the back of her right hand she passed it to me; not wanting to miss this juicy delight that still contained bits of bark and various insects, I took it eagerly and swigged a load down. I sat there with my mouth open, eyes fluttering, my head waving from side to side as the sour taste hit me; to me it tasted so dry and so sour that I thought I would either immediately vomit or shit myself, perhaps both. While I was trying to work out what my appropriate bodily reaction should be, she sat there on her heels, slapping the sand, absolutely pissing herself, some bark was stuck on my clack at the back of my throat and I started to retch and gag which sent her crazy with laughter. Needless to say, I didn't take any more of that juice, though she did, in between fits of giggles.

105

We made our way back by way of the streamside scrub where she wandered away from me over to where honeysuckle was snaking its way up and through a sallow bush. "Do you want the bast?" I asked, keen to help, "No thanks… something else." She replied almost coyly and flicked her hair away from her right ear with her right hand in a manner that looked to me as though she was hiding a blush. Thinking nothing more of it I returned to my mooching, I mooched through the scrub just looking at things, remembering where they were, so that if I next returned I already had a map in my mind of what was in here and where it was. Turning back to face her, some 20 paces away, I watched her. As she stood in the dappled light of the sallow I could see that she was slowly, deliberately collecting the yellow and white flowers of the honeysuckle, taking a while to select the most scented blossoms, visiting each flower with her nose like a butterfly tasting each bloom, before placing them carefully in a little buckskin pouch. She looked quite beautiful.

Back at camp I made a hot drink of mint tea and drank a lot, it almost got rid of the disgusting taste of the berries, almost. She was still chuckling to herself as she worked, flicking me a glance from beneath her fringe. As I sat, finally stitching my torn boot, I couldn't help chuckling myself and occasionally pretended to retch and gag just to set her off again.

That night, I sat in the dark, in the loneliness of the campfire shelter. It was a cold night and the fire had died down to embers. I could have built it up but I couldn't be arsed, so I tucked myself under the red deer skin and snuggled down into the marram grass mat as much as I could. There was a dim cosy glow coming from her house. In there, the fire would be lit and she and the dog would be nice and warm. My mind flitted back to the inside, with all her kit and things, all organised, all effective, all homely. I wanted to be in there with her, away from the cold and the dark. The patter of rain started to sound on the roof of the shelter; I shivered and re-considered my decision about the fire. But the thought of moving from under the hide and losing what little warmth I had, then getting cold as I tried to get the fire going, was not appealing. The rain grew heavier and started to hammer down, I liked that, for some reason it made me feel safe. Then, through the noise of the rain, I could hear her singing. I didn't know what she was singing; I couldn't really hear the words but I could tell that it wasn't her song because the tune was different, it was soulful, lilting and lovely, as was her voice. I let the comforting drumming of the rain and the lilting sound of her voice send me to sleep; I had tears in my eyes.

Chapter 12.

It was a north wind and there was a chill in the air this morning which surprised me. It surprised me because I thought that autumn was at least two moons away. Perhaps I had stayed here longer than I thought, the days had simply flown by and I had learned so much from her, new plants, new animals, birds and fish. I had learned how to fish for pike using gorges, learned shellfish collecting, cooking and preserving, and learned the unusual but effective basketry fence and leister fishing technique. Shivering, I moved over to the main fire, it was damp where the rain had managed to get through a gap in the sloping roof, but I was able to get it back to life. As the sun lifted itself wearily from behind the dunes and the fire started to crackle, she joined me. We sat, not saying much as we ate our break fast, above us, a great skein of geese flew from the north to the south returning for the autumn, the early morning sunlight catching their bellies and feet, which shone a pink orange colour, it was beautiful and it looked as though they were carrying glittering crystals.

For most of the day, we worked on the seal, sorting and cleaning and drying things that were wet. Fortunately, the sun was now hot and high so we let the fire die down but not go out and we cracked on finishing the work that we had started yesterday.

All in all I was very impressed with this Golden Woman; she was organised, clever, strong, generous, pragmatic, practical and very, very skilful, and though her sense of humour was a bit odd she would be a good life partner for someone. I watched her using the rocks to pound the blubber; with each strong downward thump, the muscles in her arms flexed and her breasts swung and bounced. I was suddenly aware that she had no shirt on, and no trousers or skirt, just a buckskin belt around her waist that had two short strips of buckskin hanging from it at the front and the back, just enough to cover her fanny and arse. She was just sitting there in the sun, humming a tune. Golden tanned all over, long dark hair in a ponytail, white teeth smiling occasionally as she looked at me, full lips framing them, watery blue eyes, long dark lashes, a lithe firm body, dark brown nipples. I stood and walked over to the log pile to get wood, trying not to let her see my wood which was pushing against my trousers, causing me discomfort. What had got into me? I was seeing her in a very new way, I was so aware of her skills and strengths, I had taken them at face value, but suddenly I was seeing hidden depths, suddenly I was seeing her as a sex object. Perhaps it was because I was getting to know her; I was beginning to see through all the character and skill stuff and was now seeing her for what she was, gorgeous. I didn't want to start anything, I didn't want to stop the learning of skills that I was experiencing, also she thought I had a small cock. For a moment, I thought about going into the dunes and knocking one out to rid myself of the passion, but I worried that I might get sand in my eye, so to speak. "I am going for a swim, I am much too hot." I walked to the water, took off my trousers and without turning round threw them back up the beach; I was in the water before I embarrassed myself. Smiling, she flicked her hair over her shoulder, "That's a good idea, I am finished here, I will join you." Up she stood, directly from her cross-legged position, and then bent over to wipe the sand from the top of her feet and shins, and slowly straightening carefully wiped sand from her thighs, buttocks, back, belly and breasts. I was already trying to find the coldest bit of water.

Unfortunately, my plan wasn't working. She was keen on bouncing up and down, splashing water at me, then diving under the surface to reappear behind me then splash me again. I splashed her back, but the sight of her wet tits bouncing up and down wasn't helping me in the slightest. Time passed and after a while, she looked up at the sun and told me that she had work to do. Watching her walk back to the shore, then to the camp, I watched every single drop of water leave her beautiful body.

More time passed and she shouted out to me, "You have been out there for ever, when are you coming back in?" By now, I was fucking freezing; I had no idea how long I had been messing around in the sea, but the air was getting cold as the sun started to set. Although she had got out ages ago she was only now getting dressed, so for all this time she had been walking back and forward naked. To make matters worse, she had cupped her hands with fresh water from a wood bowl by her house and had gently bathed her face, ears and neck. She then bathed her shoulders, arms and armpits, then her back, breasts, tummy and so on, all down her body. As much as I had tried to look away, I found that I was rooted to the spot.

Finally she covered herself up, thank fuck, any longer in here and I would need medicine. I waded back in, shivering my knackers off and desperate for a warm drink. As I passed the wood bowl I noticed that the honeysuckle flowers that she had collected earlier were infusing in the water, she had been making herself smell nice. I dressed hurriedly, "You really love it out there don't you?" I didn't want to give the game away so I answered as enthusiastically as I could through my chattering teeth, "It's great, there is nothing like it in my lands ... I love it." I stood there nodding, you are something special, I thought, it was as if she had read my mind, because there was that beautiful smile again. Despite being freezing cold, I wanted her so much right now, right here on this beach, with the sun setting over the mountains to the south-west, the blue-grey sea licking the sand, the breeze through the rustling marram, the fire glowing warm, the air with a hint of cold. I wanted her ... and I told her so. "I want you so much." She met my intent gaze with a frown and I thought that I had fucked up, inwardly cursing my actions. Then her eyes began to soften, her lips turned from a frown to a smile, she stepped forward and took my hands. "You have no skills, you are not that clever and you are a poor fisherman." I was concerned about where this conversation was going. "But you are a quick learner and you are good with your hands, and you can practice your fishing anytime, but most of all you are a good man and I think you would be a good life partner for me." Dropping my head to my chest, I let her words sink in. I had not expected to find someone on this journey, I had expected, at most, to catch a few salmon and it was not that long ago that I was thinking of leaving. Lifting my head, I cocked it to the left and looked upon the Golden Woman in front of me. The pink sunset lit her face as we kissed; as she exhaled through her nose, I could feel her breath on my right cheek getting stronger as she became aroused, and all around us was the subtle smell of honeysuckle.

I was already well aroused, it had been such a long time, the last time had been with my first and only partner and I was now overwhelmed with a desperate passion. Feeling as wound up as a red deer stag at the autumn rut, I nearly started bellowing as I pulled her against me. Feeling her hard body against mine, pushing against her, while she pushed against me with her hips grinding my cock, merging, two becoming one. "Hoy, hoy, hoy." We stopped, confused and in a fluster, we looked at the shore where two solid, dense, immovable lads in a fire hollowed fixed transomed log-boat were landing. "What the fuck?" Was all that I could say?

We all sat around the fire picking away the cool embers and eating the meal that I had prepared for two; seal meat, sea kale root, blackberries and various greens, she told me that it was very tasty, it was. However, this was little consolation to me, because right now I was well pissed off with things. I had been here with her for midsummer to late summer and in that time we had not seen anyone at the camp, even the fishing at the river had just been the two of us. Now, just when we were starting to get physical, these two big lads turn up and spoil things. Since they had arrived, they had been chatting to her about her canoes, asking her how she made them and comparing her techniques with the canoes that they made. I was bored shitless, I just sat there picking the seal meat from my teeth with the pointy end of pieces of marram, thinking of what I might have been up to in that cosy house of hers.

After what seemed like ages, the lads stopped rattling on about transoms and keels and bollocks like that, I thought they might be packing it in for the night and I was relieved that this uninteresting evening was about to end. Unfortunately, they had other ideas and started singing; I got up and went into the dunes for a crap. I didn't actually need one, but I needed to get away from the Nugget Twins because they were doing my head in and if they weren't careful they could end up like that seal. I smiled to myself as I imagined the dog eating one of the lad's feet while perched on the stinking fish and shell pile. Squatting in the dunes, my momentary enjoyment was interrupted as the lads upped the volume, what on earth were they singing? It was a boring tune, very repetitive, and now for good measure she was playing along with her flute. I couldn't believe it; I thought that I was her man and here she was, joining in with this pair of twats.

There was only so long that I could hide in the dunes pretending to have a crap and shortly the dog found me, then she found the dog. "What are you doing? You have been away for a long time, are you having trouble?" "No, no, I am just pissed off, we were on the edge of something there before the Nugget Twins turned up and now instead of spending time with you I am being entertained by some wankers who talk about canoes all day." "And all night by the looks of it; now they are singing about canoes, their song is very boring." "But you were joining in and playing your flute with them," I protested jealously. "I was playing my flute to drown out the bloody awful words, how did it go now? Something like, *'The canoe slips through the water, like a fish born of the water, the canoe slips through the water, like a great pike or a great eel.'* The second verse is much worse, *'The canoe slips through the water, the beaver watches in envy, his teeth cannot match the fire that makes the fixed transomed boat.'*" She started to giggle, and I chuckled, "How many verses are their?" She shook her head, "Fuck knows, as many as the stars in the sky?" I reached out anxiously for her hand, holding on to her in a desperate attempt to recapture the closeness of earlier, "Stay here with me in the dunes, let's pretend that we both have the shits, they might get the message and fuck off." "Ok," she said and squatted down next to me, giggling. "By the way, why do you call them the Nugget Twins?" she asked quietly, trying not to give our position away. "They are solid, dense, and immovable; they remind me of the yellow-brown nuggets of rock that we find near to my tribal camp. These rocks are heavy, dense, they stain the stream, we can crush them to colour our hides or ourselves." She looked interested. "What colour do they make?" "Orange, yellow, brown, and if we mix them with blood or wood ash, we can change the colours slightly." Suddenly the Nugget Twins joined us, standing above us on the crest of the dune, tanned, solid, dense, immovable, looking at us as we both squatted amongst the marram. It was silent for a while, then they told us that they had just made a hot drink of nettle leaf tea and asked if we would wish to join them by the campfire. What could we say; we joined them, it would have been childish to refuse.

I was not sure when the Nugget Twins turned in, Golden Woman went to bed after the drink, she was tired and so was I, so I tucked myself into the cold of the canoe shelter while they sat in the warmth of the campfire shelter. I lay there on my own, listening to them singing their fucking canoe songs. It was not how I thought the evening would end and I slept poorly until dawn.

To give them their due the lads were up early, had collected fresh wood and had the fire going. I joined them, "Morning," "Morning," they replied in unison, there was a ruffling noise as the house door was thrown open and she emerged into the morning light, fully dressed. She smiled at me and my heart lifted. One of the lads passed me a wood bowl full of hot water and mint leaves; it was a good strong brew and I thanked him for it. She sat down next to me to show them that despite the fact that I had slept in a canoe shelter last night, we were together. We shared our bowl of tea, passing it back to each other and smiling as we did so, each time looking into her eyes, beautiful Golden Woman. I was beginning to wonder just why these lads had decided to stay with us, so I asked them. "So what brings you here lads?" They looked at each other blankly and then one of them remembered, "Fire and smoke signals, fire at night and smoke in the day." "Signals?" I asked, "We haven't sent any signals," looking at the woman to my right I shrugged my shoulders; she curled her bottom lip and returned the shrug. "No, not you, not you and smoke signals, smoke signals from the Long Hill and the Big Step, the Big Step that points north to the Pointed Tit." While she curled her lower lip again and looked puzzled I did not, my head dropped and my heart sank, unfortunately I knew exactly what they meant. My tribal lands were bounded by the Long Hill, that ran almost north to south; it was the highest point on the west of our land and stood right on the edge of the Great Plain.

No tribes laid claim to the Great Plain so any one could hunt in there because it was so big. The distinctive Long Hill was an easy half-day's walk from one end to the other. At its highest in the middle, it dropped away at its north and south ends and it stood out as a big landmark. To the east of the Long Hill was a shallow valley then a long ridge, the Big Step was at the northernmost end of this ridge. When viewed from the Great Plain, it looked as if it pointed towards the Pointed Tit, a hill on another ridge that was about a day's walk to the north. As you worked your way across the Great Plain, these were the three dominant features in the east that you could easily see and together they guided me to my tribal home. If there had been smoke and fire signals on the Long Hill or the Big Step then it was my tribe calling its people home. "How many days have the signals been going?" They chatted; right forefingers tapped left fingers as they counted the days, three days maybe? We saw them when we were at home, we were at home for at least two days, then we came down the river in our fastest fire hollowed canoe," I nearly butted in to ask if it had a fixed transom, but I reckoned it probably had. They continued, "When we left yesterday morning they were still going, then we set off and we made a good distance, because this is our fastest canoe. It is fast because we took a lot more off the keel than normal, of course that can make it a bit less stable when you turn fast, but we are very good at." "Yes thanks," this time I did butt in, I had to, otherwise I might have nutted him. I didn't say anything for a while; I just sat there chucking shells into the fire, I was unsure what to do, I felt empty. I had got used to being here with this Golden Woman and it looked like she was used to me being here, and just when I could have settled here with her for good I get the call to go back. I had almost forgotten about my tribal camp, after all I had little reason to go back, not for a while anyway. This call back to the lands was unwelcome in its timing and meant that something had occurred that the tribe couldn't deal with on their own. Taking hold of her hands I looked at her, it was time to talk. "I know that this is shit but I must go, the signals mean that I must go, I have to go, I do not want to go, I do not want to leave you, I want to stay right here with you, but I must go and I am very sorry for this... I don't know what else to say... I am sorry." She fixed me with her eyes. "I know that you must go, I can come with you if you would like, but I know that it must be tribal business and I might be unwelcome. But if you would like I will come, and if you think that I should stay here then I will stay here and make the camp ready for the two of us this winter." She smiled, I thought for a moment before answering. "That sounds like a better idea; you stay here and make this place ready for my return, ready for two of us, for the winter." "Three if you include the dog," she added.

We hugged for a long time, then kissed once and that was enough for me, I needed to get my kit together and get focussed on doing something that I wasn't planning on doing for some time, going back home. While I made myself busy loading my pouches, quiver, sorting out my clothes, she and the lads were getting a lot of food together. I would borrow a skin canoe from her and the lads were going to drag me up the river as far as they could before I split off onto my river. I had not travelled on the rivers all the way before, I was familiar with sections of the rivers, where I crossed them or walked along side them for example, or the section that these lads had given me a lift down. I didn't want to spend any more time than was necessary with these two but they were giving me a lift, I just hoped that the tow rope was long enough so that I couldn't hear them rattling on.

Food was ready and there was plenty of it. She had done this for three reasons; one- lots of food would send me away strong. Two- it was to celebrate the fact that we wouldn't see each other for a while, and three- a good feed provided by her would make me want to come back to her, it showed that she cared for me and could, and would, provide for me.

We all sat together in the campfire shelter, an arc of us facing the fire, the Nugget Twins at one end, then me, then the dog, then her, all chewing away on the food. It was a great spread; flatbreads made of reedmace root flour containing ground dried mint leaves and fresh cranberries. I spread the seal fat on the top and the taste was excellent, a mix of savoury, smoky, oily flavours combined with the fresh mint and the tart cranberries. For the meat, we ate some of the smoked salmon, together with parts of the seal liver and kidneys, which she had gently cooked on a flat rock in the ashes. This was complimented by a mixed raw salad of sea rocket leaves, chopped sea radish leaves, scurvy grass leaves, which I thought were bitter but she liked them, sea sandwort, which was quite juicy, sea spurrey, the grey leaves of sea purslane and sea blite. On the top of this salad were sprinkled the lovely yellow flowers of dandelion. Finally, the roots of sea club rush, sea kale and sea beet were cooked in the ashes of the fire; she used the ashes at the edge of the fire so that it was a low but continual heat, she didn't want to burn the roots. I found the sea beet to be very tasty, it was quite sweet. She waved the leaves of rock samphire in the heat at the edge of the fire, causing them to become limp, which she said made them taste better, it tasted good. My upper left tooth was aching, so I had tried to chew on the right side of my mouth, which wasn't always easy, with so much food in front of me. We drank cold fresh water flavoured with mint leaves, all in all a great feed. We all prayed to the Great Spirit, thanking her for providing this food, then took the bowls and eating boards to the stream to wash up, it was a lovely way to spend my last morning here.

Sitting on the sandy shore the canoe looked ready for action; I had stashed a full bladder of water, even though I was travelling on a freshwater river, it was always wise to carry water. One of the rivers that I had walked along and crossed over on my way to the coast went through an inland salt marsh; the water in that area was undrinkable. Other gear went in; hunting kit, fire kit, clothes, my sun shield hat, the sturgeon scale, then some food; dry beaver meat, cooked reedmace roots, and some pieces of smoked salmon wrapped in burdock leaves. In went a wood bowl, the lower legs of the roe deer and its hide for cover, and finally a length of fishing cord and a couple of her gorge hooks. I was set up for my journey, though I wasn't sure how long it would take to paddle up the rivers; my main fear was that I would take the wrong river. The Great Plain was covered in rivers and streams and they weaved all over the place and because it was mainly flat there would be few chances for me to get out of the canoe and climb to a high spot so as to see where the river came from. My hope was that I would meet people who travelled the rivers of the Great Plain so that I could ask for directions, after all I didn't want to spend days paddling up a river against a current only to find that I was further away from my destination. If I was to walk home it could take at least seven or eight days to get across the wet, pool and swamp filled Great Plain, and of course, I had to cross the Great North River in the first place. With the canoe, as long as I got the right river, I guessed that I could be home at best in four to five days, at worst I could be wandering around the Great Plain until the winter. But the canoe would give me an advantage in that it would save me the need to find crossing points and as long as I got the right river it would take me right to my camp. It would also be a quicker way to get back here to Golden Woman and right now that was foremost on my mind.

Using the paddle, I propped it across the canoe from one side to the other to brace myself as I climbed in, now grabbing the paddle handle in my left hand I realised that it was wet. Smelling my hand, I was pleased to find that the dog had left me a token of his love; somehow, he had pissed on the handle. The jolt of the canoe jerked me backwards as the towrope tightened and the lads started to paddle away. I pushed off and she waved from the shore and I waved back, trying not to show my utter sadness, this place had become home and I was being dragged away. I even looked for the dog but he was lying on the sand licking his bollocks. I waved at him and laughed, he growled back.

Part Two. The Great Plain.

Chapter 1.

It had been a long day, we had paddled for ages and I was struggling just trying to keep up with these boys, they could certainly shift a canoe. Admittedly, the tide had given us a good shove up through the estuary for a while but then the tide had turned and we, well I, could feel the difference, so right now my forearms ached and the tendon in my left elbow was sore, stiff and swollen. On the few occasions when I did stop paddling, relying on them to do all the work and tow me along, they immediately noticed and took the piss out of me. They very much enjoyed this so there was no let up for me; fortunately, I couldn't hear what they were saying for most of the time so I just sat there nodding and smiling. Fuck knows what I was nodding at, for all I knew I could have been agreeing to a reedbed bumming session.

We had eaten in the boats as we went along and drank whenever we needed to; I was getting very weary and was hoping that wherever these boys were taking me, it wasn't much further. They had already pointed out that the river that I wanted was over on the south side, I could just make it out through the reedbed. I wasn't too keen as we paddled on past it, I asked why we weren't heading for it but they reckoned that I would be better off staying overnight at the camp around the corner.

As we rounded the bend of the north shore, I saw our destination; on the north side of the Great North River was a wide gently sloping sandy bank, backed by grassland, reeds and scrub woodland. At the top of this wide slope was a large camp, maybe ten or more houses, many lean-to shelters, many drying racks with fish, meat and plants hanging from them and several stalls that were simply made, off-ground racks, on which goods could be displayed. Smoke rose gently and easily from fires that were dotted around the camp, some fires were under shelters where people sat and cooked or worked, some fires were out in the open with smoking racks placed over them, some fires had people just sitting around them talking or singing. This was a busy trading camp; people were active everywhere, it was accessible by the Great North River, which flowed from the hills to the east, as well as by several small rivers that joined it along its length, to the south and north. Moreover, because of where the camp was, almost opposite the mouth of the river that I wanted, it was a good place for me to stay over. I could top up on kit, give my left arm a rest and talk to others from who knows where? I had often heard others tell me about this camp, but I had never been here before and the sights and smells fascinated me.

The Nugget Twins had already untied the towrope and were waving me off as they crossed quickly away over to the south side of the Great North River and disappeared into the mouth of the river that I would travel on tomorrow.

Stepping out I pulled the canoe up onto the sand bank and tied it off to one of several stakes that had been driven into the sand above the high tide mark along the shore. I walked past the camp ducks and they quacked at me, expecting me to throw them some food, they must have had their wings clipped because as a dog ran at them they tried to fly but couldn't. It was a simple enough task, grab a friendly greedy duck such as these mallard, extend one of its wings and, holding it against a flattish wood board, cut across the main feathers with a sharp blade. Only one wing mind, it needed to feel uneven when it tried to fly. Of course, an even simpler way of making them stay was to break one of their wings; although some people did this, I thought it unnecessarily cruel. After all, if you fed them regularly with seed that you had collected from the grasses or sedges, or gave them some bits of your surplus flatbread, they would be very happy to stay. They were normally safer in camp than out in the Great Plain. Having said that, I passed by a man who was showing a boy how to cook one, he had plucked and gutted a bird and was wrapping and sealing the body in clay, before placing it in the deep ashes of a small fire and covering it in more ashes. It clearly hadn't been a safe place for that bird.

I noticed a strong looking man with very tanned skin, thin white scars covered his arms and face. He was wearing a short sealskin skirt; around his neck were several necklaces with many shell beads on thin cords of what looked like gut. His long brown hair was streaked with blonde from the salt and the sun and was held in a ponytail. A small silver cape covered his shoulders, made from fish skin it glimmered and sparkled in the sunlight as he moved, his busy fingers stitching shells onto people's clothes. He had attracted many people, at least six stood next to him watching him at work. His stall was one where you could have coloured clay, bone, antler or wood beads, pieces of polished fish skin or shells of all sorts sewn onto your existing clothes. Some looked very effective, whereas others just looked stupid; he noticed that I was watching him. "Hey mate, do you want any beads or fish skin or a shell suit?" Shaking my head, I declined and walked on. Walking past, it felt good to stretch my legs, I probably hadn't been sitting properly in the canoe because my left arse cheek seemed to be in some sort of spasm and so I bent over and repeatedly hit the spot with my clenched left fist. It raised a few eyebrows from those nearby and a fat man walked toward me. I had not seen many fat men in my life if any, there were certainly none in my camp, we were always active, we worked hard, we walked a lot and we were not fat. "Are you ill?" I asked. He pulled his face and jerked his chins, "What do you mean?" I tried to be friendly and appear as though I was concerned about his welfare, "You are a fat man, and I can't think that I have seen a fat man before, so I thought you must be ill." He shrugged and smiled at me, "My friend, I am the leader of this trading camp. I sit in that house over there." He pointed to the biggest reed covered house, "I bargain with many traders, traders from the hills, from the coast, and from all over the Great Plain, traders and visitors from the south, east, north and west. We have elk skins, beaver skins, otter skins, marten skins, badger, fox, boar, bear, wolf, if it had a skin it is here. We have elk antler, red deer antler, roe deer antler, boar tusk, we have sinew, we have flint, we have chert, we have quartz, we have," I held up my hand to stop him, otherwise we could have been there all day. "I get it; you have everything, but what about food and drink?" He waved his left hand away to his left, "Behind my house; we have elk meat, beaver meat, otter meat, red deer…" Again, I held up my hand, I wandered if this Fat Man and the Nugget Twins were related. "Is this why you are so fat?" He nodded, "Of course, this is a sign of my wealth, my possessions." "What is wealth?" I had not heard this word before, I knew that the people who lived down on the richer flat lands to the north of the Great Plain had more resources than my tribe up in the wooded hills, but I was unfamiliar with this word. "How many bows do you have?" he asked, "Two," I replied "One for hunting and one for dancing at the ceremonies." "I have ten or more, traded from some of the finest bow makers in the area, traded for things that they don't have. I trade elk skin and meat from the coastal marshland to the north-west of here; I trade the skins, claws and teeth of wolf from the hills to the east. I trade smoked fish from the coast and send it to the hills to the far south and so on. All I do is make sure that we have a good landing place, that we have shelter if traders wish to stay, and that we always have food and water. In this way, the camp is the centre of the trade routes through our land and I am the centre of the camp, that is wealth my friend, and that is why I am fat." Placing his right arm around my shoulders, he walked me toward the food house, as we walked we chatted, stopping only as a medicine man walked past us. He was an elder, a grey haired old man, long beard, long hair tied back in a ponytail. Teeth of various animals hung on a thin hide thong around his neck. He was in another world, muttering to himself, his shaking fingers playing with the animal teeth as he walked. Moving on again we passed a stall that was full of beaver parts. As well as the skins and meat laid out on the rack, there were beaver teeth, tails and beaver stones. A beaver stone was the trade name for the inner parts of a beaver, which contained a stinking fluid that I wasn't keen on, but some people swore by it to solve various ailments and sicknesses. Whenever you were gutting a beaver, you had to make sure you got the right parts, or else you could end up with the anal glands and that fluid smelled even worse. It being late summer the beaver skins were at their thinnest, they would be thicker in the autumn and at their best in the spring, with that thick winter coat still on them. You could of course get good thick skins in winter, but that meant hunting the beaver in the ice and snow, and I wasn't that bothered about that, a spring skin would do for me.

As I neared the food house he left me and wandered off, I could smell a lousy rotten smell; it was coming from the back of the house. Nosing around the back, I found out what was the source of the awful smell. It had at one time been a little stream, but over time it had been filled with waste food, shit and any old rubbish. A stream no more, it seeped away into the grassland beyond. A strange mix of oozing crap that had long black and white strands that looked similar to the green algae that sometimes coated the ponds of the Great Plain, particularly where the aurochs stayed. The gentle fluttering of these black and white strands was the only sign that this stream still carried some flow. Flies and rats scrambled over the seeping mass. It had been a while since I had seen a rat, at one time we had quite a few around my home camp, but when foxes moved in, they seemed to keep the numbers down. Turning away from the smell of shit, I walked back to the welcoming smell of smoked fish and meat.

Men sat outside the food house drinking from hollowed aurochs horns or wooden bowls, telling dirty jokes and stories and laughing together, surprisingly it looked good. I hadn't sat around with a load of men for a long time, I was so used to being on my own that I tended to avoid crowds, but this looked like it might be a laugh. Ducking to avoid the low doorframe, I went into the round hut and stood for a while to let my eyes adjust to the dim light conditions. The walls of the food house were made of hurdles that were fairly open in their weave, so that they allowed in as much light as possible. The roof was a simple cone shape of long poles lying next to each other, which sat on the top of the hurdles and were all propped up at the centre of the roof by one long upright forked trunk, set well into the ground. The roof poles were covered in tight bundles of reeds and sedge, which were tied to the poles with anything that could be used. It looked a bit scruffy and needed patching up in places, but no one seemed bothered, after all, they were not here for comfort, they were here for food and drink. Over to the right, an old woman with wild grey hair and a ruddy face was serving a range of hot meats, these were being cooked outside, at the back of the food house on a bed of oak chippings. There was a choice of drinks; water flavoured with various berries, hot drinks such as various leaf teas, together with some fermented drinks. The drinks were easily made by allowing fruits or seeds to fester in water for four or five days till the water developed a scum on the surface and went fizzy. I tried one, it was alright, but it quickly gave me a fuzzy head and I felt a bit queasy. The trouble with these alcoholic drinks was that when you left fruits, seeds and honey in water to naturally fester or ferment, you could never be sure about the quality of the end product. Aware of this I got a hot bowl of water flavoured with roasted and ground dandelion root, I asked for it to be sweetened with a little honey to lessen the bitterness of the root. A young boy came into the hut carrying thin skewers of green hazel on which were sizzling chunks of boar meat separated by thick slices of mushrooms and crab apple. I took one and sat eating it, being careful to chew only on the right side of my mouth, not wanting to aggravate the bad tooth on my upper left jaw. An advantage of this shorter beard of mine was that I had less food in it; a longer beard gets so full of food at times, which tends to attract flies. It struck me that it might be better to keep it shorter; as I ate, I soaked up the chatter of the men around me. They talked about women, good hunting grounds, shit fishing grounds, fights, tracks, canoes. I couldn't help ear-wigging some of the conversations. To my left, a man with shoulder length grey hair and a grey beard was talking; "And you should see the women there, fantastic, big shoulders from all that pounding and hands that can crack hazelnuts, very strong women." A lean man to my right, brown hair in a ponytail, was talking sternly and slowly; "The hunting is very good, a mix of scrub woodland, heathland and grassland, it attracts everything. From here, it is a walk to the north-east of several days, but it is well worth it." Behind me, a short man with a very tanned complexion, short spiky black hair and short black beard was describing the fishing grounds along the "Black and green river." A small river a couple of days walk to the north of this camp that I had not heard of. "Its shit, don't bother." The grey bearded man to my left stood and walked out, he was immediately replaced by a wiry, strong, tough looking man who wore only a short buckskin skirt. The boy instantly placed food and water in front of him and left without looking at him or asking for payment. Out of the corner of my eye I looked at him, his long brown hair was plaited into many strands and in it were tied stone and bone beads. His beard was short apart from two, finger length plaits either side of his jaw, these too had bone and stone beads tied in. He was almost black with dirt and he stunk of shit, blood, soil and death. He wore his story all over his strong body, his arms, shoulders, chest, back and legs, were covered in strange tattoos. I tried not to look too closely, I knew what they meant. No one talked to him; no one looked at him or caught his eye. He was a ghost, he didn't exist. Moving through the world, he lived with no tribe and talked to no one but the spirits. He would be fed and sheltered here tonight and would not need to trade, the fact that he was here was payment enough.

After he had gone the conversations resumed and I remembered why I was here, after all, earlier today I had left my new partner and her lovely place to go back to my camp, summoned by the fire and smoke signals. The signals might not even be for me; it might be that someone was just signalling that they had returned home or something, though this was unlikely. The trouble was, when the signals went up it was time to go home, it was expected. A man walked between the tables carrying a little wicker basket in his left hand, at every table his right hand dipped into it and took something out, offering it. When he reached me, I could see that it was full of dried mushrooms, a mix of liberty cap and fly agaric. I told him to fuck off; I needed food, not an out of body experience. It seemed as though most of the people in the food house were smoking and whatever it was that they were smoking smelled like fox shit. I went outside with my drink and a big chunk of elk meat that was basted in a thick elderberry sauce. I looked around; there were many frames to the east of the houses, with beaver skins, elk skins and deer skins, all in the process of being de-fleshed in preparation for tanning. Buckets, made from elm bark that had been folded and stitched together using the bast of the elm, contained a mix of water and the brains of the animal that the skin had originally belonged to. These would be used on the hides, making the hides soft. The hide work area was to the east so that the dominant south-westerly winds would take the stink away from the camp, good planning by the Fat Man.

Walking past several reed screens I wondered what they were hiding. I got my answer when a man walked out wearing a small buckskin wrap that just covered his arse, cock and knackers. It was the wash area; you could trade for hot water and soaps. Looking into the now empty screened off area I noted that there was a depression in the ground which was lined with a hide. This was filled with water and then hot rocks were rolled in from a small ash rich fire about a pace away. It wasn't quite big or deep enough to lie in but you could easily squat in it and pour the hot water over you using the wood bowl next to it. A range of plants and fatty soaps lay next to the bowl on the reed mat that surrounded the bath. "Excuse me," I found that I was blocking the way of an elderly woman; she was obviously coming in for a wash. "I am sorry," she smiled at me, "No, don't be sorry, I didn't realise that part of the service was that I got a younger man to wash me down." Feeling my face flush with embarrassment, I smiled, laughed and wandered off to take a look around the camp.

A woman was kneeling down and doing something, I couldn't make out what, I passed her by and walked near to a man who was having an in-growing toe nail sorted, he wasn't too happy about it, as the man with the flint blade cut away. "I told you last time to cut a small v shape at the top, in the middle of the nail, then the nail will not grow wide, and this is what happens if you don't." Two lads were throwing a fist-sized ball of wood at two knee high sticks that were stuck in the ground next to each other, about twenty paces away. Target practice for young hunters; being able to throw accurately was a good skill to have at any age.

By now I had circled the camp and had again reached the woman who was kneeling, "Hiya, what are you doing there?" Looking up but continuing with what she was doing she replied, "Oh, hello... well I am trying to make a better soap. I am not content with just using chickweed, I saw someone up north using a much better soap, they told me how to do it but I couldn't remember the amounts, so I am working it out." I told her of the pink flowered plant that Golden Woman had used; she was interested but didn't think that she had seen it anywhere. Squatting down beside her, I asked her to explain what she was doing. She was using fat from a boar and was mixing it with warm water that she had run over warm wood ash. To do this she had placed the warm ash on a sieve made from thin criss-crossed twigs of green willow, in this way, larger pieces of ash stayed in the sieve and were not washed through into the wood bowl beneath. This mix of ash tainted water and fat was then heated in the bowl using hot stones from the fire until it simmered away leaving a strange whitish grey glob which stuck to everything and stunk pretty rank. She was working on different amounts of things; apparently the last lot that she had made had dried the skin of the young man that she was testing it on. "This mix has less ash, I think that was what dried his skin and made it sore, and I am going to add some melted pine resin for its fresh scent, because it stinks otherwise." She laughed and added, "He wasn't very happy having sore skin that stunk." Noticing that I was rubbing my left elbow, she commented, "Joint trouble?" I nodded, "Yes the whole of my elbow aches, I am not sure if it is tendon trouble, joint trouble, or both, but the paddling has really set it off." "If it is painful when you grip it sounds like the tendons, but if it is the whole elbow it could be muscular as well. What are you doing for it? I shook my head, "Nothing, nothing at all." Reaching out her right hand, she gave me a lump of boar fat, "Here, try this, rub it over your elbow it might not do anything at all, but at least the massage might help. Whenever I get tendon trouble, I stick my elbow in the coldest water that I can find, for as long as possible, it seems to help numb the pain. But try the boar fat as well, just in case it helps." Thanking her and wishing her well, I left her to it and went to find the men's hut to book a bed for the night.

A short while later with my bed booked for the night, I wandered back outside. Near to the main campfire sitting under a shelter was a young woman making baskets, beside her sat a young boy, he was sorting out rods and weavers for her and placing them in her right hand. She rotated the basket in her left hand and weaved with her right in such a fluid manner that I was surprised that she was blind. A huge hairy dog sat beside her, long legged, grey and thin but with a deep chest and big strong jaws. "I am sorry, please excuse me," I hastily apologised as an old man bumped into me as I turned without looking, it was most wrong to disrespect elders. "You are excused my friend," he said in a throaty, hoarse voice, I watched him hobble off, he had legs that bowed out like a rainbow, but not half as colourful and his feet were twisted and damaged, I guessed that he was at least 80 summers old. The two lads who had been throwing at the sticks started to take the piss out of the old man; showing disrespect in this way angered me so I went after them and slapped them both around the head. They cried out and a man ran over to me, "What's happening here, why are you hitting my lads, what's your problem?" I explained that they had shown disrespect to the old man, that I thought that they were wrong to do this and that I had intervened to make them aware that they shouldn't act in this way. He was a big man and he stood for a moment thinking about what I had said, then slapped them both around their heads and shouted at them; "Why do you do this? Why do you do this to me? Why do you let everyone see that I cannot control you both? How many times have I told you both? Do not cheek your elders; they know far more than you do, they have done more than you and they must have done it right if they have lived as long as that old man there. Do it again and I will cut off your hair so that everyone knows that you are ignorant little shits." He turned to me, "Brother, I am sorry that my sons offended both the old man and you, you did right to correct them and it is the only way if they are not bright enough to understand themselves." We shook hands and he returned to his work of repairing a skin-on-frame boat, dragging his sons behind him. I walked past two young men who were splitting timbers using bone wedges and wood clubs. They were making a good job of it, holding the ends of the lengths of timber up to the sun so it would highlight any weak points such as natural cracks. Into these they inserted the thinnest wedges and tapped them in until the next sized wedge could be used. Nearby, a man sat on the ground making birch bark tar. He was using tight rolls of dry birch bark, about half a clenched fist in size; he lay these onto a large flat scallop shell then covered the rolls with a hand sized piece of birch bark as a roof. The roof was necessary because he then covered everything with sand to a depth of two fingers. When he was sure that there were no openings to allow air in, he carefully surrounded the small sand mound with twigs and small sticks and lit them using a burning stick from another of his mounds. While that fire took hold, he carefully separated the hard-blackened sand of another mound that had cooled. Watching him, I noticed that though the little roof of birch bark was very black and charred, the rolls that were underneath were less so. He blew away the sand as he went; making sure that as little as possible ran into the shell at the bottom. He lifted the rolls and the shell away in one go then took away the rolls to reveal the dark birch bark oil, only a small amount. He took the shell and placed it into the ashes at the edge of the fire; the oil quickly began to steam and thicken. He stirred it with a small piece of reed stem until it was a black glob of gluey tar and he was happy, "Done!" he said, "Indeed," I said.

Finding myself a spare log, I sat watching two young girls who were busy burning out bowls; next to them an older woman was splitting small logs of ash in half lengthways, again using pointed bone wedges and a wooden club. It looked as though a stone axe had been used to fell the ash trunk; the trunk had then been cut through again in regular forearm lengths to produce the short lengths that the woman was now splitting. The tree would not have been very big, probably about as wide as an average head. Each split section was passed to one of the girls; they would place it on the sand with the bark downwards so that the fresh flat surface was uppermost. Then, using green twigs, they would take a glowing ember from the small fire next to them, and holding it in place, would blow gently on the ember as it burned its way into the flat surface of the split log. The charred hollow would then be regularly scraped out using a piece of pointed bone from a deer leg; they would repeat the process until the hollow was big enough. At this point they would show it to the woman who would either shrug her shoulders, roll her eyes, nod or take the piss out of them, when she did the latter they saw the funny side and sat giggling. The woman finished the bowls by taking them to the riverbank where she placed a handful of dry sand into the hollow and ground it smooth using a round stone. In the time I sat watching them I think they had produced two bowls, it looked as though they were trading them because they carried them over to a lean-to shelter where there were several more. She gave one to the Fat Man who took it willingly; it was probably a trade for the shelter and trading space.

The blue sky of this morning had given way to low dark grey clouds that were spreading from the south-west and blanketing the estuary. Smoke from the fires, that had risen gently when I arrived, was now swirling around and the sounds from the camp seemed louder than earlier. I thought of Golden Women putting things away at her camp, getting ready for the inevitable rain and I wondered whether this change in the weather would mean a change in my fortunes.

The two young lads who had been slapped were back playing again, this time one stood about twenty paces away from the sticks and the other stood in front of them. He was holding a stick about as long as his leg in both hands, the other end of the stick was resting on the floor in front of the two sticks. The one who was twenty paces away held the round piece of wood, he then threw this underarm at the two sticks and the lad with the stick in his hand stepped forward and swung it up and over his head. There was an almighty crack and the wood ball went flashing past the main campfire thudding into the food house. "What the fuck?" a stallholder shouted after nearly being brained by the lump of wood, while he went off on a rant the kid who had thrown it went to get it back. It was all quite amusing; the stallholder went after the kid with the stick while the other kid was asking at the food house if he could have his ball back. The ball was buried in the reeds of the roof somewhere, so it was unlikely that they would get that back, they would have to get carving again if they wanted another game. Dad turned up with the angry stallholder next to him, "Right, that's it, come on, how many times have I told you that if you play that game you do it in the open. You could at least aim at the bloody river and not at the camp, now go to bed, what will your mother say when we get back, she will think that she can't trust me to look after you." It seemed as though dad was having a bad time.

I sat rubbing some of the boar fat onto my troubled left elbow, wincing occasionally with the soreness. "Drink?" A young woman passed me a bowl of water, flavoured with the juice of crushed elderberries; she was very pretty and had a very good body. Her green eyes seemed big and her cheeks seemed pink, bigger eyes and pinker cheeks than normal eyes and cheeks. Her tits stuck out well, her waist was slim and her buckskin top was white and shiny. I also noticed that she had no ear lobes, I never used to look at such things until I had spotted that Golden Woman had them. "Thank you very much for the drink... you look very good, how do you do it?" Flicking her right hand through her long brown hair, which was plaited into many strands on either side, she bounced slightly on her left leg cocking her right leg to emphasise the shape of her calf. "Oh, thanks for noticing, most of them round here don't notice, but it takes work to look like this." Waving her hands down her body as if to emphasise her words she continued. "My eyes look bigger because I drew round them with a thin piece of charred twig; I also used it to darken my eyelashes. The pinkness in my cheeks is red ochre mixed with water, not too much though; I don't want to look like a holly berry." She giggled. "My nails are shiny because I wipe them against the grease of my nose, and as for my tits, I have sewn this buckskin top tight under here so it pushes them up, look." I looked to where she was demonstrating with her hands, it was great. "That's great," I said, "Thanks, and basically

I did the same with the waist," again she demonstrated but gave me a twirl as well. "How did you make the top so white and shiny?" "Ahh, I took some white clay and crushed it, then I added a little amount of water to make a paste. Then I worked it into the buckskin using my fingers and when it had dried I rubbed it with the heel of my hand so that it became polished and shiny, what do you think?" In all honesty, I was impressed, "You have done a good job, it works very well, you look very good, and I like the necklace, what are the beads made of?" "Oh thanks, they are soft limestone, it takes a while but it is easy enough, I cut the limestone into small pieces using a chert or flint blade with a saw edge and then hand drill the hole from both sides using a tiny flint blade, then I smooth and shape them on some sandstone." I was keen to learn how she had such a good yet comfortable fit with the buckskin, whenever I made my clothes I struggled to get the right balance between comfort and practicality and always ended up with clothes that were too baggy. I don't know whether it was the way that I made them, but my buckskins tended to become baggier the more I wore them so I ended up looking like I was shrinking in my skin. Holding the bottom of the skirt, she explained. "Well... I know that this is a skirt, but the waist is the same for trousers. So, the first thing you need to remember is that you have a natural curve from hip to hip across your belly, so you need to allow for that. You are quite trim but the Fat Man would need to make a heck of an allowance for his belly." She giggled again as she looked across at him waddling by, then returned to the matter in hand. "You can of course make a really simple skirt from one hide that you cut in half across the spine; you use both halves, the arse end for the back of the skirt and the neck half for the front. Then sew it halfway down on each side so that you have slits on either thigh when you wear it, and I would wear it on my waist. Now this one that I am wearing is a simple wrap-around skirt which I wear on my hips, I cut the hide in half along the spine instead of across the spine and just used one half. I wrapped the spine of the hide around the top of my hips so it makes a strong band that won't stretch that much, but because the hide isn't the same shape from its neck to its arse it means that the bottom of the skirt is wavy like this." She held up the edge for me to see, exposing the top of her left thigh. "The skirt is thicker at my hips, because the skin is thicker along the spine of the deer, and it is thinner and

130

stretchier towards the bottom of the skirt and it will get shorter the more I wear it, but it should end up being really nice. Though for the first skirt I made in this way, I put the spine at my waist instead of my hips, not realising that it would shrink so much at the edges along the bottom. Well it got shorter and shorter the more I wore it, but it was great when it was hot because it was much more practical for everything." I was nodding, "I bet it was." She continued, "For the skirts that I wear at my waist, I sew in a waistband sleeve and put a length of rawhide through it so that I can tighten it or slacken it depending on my period… I get very bloated at times." "Very impressive, very creative, you are obviously very skilled, so what do you do here?" She looked embarrassed, "Well I was thinking of trading my skills, but I am not sure if anyone would want them, what do you think?" Looking her up and down I thought about it, there were certainly a few women in my camp who would benefit from her skills, and possibly a few men. "Can you cut hair and beards as well?" "Of course," she replied, "Then I think you should sort out both men and women and I will be your first customer, please sort this hair of mine out will you?" She looked at me thoughtfully before delivering her opinion, "My friend, even with my skills there is nothing that I can do for your hair."

I sat myself down on a log bench, one of several that lay on the floor circling the main campfire; I was ready for tonight's main entertainment. I had been watching some of the games that had taken place earlier, it was fairly basic stuff; there was wrestling, mud wrestling, running and jumping, and jumping over the shitty creek at the back of the camp. As a result, there were a few people wandering around caked in mud, their eyes and teeth flashing white as they laughed or smiled. The night's entertainment started with some dickhead doing animal impressions; his range included boar, aurochs, elk, dog, cat, fox and badger. Many of them sounded very similar to me, he added to the noises by using appropriate body actions. For example, for the aurochs he extended his arms forward from his head like horns, while he got down on all fours and grubbed around in the earth when he did the badger or was it a boar. I couldn't believe that anyone could spend time doing this sort of shit, but the kids all loved it and sat there pissing themselves, even a few of the adults were chuckling. Behind me, a young lad had joined in and was wriggling along the ground pretending to be a snake, hissing. His mates were laughing and were prodding him with sticks; it all struck me as being very odd. The man obviously wasn't that daft, he got free bed and food for entertaining the people here. "What a load of crap that was," Ochre Girl sat down next to me, obviously as unimpressed as I was. I agreed, "Well I thought so, but most of this lot seemed to like it." Throwing her head back she laughed, "I know and what was all that grubbing around on the ground and sticking his arms out in front of his head like horns, as if that was helping." I was nodding, "I suppose that he thought it added to his act, made a bad act better, dressed it up a bit." She thought for a moment before replying, "Yes, I suppose so, but like they say, though you can't polish a turd, you can cover it in blossom."

The next act was much better; a slim good looking woman with reddish hair, blue eyes and a nicely tanned figure, she wore a sleeveless buckskin shirt that was open at the front low enough to see the bulge of her breasts. Her short plaited grass skirt made the most of her shapely brown legs. Unfortunately, she was with a very scruffy man who had a long beard and very long hair that was all over the place, he looked as though he had been dragged through a holly bush backwards. Her hair was plaited and all the plaits were tied at the back of her neck with a twined rush stem into which she had pushed some honeysuckle flowers, it was a pretty touch. As she sang, she gently danced and tapped a small skin drum to keep pace with the tune. It was a bit repetitive and she sang the song three times in a row but her lovely voice made up for that and it was a lovely tune. I vaguely remembered hearing it before somewhere, perhaps at my camp and it was clear that a few others knew it, they were singing along quietly.

'*Where the two rivers join*
There lives my love, lives my love
Where the two rivers join
There lives my love'

'Where the two rivers join
He waits for me, waits for me
Where the two rivers join
He waits for me'
'Where the two rivers join
I'll give my heart, give my heart
Where the two rivers join
I'll give my heart'

'Where the two rivers join
We will be one, will be one
Where the two rivers join
We will be one'

'Where the two rivers join
Our young will grow, young will grow
Where the two rivers join
Our young will grow'

'Where the two rivers join
We'll live and die, live and die
Where the two rivers join
We'll live and die'

What struck me most was that while she was a very pretty woman, what was she doing with such a scruffy bastard? I had lost count of the times that I had seen pretty women with minging men; I couldn't understand it and I probably never would. The scruffy bastard got out his bone flutes, he had several of different lengths and he began to play them, swapping from one to the other, low tones, high tones, he was actually quite good. My new friend seemed charmed by him, "Isn't he fantastic?" I nodded slightly, not wishing to appear too enthusiastic, "Yes, he is a very competent player… but it is a shame that he is such a scruffy bastard."

We chatted for a while, she was a nice girl, very wise and knowledgeable and when the sun set over the camp she went to the women's house and I went to the men's. That was normal at a trading camp unless you arrived as a couple, but even then the men and women usually slept in separate houses, in that way it avoided certain problems, such as fights. If you did arrive as a couple, you could if you wanted have a cosy lean-to all to yourselves, with everyone watching, that's why people tended to just go along with the camp rules and stick to the man house or woman house. Now in my bed in the man house, it took me a while to get to sleep, and before I did, I noticed two men who might well have been a couple, kiss each other before getting to sleep.

It had been sometime since I had slept within a group of men and surprisingly, with all the farting, burping, scratching, jokes, many dirty jokes, it felt good for a change, but during the night, someone kicked off outside. All I could hear, as I scrambled out of my bed and left the house, was, "Fuck you," "Fuck you," "Well fuck you," "Fuck you wanker," and so it went on. Two men, who were clearly pissed from drinking too much fermented fruit drink, were pushing each other around, staggering back and forth in front of the main campfire. Light from the red embers and flickering yellow flames lit them from behind so that their shadows joined in with the pushing, flitting over the houses and lean-to's like black giants. As I was marvelling at the dancing shadows, it got serious. The man on the left punched the man on the right, bang on the nose, sending him stumbling backwards with the blow and falling heavily on his arse. The man on the left moved forward while laughing at the man on the floor, who was scrambling around trying to get up, he rolled on to his right side and grabbed for something from a lean-to trade rack. Watching, I saw right man get to his feet, holding a large red deer antler; his back swing was impressive, way back past his right shoulder. Suddenly stepping toward left man, he swung the antler forward with such force and speed that two of the points struck home. One went straight into left man's left eye while the other went through left man's throat and straight out of the back of his neck. Left man didn't say too much, he just sank to his knees and gurgled, black blood flew out of his mouth, the antler still stuck firmly where it landed. As he neared the flames, I could now make out the red colour of the blood and it struck me how in the dusk or even on a bright night you couldn't see colour as well as you could in the day. He fell forward and rested on the antler, which pushed further into his shocked body; sighing and slurping, trying to raise himself while right man stood in silence his arms down at his side. Watching left man, as he raked and scrambled at the ground like some giant crazed spider, then giving up, slumping forward, yet propped up off the ground by the antlers, as he lost his life.

Fat Man came out of his house naked and saw the scene, looking at the right man then at me, "Who is at fault here?" Shaking my head, I shrugged; "It looked like both of them to me, they were being a pair of pissed twats, waking people up, shouting and pushing each other. Then he," I pointed to the right man, "He got punched on the nose and fell on his arse, he picked up a big antler and twatted him," I pointed to the left man lying on the ground, "In the face, and that was that." I felt that I had summed up the situation well. "Thanks, so he got what he gave?" He was pointing at left man, I answered, "Pretty much I reckon." Fat Man turned to right man, "At dawn you go, you take that dead man with you and you dispose of his body in the fittest way... and you owe me for the antler, no one will want to buy it now. Then make sure you fuck well off and don't come back here again, ever." With that, Fat Man turned and went back in to his house scratching his arse with his left hand. There was nothing more to do, so I went back to my bed. I lay there thinking of the words of Golden Woman, *"The trouble is that some people have forgotten that we all have that inner knowledge and they do not respect the Great Spirit or the world that they live in, instead they kill and take too much, just so they can trade for fermented drinks."* She was right, but she could take some comfort in the fact that the world was now one pisshead less.

When I awoke it was pissing it down, right man had gone and taken left man with him, I was not sure what he would do with the body, let it drift down the river? Return him to his tribe? Or leave him somewhere for the crows and ravens to get rid of? It wasn't my problem but I did wander what I would do if I was ever in the same situation, I couldn't

135

think of an answer. Jogging from the man's house to the food house as fast as I could to avoid getting too wet, I found myself a log bench and asked the boy what food there was to break my fast. "We have a fair bit of meat left over from yesterday, and some fish." I fancied something else, something different, it struck me that what I wanted was those flatbreads that Golden Woman made on those hot rocks, it seemed like ages ago since I had seen her, yet it was only yesterday.

Ochre Girl joined me; she looked as good as she did yesterday. "Did you hear the noise last night? There was a fight; we were all talking about it in the woman's house." I nodded, "Yes, I am afraid I saw it, though it wasn't much of a fight. I think that the man who was killed might be a regular here." She looked skyward, searching her memory, "Yes, I think that I saw him last year when I was here. I was with my family, we were passing through in the autumn, on our way to the coastal marshes to the north-west of here, we were going after the geese that fly in for the winter. I think he was fighting last year as well." A nearby trader must have been ear-wigging our conversation. "The girl is right, he was here then, he visited several times a year trading dry meat and skins. He would come here, trade and get pissed on that shit that they make in there." He pointed with his right thumb toward the back of the food house. "He was a trouble maker, a real trouble maker. I traded some of my chert and flint for some of his hides, after a few days they were all soft and maggoty. I don't know what he had done to them." "Probably not cleaned off all the membrane or something," I suggested. "Probably, I should have looked closely, but my eyes are not what they used to be. Anyway, he was a trouble maker, a drinker and a fighter." "He saw the world differently to you and me then," I noted. "Yes mate, I think so... it seemed to me as though he saw the world as a bone, rich in marrow and he was the stone to smash it." We all nodded in silence.

After a short while, the trader had wandered off so Ochre Girl started talking to me again. "I did not want to see the fight, so I stayed in my bed and pulled the wolf skin sleeping bag up around my shoulders." I scratched my right ear. "Wolf skin sleeping bag, that sounds warm." "It is, two skins, stitched together so that the fur is on the inside, it is so cosy and draught free that I can sleep in it totally naked, snuggling deep into the fur, it is bliss." I spent a while thinking about this good looking young woman lying totally naked in a deep fur sleeping bag, "I bet it is... I bet it is bliss." She giggled and played with the nutcracker that lay in front of us on the log plank table; it was a simple affair. A flat piece of slate with a slight hollow in it, in which you placed the flat end of the hazelnut so that the pointed end faced skyward, you then cracked it on the pointed end with a palm-sized flat stone. The boy was still hanging around, "Have you made up your mind yet?" She asked for mint tea and a fresh baked acorn flatbread with strawberries, blackberries and raspberries. "The strawberries are dried if that is okay, we ran out of fresh a while ago, it has been a poor year for them and they are so small, but the blackberries and raspberries are fresh, we grow them on the edge of the camp." He smiled at her; she reached out and stroked his hand, "Thanks." Turning to me he asked gruffly, "And you?" I looked up at him, "I will have a naked woman in a wolf skin sleeping bag please," she laughed politely at my weak attempt at a joke, the boy just looked puzzled, "Make that the same as my friend here please." He walked off into the back and passed on the order to whoever was cooking. While we waited for the food we chatted some more. She was from the east of here and had wandered down river with the Nugget Twins some time ago. It seemed that she was fed up with just messing around doing what all the other women did in her camp; flint knapping, fire making, hide tanning, making snares, making traps, making bows and arrows, hunting and fishing, all the normal stuff. It seemed that she wanted to do something different, hence the fancying up with ochre, pointy tits and tight waist. I had to hand it to her though, sitting here next to her it seemed to me that she had made the correct decision.

She asked me about my plans and I explained about my journey across the Great Plain, all the way to the coast, I told her of Golden Woman and how skilled she was and of my journey back to the camp because of the signals. "Very interesting, it sounds great, a great adventure," she seemed impressed, "Well you should do it yourself sometime, when you feel ready, travel on your own, you will enjoy it I am sure." I smiled at her; it felt good to have this conversation with someone younger than me who actually appeared to be listening. It dawned on me that one of the problems of leading a solitary life was that I denied myself such moments as I was now enjoying, it made me think.

We ate the hot acorn flatbreads with the crushed blackberries and raspberries on top, and dipped the dried strawberries into some honey that the boy had bought the girl, "Special case," I said, as she winked at him.

I treated her to the break fast and traded to cover both of us, then settled for my night's food and bed, said goodbye to her and started to get some kit sorted before I set off. First, I topped up my water bladder from the one clear part of the camp stream and helped myself to some of the raspberries and blackberries which were growing there. I could see some of the new plants of each kind that they had recently planted. Where they grew in loose soil, wild raspberries were easy enough to simply pull out of the ground with their roots intact; it didn't take a genius to work out that you could then take them and plant them in a place that you preferred. As for blackberries, where didn't they grow?

Back at the trade racks and stalls I spotted some flint, a few nice roughed out blades that I could break down into arrowheads, small knives, or just leave them as they were. I didn't really need any more flint, I had plenty of chert back at the home camp. Black chert occurred in the limestone, up in the hills just to the east of us, pieces of brown chert seemed to lie all over the place, but you can never have enough tools and flint just seemed to have a nicer edge than chert, but perhaps I was just trying to justify getting some. Fat Man joined me, "I am sorry that you witnessed the fight last night, it is not a normal occurrence and even with the fermented drinks everyone is usually pleasant to each other here." "It is alright, perhaps they just didn't like each other with or without alcohol and that is what happens when men fight, one usually loses." He put his left arm around my right shoulder, "You are right brother, you are right. It is like me with my wealth, now I have a wealth of things I worry about losing them and I worry about losing trade and customers like you. If you were to go away from here thinking that this trade camp is full of drunks who kill each other then it is unlikely that you will return." I nodded, "Fair point, but you have an excellent trade camp here with such a range of goods and you are in such a good place that I will definitely return. Besides, I wouldn't worry about it, men will always find a reason and a place to fight each other, it is what men do." "I am glad that you see it that way brother, but I do worry about it, I worry about tomorrow and the future in general. I never used to worry about tomorrow or yesterday, not until I had wealth, but with wealth I get more things than I could ever use and I have the most comfortable house imaginable. I also know that my children will have all this when I am dead, so that I know that they will have wealth." He waved his hand at the camp and pointed toward three fat children sitting on their arses outside his house, "They will be comfortable, they will be wealthy and surely that is a good thing." Giving him the briefest nod I said, "If that is what you want my friend then you should be happy that you have achieved it." We smiled at each other and he wandered off towards the food house. I got some flint; I traded the last of the smoked salmon for it, it had now all gone on food, drinks, a bed and flint, not a bad trade though, smoked salmon was always in demand because you didn't get salmon in every river.

An old man with no teeth a twisted jaw and grey almost blind eyes, sat on the ground under a lean-to shelter holding his gnarled hands out for food or water, a beggar. You didn't see a lot of them around, but this man must have been on his own, with no one to take care of him. It occurred to me that I might end up like him one day, unless I stayed with my tribe, or Golden Woman and I had youngsters who would care for us. Wandering over to a hide stall, I felt the elk skins that were hanging there, they were something else, absolutely beautiful but very big. I decided there and then that when I was next here it would be with Golden Woman and we would get one of those for our house. "Hoy, hoy, short hair fuck nuts!" Shit, the Nuggets were back, I almost fell into the lean-to stall as I tried to duck out of their line of sight... too late. "Hoy, hoy, you, short hair, hoy, we thought that you had gone, but you are still here. Is it because you cannot paddle the skin-on-frame boat on the Great North River? You need a dug-out canoe like this one; they are far better, far more stable and heavier in the water, especially if you are a beginner like you." Apologising quickly to the aggressive stall holder who was about to stick a boars tusk up my arse for falling on his hides, I got myself out of his lean-to and walked over to the Nuggets, it was still raining so I tucked all my kit under the deer skin in my canoe to keep it dry. "What do you two want then?" I wasn't particularly friendly in my manner, but these boys seemed to have the knack of turning up whenever I least expected them. "We are here for the games, we are racing in

139

our canoe, we always win, always the best." I was nodding, "I bet you are." I watched them climb out and haul the canoe well up the bank away from the strong flow of the water, then one of them piped up. "We were down the weaving river yesterday and spoke to a man from near your tribal lands, he says he saw the signals, we thought of you." Although they were in all honesty being helpful, I couldn't bring myself to be happy; after all if it wasn't for these two in the first place I would still be sitting on the sand with Golden Woman. However, I was also forgetting that if it hadn't been for these two lads I wouldn't have had a lift down the coast and I may never have met her in the first place. I owed them some decent courtesy after all, "Thanks lads, it's kind of you to think of me." "No problem, besides, we were worried about you because you are such a wank paddler," and with that they walked off to get a fermented fruit drink. As I pushed off from the bank, I thought about setting the Nugget Twins canoe off at the same time and letting it drift down the river, removable transom and all, but that would have been most disrespectful, funny, but disrespectful.

Chapter 2.

I had crossed the Great North River and was now on the south side paddling along to the west, a great reedbed on my left. I found the river that I was after, its mouth opened up, about 20 paces wide and I turned to the left and entered its waters. After a short while the reedbed on my left gave way to a dry grassy area, on this was the smouldering remains of a funeral pyre. A great pile of ash was all that remained. Kneeling in front of it was a woman, not old, about my age at a guess. She was naked but her nakedness was covered with a paint of red ochre resembling blood, she was symbolically covered in her child's blood. Whether boy or girl, they were treated the same. Laid out on a pyre of alder wood, alder smoke kept the flies away from the body in case the fire was slow to spread. The child would be fully clothed and would have their favourite toys or totems with them and then a fire was lit. Once the flames took hold under the body, green leaves or green wood or even wet wood, would be placed around the edge of the fire, this helped create a smoke screen, no parent wanted to see their child burning. The mother would stay with the smouldering pyre with no shelter, water or food, until she collapsed in exhaustion, only then, when her soul's energy had almost left her, would her family collect her and take her home, to begin to heal. I avoided looking too closely, it was her grief and she was suffering, but I noticed that her hair had been cut back, almost to her scalp, a very close cut. This haircut would show to everyone that she was in mourning, and only when her hair was long again, would her mourning have passed.

In an unfamiliar environment such as down at the coast, I had relied much upon the knowledge of Golden Woman to get around and to live. I felt that I had learned enough from her and that I could look after myself when I returned there, but here in the Great Plain I had to rely on my own knowledge. This very marshy, wet area with the reed-fringed river that I was now travelling along was an area that I had not been to before. Another thing that I was now aware of was that sitting in this canoe the Great Plain wasn't actually as flat as it seemed when seen from the Long Hill on the edge of my tribal lands, down here at river level I could make out low rolling hills to the south and east across the reedbed.

I tried to remember the old songs that we had learned from the elders at the fireside. Some told of the right plants to eat, some told of the nature of the animals, some songs told of fish and where they gathered to spawn. I could just about remember one about the lands of my tribe and I started to sing it under my breath, though it had been years since I had sat around those song fires and I had no children of my own to sing them to. I had also spent so much time on my own; it was not surprising that I had forgotten them. I tried to visualise those firesides of my childhood, safe, warm, comfortable and reassuring on a dark and stormy night in winter. All the children would gather around the main campfire while our parents did whatever they did, probably having some peace and quiet, an elder would stoke up the song fire and off we would go. Though I tried, I could not remember them word for word, the rhythm had gone. Fortunately, the one that I could remember was the map song, I used it all the time to get around the tribal lands, it told of all the rivers, the high points, the viewpoints, the valleys, the woods, the caves and shelters, I sang it now.

I wasn't singing loud, I could barely hear it myself, I was self conscious about my singing voice, it wasn't great and even though I was on my own it seemed wrong to shatter the silence that I now paddled through. For a while I thought about making up my own song, like Golden Woman, so I gave it a go.

'Here I sit in a nice canoe,
Paddling up the winding river,
I have my food, my water too,
My bow, arrows and my quiver.'

It seemed easy enough so I tried another verse.

'Travelling through the Great Plain,
On my way up to the hills,

Onwards through the sun and rain
Although I haven't any skills.'

Piss easy this song writing, I chuckled to myself as I paddled.

The rain had stopped some time ago and the sun had emerged through the now thinning cloud, its warmth was causing my clothes to steam as I dried off. Thanking it, I paddled steadily upriver against the slow current. The winding river had broadened and was about 60 paces wide here, with large reedbeds on either side, beyond that was marsh, beyond the marsh to my right was the high point of the rock step where I had taken in the view and seen the elk many days, what must have been at least two full moons ago. Water droplets splashed gently into the water as I lifted out the paddle, rippling away from where they fell like shimmering stars. The reeds along the river were blanketed with spider's webs, full of dew they were shimmering in the morning sunlight. It seemed that every reed stem was supporting four or five shining webs; it was a good year for spiders.

Two strokes of the paddle on each side of the boat, nothing manic, just nice and steady. It was a beautiful boat that she had made, light, strong, easy to lean and turn, it was beautiful, just like the maker. Feeling a shudder of something, probably affection, though I wasn't sure; I allowed myself to enjoy this part of the journey. Thinking about what Fat Man had been saying this morning I was glad that I had no wealth and that I simply appreciated each day for being a new day, a new experience, whatever came my way.

It had been a while since I had paddled for a sustained time. On the seal hunt we had been in a canoe that was big enough for two and we had shared the paddling. Here, I knew that I would soon be feeling this in my muscles, particularly my left elbow so with possibly four or five days of this I needed to make sure that I achieved it and didn't fuck myself up trying to do too much. A slap of the water from the reeds on my left caused me to look across the river; a beaver was sitting on a willow tree that it had recently felled, while another sat on the pile of branches that trailed in the water. The one on the tree hadn't seen me because it was sitting on its tail with its head between its back feet chewing its part digested shit, the one that had seen me slapped its tail in the water again before diving to safety, the other one followed close behind. Although they were in no danger from me I don't suppose that they knew that. Strange calls came from all around me as I eased my way from the world of the estuary of the Great North River and deeper into the marsh of the Great Plain. The occasional splash of fish suggested that salmon or perhaps sea trout were on the move upriver. Above me, an osprey drifted low, keeping about twenty paces in front, occasionally looking under its belly to check where I was. We stayed like this for a while, two hunters sharing a space, moving together along a river, moving together through the landscape, though without doubt the bird was a better hunter than I was. Watching it sweep low over the water it extended its talons which seemed to kiss the surface, the bird stalled for a moment then snapped them shut and lifted a silver fish that had been sitting lazily near to the surface catching flies. The fish shuddered and shook, wriggling as it tried to escape the fierce grip of the talons, the osprey lifted away with leisurely flaps of its wings. Flying over the reedbed to my left towards a distant group of trees, where it landed on the edge of a giant nest. It was a great scruffy collection of sticks, from which three heads popped up to snap at the fish, they would all be on their way soon, "Feed up while you can," I whispered. I had got the message, it was time for a food break; bringing the canoe close to a small sandy island in mid river, I pushed the paddle against the sand to check that it was firm. It would be a bad idea to get straight out and find myself in sinking sand. When I was confident that it was safe, I placed the paddle across the frame of the canoe and lifted myself out, then hauled out the canoe so that it couldn't be washed away. Cupping my hands I took several mouthfuls of cool fresh water with no hint of salt, then splashed another handful onto my face, it felt good, fresh, calming. I dipped my left elbow into the water to cool the soreness. Fetching some dry beaver meat and my wood bowl from the canoe, I sat down on the warm sand at the edge of the flow and started to chew the meat, sipping a bowl full of water every now and again to make it easier to swallow. It was good, Golden Woman had added something to it to flavour it, I couldn't tell what it was but it was slightly hot on the tongue.

144

Lying back I closed my eyes and enjoyed the moment, feeling the heat moving down the river over my face my hands and my bare feet, smelling the scents; meadowsweet, river water, warm reeds, sweet warm grasses. Opening an eye I spotted a big pile of fresh otter shit a couple of paces upwind, which explained the smell of sweet warm grass. The warm breeze caressed my skin and as I dozed birds in the reeds warbled away.

Sometime later the birds woke me up with their chattering and squawking, a large harrier hanging low over the marsh was clearly aggravating them, more splashes as more fish moved upriver, I needed to do the same.

Deeper and deeper into the marshland of the Great Plain I paddled, the river weaved like a snake across the landscape meaning that I would paddle for ages yet only make a few hundred paces in terms of a straight line to my destination. Perhaps I had made the wrong decision in taking a boat, but whenever I had walked in the Great Plain, I had crossed the many small slow flowing rivers that threaded through it by either wading, swimming, stepping over beaver dams or fording shallows where old beaver dams had collapsed and were now covered in gravel. There was plenty of evidence of beavers all around me now. Paddling past the piles of branches and vegetation of beaver dams, I admired how busy these animals were. All along this section of the river were many coppiced willows; the beavers had been changing the landscape forever it seemed, it was a perfect place for someone to collect the whippy regrowth and withy's for basketry materials but not such a good place for me to find a tree to climb up, to see where I was going.

I was getting hotter; sweating my knackers off and the stench of the eels wasn't helping. I hadn't cleaned my jacket of the eel stench from when we were on the seal hunt. It might well have masked my scent from the seals but right now, I just stunk as bad as Golden Woman's rubbish tip and I seemed to be attracting every shit fly around. Tired and with my shoulders aching my left elbow throbbing and hands starting to blister, I needed to stop again.

Pulling into a shallow sloping gravel bank, I decided that it was time to set up for the night. Surrounded by the reed and marsh this bit of gravel was about the only bit of dry land that I could stand on. I checked the taste of the river; it was fresh not brackish and looking around me it seemed as though I had left the tidal river behind. There was a lack of debris in branches along the banks and the level of the water mark along the vegetation at the water's edge looked as though it had been steady for some time. Taking my chances, I took everything out of the canoe before dragging it further up onto a small patch of dry sand then rolling it on its side and propping it up with the paddle, before stashing my kit under the shelter of the boat. It didn't look like rain but there was no need to risk getting my kit wet. This done, I stretched my back by leaning forwards and backwards, slowly and repeatedly, the round gravel was warm and pleasant under my bare feet, the small stones massaged my toes as I wriggled them.

There was still some time until the sun went down so I could try to get something to go with my dry beaver meat, it struck me that I could throw out the fishing line and try and catch something fresh. Unwinding the dry stiff willow line it dawned on me that I needed to wet it first. It would naturally become tighter and more flexible in the water while I was using it but it made sense to pre-wet it before I cast it out, as it would sit better in the water. Placing it under a stone in the margins of the flow to soak, I then got a fire going about a pace away from the paddle prop. The thin dry strips of the outer reed stems were good kindling and there were enough dry twigs scattered around along the top of the gravel bank, remnants of a previous high water flow. When the line was nice and wet, it was supple and easier to unravel; I then placed a gorge hook through the last twisted loop of the wet line, the loop held tight around the waist of the hook. Putting my boots on I scrambled up the bank, pushing my way through the reed fringe and into the marsh. Collecting the tall stems of cleavers and the low leaves of cuckoo flower, I also gathered a few stems of some tall tough nettles, snapping them off as low to the ground as I could. Gripping clumps of vegetation, I pulled plants from the earth in my attempt to find worms; I wanted a few big fat ones that I could thread onto the fine gorge hook. With several worms and my fresh leaves, I slid back down the bank onto the gravel, disturbing a heron that was investigating my upturned canoe, it croaked and drifted away down river.

The worm burst and bled as I forced it onto the thin gorge, I lay the hook parallel to the line so that some of the worm was fed along the line itself, in this way it should stay on the hook more securely and any fish eating it should take the hook into its gut. About a forearm length from the gorge, I tied the line around a little finger sized stone then gently made an underarm cast into a small deep pool in the river that lay between the gravel that I stood on and the bank that I had just slid down, plop. Fastening off the free end of the line to a large branch of dead wood, I put some loose coils on the ground so that if a fish suddenly legged it I could see the line moving and get to it, then I busied myself building up the fire using the dry wood that was scattered around. With occasional glances toward the line, I started to dig out some roots of reedmace and reed. Finding the base of the plants under the water, I felt along the root until it felt substantial enough and then slowly pulled them out, trying not to snap them and trying to be careful not to cut myself on the tough reed stems.

When I reckoned that I had enough for my meal I returned to the fire and started to spread the embers wider than the centre of the fire, into the shallow embers went the roots, I ate the leaves of the cleavers and cuckoo flower while I waited for the roots to cook. The cleavers stems were chewy, a sign of the season, as back in spring and early summer the new growth of cleavers was tender. Holding the long nettle stems at their bases, I wilted the tough leaves over the fire, it helped to get rid of the stings and make them more palatable.

Yawning as the sun started to sink I checked around that I had sufficient wood for the fire, I decided that it would be a good idea to get the wood close to hand so I spent some time bringing it together nearer to the fire. If it got cold in the night or started to piss it down, I could make up the fire quickly if the wood was nearby. Fancying a hot drink I filled my wood bowl with water, finding a stone to heat the water wasn't a problem, I was sitting on loads of them. Into the embers went several and I lifted them into the bowl using two sticks until the water was steaming, adding a few sprigs of water mint I produced a good strong tea. With the drink made and the roots cooking, I checked my sleeping arrangements. The sand was still dry under the shade and lee of the canoe therefore it wasn't just the wind that had been drying the surface, so I now knew that if I lay here it would be dry underneath me. Pushing my kit out of the way, I made enough space so that I could get under completely but not so that the kit stuck out from under the shelter of the canoe should it rain. All I needed was a pillow, I would use the deer hide for that.

Needing a crap, I wandered away from the boat, dropped my trousers and stooped on the gravel near to another big pile of otter shit, by the size of the spread it was obviously the regular place to go around here and if it was good enough for an otter then it would do for me. Typically, as I was bent over concentrating, the supple willow fishing line started to coil out into the pool. Reaching it just as it was about to tighten on the branch, I steadily pulled back against the unseen creature and it wasn't long before it lay in front of me gasping for air and bleeding from the gills where the gorge hook must have jammed. It wasn't a big fish, but fuck knows what it was, about as big as my open hand, with spines along its back and dark green skin and what looked like five fingers of black on either side. Even though it had a big mouth the gorge was wedged across ways, cracking its head on a rock to kill it I then pulled the hook out, noticing that I was bleeding from where one of the spikes from the fish had pierced the webbing of my left hand. Finding a short straight stick, I shoved one end into the mouth of the fish and the other into the gravel so that the fish hung over the edge of the fire without touching the flames. As the skin started to blacken, harden and crackle in the heat, I looked at how pretty its markings were; its yellow belly was a real contrast to its bright red fins.

Sitting on the sand next to the canoe, I gazed at the water running by and chewed the cooked roots, my fingers black from the ash of their burnt outer skin. I couldn't swallow the fibres as they were far too chewy and stringy, but chewing them released a lot of sweet juices that complimented the chunky white flesh of the fish. A tide of ants, a line of busy bodies carrying their finds back to wherever it was that they lived, picked up the bits of food that fell onto the gravel between my feet.

Sitting beneath a clear sky, I looked to the west where the last tinge of the sun coloured the horizon with layers that reminded me of the sheen that I saw on the flanks of the fresh caught salmon; silver, pink and blue. Beneath this huge sky, it seemed again that all the stars that had ever been made by the Great Spirit were coming out tonight. The

148

big moon was low over the reeds; just visible through the mist that was now forming, not quite full tonight and looking like a ghostly face in the sky. I shivered with chill as the air moved down the river like a cold breath from the Great Spirit herself, so I built up the fire to warm me. In the dusk, a huge brown harrier dropped into the reeds behind me and apart from the crackle of the fire and the occasional plop and splash of a fish, it was silent.

I had a piss, washed my hands and face in the river then kneeled down to pray for a safe journey, it had been good so far, but I wasn't travelling as fast as I had hoped. In fact, as I felt the stiffness in my shoulders and the soreness in my left elbow, I was beginning to wander if it would have been better just walking home. I could jog over the dry bits, not that there were many dry bits round here, still, I had chosen this way and as one of the elders used to say, 'I had made my bed and now I was lying in it.' After checking that the heat from the built up fire wasn't wrecking the skin on the canoe, I crawled under the shelter. The last thing to do was to bundle up the deer hide into a loose roll and tuck it under my head and go to sleep.

The occasional waft of smoke filled the canoe, which wasn't perfect but at least I could feel the heat from the fire as the night got colder. Just as I was dozing off, I heard something squeal from within the reeds, it sounded like a young boar or even a baby squealing and I wasn't happy about it, it went again, a bit nearer this time and I found it unsettling. What a young boar was doing out here was surprising and if it was a baby then whatever was happening to that baby, I didn't want to guess. It went again and I thought about stringing my bow just in case something was moving my way. Working on the belief that if I was thinking about it then it was time to do it, I did it and strung the bow. Sitting upright by the paddle prop, I reached for my boots and put them on in case I needed to leg it. Everything I needed for a quick getaway was in arms length. I could roll the canoe over, chuck my kit in, drag it down the bank and paddle like fuck down river away from whatever it was that was there. I wouldn't bother putting the fire out; it was on gravel and wouldn't spread.

I sat there for quite some time, I had noticed the moon move behind a tree, in all that time there had been no more noise and everything seemed to have settled down and returned to normal. Swallows were chittering in the reeds as they settled down to roost for the night, otters were whistling upriver and a white owl flew low over the marsh. Convincing myself that the screaming must have come from a small boar in pain, I lay back down again under the shelter of the canoe, keeping my boots on, just in case.

Chapter 3.

Throughout most of the night I was surrounded by mosquitoes, their constant buzzing and biting gave me little sleep and I tossed and turned, at one point accidentally knocking the paddle away, which caused the canoe to fall on me with a thump. As soon as the sun was up and I could see, I looked at the damage. I was covered in small pink lumps on my hands and arms, evidence of their bites; and I could feel lumps on my face and neck. As it was warm early on, I stripped off and waded into the river to bathe; using the fine wet sand from the riverbed to scrub myself. The water was cold so I didn't stay in for long, just enough time to wash the sweat and grime away and ease the itch of the mosquito bites. Standing thigh deep in the shallows facing the river, I stretched forward and back then side to side to ease the aches and get myself ready for another day sitting in a canoe.

"Ha ha, ha ha, ha, wooh, look at small cock," covering my small cock with my right hand I pointed at the water, "Its bloody freezing, that's why." The Nugget Twins bashed their canoe into the bank to the left of me. "How come you are still only here, you have got days to go yet, so how come you are still messing around, bending over naked in the shallows showing everyone your cock and balls?" Shaking my head, I tried to defend myself, "That wasn't my intention, I..." one of them butted in, "Yes everyone can see you doing it, you look stupid." Glancing around I argued my case, "Well hardly everyone, there's you two and me, and if you two hadn't been paddling past, there would have been just me, anyway I was just about to leave after I had broken my fast." They shook their heads in unison, "No need to break fast here, just around the next bend is a small camp, and they will give you a break fast." "How do you know they will?" Looking at each other they laughed, "Because it is where we live you numb nut." It struck me that at this moment I had two options; option one was to leap onto the prow of the fire hollowed fixed transomed log-boat, tip these cheeky bastards in to the river and hold their heads under the water until they drowned. Option two was to get dressed, pack my canoe and paddle off round the bend to get a free breakfast. Deciding that option two would be of greater benefit to my stomach than option one I got dressed. "We will get back and get a hot drink going, though by the time that you get there the heated water will have become clouds, see you later numb nuts, or is that no nuts? Ha, ha, ha." With that, they were off, backing off the gravel and out into the main flow before heading off upriver at a cracking pace, perhaps I should have gone for option one.

It was with a sense of trepidation that I rounded the corner to visit the Nugget camp. I knew nothing of their family though I was sure that they had talked about it at some time, I think that they had talked about everything else. The first thing that hit me was the smoke; several fires were burning across the camp, and I could see the roofs of several houses peeping above the reeds.

They had a raised wicker platform that jutted out through the reeds and into the river. It was a simple construction made from willow; three branches, which forked at the top and were about as thick as my thigh, had been driven into the riverbed, these branches supported a long straight branch as thick as my lower leg, which lay straight through them from the bank of the river. This was the same on the other side of the platform. Across these, spanning the long straight branches from one side to the other were many branches about as thick as my wrist. On top of these to fill in the gaps were smaller thinner sticks. Some of the thick upright willow posts had rooted and were growing so that the platform was anchored to the earth; I could see small twigs that were covered with leaves. On the other side of this platform was the collapsed rotting remnant of another, much older platform. It was lying as a large tangle of wet silt covered branches, almost resembling an old beaver dam. Tied up to the new platform was the Nuggets canoe, following their lead I tied mine off just behind and checked that the seal hide rope was secure. The platform was solid enough and I walked along it through the thin fringe of reeds up the shallow bank and into the camp from the south. Three houses dominated the camp, one at the east, one at the west and one north of a central fireplace, the fireplace was covered by a deer hide suspended at an angle on four upright posts at the corners. Obviously, it was important that the central fire never went out, that was why it was covered to keep off the rain. The Nugget family used fire to make their fire hollowed fixed transomed log-boats and they didn't want to have to make a new fire every day. The houses were normal in shape but were covered in reed thatch from top to bottom, after all, there was plenty of it about and you used what you could get. Between the north and west house was a large hurdle screen lean-to, about my height high and about five paces long. Six long poles were stuck into the ground at an angle at the rear of the screen from where they rose up and rested on top of the hurdle screen, then carried on to create an overhang. On the side that faced the fire, reeds had been weaved between these long poles so that the overhanging lean-to roof was as watertight as possible. Beneath the overhanging roof and scattered over the floor, was an area of reed stems which formed a base, thin branches of willow and alder then covered these, a couple of hides with the hair intact and facing up lay on top. It was an area to sit and work under the roof, protected by the screen behind you and with the fire only about three paces away, warm and wet proof. It was a great work area; I resolved to make one myself, back at the beach. Between the north and east house were three frames, on which were stretched the skins of beaver, otter and a large pike. A drying rack made from two tripods of willow rods connected by three cross pieces stood behind the east house, eels hung from this over a long fire that paralleled the cross pieces and gave off gentle smoke. Wood was stacked all over the place, some under cover and some not, it struck me that they must get through loads of the stuff if they always kept several fires going. Three scruffy dogs were rolling around in the mud on the edge of the camp, grumbling and griping at each other. Behind them the reed gave way to a marsh of mixed species; nearest were the leaf spikes of vast beds of iris, beyond these were large areas of sedge and rush, the rush spikes were already brown. Popping up through these were the seed heads of ragged robin, marsh valerian and buttercup. On the far fringe of this, where the land started to rise, individual willow trees gave rise to a dense alder and willow scrub which in turn gave way to birch and oak. Dead birch trees stood white and gnarled, covered in white bracket fungus, a buzzard sat in the top of the highest one, while two herons flapped lazily over the marsh and dragonflies flitted busily about.

About thirty paces away to my right, an area of reeds had been cut and the bank had been dug to create a slope on which several canoes lay, together with several intact pine trunks. I was very impressed; this had clearly taken a lot of effort. A group of people were huddled around a trunk, several were nodding and one was talking and waving his hands. Moving nearer until I was in earshot, I watched what was happening. It was clear that the older man, a strong man looking at his shoulders and arms, was teaching the others about the creation of fire hollowed fixed transomed log-boats. "First we find a big pine that has fallen, we get these from upriver near the sandy areas or on the edge of the sandstone hills, upriver. When we have decided on the length that we want, we mark the tree and set fires at each end of the trunk at the length marks. We stop the fire spreading by constantly pouring water where we don't want it to burn and beating any spreading flames with green plants such as bracken to stop the spread, so that the concentrated fire burns through the tree. We hack away at the burnt area with an antler pick and then carry on burning again. When we have the desired length, we roll the trunk into the river and my lads sit on it and paddle it downstream to here. We beach the trunk on this slope and start to burn along the top, using water and green plants to stop the spread, and we just keep going, burning, pouring, hacking, burning. Some people use stone tools or even beavers teeth, but we prefer this method, it is what our fathers always did." "So you have to use trunks from trees that have fallen near to the river so that you can roll them into the river easier." A young woman noted, he nodded, "Yes, absolutely vital, I have explained this to my sons on several occasions yet still they persist in doing all the burning to get the tree to length then find that they can't roll it into the river... but I think that they are a bit simple." He pointed to his head to emphasise this fatherly observation, it would explain a lot I thought. I noticed that just to the rear of the house on the east of the camp lay the remains of another reed house. It had obviously burnt down and it lay there, collapsed, rotting and covered with fresh growth, as the marsh took it back. "A problem of living in reed houses on a site with so much fire, but luckily no one was hurt." I turned to find an attractive older woman standing next to me, peering over my left shoulder at her man, "He is a good man, but a little like his sons, a bit obsessed with fire hollowed fixed transomed log-boats." I laughed, "I take it that you aren't then?" She shook her head and her light coloured hair bounced over her shoulders, "No, not at all, boats are very good tools that get me from here to there and there to here, and yes, they look nice, but they are just tools, and anyway I prefer skin-on-frame boats such as coracles, but I would never tell him. How about you, are you obsessed with fire hollowed fixed transomed log-boats, or are you the break fast man with the small cock? As my lovely sons described you." I shook my head, "No, yes and not sure, but I am the same as you with boats, they are tools and that is it. I haven't even got one of my own, the one I am using is borrowed, but I now know a thing or two about them… thanks to your sons." She laughed, "I am sure that you do, well they are helping their father with the burning demonstration, so you can keep me company and have some breakfast, come... this way." Gesturing toward the east house, she started walking, six goslings followed close behind her. "How many of you are here?" I asked, she pointed to the east house first, "Me and my partner live in there, my daughters, all three of them, live in that house and my two canoe obsessed sons live in that one on the west of the camp. We put them there so that they are as far away from us as they can be on this dry piece of land, there is only so much talk of canoes that I can take, and listening to my man is bad enough." "What about your daughters, are they obsessed with canoes?" "No, women… even girls, don't make the canoes. They cannot touch the tree, or the place where we make the canoe. They cannot go near to it, not until it is made. Then, when it is made, they can use it." "Why are they not allowed to make or help make the boats?" She seemed slightly stunned at my question and took time to answer. "Well, they are… we are, closer to the earth than men, we are closer to the Great Spirit than men. We are more fluid, more of the water, we bleed, my daughters will bleed, we give birth with water around our babies, so we don't make the boats. The boats help us to move, they need to be made by men, they need to be solid and strong, and not of the fluid and spiritual." I nodded, still not really understanding, and thinking of Golden Woman and how she made canoes and how she must be very close to the Great Spirit. She must be, because she was so beautiful. My new friend interrupted my thoughts, "Fortunately my daughters are obsessed with hunting and fishing, they should be home soon with food, and we are feeding everyone today. So, would you like a hot drink? My sons told me that you would like one." "It sounds as though it wasn't the only thing that they told you, as I said to them, the water was very cold." She laughed as she dropped some dried leaves into a wood bowl full of hot water, "Men are all the same, that thing between your legs

155

that you hold dearest is the thing that concerns and upsets you most, be assured that it is irrelevant. Have you a person who loves you?" I nodded, "Well, that person loves you for the fact that you are you, for some reason that is not always apparent there is someone who loves you, so don't dwell on things that you can't change, just accept that you are loved and enjoy that fact." With that, she thrust the wood bowl toward me, "Chamomile tea, I hope that you like it." I did like it, in fact, I liked her, we sat chatting in the sun as her man and her sons started burning, I told her of my home camp by our river and where I had been and where I was going. She seemed interested and asked many questions, she had never travelled along my river, but she had been to the trading camp on many occasions, to trade skins or even some of the boats that they made. However, nowadays people tended to come here to learn how to make their own boats, this was because the joints in the man's wrists and hands were becoming increasingly swollen and painful, and so he now traded his skills. I guessed that inside the Nugget houses were nice skins and furs, amongst other traded things. The man was an experienced teacher and it was clear that they were not going to burn one trunk through in one go, so they had several log-boats in different stages, it was a good set up. "I am impressed with all your structures around the camp; you must be very busy finding materials." "Not necessarily, we have no problem finding the timber. The river or the beaver's bring it down, we just collect it; also, wherever we push a willow branch into the ground around here it seems to grow." I nodded, "Yes I noticed that even your shelters, your racks and your house frames have rooted and are sprouting, mind, it is a great tree to have growing everywhere." "Well, we plant them wherever we can, just short rods, pushed into the ground, they grow, we use the branches, we plant more." Girl's voices from the river meant that the daughters were returning from finding food, we stood and went to meet them, the goslings followed. The girls had tied their log-boat to the platform and while one remained in the canoe passing various contraptions out onto the platform, the other two busied themselves carrying them to the shore. They had some kit; several eel traps similar to the ones that Golden Woman used on the lake, lengths of fishing line and gorge hooks, two bows, arrows, and several snares, but no spears or leisters as the slow flowing river hereabouts carried a lot of colour with it so you couldn't see the fish anyway. Taking a look at the arrows, I noticed that they were blunt, just a rounded end of the wood shaft. "What are these for, how do you kill anything with these?" One of the girls turned to me, "They are for voles or water birds, as they swim by we fire at them and the arrow knocks them out, we then paddle after them to get them." "But why don't you just use a normal arrow?" "The river is full of big pike, if we use an arrow the bird or vole will bleed into the water, the pike will smell the blood and the pike will get to it before we do." "Clever," I nodded. She walked past me with a basket which contained two coots and several water voles and frogs, none were dead. I know that I am a hunter but I don't like to see things suffer, I wouldn't want it for myself, we are all the offspring of the Great Spirit after all. I felt obliged to do something, "And how do you kill them, these voles and frogs and damaged coots?" "Why, in the pot of course." I carried the basket for her back to the main campfire making sure that I rung the necks of the gasping coots, I wasn't sure how to kill the frogs. I was just killing the third of several voles by squeezing its head between my thumb and fingers when she spotted me. "Ehm... what are you doing?" It was the woman, "I was ending their suffering, killing them before we cook them that is all." She looked at me as if I was a nutter. "But if you do that, how will we take their energy? When they die they pass their energy into the pot and when we eat from the pot we take their energy, but if you kill them first the Great Spirit will take that energy into the air instead of us, are you stupid?" Shaking my head, I apologised. "Forgive me please, but my people believe that the Great Spirit smiles on those who treat others with respect and that we should allow no suffering and that even if we eat dead meat we are still getting the energy of the life force. I am truly sorry if I have upset you or dishonoured your beliefs, please forgive me." By now I was bending as low as I could in submission, I genuinely didn't want to upset my host, besides, I was starving. She smiled, "Don't worry my friend; I am sorry that I called you stupid we get all sorts here, come and help me to charge the pot." I did, we filled a huge wood pot, that must have taken many fires to burn and shape, with water from the shallows where the flow was cleanest, she even kept the fish fry that swam into it just to add taste to the soup that she was about to make. Washing our hands in the river, we used the crushed roots of water lily as a soap

157

then sat chopping the roots of reedmace, flowering rush, water plantain and the same white water lily that had been collected by the girls and washed in the river, together with the leaves of brooklime, comfrey and watercress. I wasn't sure how those soapy roots would taste in the soup but while I chopped them it gave me a chance to look at her. Her hair was the most noticeable thing; a bit like the colour of oak smoked buckskin. But it was more complex, many strands; some white, some grey, some brown, some red, but mainly of oak smoked buckskin. Her hair reminded me of lying in dry grassland at the end of the summer and looking through all the many colours of the dry stems. She had eyes the colour of dark honey and a very clear skin, tanned but clear. "You are a Medicine Woman." I am not sure what made me say this, but her general energy seemed to suggest this to me, perhaps it was her energy that had made me say this. "Of course," it was all she said, she stayed looking down into the large bowl as I started to gut the frogs, which were twitching and moving as I did so. The girls were busy bringing over hot rocks to heat up the soup, they would lower them in and lift out the cool ones with a long spoon that was curved at the end, they called it a ladle. When the water was hot enough, two of the girls started to pluck and gut the birds, leaving one to continue with the heating stones as and when required. I wandered how they would have done this if I hadn't killed the birds first. Into the pot went the fish meat; chunks of chub and roach and a fish that was the same as the one that I had caught and eaten the night before, she called it a perch. The pot bubbled away and the meat started to cook, the dogs were having a great time lying on a grass mat crunching on the remains of the fish, I watched them eating the still gasping heads. I was glad that my tribe killed things before we gutted and cooked them, this way looked cruel, but I could understand their belief and it would be wrong of me to show them disrespect in their camp.

The grass mat was obviously where the dogs slept and it was scattered with yellow daisy like flowers that were on stems that were slightly downy, like the soft almost invisible fluff on a woman's face. I asked her what the plant was, "Fleabane, we stick the dry stems on the grass mat of the dog's bed because the juices destroy the fleas that the dogs always seem to have, it seems to work." After flavouring the soup with various leaves, some of which I recognised and some I didn't, she rubbed her hands together then down the front of her buckskin trousers and smiled at me. I noticed that everyone at the camp was wearing trousers, probably to protect themselves from the reed stems and the saw like leaves of sedge, and because of all the mosquitoes and biting insects that were in the marsh. "Right, next course," she started on the other things. At the central fire she set up four waist high tripods, two to the west of the fire and two to the east of the fire. They were arranged north and south so that a pole, lying north to south, could be propped between the tops of the tripods. With two tripods and a supporting pole on each side, several poles could then lie over the fire at just above waist height. The girls had finished the gutting and plucking, the woman now filled the body cavity of the coot and a cormorant that they must have caught earlier, with leaves of wood sage before inserting one of the cross poles into the body cavity through the arse end and out of the neck end. The girls then laid these poles over the fire onto the support poles of the tripods. I was beginning to wonder how long I would have to wait until breakfast when she asked, "Do you want to eat now before they all come over and you can't get any?" "Yes please," she gave me a bowl and a spoon and ladled out some soup, then she gave me a flat wooden plate on which were three voles and several pieces of smoked eel. I sat staring at the voles, not wishing to upset her but not having a clue what to do with them. She showed me by taking one of her own stunned voles, "Like this," taking hold of the vole by its short stubby tail she held it just above the embers of the fire, its front legs recoiled from the heat and almost immediately the fur singed away and crisped the skin, the vole gave a quick kick then pegged it. She turned it over, the fur singed away and the skin crisped, a puff of grey smoke and fluid came out of its arse as its guts boiled. Then she simply chewed on the crispy skin, nibbled the meat underneath and tossed what was left to the dogs. I did the same; there wasn't much of a taste other than the smoke from the alder wood that we had cooked it over. I was pleased to see that the three voles that she had given me were the ones that I had already killed; I didn't want to dangle one of the poor little live buggers over the fire. The smoked eels tasted good and the soup was alright, though I wasn't keen on the soft meat of the frogs and I had to spit out the skin, though I suppose in time I would get used to it if I lived here. We rounded it all off with

159

hot flatbreads made from the roots of bog bean which she had dried then bashed into a flour. A bit of water and a bit of fat gave them a simple crumbly texture. We ate these with fresh elderberries, blackberries and raspberries gathered from the woodland edge. She had mixed these fruits together with a bit of water and a thick sweet syrup that she had made by heating birch sap.

The woman excused herself and went over to the eel smoking rack, the goslings following, she took a handful of the long stems of a spiky yellow flower that were piled on the ground and threw them onto the fire beneath the fish. One of the girls told me that it was yellow loosestrife and that it seemed to be very effective at keeping the flies away from the fish. After she had checked the eels, the woman went over to feed the others by the log-boats, so I sat talking to the girls, as they were keen to ask me about my hunting. I told them; trout, salmon, hare, black grouse, red deer, roe deer, boar, sometimes wolf, sometimes lynx, very rarely bear. What I used? I showed them my flat bow, they handled it eagerly, passing it between them and running their eyes and hands all over it. They used round bows, made from willow regrowth from beaver coppice, only the eldest girl could draw my bow properly and she was a natural. I would have liked to see her hunt through the marsh, slim and slight she would have been good to watch, moving softly through the reedbed like a heron ready to strike. What fascinated me, was how they killed the birds and beasts of the water, they drowned them. To catch cormorants they used a post driven into the riverbed in water that was about waist deep, so that the top of post was about a foot length above the water. Cormorants would perch on this post as they dried their wings after fishing, every now and then, the girls would place a snare on the top of the post, if they were lucky, as the bird moved its feet on takeoff the snare would start to tighten. This snare was a simple slipknot and the fixed end was tied to a heavy stone that was balanced on top of another shorter post next to the perch post. As the snare tightened, the cord pulled and the stone tipped off and into the water, dragging the bird behind it. The setting of the post in the right depth of water was critical, too deep, the bird would be out of your reach, not deep enough, and the bird just stood on the bed of the river with its head above the water wandering why it couldn't move. They used similar methods for both beaver and otter, but placed the snares on

160

regular trails where logs jutted out over the water so that the animal was dragged in to deeper water from a clear fall. The main difference between these methods was that the beaver and otter snares needed lengths of strong rope that were attached to the stone so that the stone could be lifted from the bed first followed by the length of snare and then the animal. Often, once the rock had been lifted, the gas-filled body of the drowned animal would float up anyway. They used snares for many things, even grass snakes, they pointed to a large grass snake skin that hung from a frame in the work area. The most interesting trap that they used was very clever. They would take a large piece of wood about as long as my arm and as wide as my head and burn and pick it out like a small fire hollowed boat. They would then weave a lid that covered this hollowed out log, the lid was made from thin willow but they left a hole in the centre that was about as long as an adults hand and about four fingers wide. Several pointed sticks as thick and as long as fingers were attached to the lid using cord, so that the points just overlapped the central hole, this lid was then secured to the log using strong cord. These traps were placed just under the surface of the water at deer drinking places. A deer could step onto the hidden trap and its foot would go through the hole into the hollow of the log, the short pointed sticks would stick into the animal's foot or lower leg and prevent the animal from removing its leg from the trap. The newly attached log would hinder its escape as the hunters closed in; several of these traps were used at a time. I asked them about the drowning method of trapping for the beaver, otter and cormorant as it surprised me that they would eat things that were already dead given their beliefs. "Cormorants are too difficult to shoot using arrows and beaver and otter skins get damaged when we use arrows... besides, they are like fish, they are all water animals." This argument didn't make sense to me, "What difference does that make? You eat only live fish, but you eat cormorants, beavers and otters when they are dead." They all looked pissed off with me and the eldest gave me my bow back in a huff, "Well that is what our parents tell us, that is their explanation." Leaving it at that I thanked them for their hospitality and praised them on their hunting skills, and, because I felt that I had upset her by challenging her beliefs, I gave the eldest daughter one of my flint blades that I had got from the trading camp, so that she could make several arrows to compliment her bow. She seemed happy enough with that and I felt better about it. I changed the subject, "What's with the goslings?" They all laughed, "Every year mother collects a few greylag eggs from the geese that nest over in the grassland, she keeps them warm until they hatch, and the first thing that they see they follow. They stay with us all summer and autumn and then we eat them over winter. Then next year she will do the same and so on and so on, easy food, lots of feathers and they are fun."

The woman returned and I again asked her about my river, she answered using her hands to emphasise the directions. "Just around the bend is a little river on the left, go past that then around two bends and it is on the left, that is where your river comes from, it has been raining well in the hills so it should have enough water for you to go quite a way up." She had half turned away from me and I from her, but then she turned back and added, "I hope that you have a safe journey, take care with your tasks and that you get back to the Golden Woman soon." With that, she smiled and walked over to her house while I took one more look at the boat making session, then walked out on to the platform and made ready to go. As I was about to leave, the woman returned carrying a whole smoked eel and a small coiled rush basket that was held together with a binding of stripped clematis bark. Giving me the eel, she reached into the basket taking out some leaves.

 "Some people don't get on with frogs the first time that they eat them so take these with you." I looked at the ripped pieces of leaves that I was now holding, "What are they?" "They are bistort leaves, and they can help stop the shits, you might need them, having the shits when you are stuck in a canoe all day paddling and putting pressure on your belly is not much fun." "How do I take them?" "Use them in hot water as a tea or simply chew them to get the juice out and spit out the pulp, oh and if you want to, just break up some of the cold charred wood from your fire and chew on that as well." Gladly taking the eel and the leaves, I thanked her for the food and her kindness then added, "Please thank your sons for inviting me."

Chapter 4.

I had taken her advice and was now paddling along the second river on the left; in theory, this was my river. It didn't look anything like my river in its young form, up in the hills, but I was fairly sure that it was my river. Reed buntings flitted along the banks, in and out of the reeds and the stems of flowering rush, the many pink flowers of which I had passed when travelling to the coast, the vibrant pink had now changed to purple seed heads. Occasional clusters of arrowhead grew in between the rushes, and I could just make out the small six pointed star-like seed heads of star fruit. Pungent smells came from the wet soil, rotting vegetation probably, and quiet, but for the rippling and light rhythmic drumming of the water against the tight skin of the canoe… beautiful. I was thinking of the Medicine Woman, I wasn't sure why I had to take care with my tasks; I didn't know what she had meant by that. Perhaps it was something that she said to everyone? My guts weren't too bad, so I didn't need to chew on the bistort leaves; I think that it was because I had spat out the frog skins. I was already aware that charred wood could help if you had the farts; my tribe reckoned that it sweetened our guts. We would also use broken up charred wood in other things; for example to draw with, or to add to pine resin to make glue, like when I had fixed my water bladder on my way to the coast.

The valley was beginning to close in, gone were the extensive reeds, this part of the river was only edged by reed, grasses and reedmace, beyond this edge was either grassland that was grazed and kept low by deer and aurochs, or scrub or marsh then low wooded slopes. Around a south bend in the river, I found another river coming in on the left. My head told me that I should still travel south on the river that I had been paddling on as I didn't feel that I had gone far enough south. Up till now I thought that I had been travelling in a roughly south-easterly direction, the question was should I continue south then hope that my river was further on? From the map in my head I knew that a main river ran south to north across the Great Plain. When I had set out on this trip, I had walked along my river on its south bank, and then where it had joined another river that

163

was flowing north I broke away to the south-west. I had crossed the north flowing river and a short time later I had crossed another river that flowed north, this second river had seemed bigger than the first so I guessed that it was the one on which I had been travelling upstream from the estuary to just past the Nugget camp. I had been travelling up my river since just after the Nugget camp so if I took this river on the left I reasoned that it must be my river because my river joined a river that flowed north. I just hoped that there weren't lots of rivers in this area because if there were then I might spend many days pointlessly travelling up and down. I paddled around for a bit trying to look for a land mark then remembered something; when I was walking across the Great Plain and I had crossed the river that my river had joined, I had climbed a dying alder tree to try to get a view across the land. The end of a branch had broken off on my way back down causing me to fall and I had kicked out at it in anger and had broken it off completely.

Beaching the boat on a muddy bank my boots slipped as I scrambled madly up and crashed through the thin edge of reed with the momentum. A bittern was standing looking at me, it jumped and I jumped, nearly falling back down the mud bank, it flew off silently and landed beyond some alder scrub in the marsh to my right. Unfortunately for the bittern that was where the tree was, about 100 paces away. After about 120 wet paces, I pushed through the scrub and got to the tree, muttering my apologies to the bittern that I had disturbed again. Sure enough there was the scar just above hip height, and down amongst the plants were the smashed up bits of the branch. Already covered in moss and being chewed away by various little beetles and slugs, all doing their work in turning dead things back into earth so that other things could grow; the Great Spirit was skilled and clever. I climbed up as high as I could go and it was with some relief that as I turned to face the east I saw the Great Step and the Pointed Tit, in between these two hills was my camp.

The sun was still high so I could push on up river, but I knew this area now and I decided to stay the night to give my left elbow a rest, get a decent feed and an early night, and then crack on in the morning as soon as I could see. I knew that an ant's nest

164

was at the base of the rotten alder, I had eaten from it the last time I was here. I kicked away at the soft rotting bark and out came the ants giving me grief, under the bark were the white grubs, collecting a handful I shoved them in my mouth, along with a few ants at the same time. I tried a few slug eggs, round and white I didn't much care for them so I spat them out. Next it was reed root collecting, while I was at it I collected several stems of mint. In one of the small pools that littered the marsh I waded out to chest deep to pull up the roots of water lilies, they had tasted alright back at the Nugget camp, and their white flowers had looked stunning when I was last here. I only collected a few; it was enough to provide me with some variety in my food. Even though I was all alone I looked around me just in case the Nugget Twins were about to turn up and see me naked again, but no one was within sight so I lay in the grass and soaked up the heat of the sun, first on my front then on my back.

Getting dressed, I watched a grass snake slip past me through the reed and get into the river. Swimming strongly against the flow it was quickly on the other side, where it wound its way up the bank and into the reeds, amazing animals, on land or water, amazing. I collected some other leaves; marsh violet, watercress, bog stitchwort, as well as the small green seedpods of white clover. Some welcome raspberries from the few canes near to the alder scrub would add some fleshy sweetness and finally some stems of chickweed, which seemed to grow wherever I went. I wasn't happy with the muddy bank as a base camp so I climbed back into the canoe then paddled about 50 paces up my river to where a sandy gravel bank lay on the south side. On this more accommodating bank, I hauled out the canoe, emptied my gear to lighten the weight, and then hauled the canoe up some more. Once it was far enough away from the water, I turned it over and propped it up on its paddle for my shelter for the night. I walked back along the bank to collect my food, pushing my way through willow herb and rushes. On returning to the boat I found an otter sniffing at the canoe, I don't suppose it had ever smelled seal before and it appeared to like it. It was also very interested in my whole smoked eel and I cursed it as it disappeared into the river with the long fish trailing out of its mouth. I needed to rethink the meal.

Scraping a hollow in the sand just bigger than my head, I lined it with my roe hide to create a large bowl, then using my wood bowl I scooped up the cleanest water from the shallows and filled the hide bowl. Out came my fire kit and I got a fire going, several stones went into the ashes and then into the water in the hide bowl. After a while, I had heated the water in the hide, I filled my wood bowl with some of the hot water and dropped in some of the mint leaves. All the other leaves went into the hide bowl to make a simple soup while the roots went into the embers. I was really pissed off with the otter, if I had had my bow and arrow with me when I saw it I would have shot the cheeky bastard, now I needed to get some more fish. While everything cooked, I got out the fishing line and baited up the gorge by wrapping a thin strip of the dried beaver meat around it, making sure that the gorge speared the meat so that it wouldn't fall off. I lowered it into the margins to see what it looked like, in the water it looked like a great fat red worm. Tying a small stone to the line, I swung it out into the channel, sat back to relax and took a sip of my hot mint tea. Almost immediately, the line tightened and interrupted my relaxation. As I pulled on the line, the silver fish shot out and into the air and used its tail to dance across the water towards the other bank. Then it plunged beneath the surface and got its head down shaking from side to side, like a dog ragging a white hare. The line bounced and skipped, I could feel it snagging and catching against the riverbed as the fish fought to stay in the river. Just when I was expecting the line to break against the stones the fish gave up, as it drifted across the shallows and onto the edge of the bank, I could see why. The gorge had punctured the gills on the left side of the fish's head and a trail of blood was leaking into the water. Leaning forward I reached down to grab the fish in case it tried to leg it again, as I lifted it from the water a flash of gold and green shot away, a pike only a hand width away from stealing my fish. Killing the fish by hitting its head against a stone, I gutted it straight away using a flint blade, then simply laid it skin down in the shallow bed of cooler embers right at the edge of the fire. The sea trout smoked and hissed gently, its pink flesh hardening as it cooked; its smell was wonderful because it reminded me of my time with Golden Woman.

As I ate my soup, roasted roots and fresh sea trout I listened to what was happening around me. Noises in the marsh and scrub told me that something was moving my way, birds would call then fly away, their alarm calls trailing off into the distance, a flight of ducks took off from one of the small ponds to my rear and flew low over me quacking. Whatever it was that was coming my way, it stopped now and again, before walking towards where I was sitting. I could hear it moving heavily through the vegetation, it was big. Unsure whether to prepare myself for a hostile encounter or simply to sit quietly and eat, I chose the latter and remained seated. It arrived at the bank behind me and the sun went out; turning my head slowly to the left, I saw the huge bull elk only five paces away, standing with his head craning up tilted back and straining to get his nose as high in the air as he could. He was sniffing the air, looking for a cow elk, his antlers blocked out the sun like two giant open hands plucking it from the sky. Never had I been this close to a bull elk before, I froze, wanting to absorb the image of this grey brown animal. The strong muscles in his neck stood out as they held aloft his huge head and enormous antlers, his tongue kept licking his nose, seeming almost to taste the air. Flies buzzed around the damp of his eyes as he blinked his long eyelashes, he snorted and flies that were hanging around his long muzzle and nostrils flew off then landed on his head. My eyes followed his long forelegs, which extended down from those muscular shoulders as tall as me, if not taller, and primed with such raw power. A dark brown ridge of coarse hair ran from the mane on his neck down his shoulders and all along his back to the solid massive power of his arse. Under his neck was this strange dangling thing, it looked as though it was long hair but I couldn't be sure. Shuddering at the closeness, the intenseness of this interaction, I was overwhelmed by him, in awe of what the Great Spirit could create, and as before, I had no desire to kill him but just to marvel in his strength, power, scent and beauty. As he stood there filling the sky, I thought back to the old story that Golden Woman had told me about the women fighting one off with barbed points, I hoped I didn't need to take any such action.

He had a great big crap then widened his back legs and had a piss, the strong smell wafted by me, he probably did it just to scent this spot so that he knew where he had been and any other elk in the area knew where he had been. It was probably a better

167

system of marking an area than mine, of smashing up tree branches in a childish tantrum. My right foot slipped as I tried to turn further, he heard the crunch of the gravel and immediately dropped his head to look at me sitting below. We looked at each other, I thought that he looked angry and pissed off. Angry because he hadn't seen me till now and I could have killed him, pissed off because I was an irritating thing that he now might have to deal with. He pawed at the ground with his right leg then snorted at me twice scattering the flies from his nose, I reckoned that my best option if he decided to charge me was to jump in the river, though I knew that elk were good swimmers. Fortunately for me he had other things on his mind, so after another steaming piss he snorted and ambled off along the bank to the west crashing through the vegetation. Taking a deep breath, I quickly drew a life size image of his head in the sand, just to remind myself how big he actually was.

As I finished my food an enormous splash told me that he had jumped into the river that flowed north, sure enough I watched him float from south to north past the junction of my river and another splash told me that he was getting out somewhere on the far bank.

I was all alone again with just the jingle of the river and the shuffle of the reeds and a low dark cloud emerging from the distance to my right. A large cloud, then two, three, four clouds that changed; immense, swooping and sweeping, to-ing and fro-ing, curling and leaping, endlessly going… back and forth, over and into the reedbed. Beautiful, magnificent, timeless.

Washing my hide and wood bowl in the river, I topped up the fire and settled down for the night; real clouds were now rolling in from the west, which looked like rain, possibly a bad sign. But, the sea trout must have been a good sign, after all, she and I had fished for them together and here they were following me up my river, taking me home, connecting Golden Woman and my home, connecting Golden Woman and me. This river and all its water connected the two of us, all I needed to do was lie on its surface and float downstream with it, and if I was lucky I would eventually wash up on the north bank of the Great North River, right at her feet. As darkness fell, other than the jingle of

168

the river and the shuffle of the reeds, all I could hear from the reedbed was the strange mix of burbles, whistles and clicks of all the worlds' starlings.

Chapter 5.

As soon as I could see, I packed up. Although it was now dry, rain had put the fire out sometime during the night and washed away my image of the elk. A couple of crows flew low over the marsh, croaking at the morning while two storks flew over the river, landing in the reedy grass on the other side. Everything seemed to be waking up as I slipped the canoe into the water, it was bearing up well, the seams were intact but the skin seemed to be stiffer along the top of one side. Perhaps I had placed the fire too close to the canoe last night and it had dried the top of my temporary shelter. A strange thing about this wet marshy area of the Great Plain was that one of the many small streams tasted slightly salty and there were springs that tasted as salty as the sea and were red in colour. Whenever I found myself at that point I knew that I was only about a good days walk from home. Another unusual thing had happened during the night. I had seen several lights across the marsh, little blue green ghosts, there for a moment then gone. We knew that boggarts lived in these wet, marshy places, the lights were eerie, unnatural and I had shut my eyes as tight as I could, in case it was something not of this earth, something that I should not see.

Out in mid flow I topped up my bladder, the water looked clean here apart from all the little flies that scooted across the surface. It was a steady pull up the river, the frequency of right and left bends pissed me off and I seemed to have been paddling for ages yet was not actually getting anywhere. At one point I passed a large grassland on my left where many aurochs grazed and called, most of them lay on the ground lazily flicking their tails as the flies aggravated them, while two stood tall, watching for anything that might attack them. Standing as high as me, if not higher, starlings were busy pecking insects off their backs and swallows fattened up for their journey away from here by flying over the herd, feeding on the insects that were attracted by the heat of these huge animals and the piles of shit that they left. There was a big swampy area where they came down the bank to drink, the result of which was that there was a lot of shit in the water so I wouldn't be drinking here, but a great shoal of fish fry were busy feeding around it. As I passed the shitty water area I was bitten on my chest by a furry yellow shit fly, it felt like the barb of a blackberry thorn and was immediately sore. If I had been wearing my shirt it wouldn't have happened, but the day was so warm and I was sweating so much that it was more comfortable to be travelling naked. Slapping and flattening another shit fly that was biting my left arm I pulled into the right bank and stopped for something to eat. I had still got some of the fish from last night and a couple of the cooked roots, I ate them hurriedly as I wanted to crack on but I made sure that I had a good drink of water before I set off again to make sure that I was hydrated.

Now that I was still I could hear that several of the aurochs were making a racket. It looked as though they were standing around and looking at a fixed spot on the ground in front of them. Carefully lifting myself up to get a better view, I saw that a calf aurochs was stuck up to its neck in a soft spot in the marsh. It was in a panic, calling and trying to free itself, its mother and the others were stamping on the ground with their forelegs and calling back. None of them were happy and neither was I. Deciding to move on, I rounded the next bend with the calls of the little one still ringing in my ears, wandering why the fuck it was about to die in such a scary and shit way. As a hunter, I could understand why animals died when they were killed for food, that was just the nature of things. But when animals died for no apparent reason, it seemed such a waste, perhaps the Great Spirit needed some sort of gift, some sort of exchange, a life given back that was not a life taken by a hunter. A life simply returned to the Great Spirit, no reason, just a life given. The little aurochs calf would be meeting the Great Spirit soon enough so it could ask her directly. But it seemed to me that the aurochs was dying because it had left the others, the penalty for straying onto soft ground and not staying with the herd. I thought of myself not staying with the herd and I thought of the man at the trading camp, needlessly killed by the man wielding the antlers.

A peewit drifted up out of the rushes to my right, its lopped wings barely seemed to carry it. It flapped over me, taking a look at this animal in a boat then gave its distinctive call and returned to the rushes. As I was paddling along, looking at a family of long-tailed tits flitting through the branches of some scrubby willow, a skin-on-frame canoe came round the bend toward me. It wasn't the Nuggets and I didn't recognise the paddler, so I moved over to the shallows on my right gently allowing my canoe to beach, giving him the opportunity to paddle over and talk if he wanted to, he did. "Hello brother," I returned his greeting, "Hello brother, have you travelled far?" he slid his canoe onto the beach beside me. "From not far up river, I was hunting beaver and otter, but there's nothing much around up there, the river is too young, not the right place for them. I was going to trade the skins at the camp on the Great North River, do you know it?" I nodded, "Yes, it is a... very interesting place; I went a few days ago... would you care for some water?" I held out my bladder, he shook his head, "No thanks, I have plenty... where are you travelling to?" I told him about my journey to my camp because of the smoke and fire signals from the Great Step. He nodded, "The signals have stopped, a day or so ago, I have been watching them in case I was hunting in some tribal land and the signals were a warning to me, in the end it was why I packed up and moved." I let this sink in for a moment; if they had stopped then perhaps I could turn round and get back to the coast instead of getting back to the camp. "Was there any tribal activity at all?" I wanted to see if the signals were simply to drive away this hunter. "No, I didn't see anyone or anything at all other than the signals." Nodding again, I reasoned that as I had come so far I might as well return to the camp, besides I needed to check on my strawberries. I asked him if he always travelled by canoe across the Great Plain, "Yes, I think that this is the best way to travel, there aren't many animal trails across the Great Plain, the elk tend to move around on their own so they don't make good trails to walk along. Aurochs make decent trails but they are lazy so their trails just link grazing areas, which is alright if you are hunting aurochs but not if you are trying to walk in a straight path across the Great Plain. Then of course there are so many rivers and streams to cross, I got fed up of relying on finding a beaver dam as a crossing point so I chose to use a canoe instead." I knew what he meant and I thought back to my time spent pissing around in the reedbed of the Great North River before the Nugget Twins gave me a lift. My tactic for crossing the Great Plain had always been to try to link up as many of the trails of badger, fox, aurochs, elk and deer that I could find.

172

As long as the various trails were pointing in roughly the direction that I wanted to travel, I could then make my own way in between. It was surprising just how much headway I could make by following the regular trails made by other animals.

We chatted about good and bad hunting areas, I told him about the aurochs just down river, then we both looked to the sky at the grey clouds that were gathering on the horizon to the west of us, "Time to go" he said, "Time to go" I said, "Good to meet you, take care brother," "And you brother".

For the rest of the day I got my head down and paddled, the lightweight canoe meant that I sat high in the water; I was sitting just to the rear of the mid-point of the canoe, so that the front was lifted slightly from the surface of the water. This seemed to present less of the canoe surface to the water and I felt that it helped as I pushed against the increasing flow. Even so I occasionally had to shift my kit to get a better balance and their was only so long that I could sustain my rate of paddling, it was time to stop.

This area was much more wooded, with oak, elm and lime as the main trees and dense areas of hazel along the scrubby edges of the drier parts of the river bank. A flat beach with sand and shingle looked good, so I landed, turned the canoe over then propped it up with the paddle. I was so tired that I lay down under the canoe shelter and fell asleep.

It was dusk when I woke, I had fucked up. I had made no fire and had collected no food, I had no supplies other than water and there was plenty of that around anyway. I could do something quick and try to get a fire going then grab some food before it became dark, or I could just do one of those tasks. Despite the low grey clouds that stretched from one side of the sky to the other it was still warm and I was hungry, so I decided that I would forget about the fire and look for food.

By the time that it was dark, I was back at the boat with food. I chewed the acorns that I had gathered just enough to crack the outer shell, and then peeled this off with my nails. The bitterness of the green acorns was intense and they quickly dried my mouth, but they were full of energy and I needed that now. If I had made a fire, I could have at least roasted them in the ashes, which would have made them a bit sweeter, after eating a handful of them I switched to the hazelnuts, which tasted excellent after the acorns. There was sorrel growing on the riverbank so I ate the leaves together with a few blackberries and dewberries that sweetened the sour sorrel. After a gulp of water to rinse the powdery remains of bitter acorns from my mouth I looked east. In the darkness, there was no sign of fire on the Great Step and during my journey I had not seen any signals at all, crawling under the boat I got my head down on my rolled up hide and fell asleep almost immediately. A cool steady breeze came down the river and it started to drizzle, waking me and making it uncomfortable, but at least the breeze kept the midges away. Sometime in the night, I woke again to find that the drizzle had stopped, the clouds had cleared and that I could see very well in the light from the full moon. Looking up at the bright silver disc, I now knew, with what she had taught me, that it would be pulling at the sea and bringing it in to the land at its highest and drawing it back out again at its lowest. I thought of her there all alone, listening to the crash and crunch of the breakers as they clawed at the sand and shingle and I longed to be listening to them with her. It was cool now and I very much regretted not having a fire, I managed to doze off again, but I was having trouble sleeping, shuffling uncomfortably on the shingle. An occasional sea trout or salmon splashed in the deep pool under the trees and with a yawn I opened a drowsy eye to see the rings of ripples move out across the pool in the moonlight; seeing my yawn and meeting my drowsy eye, a lynx slowly backed away into the trees and was gone.

At dawn, it felt as though someone had hit me over my head with a rock, it was banging away like a tight skin drum, and so to rehydrate my complaining body I drank as much water as I could stand. I was also very hungry, but it was a tossup between time spent looking for food, or time spent getting back to camp. The sooner I was at back camp the sooner I could go to the coast it seemed that simple. Pushing off into the stronger flow I bashed the paddle against a rock and jarred my right hand, nothing serious but it served to remind me of just how easy it was to damage myself. I needed to concentrate, the water that I had drunk started to help and my eyes could begin to focus properly. Taking the main flow wherever possible meant that I was in faster water but it seemed to be the deeper water, well, nowhere was deep, there were just fewer rocks showing above the surface. It would be a crap thing now if I put a hole in the boat, having come so far. It

174

was too rocky in places so I got out of the canoe and pushed it in front of me, it was hard going at times having to step over the slippery boulders of the riverbank, the canoe longing to run away back down the river, downstream to the estuary, downstream to the coast and its maker, Golden Woman. I would happily let it go and find her, but only when I was sitting in it.

I was now rounding the Great Step to the south of me and was not far from the camp. In the time that the sun had travelled from directly above me to dropping into the trees I had got in and out of the canoe several times and I was now paddling up the last long flat of water toward my camp. Passing the tribal totem tree, looking up at the collection of deer skulls, antlers and wind rattles made from deer feet that were all tied to many of the branches, it was a welcome sight. Just past the totem pole on the south bank to my right was a sandy beach with two upturned canoes, made from deer hide and held down by ropes of lime bast tied to heavy rocks. Another, older canoe lay rotting nearby; its frame had been made from willow withy's and thin branches of birch then covered with birch bark.

As I beached it on the soft sand my canoe seemed to sigh in relief, I did the same, dropping my head onto my chest. After emptying all my kit, I hauled up the canoe to well above the water line laying it next to the two canoes. Moving the stone weight, I pulled the lime rope over the canoe so that it too was held down, then turning south I trudged wearily into the camp.

Part Three; Home Camp.
Chapter 1.

Walking slowly towards the camp I cast my gaze about, checking that everything was alright, that everything was here and that I was in the right camp, which could have been embarrassing. As I walked into the camp I passed a naked young man, not an unusual thing in itself apart from the fact that this man was tied to an oak tree. He was standing facing it and the rope passed round the tree and was fixed to both hands, he wasn't going anywhere. This tree, just on the edge of the camp was the punishment tree. I approached a brother of mine who was snapping over and breaking off branches of hazel to get himself some poles for a frame, nodding toward the tree I asked, "What's he been up to?" He smiled and shook my hand then walked with me to the centre of the camp some forty paces away. "Magic mushrooms, he ate a load and went into a frenzy of screaming, running around the place and frightening the kids. Well, as you know, we don't tolerate such behaviour, so he has been there for three days. We feed him a little and give him water but that is it, and every now and again the kids hit him across his back, his arse and his legs with nettles." I nodded, "That'll teach him," I said. We chatted for a bit, catching up on his partner and kids, she was away for a few days with some other women. They were collecting some tinder fungus from a place just to the south of here, where the old birch trees were riddled with the hoof one and the great brown/black cinder with a yellowish base. He added that there was quite enough around here and that the women were probably just off on a trip, leaving the men to stay at home and look after the kids. Though from the sounds of it, the kids didn't need too much looking after, they would be having great fun punishing the lad tied to the tree.

Like Golden Woman's house on the beach, with a little fire in it and her main campfire a few paces away, each house in our camp also had a fire inside, though our main campfire was in the middle of the camp, in a big house. Our main campfire was again circular almost two paces across, edged by stones; the campfire house was made of four trunks as thick as a man's thigh and just under twice my length above ground, though they were an arm's length in the ground. The fireplace was in the middle of these four trunks but not close enough to set fire to them. At the top of each of the trunks was a fork, where in life the tree had branched, which was why we had chosen and felled these trees in the first place. Through these forks we had weaved a circle by using several lengths of willow, so that the circle of rods held tight against the trunks at the top and the trunks held the willow circle in the air. Against this circular support, long thin poles of green hazel were propped from the ground, making a cone, at a gap of about a hand width, rods of willow were tied across these poles from the top to the ground all the way round. The thatch of the roof was made from coarse pieces of gorse shoved in between the poles and rods, then bracken fronds had been stuffed stalk first into the gorse, the more bracken you stuffed in, the tighter the whole thing got. The bracken fronds were set first at the bottom then overlaid up the cone towards the top so that they overlapped from the top downwards like feathers on a bird's wing and shed water easily. On the southeast side, was the door there were no poles and the gap here was wide enough for two people to pass through at the same time. A head size hole in the top let the smoke out when we were sitting in here for meetings, which was fine for me, but of course, people who sat smoking in here buggered up that advantage. Parts of the roof had started to rot, and the lowest layer was damp and smelled like the forest floor, but on a positive note, it meant that the damp reduced its chances of setting alight.

Passing the communal raspberry plot, I approached my house, conscious of the fact that it was beginning to look like a shit tip; my lack of house maintenance was letting the tribe down. All round the left and rear of the house, the nettles were dense. I didn't mind the nettles, in fact I encouraged them by pissing on them, why wander around looking for your greens when they would happily grow outside, particularly if you gave them a hand. Besides, nettles were not only a staple green for me; I also drank a lot of nettle tea and of course the fibres were always useful, however they had grown so dense that they had choked out my other plants. I started to remove some of the nettles, trying to find the strawberries that I had planted earlier in the year. I had dug some shallow rooted strawberries that I had found growing on some rough dry ground, where aurochs occasionally gathered and turned it over, carrying the plants carefully back and keeping the roots damp by wrapping them in moss. Back at camp I had planted them in the partial shade at the rear of the house, watered them every day and weeded them until they were growing well, but then I had buggered off and left them. Grabbing the base of the nettle stems, I yanked them out chucking them behind me to eat later. There at the base were the remains of the strawberries, the nettles had outgrown them and the dampness at the base of the nettles had enabled the slugs to feast on them. Some of the other houses in the camp had made several loose weaved stiff baskets which they had lined with moss and filled with soil, they had then planted the strawberries into these. It meant that they could keep an eye on the fruit, check for slugs and snails and the baskets had less chance of getting full of nettles. With hindsight, perhaps I should have left the strawberries where they were growing in the first place. It wasn't that I was lazy; it was just that I had to pick, get, catch, kill, cook, and make everything on my own, so I tried to cut corners where possible. When my partner was alive, we shared the workload. If she was out, she would return to find the fire lit, the house tidy, the food being prepared or cooked, kit being repaired, our clothes being cleaned or repaired. If I was out, then I would return to find the same. Living on my own meant that when I returned from a trip, piss wet through, stinking and knackered I had to start all over again, and now was no different. Pulling away the weaved willow door which was hampered by cleavers, I waved the cobwebs away from the entrance. It smelled musty inside, something was damp and rotting by the smell of it. Letting my eyes adjust to the dark the cause of the dampness became apparent. The small hole in the top of the roof had become wider, about half a pace across. Rain must have poured in and wetted a lot of the floor and my kit. Also, the fact that the door had been shut for ages meant that the air flow had been lacking, the warm wet airless conditions meant that must and mould had had a great time. Up above me hanging from the topmost willow roof bracings, several bats looked agitated, I had obviously woken them up. On the floor was a small pile of bat shit, looking very much like the mouse shit that was everywhere else. It looked as though on the day that I had moved out the bats and the mice had moved in. Scrambling around for a rush light I took several out to the house of the main campfire, where a small fire was always kept burning. Despite the size of the main campfire hearth, the lit fire was very small; this was the mother fire for the camp. The mother fire was there so that anyone

178

could get a light at anytime. It was where we lit our torches; birch branches dipped in fat that we used to set light to dry bracken or scrub when we were burning in the autumn. It also meant that when people returned wet and cold they could sit there and warm up, perhaps cook something and get themselves sorted. The mother fire never went out, there was always a small log smouldering away, it would always be there, unless the camp was dead. Returning to my house with one rush light lit, I glanced around. Fortunately, I had placed my kindling to one side on top of a log together with several cramp balls that were drying out so that they could catch a spark or hold a flame when I needed them to. If they were too moist they would go mouldy, a greenish dust would form on them and they would crumble into a green black powder and be useless. All my tinder and kindling was bone dry so I cleared the hearth of leaves and twigs, laid some short sticks parallel to each other, placed a few small sticks on top in a cone shape and pushed some dry grass between them, which I lit. The fire crackled and spat as the dry birch bark took light; I lit another rush light, picked up and shook out my slightly chewed furs, laid them out on the dry side of the house and collapsed face down on to them.

I awoke sometime later, it was getting cool and I could see through the hole in the roof that large rain clouds were moving in from the south, the fire had almost died down so I placed some more of my stash of sticks on to it and rubbed my hands in the heat. Thinking of making a hot drink I reached for a small wooden bowl then untied the neck of the water bladder, poured some water into it, and rolled one of my small heating stones into the fire. The stone heated quickly, I got it out with my stone carrying sticks and dropped it into the bowl of water, it hissed and steamed. Behind me, my dried leaves hung from the roof, nettle and bramble; blowing the dust off them, I dropped some bramble leaves into the water and let them soak. Unhooking the bowstring from my bow, I hung it under a lower roof support; my quiver went next to it. The fire kit pouch went to the right of that, the blade pouch to the right of that, the odds and ends pouch to the right of that. Everything in order and available if I needed it suddenly or in the dark. As long as I could find the bow in the dark, I knew what was next to it on the right and so on. The place looked neater and smelled better now that the pleasant drink was ready, I lay back, leaning against the weaved hazel frame of my back rest, stretched out my legs, kicked of my boots and took a sip sieving the powdery leaves and small flecks of wood ash through my teeth. Feeling a little more relaxed I lifted my left arse cheek off the floor and farted.

I lay there listening to the familiar sounds of my tribal camp, sounds that I had not heard for some time. A mix of voices, kids, women, men; were chattering, laughing, singing, and arguing. Something that I had forgotten while I had been on my travels was that tribal camps like this were often noisy; they could be places of petty jealousies. They were also of course full of caring people who looked after each other. One now knocked on my door. "Come in, whoever it is." She entered, wafting her right hand in front of her nose, "Pooh, it smells in here, is something rotten?" I apologised, "It's the bats and the mice I think, they smell, sorry about that." Waving her head, she dismissed my apology, "Don't worry, it is really good to see you, where did you get to this time?" I told her of my journey across the Great Plain, to the shelter, the walk along the north pointing sandstone ridge, the journey in the fire hollowed fixed transomed log-boat with the Nugget Twins. Funnily enough, I left out the bit about the time spent with Golden Woman, my new partner. I did tell her of the trading camp, which I promised I would take her to so that she could trade things and I told her of my journey back up our river and of meeting the elk. She sat listening patiently, long brown hair tucked behind her ears which I now noticed were without ear lobes and over her shoulders, freckles on her face, her beautiful hazel eyes and mouth opening wider whenever I spoke of something particularly exciting or different. She was wearing a long buckskin skirt with slits up both thighs so that she could sit cross-legged, she was barefoot and her feet were black with dirt. Up top, she was wearing a simple tabard, which she had made by weaving thin single ply nettle yarn into a straight length of material. She had then cut a hole in the middle for her head, and to stop the warp and weft coming apart, she had stitched round this hole with nettle yarn several times to reinforce the collar. The tabard was held together under her arms by the use of nettle cord lacing; across the front, she had

180

stitched small clumps of red pine marten fur. The patterned top suited her and was very different to the usual buckskin. I wondered if it was her small way of demonstrating her independence, not simply wearing the buckskin that her partner made.

After a while, she asked me if I had seen the signals on the top of the Great Step, "That is why I came back, the lads in the canoe had seen them, they told me and I came back." "And is the skin canoe yours?" I nodded, "Well... I borrowed it, from someone at the coast, so I must return it someday." Changing the subject, I asked what the signals were for. "One of the families has a problem, they need it sorting, I will let them tell you, it is they who sent the signals and they wanted everyone back here." I sat nodding, but she could see that I was tired so she made to leave; before she did, we hugged close and tight. I don't know why I hadn't told her of my new partner, but me and Beautiful Eyes had grown up together, we were very close, she was like a sister to me and I was like a brother to her. The trouble was that she might actually be my sister and I her brother, so though we clearly felt very deeply for each other we couldn't act on it, it was what the tribe had decided. The problem had arisen because her mother's partner had died young, so her mother, who was young herself, had immediately moved into our house with my mother and father. She then found that she was pregnant, but no one could be certain whether the woman had become pregnant from my father or whether she had already been pregnant by her former partner. It was a great shame because Beautiful Eyes and me had always got on and she was not happy with her partner. He was very good at tanning hides and making fine buckskin, so that is what he did and he had a decent trade going so that he could trade for good flint or even food, but the trouble was he often gambled away the skins that he had prepared.

A popular pastime in the camp was to throw either a stick or stone at a target such as a deer skull. To make it interesting, a young lad would go back and forward behind a low bank, carrying the top of the skull of a red deer with antlers still attached at which the game players would throw. So that the carrier wasn't hit, the skull and antlers were set on a stick which had a bend at the top, and in order that the skull didn't fall off, two holes were drilled through the skull. A strong cord was passed through these holes and back through the natural holes in the skull, the entire thing could then be lashed to the stick.

Personally, I thought that it was a kid's game, after all, kids needed to practice their throwing skills for when they started to hunt, and games like this did nothing for me. For me, life was hunting and hunting was life. Perhaps the reason that I didn't tell Beautiful Eyes of my new partner was that I didn't want her to be feeling bad about her partner... Tanner. Perhaps if she thought that I had found someone, it might make her feel worse than normal.

Wafting the rest of the lingering fart smell out of the door, I lit another rush light and noticed that the coiled basket that I had made from last year's growth of bryony was beginning to break up. I needed to collect some more of the long bryony shoots and make another, they were simple to make, just coiling round and round into shape, and to keep its shape I usually used nettle fibre as the stitching.

I began to sort myself out; stripping off my over jacket I then placed my boots by the fire, sticking them upside down on two sticks so that the heat of the ashes could rise gently into them and dry them out. I had to be careful though, I didn't want them to dry too quickly or be heated too intensely or they would crack and shrink. I patched up the hole in the roof by taking some loose bracken from the base and pushed it into the top. It would have to do for know, I couldn't be arsed to go off looking for dry bracken now, and I was starving. The trouble was I hadn't got any food, so I now needed to decide whether to go and find some, I had got nettles but nettles on their own aren't the best at filling an empty gut. I had a plan; this involved getting food from someone else. Tottering out of the doorway, I wandered across to the campfire house with my nettles. I sat for a while but no one came over, I started to whistle, still no one came, I started singing, and that did it. "What the fuck is that row? When did you get back?" He walked toward me, arms wide apart ready to hug me, I stood still and we hugged, nearly crushing the air from each other. "Brother, it is good to see you, where have you been? Please tell me." I took my time and told him almost every detail, but throughout my

182

story I could tell that he was thinking of something else, he was distant from me, I could see it in his grey eyes. "The signals brought me back, but I was told that they stopped a few days ago, did I need to come back?" "Well, yeah, the signals stopped because after several days they thought that everyone would have seen them, and besides, they had run out of wood to burn, up on the ridge. They also needed everyone back at camp in case the men came back."

"The men? What is the problem?" he shifted restlessly from foot to foot, "Can we sit please," we sat. "One of my daughters has been taken, as you know this is unusual, five men came from the east, from over the hills, I am not sure where they are from but they were not recognised by anyone, even by the elders. They had wolf skin capes and a different accent to us; the elders think that they may be long distance traders." "Or long distance thieves," I interrupted, before adding, "I take it that you sent someone after her?" it was an obvious question, but it needed asking. "We thought about it for a few days, the elders needed to think about it first." This surprised me, "What the fuck was there to think about? Someone had taken your daughter." "Yes, well, I felt very much the same, but the elders wanted to see if it was because we had wronged the Great Spirit in some way." "Like what?" Looking around him, he shrugged his shoulders, "I don't know, they thought that perhaps it was because we had burnt an area of woodland that we shouldn't have. Anyway, they thought about it for two days then sent two young men to follow and bring her back, they have not returned and it is many days since we had any sign from them." I guessed that there were several reasons for it now being someone else's turn to go and look for her, and as he explained each of his reasons I found that I was right. "We have thought about this greatly and we think that you are the best man for the task." My jaw dropped, I wasn't against the idea but I did need a good reason for risking my life. "Why me in particular?" His answer was well prepared and it was obvious that he had considered it for some time. "You are a good hunter with a wise head, you see things that others do not see, you know this area as well as anyone, you spend much time on your own and you have no one to care for." That pretty much summed me up, he wasn't wrong and these words, though largely flattering, were tinged with sadness, I had never thought that being alone and not having any one to care for

183

were positives, but here in this situation I supposed that they were. After all, there were people here who would miss the young men, but hardly anyone would miss me, I had pretty much made sure of that by not hanging round since the death of my partner. My mind did return to the coast for a moment and my new partner, but then I snapped it back into focus, for I was conscious of the fact that if the young men had wanted to communicate with the tribe they would have had to be subtle. After all, they wouldn't want to highlight to the kidnappers the fact that they were on their trail. I sought clarity on this point, "How were they keeping in touch with the tribe?" He turned and pointed at the river, "It was a bit hit and miss; they were collecting three sticks, the length of an outstretched hand and tying pieces of white birch bark around them. They were regularly placing them in the middle of the river in the hope that we would see them as they floated by, if one of the kidnappers had seen them float by, they would just have looked like twigs floating down the river." "Has the river flow been regular?" I asked, aware that an irregular flow may have washed the sticks into or over the bank. "Yes, we have had a lot of rain but it has been rolling by, nice and steady... we had the kids sitting on the bank staring out looking for the sticks, it was a bit of a competition, whoever saw the most sticks could fire my bow. But it has been several days since any were seen; I don't think that is a good sign." He shook his head and ran his right hand through his long greying hair. I tried to be positive, "It is more than likely that the sticks just washed up somewhere else, or into the bank, the river is very winding further up, I would find it difficult to believe that any stick bundles placed in the river would get this far. The lads are probably fine, and somewhere up river there is probably a great pile of hand-sized birch twigs collecting on the bank. And, what if they are not walking along the river, they may be in the woods or up on the moors, so they won't be putting sticks in the river." Looking up at me, I could see that he was deep in thought, "I hope that you are right, but I fear the worst, and of course I fear for my daughter, is she alive? Is she as we speak being fucked by the men? Or is she already lying on the earth rotting away...?" His head had dropped, "For fucks sake stop it, don't torture yourself, this will get you nowhere, the lads might be fine, your daughter might be fine, there is no point worrying unnecessarily about things that you can't see, the Great Spirit will know, leave it at that." Nodding, he agreed, lifting his head and looking at me, "So what did happen to your hair? You look like a mangled wild cat."

His partner joined us, she carried a close-weaved willow tray on which were small chunks of dried roe meat and three wood bowls filled with hot water in which ramsons leaves steeped. While the meat rehydrated in the hot water we chatted, he apologised for not fixing the hole in my roof, though he had patched it up on one side where a branch had fallen against it. Fixing the hole in my roof was a task that he was about to do, then the men came and took his daughter so it was understandable that he forgot. It was normal to repair each other's houses, if people were away on a long hunting trip or off trading somewhere it was nice to know that everything was fine back home. When the meal was ready, we sat in silence, subdued by the discussion and possible connotations, chewing the meat, drinking the broth and eating the heated wilted nettles.

Chapter 2.

Cold water was dripping down my neck, I hated having cold water down my neck and I couldn't put up with it anymore, so I roused myself from my slumber, threw off the deer hide and immediately felt the cool air. It had been raining for some time by the look of it, the deer hair side, which was against me, was dry but the skin side was quite damp. The fire was out, extinguished by the rain dripping in some time ago and a puddle had developed on the hearth. I sighed, thinking again of how, if I was living with someone, we would have shared the tasks and one of us would have kept the fire in, got the food that broke the fast and made a hot drink, whereas on my own I would have to go and do everything. As I saw it I had two options; option one was to get up and dry everything, go and get bracken to seal the hole, get a fire going, get a hot drink made and eat something. Option two was to shuffle over to a drier spot in the house, crawl back under the warm deer hair and go back to sleep. I went for option two.

Option two seemed to be a good choice until sometime later when the puddle in the hearth overflowed the stone surround and ran toward me, it was time for option one. The first thing I needed to do was to get some new roofing materials. As it was still pissing it down I needed to put my wet weather gear on. I chose my thickest smoked rawhide coat with a big hood; it was becoming darker and greasier with each season and was almost as stiff as a tree. The hood stood up higher than my head, but it was very wind and rainproof, it was also good for scrambling through rough vegetation. To go with this I chose my rawhide trousers and rawhide boots. The trousers were stiff as well and if I bent down quick, there was a very real danger of crushing my bollocks. I didn't wear this gear when I was going hunting or dancing, nothing active, it was for bad weather and rough vegetation only. After struggling into the stiff slightly mouldy clothes I backed out, arse first, so that I didn't catch my hood on the sticks of the doorway. Already sweating in this get up, this was quite possibly the most ridiculous looking and uncomfortable gear that I had, but I wasn't a fan of getting cold and wet, it was always a bad way to start the day, especially when you had no heat. For a moment, I thought about Ochre Girl at the trading camp and her clothes making skills, "Where are you when I need you?" I muttered. Behind me came an eruption of laughter, kid's laughter, turning round I saw three of them sitting by the campfire house, pointing at me and pissing themselves. Frowning at them I pointed skywards to the clouds, looking up to find that the rain had stopped, they laughed even more. I couldn't be arsed to go and change and besides, the vegetation would be wet anyway, so I tucked the outer edge of the stiff upright hood back behind my ears so that I could hear above the rustling and creaking of the hide and off I went. I went south-east into the dense wood of oak and birch that covered the slopes of the southern part of the valley. The bracken grew thickest toward the top of the slope, only a short walk away; even so, wearing this restrictive stuff meant that when I got there I had to sit down for a while to get my breath back. Nearby I noticed a small hole in the dry clay of the bank of a small stream where a badger had raided a wasp nest, there were still a few wasp grubs wriggling around. I finished them off in between mouthfuls of water, sharp tasting wood sorrel and the heart shaped green leaves from hedge garlic. Carrying on up the hill I gathered a handful of rowanberries and ate them, chewing the pulp and spitting out the coarse bits, I found the occasional dewberry, which tasted much better than the rowan.

At this time of the year, the woods were full of mushrooms, so I gathered a few and ate them fresh, and then had an idea. Removing the restrictive jacket, I tied the sleeves around my waist so that the inside of the jacket faced my gut. Reaching down to grab the bottom of the jacket I pulled it up and tucked it into the belt of my trousers, making sure that it wouldn't come out. I now had a makeshift bag in which I could collect food; it was a better use of time to combine the tasks of roof material collection and food gathering. I began to fill the coat bag with mushrooms, yellow ones, brown ones, grey ones but not the poisonous ones. We were fortunate in that only one deadly mushroom seemed to grow around here, the death cap. A hawthorn bush was full of red berries; I took as many as I could and made sure that the hem of the jacket was still tucked into my trousers. A few small green crab apples went into the coat bag and then it was full. Of course, if I had thought about it I should have collected the bracken first as I now had a great big bag of food in front of me that limited my mobility. Just as I was considering emptying my jacket of food and getting the bracken instead, luck visited me. Two young girls were collecting lengths of clematis for some 'project' that one of the elders had set them and they were only too glad to collect the bracken for me as long as I traded with them. The trade was easy enough to make, I told them where the best clematis grew. Back at the camp, the girls dropped off their armfuls of bracken outside my house, before walking to the main campfire house with their clematis. I could see through the doorway that one of the elders was stoking the fire in readiness for the teaching session, she turned and waved at me, I waved back. Carefully removing and placing the jacket bag inside my house I went back outside and set about repairing my roof. Gathering handfuls of bracken by their stems and pushing them in between the roof spars, then packing them tight until the gap was filled, I made sure that I still left a hole in the top for the smoke to pass out. It was a maul doing it and I had to clamber up onto the roof to fix it, I could feel that the roof was giving way in some areas; it was obvious that the bracken was rotting away too much in places and I thought about reroofing with turf before winter. The elders lived in turf houses; turf instead of bracken covered the poles and spars. They were warmer and were more robust, all of the tribe helped to build and repair the elder's houses, that was why they were the best houses. It would be a big job to do it on my own, though I could ask for help if I needed it, but everyone in the camp was always busy and I didn't want to take him or her away from his or her own tasks, particularly at this time of year when everyone was preparing for winter.

Although the roof was clearly rotting in places, it was still largely effective at shedding the water and the compacted drip line on the ground all round the outside of the house was evidence of this. The next job was to dry out the hearth, I took off my boots and my bollock splitting trousers and kneeled down by the puddle, what a mess. Fortunately the ashes had soaked up most of the water so I was able to carry handfuls out and chuck them at the back of the house; this took quite a few trips back and forth and in my haste I accidently caught my bare legs and arse on the nettles. When the hearth was dry, I took a piece of slate over to the main campfire. I had found several pieces of slate on the Great Plain a year ago, I don't know where they had come from but everyone was jealous of me. On the slates I could carry things like the ashes from the main campfire, something that I was about to do now, I could also cook on the slates and make excellent flatbreads.

I sometimes drew on them by scratching a thin piece of stone across their surface, but they were best used for another thing, something that I would do once I had lit the fire. Several trips to the main campfire enabled me to build up a dry and warm ash bed in my hearth, and then it was easy. I lit my fire by borrowing a lit stick from the main campfire which I used to light my kindling, once lit I returned the borrowed stick. At the back of my house was my wood stack, it was very simple in construction. Two logs three paces in length lay on the floor, half a pace apart. Across these lay my sticks and logs, arranged so that I could help myself to whatever I needed, whenever I needed them. The stack was about as high as my chest, and was covered by two red deer hides that had seen better days; several stones placed on the edges of the hides held them down. Gathering enough fuel for the rest of the day and a large log for the night, I rolled my heating stone into the ashes and made a fresh bowl of nettle tea. I got a little blaze going by using many smallish birch branches, it threw out a lot of heat and light and I was able to tidy up and begin drying my place out. Alright, I might be legging it down to the coast in a few days, but I still needed to keep the place sorted and ready for winter, just in case. After all, it was my home and this was the house that we had built together, what seemed like a long time ago. Looking above me, I reached up to one of the roof supports, my left hand held on to the length of hair that I had taken from her head when she had died. Her hair was wrapped around the small peg loom that she used to use, when she weaved with nettle yarn or lime tree bast.

Brushing the tears away with my right hand, I replaced her hair back over the pole and focussed on my next task.

I sliced the little green apples and mushrooms on my slate by using the thinnest blade that I could find; I then threaded these slices onto several very thin green sticks of willow. I placed these so that they spanned the bars that were tied across the roof beams over the fire. Left here out of the rain and over the smoke, they would dry quickly and I could eat them over winter. If any went mouldy, I would add them to hot water or soups, the mould would wash out and they would be more edible. As for the hawthorn berries, I sat outside pounding them with a cobble in my largest wooden bowl. I wasn't bothered about all the small pips as I didn't have time to sit there picking them out, so I left them in, occasionally adding a mushy apple to the mixture to add some moisture to the dry pithy berries. When all of them were done, I spread out the mixture thinly onto the slates, less than half a finger thickness was what I was aiming at, thinner than that if possible; they needed to be thin so that they would dry quickly. Placed around the fire, with the slates sitting in the ashes, the heat quickly started to dry out the mix. There was no chance of the fire spreading from the stone surround, so I left it to it and went outside. I had already achieved a lot today; it was time to relax; besides, I needed to start thinking about how to get this girl back and not get myself killed in the process.

Chapter 3.

The camp was busy; everyone was making the best of the weather and working outside while it was dry. People were airing their homes by leaving the doors wide open and shaking out their grass and hide mats, using heather brushes to brush off the dust and crap and sweeping out their houses. Roofs were being repaired, windbreaks, hurdles, whatever could be repaired was being repaired because it was now autumn and we needed to get ready for winter. Two women were using stones to smash the long leg bones of red deer, exposing the marrow to extract the grease. They sat facing each other on either side of a rawhide-lined depression in the ground that was filled with water. Using forked sticks, they lifted hot rocks from the small ash rich fire that was next to it and placed them into the water, till it was boiling. The right-handed woman sat with the fire to her right, in this way she could transfer rocks and the bones to the water in front of her. The other woman was left-handed so she sat with the fire on her left so that she could transfer rocks and broken bones into the water in front of her. It was a good system because they didn't get in each other's way. Once the water was boiling, the marrow would begin to break down and they could skim off the floating grease from the surface of the water into a birch bark container. When it was cool, the grease would be stiff and we would use it through the winter in a similar way to Golden Woman's seal fat.

Tanners work area was very active; and I stood and watched for a while. What looked like three small fire hollowed log-boats about as long and as wide as me, were in fact hide soaks. In two of these, freshly skinned hides had been soaking in water mixed with wood ash for several days; they had become slimy and swollen with a yellowish-brown colour and you didn't want to smell the water, it was rank. While in the third, hides that had had their hair and membrane removed were soaking overnight in a mix of water and crushed deer brains and birch bark. One of his kids was removing the hair and membrane from another hide that had come out of the first soak and was now draped over a log. Sitting astride the log, her arse trapping the hide at its base, the girl pushed the hair off the hide by using a deer leg bone, pushing it away from her then occasionally pulling toward her. Making use of the stretch and tautness that the log provided, clumps of deer hair coming out with each stroke, the ground covered in a thick layer of wet deer hair. Meanwhile, Tanner was busy using a cobble to pulp deer brains in a hide-lined hollow in the ground, he also added some powder made from the crushed yellow-brown nuggets from the river, then pissed into the mix and stirred it with a stick. I was never sure that his piss was necessary, but he swore by it and he did make excellent buckskin. He stretched his back, first forward then back as far as he could, his hands on his buttocks. He suffered from neck and shoulder pain, from all his years spent hunched over, working skins. Behind him several hides were stretched across simple frames, one of the hides was being softened by his son, using a de-barked stick about as long as his arm. The end that he used to work and soften the hide was wider than the handle end and it looked a bit like a short canoe paddle. Every now and again, he would scuff and work an area of the skin with a palm sized piece of sandstone to aid in the softening. Nearby, finished skins were being smoked over a fire made from rotten pieces of oak or birch that produced a thick acrid smoke. Some of these skins were already changing shade from white into the honey colour that meant we could blend into the woods, particularly in autumn, when our colour would match the leaves as we hunted deer to stock up on meat for winter. This final smoking part was very important as it also made the buckskin able to be worn in the rain and to get wet without going stiff or shrinking. As I walked past them all, I was conscious of how strong Tanners kids were in their hands, arms and shoulders, unfortunately they also had short teeth, because of all the chewing that they did on the hides, to make them supple.

As I neared the main campfire, another girl was just finishing stripping ripe seeds from the stalks of plantain and goosefoot into a wooden bowl, which contained a small amount of water. Then, cupping her right hand, she lifted seeds from another bowl in which seeds had been soaking for the morning and turned them out onto a flat stone that was sitting in ashes on the edge of a small fire. Patting them flat with her fingers, the damp seeds bound together forming a flat round cake. She roasted them in the heat of the fire, watching as they baked into crisp seed cakes. Two kids sat nearby making a birch bark sheath for a long flint blade, they were arguing and laughing as each of them tried to remember how to bend and tuck the bark. Someone shouted over to them, "Warm the bark over the fire; it will bend much easier when it is warm, remember?" They ran over to the main campfire to do what they were told, passing a young girl who was sitting and knapping a hand sized piece of chert into small blades for arrows.

By the look of the piles of dry bracken that were being brought into the camp, the summer bedding in each house was being changed. The old summer bedding would be burned in one big fire on the edge of the camp, getting rid of the lice, fleas and ticks in one go. We would also have fires in the spring when we burned the winter bedding, we enjoyed these tribal fires, they represented the turning points of the year for us, the ending and the beginning. Autumn and spring were times of cleaning; cleaning the homes, cleaning the camp, preparing for winter, preparing for summer. Soon the new dry bracken would be layered with the dried pink flowers and stems of lousewort, to help keep away the lice and fleas. It was good to see such activity in the camp, I always felt very positive at this time of year, despite the fact that winter was rolling in with her cold icy blanket. When we were all ready for winter, as it looked as though we were this year, we would have solid houses, fuel aplenty, tinder, kindling, dried fruits and mushrooms, cowberries stored in wood bowls full of water, dried and smoked fish and meat, tubs of marrowfat, dried and powdered roots, dried leaves and lots of roast acorns and roast hazelnuts. The acorns and nuts tasted much sweeter when roasted and kept better as well because the moisture had been driven off. I would usually grind them into a powder and hang them off the floor in sealed birch bark containers so that the insects didn't get in. Then I could add either the roasted acorn or roasted hazelnut powder to other things that I was cooking, to thicken stews or soups, or I would use them to make simple flatbreads like the acorn ones that I had eaten with Ochre Girl at the trading camp..., what again seemed like ages ago.

We sat in the open, in the centre of the camp; the warm sun caressed my face. As we chatted bees flew busily back and forth from the ivy into the several hollows that the tribe had dug along a south facing bank. The opening of each hollow was covered with a weaved grass mat which had a small hole at its centre. The small black honeybees landed on the mat and crept toward the hole into which they disappeared. A young woman was holding a smouldering stick at the entrance of one of the hollows to make the bees drowsy; the grass mat had been removed to reveal the structure inside. The hollows were all the same, each was a forearm wide and high and an arm's length deep. Inside each hollow near to the top, flat sticks were wedged into the soil to span the width of the hollow and enable the bees to suspend their heart shape wax combs from them. Within these combs were the bee grubs and honey. A young boy carefully inserted a stick with a thin flattened end into the hollow, slowly moving it along one then another of the comb suspender sticks. The small combs fell into a rush basket that he held in his left hand, he made sure that there were still other combs in the hollow, there was no need to be greedy. The old man turned to me, "That is yours my friend, they are collecting it for you; we want you to be fit and strong for your hunt." I smiled and nodded my head slowly and appreciatively, "I look forward to that; please thank them for me, and thank you for giving it to me." Making the most of the opportunity to talk to this elder, I explained about my time at the coast and about my new friend, it took a while, but it was his turn to nod appreciatively as I described her virtues and skills. "She sounds very good, but how big are her tits?" I laughed and answered, "Although the winds, the sun, the moon, the plants, animals and seasons all change, it is good to see that some things don't."

I caught up with what had been happening in the camp, he told me that one of the old women was coming to the end of her life; it was time to visit her.

Knocking on the wood frame of the entrance to her house I was called in; ducking through the door I went inside. She was lying on her bed with her head and shoulders propped up so that she could see out through the door. The door was permanently open so that she could see the sky, feel the wind on her face, see the kids playing outside, see life and hear life. In this way, the Great Spirit could visit her and take her away when it was ready for her. Several people were already in the house and she was surrounded, surrounded by chatter, by songs, by kids, by flowers, some women were making baskets,

194

others were stitching buckskin together to make clothes. Her old stinky dog was curled up on her bed, fast asleep and she stroked it with her left hand. All this noise, chatter and activity served to remind her of her place within our tribe, of her importance to us, as a people. Apparently, she was off her food, but they were still giving her simple hot soups and hot drinks made of marrow, meat fats and blood, as well as lots of yarrow tea. I excused myself as I pushed past everyone to get nearer to her; I needed to pay my respects. Things like this were never easy; she was a tribal elder and as such, she had been responsible for much of our education. Her great grandfather and great grandmother had found this place. They had travelled from the south, along another river. As a couple, they had followed the spawning salmon from a broad marshy plain with many rivers, up along the main river by canoe until the river forked. They chose to travel northwards along the lesser river, passing other smaller rivers on their way, until they reached two limestone gorges. The river in the eastern gorge was fast flowing and rocky, the gorge was narrow and full of tors. They then tried the western gorge, which had caves along its narrow valley. These caves had been lived in for many years and people were still living in some of them and bears were living in others, so they turned tail, dropped back down river past both limestone gorges and turned north up another river. This one wound through a densely wooded gorge of sandstone, emerging at the top of the gorge into a broader valley with several headstreams. They had pulled out their canoes and had spent many days wandering around looking for a good spot to settle. Their totem was the red deer and a large herd were moving slowly through a marshy valley that went away to the north-west, so they followed them, paddling where they could and carrying where they ran out of water. Eventually they arrived here, by this river, on this dry low slope open to the south, the east and the north-west, surrounded by birch, oak, hazel, some small lime trees, elm, cherry and many others. It was a beautiful warm spot, with high moors to the east and west, and a valley and a river flowing south just to the south of us. Our river ran steady and clear, winding its way down from the moors to the east, past our camp and north-west out onto the Great Plain just around the corner of the ridge of the Great Step, and nearby were streams and clear springs. Everything that we could ever need was here, they had chosen well. They made their camp, organised themselves, and had children, and whenever they went out onto the Great Plain or south on the rivers, if they met people who they liked, they would tell them of this place. Slowly, other people came and soon there were nine houses here, at that point they decided to stop telling people how good it was because they didn't want it crowded.

About thirty people lived here now; two of the houses had one person in each of them, and I was one of them. Another house had a man and a woman, a young girl and a new baby; another had a man and woman, two young men and a girl. Then there was Tanner and Beautiful Eyes who had two girls, and a boy. Two more houses had three elders in one and two in another and a young man who moved between the elders houses looking after them. The other houses were a bit more complicated; in one were two men and one woman, a boy and a girl and the final house had a woman another woman and two boys. This house in which the old woman lived would soon be empty, which would leave me as the odd one out, on my own in a house, I thought of getting my new partner up here, just to even things out.

Sitting by the old woman, I reminded her of how she had taught me so many things over the years. How, when I was a young boy, she taught me to make snares and the finest cord, how to clean a fish skin by placing it on an ant nest, or how to strip and work sinew, and how to choose the best woods for my fire kit. I also told her how she used to tell me off and scuft me round the ear hole when I was messing around. Smiling, she laughed weakly, "I can still tell you off … what have you done to your hair? You look like a badgers arse."

I left the old woman's house when they all lit up; some were smoking lit sections of hollow clematis stem. Others were following what the old woman was doing, passing around a wooden bowl in which dried coltsfoot leaves were smouldering, sucking the smoke into their bodies through a hollow piece of reed. The combined smoke stunk the place out and I couldn't stand it any more.

Back home, I checked on the small fire in my hearth, it was burning steadily and slowly, so I rolled a couple of sticks from the centre using my fire stick and bashed them gently so that they broke up into coarse ash. My fire stick was the stick that I used to poke and prod the fire, to move logs around, to turn sticks and logs over and so on. The fire stick would occasionally set alight and I would blow on it and shove it in to the sand by the hearth to put out the flames. Over time, through use, the fire stick would get shorter and shorter and would end up being chucked on the fire itself and I would then have to get myself a new fire stick.

Into the coarse ashes I rolled one of my heating stones, it was time for a hot drink. I felt tired; my journey back was catching up with me. I hadn't slept too well during my journey, the noises in the marshes had been unfamiliar and the screaming thing that night had scared me, what the fuck was that? Furthermore, my shoulders ached and my left elbow was still sore. The stone heated quickly and caught me unawares, my bladder was empty and I needed to get some water, I jogged over to the drinking stream. Two small streams ran down to the river on either side of the camp, one to the east one to the west, they were about 150 paces apart. The closest one was the west one and this was the drinking stream; I topped up all my four bladders, took a good drink of the cool clear water and splashed some on my face. We marked the best drinking place with a stone, the largest that we could shift, it marked a gravelly area that was always clear of weed. Anyone found to be washing or doing anything odd in the stream upstream of this rock would get in to trouble. Over in the east stream was the washing place, marked by a smaller rock, downstream of that was the dirty preparation area. Grubby, shitty, bloody work was done there and it was marked by two rocks. It was also where we laid our hides to wash off the slime and the remnants of the wood ash or brains in which they had soaked. This dirty preparation area was by the east stream because the winds tended to come from the south-west, the smells would therefore be blowing away from the camp rather than toward it, the flies would be away from the camp and any animals that might have been attracted to blood and scraps would also be away from the camp. The bears in our area tended to be up in the peaks to the east, but wolves did nose around here occasionally, particularly in the winter when they followed the red deer down from the hills into these woods. Our dogs would normally see them off, but I had to admit that it still made my spine tingle when I heard a wolf call, especially on a cold, black, windy winter's night.

Back in the house, I poured water into the wooden bowl and lifted out the stone with my green stick tongues. Rummaging around to the left of the hearth I found my storage box, it was very simply made of several pieces of pine bark. About a forearms length overall, it had a bottom, two sides and two ends, it was held together with pine root stitching, I had bored the holes through the bark by using a pointed chert blade hafted on to the end of a short hazel stick. The lid was another piece of bark, which was held on by a strip of rawhide wrapped around the box several times. Inside this box was my roasted and ground dandelion root powder, I put in half a handful and stirred it with my finger, it was hot, it smelled good. Letting it brew for a bit, I rearranged the slates to maximise the heat. The fruit was already drying and hardening into fruit leather, I usually made as much as I could at this time of year, when I dried fruit like this it would last me through the winter. I could eat it dry, or if I placed it into warm water and left it to soak, it would go mushy and turn into a type of fruit soup. Taking my drink outside I sat and soaked up the sun, my gut and the position of the sun told me that it was well after feeding time. I had done a lot so far, collected roofing material, collected food, repaired the roof, sorted out the hearth, made fruit leather, sliced the mushrooms for drying, chatted with an elder, seen the old woman, topped up my water bladders, made a hot drink. Taking a sip, I savoured the hot wholesome flavour, glad that I had used the biggest bowl.

Somehow, by being back in camp, the fact that I was on my own was emphasised. For example, glancing around I could see men and women working in pairs or teams, sharing tasks. While one cooked, another prepared food, while one swept the front of the house and cleaned the area so it didn't collect damp or vermin, the others were patching up the roof, or collecting wood, or carrying water, or… "Hi." I turned to where the voice came from to see Tanners son walking toward me. "Hiya mate, apart from being about half a hand taller than when I last saw you, how are you?" He blushed, he was a nice lad, getting tall, a good-looking lad who got his looks from his mother Beautiful Eyes and definitely not his hide-tanning father. While I had been away, he had been working on his hunting techniques; his father spent much of his time working hides and not actually hunting and his mother made many of the baskets in the camp. Everyone could make baskets or hunt, but we were practical people, if one of us here in the camp excelled in something then why not let them specialise? When we were out, we could all turn our hand to anything, after all, we needed to in order to live well. I had been teaching this lad stalking techniques; he had made himself a good bow, he had good arrows, the heads were a bit on the large side for me, but they were effective. However, where I thought that he could increase his skills was in getting close to the animal. I had been getting him to stand on one leg for as long as he could, then move as slowly as possible onto standing on the other leg for as long as he could. He would laugh at first as he fell over, thinking that I was crazy, but he soon realised that by doing this he was strengthening his leg muscles, focussing his concentration and keeping his body under control. I told him that animals had senses that we did not have, they could tell when the weather was turning bad, they could hear and smell things that we could not even see, they could find their way to places and be there at the same time each season. I had once asked him, "Why would you be so arrogant to think that you are a better animal than them? You need shelter, water, food, you piss, you shit, you are scared, and you want a partner to raise young, you are the same as all other animals, so respect them as you would respect me and as you would yourself want to be respected." At first, I think he thought that these sentiments were a load of aurochs crap, but gradually he got it. The last time that I had seen him, I had taken him with me on a stalk, we had tracked a heavy roe doe into a glade of hazel, it was early evening. I had made him stay put, then I moved on toward where she was grazing, immediately behind her was a load of pink cuckoo flowers. When I returned to him some time later at dusk, she was still grazing; he immediately doubted that I had been anywhere near to her, until I produced the cuckoo flowers. As I told him; "When hunting, you need to be near to your animal and you can only achieve this if you are an animal, so remember that you are." He had asked me at the time why I hadn't killed her. My reply was that I could see that she was a heavy doe, and as such, she would soon drop one or two kids. That meant that if all three survived the winter, we would have three deer to kill next year, if I took her now, there would be none. He stood next to me now and we shook hands, "Good to see you again, how long are you back for?" I shook my head, "Not sure, I have a task to do, and then I might go away again, to the coast." He dropped his head, "It is a shame, I don't seem to see much of you now," he looked up then continued, "I have practiced the walk, watch." Standing on his left leg he stood until he started to wobble slightly, at this point he slowly lowered his right leg to the floor, took up the weight of his body and slowly lifted his left leg. He had walked about half a pace toward me. I clapped my hands, "Good work, you look like a heron stalking tiddlers with those long legs of yours, very good." He looked at the ground again and blushed, "Thank you." Finishing my drink, I asked him to give me a hand collecting some food, he was happy to.

We walked along the rutted track that led from the camp down to the river; it was amazing just how rutted it was. A herd of aurochs that had crashed through here last winter had first formed the ruts, they were moving from the flooded grasslands of the Great Plain up onto the drier wooded slopes. We had all run out of our houses wandering what on earth was going on, it was just getting light and there was this great rumbling noise, gathering like thunder. Then a crashing, splashing roar as they piled across the river, their hooves grinding into the gravel, up to their necks, twenty strong, waves and spray flying around, water streaming from their broad backs. Foaming away, a froth of white and brown as the huge animals waded through, pushing waves up and onto the bank in front of them. Snorting and roaring, the grey-muzzled lead bull was at the front and he didn't give a shit that we were here. He went right past me, as black as night, apart from the white stripe all along his spine, horns that pointed forward then up at the tips, the strong mound behind his horns, the mound of his shoulders rippling and juddering with each heavy footfall. A slim belly and slender waist carried on long powerful legs and behind him were several young bulls, some dark brown rather than black. Then the cows followed, smaller and all of them reddish brown, no mound behind their horns and their udders hardly visible. The herd drove up the muddy bank then ploughed through the camp, unstoppable. Kids stood wide eyed as these monsters shouldered their way past the houses, steam rising from their backs and flanks, great horns gouging, scraping and ripping bracken from the roofs. Dogs going mental; running around and barking, noisy but ineffective, I remember just standing in awe of these amazing animals, watching as they crashed their way into the woodland, smashing through the tangle of bracken and branches, and then they were gone.

At the time we had stood together after and discussed what we had seen, then gathered as much of their shit as possible, which we put aside to dry so that we could burn it as fuel in the future. Together we then repaired the damage that they had caused and laughed at how none of us, not one of us had thought of getting a bow and arrow, so impressed had we been with these giants and so surprised that they were right in our camp. The aurochs ruts had been exaggerated by our own movements around the camp, and now every time it rained, the clay rutted and pitted even more. One result was that a range of plants grew along the rutted and pitted track; and we collected plenty for the two of us. When we were happy with our lot, we went and prepared the food, scrubbing the dandelion and woundwort roots at the washing place, and rinsing off the worst of the soil from the various leaves.

Chapter 4.

Back in my house I asked him to pass me the basket that contained my cooking kit, the weaved willow basket was a forearm long and wide, and a hand width deep, in it were containers made from birch bark. These were simple coils of bark with two or three arrow shapes cut along one edge; these tucked into corresponding cuts on the opposite edge so that they interlocked to make a tube and stayed closed. Whenever I cooked meat, I would scrape any of what little marrow, fat or grease was on it into some of these tubes, the fat would stay in the tubes until I needed to use it to cook. The other tube containers held dried leaves, or dried berries, the whole cooking basket was covered by burdock leaves to keep dust off it, then it was hung from the rafters and suspended by clematis cord at head height, in this way there was less chance of the mice getting in, and it seemed to have worked.

Slicing the dandelion and woundwort roots into thin rings, I then used one of the slates which had a slight depression in the middle; I had pecked this out last year using a piece of hard sandstone. Into this depression I put some deer fat, moved the slate so that it sat on the hot ashes, then dropped in the sliced roots. As they sizzled away gently on the hot slate we smiled at each other, I had to ask. "How is your mother?" he cocked his head to the right, "Oh... ok I think, you know how she gets, she argues with my father, he argues back... she misses you when you go away... but so do I." Sighing I nodded, "Yes... she isn't happy is she, it is sad because everyone knows it." He pushed a glowing stick around the hearth with my fire stick, "She says that by rights you should have been my father, but the elders did not allow it." I sighed again, "That is true, we grew up together and it was only a matter of time until we got together, we should have been together, but... well... you know why we couldn't." He dropped the stick into the hearth cursing; it was time to rescue this conversation. "The good thing is that here we are all part of the tribe, we are all brothers and sisters, all mothers and fathers, and we look after each other as one family, so perhaps things are not as different as they could have been." He shook his head, "My mother used to talk to your partner about the noise that your partner made when you fucked, your partner said that you were like a bull aurochs with a cock to match and that is why she made such a noise. I think that my mother wishes that she could find out for herself." Though flattered by the comments made by my partner, I took no joy from them, she was dead and we could no longer love each other in the way we had. The sad fact was that she probably made such a noise when we made love because of some problem with her body. Perhaps she was too tight down there and that was why she died giving birth. The jealousy displayed by Beautiful Eyes slightly lessened her in my mind, lessened her as a woman, and it pissed me off that she had talked to her son of these things, these things that were private.

When the roots were cooked, I fried the plantain, goosefoot, nettle and dock leaves on the slate in some more fat until the leaves were hot and crispy. Raw mixed leaves of dandelion, watercress, violets and sorrel complimented the fried roots and crispy leaves; we swilled it all down with a big bowl of fresh strawberry leaf tea.

That night I couldn't sleep, so I spent most of my time sorting out my house; I was starting to worry about my task, the words of the Medicine woman played on my mind. She had told me to take care with my tasks, did she mean tasks in general or was she aware that I had been chosen for a task? Either way, I was uncomfortable with it. I was thinking that I had been dealing with things fairly well, but now it dawned on me that I wasn't keen on getting myself killed, in fact it didn't appeal to me at all. Perhaps a better idea was to send me and two other men to get the girl back, me against five men sounded like a bad idea, I decided that I would suggest this to the elders.

Needing a crap I slipped from under my deer hide and trotted outside, the dawn was spreading across the camp as I made for the screen. The shit screen was over by the east stream, so that you could have a shit and sort yourself out afterwards using the stream. They had moved it since last time, so I had to pick it out against the trees. There it was, a willow hurdle, chest high and two paces long supported by three poles that had been pushed into the soft soil of the woodland edge, the ditch would be behind it. This was a new ditch; the lads would have dug it out using digging sticks and antler picks and removing the soil from the ditch with flat pieces of bark. It was only as deep as an arm and as wide as one pace and two paces long, nothing drastic. I stepped onto the freshly snapped thick branches of willow that lay across the ditch as a platform, crouched down and crapped through the gap. The platform was essential in summer, it reduced the number of flies that were buzzing around and limited the smell. It also meant there was little danger of falling in the shit tip, as long as the platform was regularly maintained. The platform was moved along the ditch as the ditch filled with shit; the idea was that we would cover the exposed areas of shit with leaves, soil or just general rubbish. When the whole ditch was full it would be topped with leaves and branches and a marker post was placed at each end so that no one could walk into it by accident. As for the screen, while we didn't mind seeing each other crouching anywhere for a piss, watching an old man or a pregnant woman trying to stoop for a shit was not that great a spectacle, the screen gave the squatter some privacy and these kinds of toilets were essential in a permanent camp such as ours.

Yawning and rubbing the sleep from my eyes, I walked to the main campfire and threw a log onto it to make sure that it was still burning. In the winter, one of the kids would be in here all night, making sure that the fire never went out. If the weather turned very bad this is where everyone would come and shelter, to be together, food would be made and people would stay here till they were able to go back to their own houses.

As I came out of the main campfire house several boar came wandering through the camp, snuffling around for scraps, one younger one made a start to run away as it saw me. The sow made a noise; I guess that she must have said something to it because it got back in line and ignored me. Stooping down onto my heels, I chucked the sow an apple that was lying on the floor, probably one that I had dropped the day before. She ate it, chomping through it while making contented grunts. I had no inclination whatsoever to kill any of these boar, these were part of our family. About three years ago, one of us had killed a sow only to find that she had several piglets nearby. We ate the sow and two of the piglets, but when one of the kids asked to keep the other three the parents relented and the piglets joined the tribe. They got used to being around us and we got used to seeing them here. Last year all three toddled off, the two males went south down the valley but the sow got pregnant and here she was with her family, how long they would stay was up to them. A result of this was that no one killed any boar in any direction within a day's walk of here; it would be like killing one of our own. They shuffled off into the woodland grunting and chuckling, I waved them goodbye, it was nice to see them.

It seemed as though everything was waking up; several mallard wandered through the camp, scrabbling for scraps, they spent a while dabbing at the ground where the girl had been stripping seeds, then waddled down to the west stream for a drink. Then it got noisy, three dogs started scrapping over a piece of aurochs rib, they must have got it from an old carcass because none had been killed in the area for a while, probably since spring last year. It was funny to watch them scrap, the smallest one was the loudest and he was giving it to the other two, he was going bonkers barking and growling then lunging and grabbing the thing, what was funny was that he could hardly get it into his mouth. Turning away I left them to it, but suddenly there was an almighty wailing, I turned back to see the dogs legging it and the camp cat carrying away the rib. It had been here since someone found it as a kitten. We had lynx around here, they were all through the woods and kept themselves to themselves, but we also had the smaller more vicious cats. Long thick tails ringed all the way down, very impressive for a small animal, the dogs didn't stand a chance. The cat lived in the base of an old oak tree that was rotten at the top. Even though the tree itself was dying the tree was full of life, insects burrowed into it, birds nested in it and all sorts of fungus grew on it. It was about three paces across and many more around, though it was only about three times as high as me because most of the branches had fallen a long time ago. The elders said that this tree was probably as old as the world, which seemed to make sense. It was the oldest tree in all of the area, the oldest that I had seen on all my travels, so that must mean that it was the first tree, and if it was the first tree then it must be as old as the world, certainly our world anyway. When we wanted something or needed something physical to pray to, we would sometimes go to this Mother Oak. We never ate the acorns from this Mother Oak; instead, we took them and planted them all around the woods, so that her young, the descendants of the first tree, would be all around us. It made us as a people feel safer somehow, as though if she had sons and daughters all around us, something from when the world was made was with us, around us, protecting us. If the Mother Oak had survived for so long, then perhaps her sons and daughters would, and perhaps with more of her around, so would we.

An otter came chattering toward me, I sat down on my heels and held out my left hand, it nuzzled and nibbled my fingers before rolling on its back. Stroking its belly, I chuckled to myself, if this animal had been on the Great Plain I would have killed it by now, but here it was part of the tribe. One of the young girls was training it to catch fish, apparently, she had seen an old woman doing this downstream, on the edge of the Great Plain, no one else had seen this old woman and her otter but the girl was positive that she had. The training wasn't going that well because the otter just kept bringing back frogs and newts from the margins of the river and from the old ponds where the river used to flow. It righted itself and trotted off toward a man who was entering the camp, he had been to check snares that he had set last night. Over his shoulder were two pine marten, their beautiful coats matched the autumn colours of the trees. He would make a stew from the meat and flavour it with ramsons, the skins would be sewn onto a ceremonial cape as part of the midwinter celebrations. I looked forward to those days and nights, when we knew that the year had turned, even though the winter might still be with us for a while. The fire in the main campfire house would be blazing and everyone would be sitting around eating, drinking, chatting, singing, farting, laughing and telling stories, just as our people always had. Then the elders would gather the kids around the fire and tell old tales while the parents went back to their own houses for some peace and quiet. The elders would teach the youngsters songs, stories and skills. The main campfire house would be decorated with things that reminded us of warmer, more fruitful times, such as the stems and colourful berries of bryony, the green and white of mistletoe and the green and red of holly. Slices of dried apple would hang from the rafters, and the evergreen branches of juniper, holly and yew would be tied above the door so that we welcomed spring back to us. This house would at times, be packed tight with all of us and would be the centre of our world for several days of warm, comfortable, funny, sad, bonding times. In bad winters, most of the tribe lived together in this house through the cold, making sure that the sick and the elderly were with us, warm and loved. And above and outside this warm, comfortable, love filled main house, the cold white snow would lie on the roof, sometimes so deep that we thought that the world had ended and that the ice had come back to cloak the land.

Chapter 5.

I managed to get some sleep after my early morning visit to the pit and awoke when the sun was already well up, yawning and stretching I ducked through the door and walked out squinting. Outside my house, one of the elders was waiting for me. "You need to decide when you are going to get her back; we have a family waiting to find out what has happened to their sons and every day that passes means that she will be further away. You have been here for two or three days now, messing around, cleaning your house, weeding it and repairing it. It is obvious to everyone that you don't want to go and that you are wasting time. I suppose it might be that you feel that you need to get your house in order in case you get killed in the next few days and to an extent that is understandable." This was not the first thing that I had expected to hear as I wandered out into the sunlight and so I reacted badly to the old woman. "Why am I to go? Why not the other men? Why not me and two others? Why me on my own?" She held up her right hand to stop me and I did so immediately, dropping my flailing arms to my sides. "You know why you are to go, are you vain and stupid?" I shook my head, "No... no I am not." "Your brother told you why you should go, you are a good hunter and you have no one to care for. There, in a nutshell is what he said, in case you had forgotten. I have told you that you are a good hunter, if you are not vain then you did not need me to say that; you have no one to care for, if you are not stupid why did you ask me to explain why you should go? And besides, you are not on your own; the two lads will be with you." Biting my lower lip, I looked at the floor and nodded while running my right hand through my hair. She was right and I was wrong, but I didn't feel good about it, in fact I felt very pissed off and wondered why the fuck I had left that gorgeous Golden Woman on the beach to come back home to sort out some shit that should have been sorted out by the men already here. Nevertheless, how I felt at this moment in time didn't change a single thing, so I nodded again, "I will leave tomorrow," I turned back into my house and started to get ready.

There was a knock on the door, it was the lad who I had been teaching to hunt, I waved him in and asked him if he wanted a drink, he helped himself to some water and thanked me, I carried on sorting myself out. "The elders have asked if you want a party tonight before you go… when are you going?" I wasn't in the mood for parties or questions, but it wasn't his fault so I tried to stay calm even though I was pissed off. "No party, just the sweat house on my own, food, drink and someone to beat out… I will go tomorrow at mid day." I was lying, about when I would leave. He could see that I was busy so he thanked me for the water and left, leaving me to concentrate on my gear.

My problem was that I needed to travel light, light enough to catch up with them but have enough gear to eat and drink, make fire, and enough options to kill five men should the need arise. I figured that the chances of me even catching up with them were slim. I was days behind. Casting my mind back, the Nugget Twins had said that they had seen the signal for three days prior to them telling me. I had then taken five days to travel up river and I had been home for two days, this was the third and I wouldn't leave till tomorrow. That made a total of about 12 or 13 days that they were in front of me; if they had walked along the tracks to the east then they would be very far away by now. Yet I was supposed to track and catch up with them, I reckoned that it was a waste of time even trying, and even if I did manage to run after them and catch up, I would be so bloody knackered that I wouldn't be able to fight. My only chance was if they had hung around in the deer rutting grounds, perhaps waiting to take the best stags. If they were traders, a few big stags would give them decent antlers, hides and sinew to carry back with them. It also occurred to me that where the red deer were rutting there might be wolves hanging around. The men had been wearing wolf capes, so they might target the wolves and this seemed to make sense. The deer rutting grounds were only about two days walk from here, if that, it was a long shot that the men would still be there after so many days but the few swallows that were still around told me that the rut might not yet have started. Therefore, perhaps the men were waiting out until the deer and wolves were in the area, or perhaps they had just buggered off. In addition, the fact that the two young men hadn't returned might mean one of two things.

One; that the men had left the river headwaters and crossed the ridge right at the top of the river valley then moved into another river valley to the east with the lads following them.

Or two; the men had killed them and didn't give a shit that anyone else was following.

If it was the latter then they may still be sitting only two days walk from here and if there were five of them, they could sit where they wanted.

I chose my thick trousers, reasoning that they would protect me in the rough heather that was on the higher slopes. It made sense that I would therefore need my stiff jacket, as it was fairly weather proof and snag resistant. To this, I added my stiffest boots. I made a hot drink of fresh nettle leaf tea and sat back on my heels in the doorway facing into the house, in front of me was so much stuff it was unbelievable, if I took all this with me I wouldn't be able to carry it never mind hunt down five men. I had a rethink and focussed on the task, breaking it down into stages:

Shelter; there would be plenty; old hollow trees, fallen trees, rockshelters and small caves, therefore I didn't need my raw hide sheet, so it went to one side.

Fire; if I lit one they might see me, but if I got cold and wet I couldn't function, into a small pouch I put in some dry grass, lichen and small strips of birch bark together with cramp balls, a piece of flint and a piece of rough iron pyrite, it would have to do.

Water; there was plenty, streams were everywhere, it rained a lot at this time of year, there would be puddles and water would collect in the clefts and cavities of trees. But, if the men were out in the open I might have to spend time getting near to them or have to lie up for a while, in went the small bladder. I would take the opportunity to drink from streams whenever I could and make sure that this was full at all times.

Food; there would be plenty on the ground at this time of year, I placed some dried meat and dried dandelion root powder into a pouch, that was all. I would follow my new partner's advice that a hungry body has a sharper mind. I also put in a small wooden bowl about the size of my cupped hand; water in it would be quick to heat up with a stone and therefore wouldn't require a big fire.

Hunting gear; my bow, two spare bowstrings which went into the odds and ends pouch and my buckskin quiver which didn't rustle as much as the rush one. As for the arrows, I chose ten of my heaviest; slightly thicker stems than normal with a pointed thumbnail size chert blade at the tip, and a sliver of chert set on the side of the shaft just behind the tip. These heavier arrows had better penetration than my lighter ones, I used them for larger animals like boar, they were also quieter on the bow and seemed to mute the 'whish' noise of the string as I fired. I don't know if it made a difference to what I was shooting at but it made me feel better. If I was intending to kill these men with the minimum of fuss, I needed to be as close and quiet as I could then let the heavy arrow do the rest. I left the three swan feathers in the quiver, they were part of my hunting kit and they seemed to bring me luck.

Clothes; this last line of thought had made me re-think my choice of clothes. Apart from the stiff boots in came a simple buckskin shirt with a hood and my buckskin trousers with a rawhide belt. These were my autumn clothes; in the spring, I would collect handfuls of the green algae from rocks in the river, then collect handfuls of fresh grass, ripped out so that the sap was exposed. Then I would sit myself on the sand of the bank and rub the algae and the grass stems onto my buckskins, so that I could move unseen through the freshly green woods. With green hands and a green face, the green man of the woods, bringing death at a time of birth. With these autumn clothes, I would be moving, hopefully unseen, through the autumn woods, bringing death at a time of death. I put in another rawhide belt as a spare, then out went the heavy gear, I needed stealth. I was up against five animals that would think like me, it was unlikely that we would end up in a straight shoot out with me in a good position and them being sitting ducks. The most suitable situation for me was one where I would try to pick them off one by one, though this was unlikely to happen, what was more likely to happen was that as I was fighting with one man, one of his mates would fire an arrow up my arse.

The final thing was small stuff; a small pouch with a few flint blades wrapped in a small piece of buckskin, the odds and ends pouch that now contained the two spare bowstrings as well as pine resin, sinew and stuff for running repairs. Then as an afterthought, I grabbed my camouflage daub, a mix of my own; ground up charred wood, ground up green lichen from the trees, some damp brown soil, all mixed with deer fat. It was in a birch bark container as big as my clenched fist, scooping some onto my fingers I began working it into my buckskins to break up my shape in the woods. When I had done, I took the container and shoved it into a pouch of its own; I then went through everything again and decided that I wasn't happy with the fire kit. Out came the pyrite and the flint and in went my bow drill set, if I wanted a fire I needed my best fire kit, I didn't want to sit there pissing around knocking rocks together like some primitive.

Laid out in front of me it looked good, and what's more, it was now manageable. All these pouches could hang from my rawhide belt around my waist, or I could hang them from the other rawhide belt and loop it over my shoulder. However, I chose to carry the kit, there was now a lot less to carry than my original plan. Drinking the rest of my drink I kissed my deer totem necklace, it would be going with me, it went everywhere. If I was killed, by the time they found me it might be the only thing that would identify my remains to my tribe.

My right forefinger was itching along its outer edge, not itching in the way that a nettle sting itches after a day or so, but just enough to aggravate me. I looked at the rough skin, hardened and cracked; a couple of my fingernails were broken and all of them were full of soil. Chewing at the calloused skin seemed to ease the itch, I used my thumbnails to pick out the bulk of the soil and crap from under all my fingernails. It was a good idea to do this every now and then, to prevent soreness and the development of pus.

I needed fresh air; outside I sat cross-legged just by my door, shutting my eyes to let the warm sun kiss my face, let the bird song, the rustle of the leaves and the sound of the camp wash over me. This might be the last time that I ever heard it; I needed to make sure that I carried all these sounds and images with me wherever my journey took me. A regular cracking noise to my left stirred me from my meditation; I wandered over to its point of origin. One of the young girls was breaking hazelnut shells by placing them on a flat wood block and using a little stone as a hammer; she would break them quickly and pass the nut to a boy on her right, sweeping away the shell with her left hand. The boy was breaking up the nuts between two flat stones. In a wood bowl, honey was being heated by the use of small round stones, taken from the fire as and when they were needed. When the stones were cool enough to lift from the honey the boy would pick them out, licking the honey from them only to get a slap around the ear from the girl. You couldn't waste honey on young lads. As the honey got hotter it began to change colour to a brownish gloop, it was at this point that the boy added the crushed nuts and stirred them in using a thick twig, the twig had previously had its bark removed so that it was clean. The mix was then turned out onto a large burdock leaf and left to cool and stiffen, I took a small piece from one that they had cooked earlier, it was alright, it was very sweet and crunchy, perhaps a bit too sweet for me.

My beautiful eyed friend came over, "So, you are leaving tomorrow... are you ready... do you need anything?" Taking a deep breath and letting out an even bigger sigh I replied, "Yes I am going tomorrow, and no I don't think that I need anything and I am well prepared, at least I think I am." Smiling weakly at her, I took her hand and kissed it, "But I will take the taste of your skin with me to remind me of here," she smiled, with those beautiful eyes.

Chapter 6.

Everything was packed, I was ready to go, I just needed to relax and get my mind straight and that is where the sweathouse came in. It was a simple dome-shaped willow frame, lashed together and covered in rawhide so that it was fairly airtight but was transportable. This transportable roof covered a circular pit, about an arm's length deep and two paces wide, which was lined with flat stones. At a push four people sitting cross-legged could squeeze in. The way that we heated it was very simple, the pit would have a fire lit in it and the logs would burn for a while until they reduced to ash. At this point the ashes were removed by scooping them out using lengths of bark, when as much of the ash was removed as was possible the roof was placed over the pit and any gaps at the base were sealed with soil or turf. The flap of hide that acted as the door was opened and water was poured inside onto the hot rocks, the result was a hissing frenzy of steam, which was captured beneath the dome. A young man periodically tested the stones to see if they were safe to sit on, when they were, grass mats were placed on them and the sweaters could go inside. A bark bucket full of water meant that the sweater could occasionally drip water onto the rocks on which they sat to produce more steam. When it wasn't being used as a sweat house it was the main cooking pit for the camp. If we got something big, or there was a feast, we did exactly the same. A fire was lit, it would burn out, the ashes were removed from the rocks, the food went in, it was covered with large green leaves such as burdock or butterbur, green sticks on top of these then turf or soil and more leaves, depending on what we were cooking and what time of the year it was.

Sitting in here naked I looked up at the hide dome, the rush light to my right showed the black and grey moulds that were growing across it, probably a result of the damp conditions that this hide frequently endured. It got wet from rain on one side and wet from hot steam on the inside so that it was beginning to warp and tighten on its frame, it was probably time for a new one. I poured out the water onto the rocks on either side of me and steam rose, someone had broken up mint leaves and placed them in the bucket so that with each bowl of water, the fresh smell of mint lifted all around me, breathing slowly and deeply I filled my lungs and body with the scent.

I had already eaten; Beautiful Eyes had visited my house and bought me a bowl full of a hot venison stew. She had cut the meat, liver and kidneys into chunks and had cooked them slowly in hot water, it had taken most of the day and it was beautifully soft. In the stew were various chopped green leaves, chopped mushrooms and chopped thistle roots, the roots had broken down during the slow cooking and had thickened the stew. She had also made flat biscuits made from acorn flour flavoured with ramson roots; we dipped these in to the thick stew. We had chatted about life in general, and laughed quite a lot, I finally told her about the woman, she was impressed and said that the Golden Woman sounded like a good partner for me. She seemed alright about it, I think she just wanted me to be happy, I just wished that she could be. We then ate a mix of fruits that were still around in the area; redcurrants, blackcurrants, a few raspberries and blackberries; dipping them into a small bowl of honey. After this meal, we hugged tightly for a while and then she left me and returned to her man.

Pouring more mint water onto the stones I waved the steam toward me, the sweat was streaming from my body, my eyes stung with it and my scalp itched, this was supposed to be good for me. I drank a tea of ground valerian root to calm my nerves, it was a lousy taste and I sweetened it with honey to make it more palatable. I ate the waxy part of the honey greedily, the wax and a few bee grubs stuck to my teeth. I sat chewing and thinking for some time, until the last vestiges of honey were wrung from the wax and it had become a tasteless glob, I spat it out into my hand and placed the chewed wax to one side. It would later go into my odds and ends kit pouch; it could come in handy at some point. The rush light flickered then went out and I was left sitting in the dark, in the warm moist heat… comfy… safe… covered by the dome… anchored to the earth. All this time, people outside took it in turns to walk round the sweat house, softly beating out a slow constant rhythm on a small hand held skin drum. The first strike of the drum was always the loudest, the beats descending in strength, softening… the heart beat of the earth, with me in the mother's womb. 'Bah, bah, bah, bah…Bah, bah, bah, bah… Bah, bah, bah, bah," constantly, endlessly, mesmeric, hypnotic, sleep inducing, sleep….

I awoke a different man; refreshed, relaxed, keen and committed to the hunt.

Back in my house I drank a tea made from dandelion leaves and ate even more, they would make me pee and I would lose body fluid. The negative side of this was that I would be thirsty for a lot of the time; the plus side was that I would be travelling as light as I possibly could be to start with. To travel light meant that I was literally light on the ground, which gave me a light footfall and meant that I could jog quicker. It also meant that I wouldn't have to keep stopping for a piss later, just in case I was close to the men, I didn't want the dogs to smell it and I didn't want to be a standing, pissing target. Slipping out of the house I deliberately left the door open; it was my intention to return soon so I didn't want to tempt fate. Wanting to leave before it got light and before anyone saw me, I made for the Mother Oak. I didn't want anyone to talk to me, I wanted no distractions, nothing to cloud my mind, I had a task to achieve, I would achieve it, I would be back.

Having made sure that the camp cat wasn't in there I kneeled in front of the great tree and held my antler deer necklace, I shut my eyes and rocked forward so that my forehead touched the trunk, I had thoughts about what I wanted and what I expected, no words just thoughts. I was never sure if the tree could understand my language, probably not actually, but I was sure that it understood thoughts and in particular pictures of thoughts. I thought in as many pictures as I could, I even thought of my new partner naked, then apologised to the tree. When I was done, I breathed in deeply, taking in the scent of the bark and the moss, again something to remember if I was to find myself in danger sometime soon. When I felt that I had expressed my wishes and hopes to the great tree I stood up, as I did so I noticed that something had been placed at the heart of the oak in a rotten cavity. It was a small weaved man made from rushes, with long brown hair wrapped round him for protection, my beautiful eyed friend was praying for me.

Part Four; The Hunting of The Dog Men.
Chapter 1.

They had dogs, three by the look of it; I knew that because they had shit on the track that I was following. I was wondering how the five men had found our camp in the first place, there were several obvious tracks leading to and from the camp, branching out in all directions. The other animals that lived here had originally made the main tracks; it made sense for us to use them as well. The problem was that these tracks often divided into smaller tracks, and we had added to the other animal tracks by making ones of our own, ones which led to favourite collecting areas or favourite hunting areas. Taken together all these tracks were like the veins on a leaf, spreading out here and there from our camp. Mulling it over I thought that it was most likely that the men had been following stream headwaters to cross the peaks and moors, using the steep river valleys to navigate. Based on this assumption I reckoned that they had come across our main track that led to and from the river by accident. When they found it, they had turned left along it and into the camp. Though it struck me that the kidnap of the girl seemed a bit foggy, I wondered why no one had taken the opportunity to tackle them at the time. Perhaps they had sat in one place watching our camp for several days, making sure that they knew how many of us were there. Perhaps the girl had been away from the camp and no one realised that she was missing until it was too late; whatever the circumstances of the kidnap the fact that I was about 12 days behind them wasn't good. Of course, if I had got off my arse sooner and not spent three days faffing around in the camp I would only be about nine days behind. But, let's be honest, part of me was hoping that these boys had fucked off sharpish and were well on their way to somewhere else, preferably somewhere far away. I was upset they had taken one of my tribe, but I wasn't happy that I had to go and sort it. Good enough reasons to stay in the camp for three days? Certainly, they were, and besides, I wanted my house to be in one piece when I returned. It gave me a focus, thinking that my house was in order, ready for me, even if I was about to die.

They had left good signs of their movement back up the track, five sets of prints from men and a smaller set; I presumed that this was the girl. I could see that the men were wearing hide boots that had strong 2-ply cord as a wrapping around the feet; this was to keep the boot tight to the foot and to act as an aid in wet and slippy ground. An advantage for them and a distinct advantage for me, as no one in my camp wore their boots like this, it meant that I could travel fairly quickly, as any imprint in any wet mud or sand that had a 2-ply cord impression must be the men. I could see no sign of the two lads; perhaps they hadn't come this way, not that I needed to look for them, the tracks of the Dog Men were enough to follow. Pacing myself into a steady jog, not too fast, not too slow, my head down I looked forward, concentrating on the way ahead. Another reason for not running after them was that I was carrying my bow in my left hand parallel to the ground so I didn't want to catch it as I ran. The bowstring was only attached at the bottom end of the bow so that it wasn't under stress as I ran, the string was bunched up in my left hand so there was less chance of it snagging on something. I was now standing where the path divided which meant that it required a different approach. If the men were holding up in the red deer rutting grounds they may simply have followed the main trail up through the valley, paralleling the river on its south side to near its source. The rut always took place in open country on the break of slope at the top of the valley just under two days walk from here through the dense and often scrubby woods. We would hunt there ourselves sometimes. If the men were there they would have set up camp by now, shelter, kit, whatever they needed they would have probably organised. They would have dogs that would sense if anyone was following them, I could really be in the shit here if I wasn't careful so I needed to make sure that if they caught me I just looked like a fellow traveller. After all, they hadn't seen me at the camp, so if they had been watching the camp they wouldn't have me down as a member of the tribe. I might get away with it, I had genuine stories to tell about the coast and the trading camp on the Great North River and I was very tanned, much more than most of the people in my camp. They spent their lives amongst the trees and the glade of the camp; I had just spent ages by the sea in the open. I might have difficulty explaining the camouflage gear and paint, but I could pass that off as part of my hunting kit. Deciding that this story would hold up even if someone was squeezing my bollocks, I picked a more definite track and jogged along it because if I went too slowly I would never catch them. If I jogged into a trap, I would try to look innocent and just spin the yarn asking to pass by to continue my journey.

The track began to fade out, the days that had passed and the autumn leaf fall had covered the tracks of the men, girl and dogs, I needed to look for other signs. I got down on my knees as close to the ground as possible and cocked my head to one side parallel to the ground. Nothing, I scanned the vegetation along the path at ground level, at ankle level, at knee level and at thigh level. A clump of campion was pushed to one side at just below knee level; I stepped off the track into the vegetation and looked at the base of the campion, sure enough, there were dog prints. I imagined what had happened here, they would have been walking along the track in single file; the dogs would have been with them, probably two at the front and one at the back. To the right an animal, possibly a roe deer, got up and ran away, one of the dogs, leapt from the track and landed at the base of the campion, as it then charged on it pushed the campion to one side. Stepping back on to the track I continued, persisting with this now tiny trail, I slowed right down as I strained for detail. A small stick that had been lying in the ground long enough to make a depression was now cocked up at a funny angle; someone had stood on one end. A small stone that had grass growing around it now lay next to a small grass-less depression, someone had accidently kicked it out. Anything might be of use to me. I was looking at tiny branches that had broken as someone had snagged them, leaves that had been turned over in one direction as a boot dragged over them. Tiny puddles where leaves had been compacted when someone had stood on them and they had retained water, I carried on in this way for some time until I was becoming mentally exhausted. My eyes were straining and I was getting a headache from all the close work, I sat down by a big ash tree and rolled my head on my shoulders, slowly around one way then the other, back and forth, rubbing my neck then my temples in an attempt to ease the ache. It occurred to me that I hadn't had a drink in ages and I was getting dehydrated. There was a small stream about 60 paces down the slope from me, I didn't want to lose my spot on this tiny trail so I broke off six small twigs from the ash tree and weaved a cross shape then hung it at eye level from the tree. I then moved in as straight a line as I could down the slope toward a large rock in the stream course, occasionally turning to keep my eye on the cross.

The stream was clear and cool; I immersed my hands up to my wrists so that my body felt the benefit of the cooling water. I then pushed my face into the water, but not my ears, I didn't want ears full of water when I needed my hearing to be working. After a few mouthfuls, I wiped a cool but not wet hand around the back of my neck, it felt good and seemed to ease the strain in my eyes and head. Standing slowly just in case anyone had spotted me, I moved back toward the cross, turning occasionally to look at the large rock, knowing that as long as I was in line with the cross in the tree and the large rock I would get back to the exact spot from which I set out from the small trail. I did.

Back at the tree I decided that I had come far enough for one day, the fact was that I could have come this far in no time at all if I had been walking as normal, but this close tracking had really slowed me down. If as I thought, the men were camped at the rutting grounds waiting for the deer to arrive, I would find them soon enough, after all, I could only do what I could do.

Climbing up into the branches of the great ash tree I nestled down in a broad cleft, through a break in the trees I saw my first view of the high moors and the ridge with the large strange rocks. Finally, after checking that all my kit was still with me and that my arrows and bow lay together, I fell asleep. I must have been knackered; it was probably the mix of emotions, fear, anger and nerves, combined with the mental exhaustion of concentrating so hard on tiny signs.

Chapter 2.

I slept so well up in the tree that it was just before dawn when I heard a wren calling, not to welcome the day but churring at the approach of an intruder. A blackbird started to call, "Chup, chup, chup," then exploded out of the blackthorn below me. Something was approaching; readying myself for action I pressed against the thick trunk trying to present less of a target to the hunter below. A rustling below me, the bilberry bush shook and out popped a small black and white head. The polecat never saw me; he just wandered on his way down the slope to the stream for his early morning drink. I let him get on with it and watched him toddle back up the same way then return into the blackthorn bush and off up the slope where he disappeared into the vegetation. Down at the stream I sat on a dry rock and chewed on some of my dry meat, taking regular handfuls of water to help me swallow the stuff. I did think about getting a fire going and having a hot drink but that would take too long. Instead, I contented myself with taking a mouthful of over ripe and very soft bilberries together with a few soft cowberries. We called them cowberries because they had the same red colour as a cow aurochs that we had once seen grazing on them. These berries were a bit later ripening up here because of where they grew; on a slope, facing north surrounded by light woodland meant that they were ready later than elsewhere. This was useful to know as it extended the berry-picking season, we had areas where berries ripened early and areas where they ripened late; we made sure that we visited all the areas at the right time of the year and in that way we had more berries over a longer season. Although cowberries were dry and sharp to the taste, the fact that we could store them for much of the winter in a bowl of water meant that they were a good berry for over-winter use.

I had a small crap that was quite hard and painful, I hadn't drunk enough yesterday and I knew that it was important that I did, but I didn't want to have to keep stopping for a piss. For now, I would put up with the small hard shits, besides if the men spotted it they would think it was from a polecat and not a man.

When I was sorted and it was light enough to see properly, I returned to the tree and removed the cross, breaking it up and scattering the branches into the undergrowth; I then got down on all fours and again focussed on details. The ash tree had a huge base, which had forced the men to walk to the right and scrape along the edge of a blackthorn bush; grey hairs on the thorns at knee height came from the dogs. Long, about as long as my index finger, these came from big hairy dogs that hunted deer and wolves, and possibly me, I didn't like the thought of that. Moving onwards slowly uphill, finding areas where the men had picked the bilberries, they had picked them in handfuls, some of the fine branches were torn and many bilberries lay on the floor squashed. I don't have the greatest sense of smell, but it was obvious to me that someone had pissed on this bush, which was poor, you did not piss or shit on berry bushes; obviously these men didn't care about such rules. I thought about this and reckoned that it couldn't have been 12 or 13 days since someone had passed this way, perhaps three or four or even less. Pausing for a moment it struck me that they might be close at hand, I backtracked very slowly four paces, then moved off the track and into a dense patch of heather to my right. Moving slowly backwards, I sank into the dense cover of a coppiced hawthorn. It had been cut off at the base several years before during an axe demonstration, a man was testing antler axes against stone axes, it seemed to take so long for both that I wandered off, I couldn't see the point of it. After all, fire did the same thing and we used fire all the time, and, as I had seen from the coastal marsh and the Great Plain, beaver did an even better job of coppicing than we ever could.

There was movement to my right, if I had continued to walk on the line that I had been working I would have bumped into them. Two men, well one man carrying another man, I thought I recognised them but I had to stay put, they might be being followed by the men and their dogs. Sitting motionless I watched the young man pass by, he would occasionally stumble and cry out, the dead body that he was carrying didn't object to the rough treatment. Not knowing what to do at this moment in time, I thought about running over to him to assist if I could, but it might be a trap and he might be the bait. The Dog Men might be sitting watching, they would think that if I recognised the young man it meant that I was from the camp. The trouble was he might be able to tell me about the Dog Men and where I could find them, so if I just let him go past I might miss out on some useful information. I went for it in as casual manner as I could, just in case I was being watched. "Friend," he jumped in shock and dropped the body, running over to help him I muttered, "Do not show me any emotion, pretend that you do not know me, we may be being watched." Sinking to his knees, he raised his arms in front of his face pretending to be in fear for his life, "It is good to see you… my brother is dead, those bastards did this to him while he was alive, he died from the pain, they threw his skin to the dogs and sat laughing, how could they?" Joining him on the floor, I saw what he was on about. They had sliced thin strips of skin from his face and neck, it was a messy job, they hadn't been neat and there were still pieces of skin attached in places. The bloody mess underneath was riddled with small maggots that were eating into the muscle, fat and meat, it wasn't good, it wasn't good at all. As he sat there sobbing I picked out as many of the maggots as I could from his brothers face and neck, some of the smaller ones required me to use a thorn from the hawthorn bush. Even though he was breathless and exhausted, I asked him what had happened. "We took the track along the river and came across them a lot sooner than we had thought… we expected them to be well up on the moors… but they were just up river… where the river splits… they were on the south side of the river opposite the river that flows from the Valley of the Boar… from down past the Pointed Tit. We walked straight into them, we didn't have a chance… they hit us with the dogs then grabbed us and tied us to a tree." He showed me a large bite wound on the front of his leg; it was in a right state, green, yellow, full of puss and black with rotten blood, no wonder he could hardly walk. Picking up some of the maggots that I had just removed from his brother's face, I placed them into the festering wound on his leg, then took a blade from my pouch and cut the ripped buckskin from his trousers. A few paces away a patch of moss was growing on the base of a tree, I collected a handful and placed it over the maggots to make sure that they didn't fall from the wound. Finally, I took the ripped piece of buckskin that I had cut away and wrapped it round his leg, tight enough to secure the moss and the maggots, but not so tight that his leg fell off. The maggots would clean up the rotting flesh and they could get him properly cleaned up back at the camp. He was about to continue but I stopped him, "How many of them?" "Five," "Are they still nearby?" I wanted to make sure that we weren't the next thing on the dogs daily feed. He shook his head, "No; they left yesterday, they were heading for the rutting grounds, they untied me and left me for dead." This didn't make sense to me at all so I questioned him, "Why were they still hanging around at the fork in the river, were they waiting for someone else?" he shook his head, "I don't think so… I think they were just hanging around." "Why did they come to our camp?" He shook his head again, "Perhaps it was an accident, perhaps they overshot the rutting grounds, perhaps they were after the rutting grounds for the deer and the wolves… perhaps that's it, but when they found us they watched us for a while and decided that the only thing worth taking was the girl." "Yes, but why hang around just up river? They must have thought that we would send men after them, so why hang around?" he shook his head, "I don't know… I really don't know, but they are bad men, very bad men… how could they do this to my brother, how could they do this?" Running the fingers of my left hand through my hair I looked at the fucked up face of his brother, my stomach turned over as I recognised him through the mess, I looked away quickly, not wanting to throw up. This simply didn't make sense to me, if you had just nicked something from a tribe you wouldn't hang around waiting for them to follow you; not unless you didn't give a shit, or you were waiting for someone, or you had nowhere to go. Then it struck me. If these men were outcasts from their tribe, it may be that they spotted what they thought was an opportunity to get back in with their tribe, and what better way than to take a young woman back as a gift for someone. They might have been hanging around because they didn't know what to do with her; go back home together, or in dribs and drabs, one man could take the girl back and if he was accepted back in the tribe because of his 'gift', he could go and fetch the rest of them, who knows? I didn't.

"What hunting kit are they carrying?" "Just bows." "Are you sure? No spears or ropes or anything?" "No: just bows... and three big dogs." This made sense; five men with three hunting dogs, their hunting gear, on a hunting trip to the rutting grounds, they haven't been here before so they overshoot the grounds and find a camp, they watch it to see what is happening and take the girl who is about to become a woman. They kill one of these two lads, leave the other for dead and are confident that they can take care of themselves if anyone else shows up, so they carry on doing what they originally came here to do and go to the rutting grounds. But why they had been pissing around at the fork in the river for days didn't make sense. I needed to ask more questions. "Have there been any other tribes moving through our grounds or even just lone hunters from other areas?" "I don't think so, we didn't see anyone else at all, no tracks, no skulls on trees showing that someone had been hunting, nothing. But as you know, we have never had problems with other tribes; they normally stay in their areas, even when the rut is on." He was right, we had such massive areas of land in which to live and everything that we needed was all around us, there was no need for any tribe to overlap other than when we wanted new blood in the family or wanted to trade for something. "Were the salmon at the fork in the river?" Sometimes the salmon would hold up in a large pool at the fork before they decided which fork to travel up, "Yes, yes they were, it was packed with them." "Well that might be it then, perhaps they were making the most of the fish." I could now imagine the men; on their return to wherever it was that they came from, they would have wolf furs, salmon skins, deer hides and a nice young present for someone. I now knew a few things about these men; they were hunters, they were nasty bastards, they were capable of immense cruelty to a young lad and they didn't give a shit about berry bushes. "Can you make it back to the camp?" he nodded, I let him drink from my bladder and gave him some meat. "Right, you know where you are going? Downhill and keep the stream to your right and you will hit the main track back to the camp." He nodded again. "Make sure you rest whenever you need to, you need to get back, that is your priority and your family need you back safe, and make sure you cover his face."

Watching him stagger back towards the camp carrying the body of his dead brother I didn't know what to think. Crouching on my haunches I gazed at nothing, I was not looking at anything; struck dumb by the situation. Only a few days ago I was hugging my new partner on a sun kissed beach, then the Nugget Twins turn up and here I am, tracking five men and three dogs. Five men, who had dealt with a young man by slicing pieces of skin from his face and neck with a stone blade while he was still alive. Whoever had done this, had to peel away the skin, cutting it away, their hands would have been holding his face, fingertips pressing against his skin, a close contact, an intimate act, a brutal and ultimately fatal invasion of his space. While someone was holding him down, the skinner was cutting his face away, slice after slice and then throwing it to the dogs; he would have watched this and seen this, until his young life left him. Rubbing my forehead with my right hand, I thought about my options. I could go back to the camp under cover of darkness and slip away down river, get to Golden Woman and just bloody stay there. On the other hand, I could go back to the camp and ask for people to come with me. Alternatively, I could go after them and simply accept my destiny, simply accept whatever happened to me.

I don't know how long I sat there doing nothing, but suddenly a great wave of decision hit me. So strong was it, that I thought it must be the Great Spirit telling me what to do, so I responded. I responded by doing what I felt was right even though it scared me shitless, I made myself ready.

Taking the bark roll container of camouflage daub from the pouch I carefully and methodically rubbed it all over my face, neck, ears, hands, wherever my skin showed. I looked into a clear still puddle at my reflection, the daub stunk pretty rank and it didn't have quite the same enhancing qualities as did the makeup on Ochre Girl, but for me it was as effective.

Resting one end of my bow against a fallen bough, I leaned onto it to put the curve into it and turn it from a stick into the thing that would save my life. As I hooked the bowstring over the notch at the top, the dead stick shook itself and became alive, taught and receptive, almost quivering with an inherent power, a power that would be unleashed once I had placed another dead stick against the bowstring. The smaller dead stick would carry a small dead piece of flint or chert; this dead stick would fly because I had given it the wings to do so. I had given it feathers to fly straight and I had given it power to fly by transferring the sprung power of the dead bow through the bowstring and into the arrow. These dead sticks, feathers and stones would themselves cause death and paradoxically bring me life. I treated all my kit with respect and humility, without them I could not live and without me, they would never have existed; we were a product of each other.

When I was hunting, I did not think of anything else, I became the animal that I was hunting. When I hunted deer I behaved like deer, I drank where the deer drank, I lay where the deer lay, and I fed where the deer fed. By mimicking the deer, I knew where they would be, what they would do, what they thought. In this way, I hunted and killed deer whenever I needed to, and in this way, the deer knew that this animal that hunted them, respected them. I did this with all the animals that I hunted; I knew them, respected them and they kept me alive. The problem that I had here was that although I knew the quarry, the men, I did not respect them. This lack of respect was a potential weakness for me; if my main guide on this hunt was anger then I might make poor decisions. I needed to be calm at all times, which was not going to be easy, I needed to be focussed at all times. One slip up and I was dead meat. Getting onto my knees and holding my antler deer head necklace in my right hand I prayed to the Great Spirit.

"Great Spirit...
Great Spirit, please guide me throughout this hunt.
Please let my eyes see and let my ears hear.
Let my fingers feel, and my nose sense the air for direction.
Please let my feet fall gently upon the earth so that no one can hear me...
But let me run fast and let me run far.
And let me avenge those that have been hurt and return the one who has been taken,
... And please, please... let me return safely to my Golden Woman."

By the time that I had finished this prayer, I had tears in my eyes. From now on, my future was in the hands of the Great Spirit and as long as I did what felt right at the time and trusted myself, I could be happy that the Great Spirit would deliver to me whatever was due.

Chapter 3.

For the remainder of the day I continued with my slow progress, at the main fork in the river I had found the tree on which the young men had been tied; I also found the camp that the Dog Men had used, several rough tree shelters. They had chosen to use the fallen trunks of trees that were resting on the ground for the long horizontal support and had built the shelters by leaning branches and sticks at an angle along either side of the trunk. These branches were then covered with leaves and vegetation with two men per shelter, though it appeared that one of the men had a shelter to himself, I wasn't sure what had happened to the girl.

From here, the river became channelled through something of a gorge, dense scrubby oak woodland rose up on both sides of me, good cover to hide in, for both me and the Dog Men, so I moved through here slowly and with some uncertainty. This dense woodland in the gorge with its damp soils seemed to hold the moisture in the warm air making it almost difficult to breathe. Entering slowly into a little glade I noticed that there was evidence of another small camp; a fire, the remains of salmon heads and tails, large stones scattered around on which they had sat, and plenty of dog shit. It looked as though one of the men had been making an arrow; there were wood shavings on the floor where I reckoned he had been smoothing a shaft. The fish bones had been chewed on by animals and the shavings and wood ash were wet and had swollen, while others were compacted by badger prints, so the shavings and ash weren't fresh, perhaps three days? I was now in their area and my gut was telling me that they were hanging around in the rutting grounds just over the hill and moor to the north-east from here, about half a day's walk if I took a direct route. The winds at the moment were coming from the south-west so if I did take a direct route I would be upwind of them and my scent would arrive on the dogs noses some time before I did and they would be waiting for me. I needed to go all the way around them, behind them and work my way from downwind so that my scent was blowing away from me and I had some element of surprise.

I followed their trail; it hugged the edge of the river. I noticed that several of our boulder fish traps needed repair. We built them to make large pools where salmon would hold up, when the river level dropped we could then wade in and spear them. Working my way through ancient alders and wet flushes of willow and rush, I was conscious of the towers of rock that were appearing on my right, we knew them as Fox Tor, because foxes had always lived amongst the sandstone blocks. Just along from these a ridge started which at the eastern end had strangely carved gritstone rocks that were as big as our houses. The elders said that giants had carved them in the time of the ice and I wasn't going to argue with the elders. Some of the rocks there looked like the sand dunes at Golden Woman's beach, layers of sand frozen in stone; it was an awesome place, particularly when the wind was howling through them.

I moved forward into the gorge, high above me now was the entrance to the strange channel through the rocks, a narrow but deep gorge that was drenched in ferns, mosses and slimy green things that made the walls wet and cold. I had only been in there once, a long time ago and I had almost shit myself. I had been working my way through the ferns trying to see where this strange, cold damp gorge went to when I came face to face with a bear cub. That wasn't what had made me shit myself, it was the fact that the mother was standing just behind, it was at that moment that I discovered how fast I could run.

Reaching another fork in the river I scouted around for signs, it seemed as though they had chosen the northerly direction rather than the easterly direction and had set off parallel to a series of noisy rapids and into another sandstone gorge. I followed their trail then stopped, took off my boots and crossed the river at a shallow riffle where I sat in the sun on the western side and let the warm breeze dry my feet. I wasn't sure why they had taken this route, it led up into the headwaters of the river which were split and led in to several different smaller valleys. The rutting grounds were along the other fork on the river, perhaps they weren't going to the rutting grounds or perhaps they hadn't got a clue where they were going. Finding a little rockshelter, I tucked myself into it and decided to stay here for the night.

It began to grow dark and as the cool mist floated past me and on down the river, a white owl drifted over the short rough grasses of the riverbank and an otter whistled below my shelter.

A clear sky meant a warm day or at least a warm morning, though in my experience up here in these hills it could cloud up very quickly and a nice day could become a bad one fairly fast. Clouds would often roll in across the Great Plain and stop as they hit these hills; they would then dump everything that they were carrying. Crossing the river back to the point at which I had left their track last night I picked it up again, I was able to move fairly quickly along the bank because the track was obvious; dog fur, dog shit, broken branches, damaged vegetation, it was almost a bit too obvious. As I walked I made sure that I looked up and forward regularly so that I wasn't about to walk into them like the two lads had. Unfortunately as I was looking up I lost the track, it had totally gone, no sign whatsoever. I was very tired this morning because I had been regularly disturbed throughout the night. The otter had kept on whistling for some time and then a badger had come wandering past, and sometime in the night a wolf had called, unless it was my imagination. Backtracking to where I could find the last sign of them I could find no direction, so I walked back along their track about 10 paces then circled back around, parallel to the river and their track. I was thinking that they might have simply branched off their track along the riverbank and gone up the slope to the right, but after several attempts where I circled back and forward around their last sign on the ground I still hadn't found their track. The only other option was that they had crossed the river, so off came my boots again and over I went, bashing the arch of my right foot as I crossed. Sure enough, I picked up their track just along the west bank, upstream of the shelter, the track then continued for about 60 paces to where a dead roe deer lay. From the state of the deer it was clear that the dogs had caught it and had ripped out its throat, it then looked as though the men had camped here and had eaten what they could. It seemed as though the only reason that they had come onto this side of the river was to eat the deer, they had simply followed the kill. They hadn't got a plan; they were just wandering up the valley. Filling my hands, I took on some water from the river being careful not to wash the camouflage daub from my face. Sitting on my heels, I let my mind work on this. If they had only crossed the river because the dogs had caught the deer then I guessed that they had gone back across the river afterward. Crossing back again, I found their scrambled foot and hand prints on the mud of the bank. Their trail went along the east bank of the river through knee high heather and bracken. In places, they had been very close to the river bank and I wandered if they had crossed again, it struck me that they may have been crossing the river to throw in an element of confusion for anyone tracking them. If that was their plan it was certainly working, but then it didn't take a lot to confuse me. At yet another fork in the river I stopped, they had taken the easterly fork, this led up into a valley that opened out as it got higher; I took another drink and ate as many berries as I could as I walked. By now, I was again getting a headache from concentrating and I was very hungry, a damn site more hungry than berries could sort. Having little option and always aware that I might walk straight into them and their dogs I continued on my journey through the rough vegetation.

This slow progress was ridiculous; but I was stuck between a rock and a hard place. If I followed my gut instincts, I would just leg it to the rutting grounds where I was convinced that they would be, but if they weren't at the rutting grounds then I would have to come back here and look for their tracks and start all over again. It was wiser that I made sure that I tracked them, even if I was days behind them, at least this way I had a better chance of getting to them eventually.

A steep cliff faced me on this east bank, where the river was cutting away into the soft shale, it was clear that they hadn't gone toward it, instead their trail went straight up the slope to my right over a solid rock outcrop and into an area of low birch and pine scrub. As I walked I was constantly disturbing little white moths that must have been sleeping on the twigs. There were so many of them that at one point it looked as though I was in a flurry of snow. A black grouse flew up in front of me causing me to drop to my knees; I had to be very careful in here. Yet again, it was good cover as it made it hard for anyone to see me, but equally it made it hard for me to see out and I might appear right in front of them like a numb nut. I took it slowly, one foot then the other and so on, so that after a breathless climb where I was straining to be quiet as I walked, I reached the far side of the scrub to find a stand of pine trees. The wind here was blowing through the high branches quite strongly and I realised that I must be near the top of the hill, close to the moors and the rutting grounds, close to the men, close to their dogs. Sinking to my knees in the moist moss and leaves of the earth, I was so tired and felt very low; and although I realised that I must be very close to them, now was not the time for a fight, now was the time for shelter, food, drink and rest.

I could hear crows calling from out on the moor possibly preparing to roost, as I was so close to the edge of the moor I dropped back a way into the denser birch scrub and found some trees that were growing very close together which would provide me with shelter. Mostly young trees, their branches were springing gently in the breeze, full of life, nearby on the stems of some older dead birch, were clusters of hoof and cinder fungus. I was tempted to gather some, I could get carried away collecting tinder fungus, it was essential kit. But not today, instead I would remember the trees and remember the place, and come here sometime in the future. A short distance to the right were some pine trees about twice my height, they were growing close together and the ground beneath them was nice and dry, so I walked over and set myself down, tucked under the branches and leaned back against a trunk. Only a few paces away was a thicket of aspen, they had suckered extensively and the leaves rippled in the wind, making a never ending shimmering sound. Listening to the leaves of the aspen, their sound reminded me of the rain gently tapping on the hides of Golden Woman's house. If I snored or for some strange reason started singing in my sleep, their constant noise should cover me.

I awoke suddenly, rubbing my face with my left hand and yawning, I was knackered and I hadn't intended to drop off like that, it was a dangerous thing to do. Nerves must have been affecting me because I found myself biting my nails. I didn't normally do this because fingernails were very useful tools. Holding my head in both hands, I began to feel that I was not up to this task and started to get down about it. My mind started to spin and I questioned my resolve, questioned why I was on my own, questioned what the fuck I was doing here. Perhaps it was simply because I was brutally tired, my mind was often in its worst state when I was tired or weary and here I was both. Perhaps once I had found the Dog Men I would get myself up for it again, perhaps I would feel more positive. I wasn't sure why it seemed so difficult to have a more positive attitude when only the other day I felt as though the Great Spirit had set my mind straight, yet here again I was doubting myself.

I sat thinking about it for a while and gradually my thoughts became ordered. I reckoned that it was simply because I was in love with Golden Woman and was missing her, and I was very tired. As soon as I had reached this conclusion, my mind cleared, I was in fact, very much in love with Golden Woman. As I thought about her, it struck me that I very much wanted to be there with her, on the sand, by the fire, in the canoe, fishing, seal hunting... I think I even missed Shit Bag. I thought of the dog, lying there in the sun sitting on the rubbish tip, licking his bollocks and only thinking of the moment, only thinking of his bollocks. I had to be more like that dog, not so much able to lick my bollocks or spend time thinking about my bollocks, but more able to live in the moment, no forward or backward thinking. No thought of yesterday and no thought of tomorrow, just now, just this moment, focussed calm and ready, focussed on the bollocks of things. It was all very simple really, the fact was that I wanted to be with her and it was my intention to be with her, once I had sorted out this shit on behalf of the tribe... if I was still alive. If I was still alive after this I would go to her as soon as possible, and the thing that was stopping me from going to her was these arseholes, so I needed to sort them out and get gone.

It is amazing just how the mind can switch on, there I was a moment ago feeling sorry for myself and wondering what the fuck I was doing here, and why it was me and why and why and why? Then my mind tells me that I am moping around feeling sorry for myself simply because I am in love with Golden Woman and I am missing her, and it is that emotion, love… that is making me feel hollow. Suddenly, because I have identified the cause of my misery, missing her, I box it up and concentrate on the matter in hand; suddenly I feel more positive and up for anything. The daft thing was it was my mind telling my body what is what. Well given that my mind is already in my body, why didn't I already know that I was feeling so miserable because I was missing her? Things like this made me believe in the Great Spirit all the more, because when my mind came up with things out of nowhere I reckoned it must have come from somewhere else, and that must be the Great Spirit. I thought of Golden Woman in the scrub woodland by the stream, watching her bathed in the dappled light as she collected a handful of honeysuckle flowers; I smiled to myself at the thought of this image. Turning to the north-west, I whispered down the wind. "Right Golden Woman, I am going to sort these bastards out, get the girl back home and I will be with you as soon as I can be, you can be sure of that." I paused for thought before adding, "And the ever so gentle breath of wind that lifts a few strands of your hair softly away from your eyes, and that gentle touch that you now feel upon your forehead, are from me." I blew her a kiss down the wind, for good measure.

It was time to sort myself out. I guessed that by tomorrow I would be right on them, I was already at the edge of the rutting grounds and if the men were still around then they could be close. I was getting cold and needed hot food and drink inside me. The problem was that a fire could give away my position; the smell of the food could bring the dogs and behind the dogs would be the men. Funnily enough, in my new positive mood I didn't give a flying fuck, no one was coming between me and my food and drink. I needed to risk it so that I had energy tomorrow so that I could sort them out, if they came to me while I was eating I would have to kill them here, I nodded to myself, seeing it in my mind, convinced that it would happen, so I got started.

The peat that I sat on was a problem, if I set fire to that I would have a big fire, dry peat could burn for many days underground with no sign above ground. I remember some years ago, seeing a half-cooked deer that had gone through the surface into a hot spot. We had been burning the moorland scrub to try to keep the trees down and encourage the open heather and grasses for the deer to graze on, the peat had caught fire but we beat it down with our birch branches and thought it had gone out. Two full moons later when we were back up there, we found the poor thing sticking out of the hole where the burning peat underneath had eaten away a chamber into which it had fallen. Its arse and back legs had cooked while it was still alive and struggling to get out. It made me shudder just thinking about it, no animal should die like that. It also showed me just how what we did as men affected the world in ways that we could not imagine at the time. "The great web of life," one of the elders would say when I was a child; I never really understood what she had meant until that day with the deer. Using fire in this way was a quick way to manage the growth of vegetation. I can well remember the looks on the faces of the young men who had never used fire before. A mix of surprise, fear, excitement and the realisation of what power they possessed. How with this skill they could burn entire moorland, grassland, heathland or scrub woodland. The bracken tended to come back well a year or two after a burn, which was a good resource for our house roofs and bedding. Of course, there would always be some dickhead who would set fire to things, just for the sake of it, but generally after the deer incident, we only burned the moors when it had been raining for a while. In that way the peat was wet underfoot and there was less chance of it setting alight, but the vegetation above ground would still burn. With this in mind, I scraped away a small pit about as deep as my fingers are long, about a forearms length and width. Into the bottom of this, I placed as many small stones as I could find, so that the bottom was fairly well sealed and the peat was covered. I then laid short dry sticks on the stones and built up a little tinder dome of dry moss, birch bark scrapings and small pieces of cramp ball that I had broken up using a hand sized stone. Out came my trusted bow drill kit and in no time at all I had a nice little fire going, with the added advantage that when the sticks had burnt down the stones would still retain heat and give me some warmth for the night and I wouldn't need to keep looking for fuel.

By now, I was starving; I needed some stodge. Wondering off into the woodland fringe, I nearly stood on a woodcock, which had tucked itself down for the night. It shot off low through the trees and out onto the open moor, before entering the woodland fringe some way in front of me. By the time I had collected my food, the fire had settled down into a nice slow burn, I added some dry branches as wide as two of my fingers and as long as the fire hollow, so that they would tick away in the embers, giving me a slower burn and something to rest the food on. I started by cleaning the soil from the bracken roots and laid them over the sticks so that they were off the embers but were in the heat. In this way, they roasted slower and didn't set alight as they dried and cooked. While they cooked, I sat peeling the bast from several pieces of birch bark, waving the bast over the heat to warm it up and dry it a little before I began to chew it. Ideally, if I had time, I would have boiled the bark first so that it became gelatinous, I would then let it dry and once dry I would pound it into flour. Like this, it just tasted like warm chewy bark, so I ate a handful of cowberries and they helped to provide flavour. In my little bowl I heated the water with a pebble and tore off small pieces of my dried meat, putting them in with some small leaves of sorrel and slices of a mushroom that I had taken from beneath the birch, it was a slimy mushroom without gills, it tasted like a slug probably does. At least it was a warm soup and I had plenty of stodge with the bark and the bracken roots. I had thought about shooting a blue hare or a grouse, but if I had winged them they could have headed off onto the moor towards the men and given me away. After all, if a hare comes running at you with an arrow sticking out of its arse, you are unlikely to think that it had had an accident.

A short while later, as I was allowing myself to think of her again, I had the pleasure of the gentlest scent of honeysuckle reaching my nose, I hadn't noticed any when I was gathering food so I was surprised. For a moment, it lingered all around me before moving away, its passing marked only by the slightest movement of the grasses behind me.

After the meal, I had a hot drink using my powdered dandelion root and then had another just to make sure that I was warm before I let the fire go out, the stones began to give out a gentle warmth. When I was done and as darkness fell, I settled back against the trunk of the tree, I looked about me just to be sure that I was alone, the young birch trees had already slumped, the tips of their branches hanging slightly lower, ready for sleep. Piling up bracken around me as insulation, I used the fronds whose roots I had eaten earlier, and then fell asleep with my bow by my side and three arrows lying next to that.

Chapter 4.

The cloud cloaked the moor, dense and low, a wet, cold, grey spectre. Feeling its way into every nook and cranny, around every tree, every rock, and every blade of grass, through my clothes, through my skin and deep into my bones. I sat shivering, I think it was the cold damp that was causing me to shiver, or perhaps it was because I was scared. As the drizzle hissed around me like a great grey snake, I could at least console myself that this weather normally cleared into fine weather as the day wore on. I did not want to die on a cold drizzly day, ending up face down in wet shit with an arrow in my back; I hoped it would get drier or at least warmer. One of the reasons that I was cold, was that because of the two hot bowls of dandelion root that I had drunk before I went to sleep, I had to get up for a piss in the night. When I had sat back down under the tree I couldn't see well enough to pull the bracken around me, the result was less insulation and more exposure. I now got the fire going by blowing on some of the embers that had nestled between the stones at the bottom of the pit. I was fortunate that the drizzle hadn't managed to get under the cover of branches and put them out, I thanked the Great Spirit for that. I made a tea of birch leaves and drank it, then made another bowl full but instead of drinking it, and before it got too hot, I used it to wash my hands, face and neck to reduce my scent to the dogs. I would use other things to mask my scent when and where I found something suitable. The birch tea wash also eased the midge bites that I had received during the night. My face and hands were itching from the bites, with pink spots all over my hands; if my face was as bad as my hands then I reckoned I must look terrifying. Next, I got out my camouflage mix and daubed it over my face, neck and hands, trying to check my image in what remained of the water in the bowl. Squatting beneath the tree, I had another squirt of a crap, a product of nerves rather than a regular bowel movement, and then covered it with the bracken fronds. I then spat on the stones in the fire pit, they were still hot and so I stood up, pulled my trousers down and pissed onto the stones. They hissed as the heat left them, when I was done I put my hand over them to assess the heat that remained, not much and I could easily pick up a piss drenched stone and hold it. Doing this with several of them, I felt confident that the heat from this pit would not spread into the peat. Finally, I wiped the damp from the three arrows that had been at the ready and placed them back into my quiver. I stood and brushed away several deer ticks that were wandering up my trousers and along my sleeves. I felt sure that some would have managed to get stuck into me during the night, the bracken that I had used to cover myself seemed to be crawling with them. I noticed that all about me spider webs were dusted with midges, loads of them were stuck to the fibres of the webs yet they were surely not big enough for the spiders to eat, not much meat on them. In addition, they had the unfortunate effect of highlighting the trap to other insects so that they could see and avoid them. I needed any potential traps that I might walk into to be as obvious as these midge-dusted webs.

My plan was to walk north-east to gain height, leaving the river below me and then track across the ridge to the south-east. If I had this right and they were camping at the rutting grounds, then by gaining height to the north-east and then walking south-east it should put me behind them so to speak. Looking around me to check that I had everything I took several deep breaths to slow my beating heart then set off uphill through the ever-diminishing cover of birch trees, past the tall pines and out onto the open moor. I didn't like being out in the open so I headed left and up towards a ridge of rocks and a little rocky valley, it was a natural route to the tops of the hills, anyone would have followed it. The valley seemed ancient; it was obviously an old pathway, not just for deer but also for man. The brooding rocks on either side seemed to narrow the further I walked through it, closing me out, almost sneaking up on me, squeezing in on me. The constant drizzle blown by the cold wind, spat into my face, forcing me to squint; it meant that I was unable to see these rocks as they moved. I am not a man stupid enough to believe that rocks move, but in this narrow cold valley, they seemed to. The path, the valley and the rocks all had a feeling about them, a feeling of timelessness. A feeling that the ghosts of the ancients still lived here, in amongst the rocks, moving through the heather, whispering their stories over the stones and the ground on which I trod. I sensed that in this valley, people had felt the wind on their face for a very long time.

The drizzle was becoming a real problem and as I moved low to the ground I could see my breath, which told me just how cool it was up here. The cold water constantly running down my neck was chilling my back; I could not stand water down my neck. If my hair had been its normal length it would have at least given me some protection, particularly as it was now so greasy. Shrugging my shoulders, I tried to make myself more comfortable but without success so I sat myself down under a pine that had dense branches at head height. It was dry underneath so I decided to sit the rain out, there was no point getting myself so wet that my buckskin started to squeak as I was stalking the Dog Men. Also, wet gear didn't work as well as dry gear. For example, my sinew stitching on my clothes would loosen the more they got wet, while my bast stitching along the base of my quiver would tighten and could start to warp the shape of it, making it difficult to get the arrows out smoothly. Either way, it was not a good idea to get wet. The other thing was that the drizzle was still hissing all around me, and that was all that I could hear, so if there was anyone around I wouldn't hear them till it was too late. There was no point just sitting here moping in the rain, so I did a kit check. My bow was fine, I flexed it a couple of times just to remind it what it felt like to bend under strain, it was as much for my benefit as it was the bows. I needed to remember what it felt like to hold the bow tight, under tension... to feel that tension in my arms, the extension of my arms into my bow, an extension of my body, an extension that would project that tension, that energy away from me and toward my target. I could get quite emotional about my bow. But when you had cut something down and shaped it with tools that you had made yourself, then sanded it with different grades of sandstone, then strung it using cord that you had made yourself, why wouldn't you get emotional about it? I had made it, it was a product of me; and for me as a hunter it was an extension of my muscles, my bones and my mind... it was probably the most important thing that I had ever made.

Checking through my pouches, everything was in order; I thought about hoarding some of my kit beneath this pine, it stood out given its unusual shape so it would be easy to find on my way back. However, I wasn't sure how far these men would be from here, if they were several days away then I would need this kit just to live day to day. I decided to persist carrying all my kit until I had spotted the men, then I could dump stuff if I thought I didn't need it and it would be close at hand if I did. I sat chewing some of the bast from the pine; I had torn off a branch and hacked away the tough scaly outer bark. I wasn't a fan of pine bast but it served a purpose and went some way to staving my hunger. I really hoped that Golden Woman was right in her theory about an empty stomach giving a sharper mind, because right now I wanted to fill my face with a big chunk of roast boar, with plenty of crackling to crunch through. As my mouth started to water and my mind was somewhere else the rain stopped, time to move, thank fuck! Looking up into the branches of the pine, I noticed that a decent limb stuck out almost level, about three times my height up the tree; it would be an ideal viewpoint. Struggling up through the wet slippy branches, I perched my arse on the limb, easing my way along it, not wanting to appear suddenly to anyone on the ground. There was nothing obvious out there, just moorland and the grey cloud so I began to climb down. As ever, the climb down from the limb was harder than the climb up. Going up through branches that were reaching for the sky was far easier than scrambling back down through the up-stretched arms of the tree. Every time I looked down for my next foothold, I got a face full of twigs and needles, so I shut my eyes and let my feet feel for strong branches on which to stand. In this way, I was able to clamber down through the spiky thing and not risk scratching my eyes. It seemed a slow process, and my hands were getting tired, but it was probably due to the cold water on the twigs, needles and branches, and the fact that the branches were scaly and rubbed away at my hands. Opening my eyes just to see where I was I found that I was near to the bottom of the tree. Beneath me was a mossy spot so I dropped the half-length of me onto the soft floor, hands throbbing from the cold of the water and the roughness of the branches.

Padding through the wet heather and bilberry wasn't pleasant; it was waist high in places and I kept being tangled up in the stiff woody stems, which seemed to snatch at my clothes and kit. Snipe and curlew took off as I trudged on, their alarm calls echoing around me, it was almost impossible to be unnoticed and I was worried that it was only a matter of time before these birds would give me away. I passed the cloudberry beds on the edge of a large wet grassy area of moor, feeling slightly sad that I had missed out on the succulent berries. They would have ripened and been picked while I was still at the coast. A slow stream crossed the moor in front of me. I jumped across but the peat held my trailing right foot so that I didn't get the speed and height that I needed to make the distance so I landed heavily on the other side, sinking into the wet peat and jarring myself as I fell forward into the heather. "For fucks sake, what the fuck is going on?" I was really pissed off by now and pushed myself up out of the rough stems, rolled onto my left and pulled my feet out of the wet shitty peat in which they were stuck. Beside me was a patch of crowberry, I ate what I could gather then noticed to my right the bones of a red deer scattered about, as white as Golden Woman's teeth, but not as attractive as Golden Woman's smile. By the looks of it, it had done something similar to me, jumped and become stuck, the difference was that the wolves had ripped the poor bastard apart, probably while it was alive. That was definitely no way to die.

I loved wolves; I loved their call... on a windy winter's night with the rain lashing down on my house and the fire crackling away in the hearth. It was the sound of the ancients. I could imagine our people, the original people, possibly even before the ice came and went, walking across a high valley pass such as this and coming to the edge of everything that they knew. A new land lay stretched out before them, they could see rivers, trees, marshes and lakes, and they would look at this and think that they could move into that landscape and live there, the first people. Then they would hear that call... the call of the wolf and they would know that they were not the first people here, they would know that they would only ever be the second people here and that they would have to take second place to the wolf. Yes, I loved wolves, they were supreme hunters and they possessed skills that I could only envy and dream of. They could smell, see, and hear far better than any man could. They worked as a team; one would chase and direct a deer until it was tired then another that had been waiting would take up the chase and so on, until the deer succumbed to yet another wolf. They had a system and the system worked; they had an ordered tribe consisting of a leader and those that were led, some years it was a bitch leading and some years it was a dog leading. They sorted it out through aggression, and when it came to hunting, they were merciless. Looking at the scattered bones of the deer lying next to me, as much as I admired the wolf, I didn't like the way they did some things and they seemed to lack respect for the animals that they hunted. But what did I know of the mind of the wolf? Fuck all.

Chapter 5.

Trudging up through the wet peat of the valley was difficult. Slipping regularly, the wet peat clinging to my boots slowed me down. I was aiming for Wolf Edge; we called it Wolf Edge because it was a rocky edge with several gritstone tors along its crest, where the wolves seemed to hang around. I didn't want to visit them, I wanted to keep it well to my right and skirt its northern flanks in case the men were on the top keeping an eye open for anything unusual. The rutting grounds of the red deer were to the south of Wolf Edge and the narrow valley that I was walking up was an obvious trail toward the top of the ridge. I was heading roughly north-east and I knew that at the top, this coarse gritstone would suddenly give way to the white limestone where the black chert came from; it was a dramatic change in the landscape. On the other side, the rivers of the limestone flowed south-east, if the men had already got to those headwaters then they could be well on their way down river or off over the hills on the other side. As I walked uphill the valley opened out, becoming shallower, the scrub of birch, oak and pine gave way to deep heather and patches of wet grassland. Two red grouse belted away low over the heather, telling me to 'Go back, go back, go back' and a curlew called and took off from in front of me causing me to drop to my knees in case any eyes were turning to see what had scared the birds. When I was happy that no one was around, I carried on.

Walking along a small stream, I looked at its peaty almost black waters. Frothing and foaming its way down the moor, slavering like a lithe black dog, licking the sand and quartz from the gritstone cobbles and boulders. In the shallows, where it ran clearer, I noticed many small round pebbles of white quartz. Very pretty, they sat like stars in the peat black night. There were otter tracks on a sand bank; the sand was as pure as that upon which Golden Woman and I had been walking, only days ago.

At the top of the valley I arrived at the ridge, I sat for a while chewing some thyme and looking over to the white hills and valleys of the limestone. It was yet another spectacular view; this area was full of spectacular views. It occurred to me that if I stood on the top of the Pointed Tit to the west of me, I might be able to see all the way to the coast and Golden Woman. Below me was the head of one of the rivers that the great grandfather and great grandmother of the elder who was dying had travelled up all those years ago, the narrow valley with ancient caves.

A golden eagle was quartering the ground to my left, roaming between the trees and out across the grassy slopes. Several hares legged it into the gorse bushes that fringed the slopes, not yet white for winter these hares had managed to escape, all apart from the one that the eagle had its eyes on. Its squeals and cries rang out once the eagle had wrapped its talons around it, but soon faded as the eagle turned away from me. A young one came my way at pace stopping suddenly as it saw me. It changed its shape immediately so that my eyes lost it, scanning slowly back I saw it lying flat to the ground, ears back along its head, it had become like a log. "You need have no fear from me little one, I am not after you and I have no dogs, go back and keep your head down away from the eagles and grow bigger." I never realised that I could speak hare language but it took me at my word, lifted its ears, turned tail and legged it through the bilberries and scrub leaving me to chuckle to myself.

There was no sign of the Dog Men anywhere along the ridge as I walked; Wolf Edge was now slightly behind me on my right, to the west of me. To my left the steep slopes fell down to the small rivers of the limestone, in front of me hills stretched out into the distance. To my right many gritstone tors poked out of the crests and ridges, rupturing the skin of the earth, raking the sky. Continuing along the ridge, I snacked on the last of my dry meat and whatever leaves I could find, hugging the scrub woodland wherever it grew and jogging over the open spaces when there was no cover. I was beginning to think that I had taken too wide a loop to get to where I was now and that I had simply missed them, when I noticed three ravens trying to fight off another eagle. I moved south-west about 300 paces to where they were scrapping. On the ground were the remains of two red deer and a wolf, all had been skinned, most of the meat had gone from the deer, the bulk of the meat was still on the wolf. The men wouldn't eat wolf meat, none of us did, it wasn't good for us, our ancestors had learned that a long time ago. Taking a blade from my blade pouch I sliced off several chunks of what remained of the deer flesh from the underside of the deer where it had been covered and was not yet tough from being air dried. I may as well make use of it, as I didn't know when I would be eating again. It was clear from the remains that these weren't that old on the ground, there were no maggots but the bodies were blown with fly eggs and the ravens, eagles and hooded crows hadn't cleared off all the flesh. Tracking back to the ridge I dropped down into the heather, they might still be in the area hanging around to get more skins, the wolf skin was a better trade than deer, everywhere had deer but not everywhere had wolves.

Of course, they may have got these three skins and buggered off, but the fact that they had been hanging around for several days made me think that they were here for more skins, preferably wolf. After all, five men and a girl could carry a few skins between them.

Sitting for a while, I soaked in what was happening; a skylark to my right was up high and singing, while to my left pipits flew low over the heather. A short eared owl hovered low over some grasses on the edge of the birch scrub and, as everything settled down again and started to accept my presence, voles started to scurry around. A buzzard called from a tall birch tree and one of the eagles that was feeding at the deer and wolf carcasses took off among the three pestering ravens. The sun had broken through the cloud some time ago and the earth was now hot beneath me. An adder was basking in the sun; nearby her small young were doing the same, orb spiders began to gently quake in their webs as the south-westerly breeze began to lift and strengthen.

Nearby, the seedpods of gorse cracked in the sun, shedding their seed into the tangle of heather that had recently finished flowering. A bumblebee buzzed past me over my right shoulder, the birch leaves rustling on my left as the breeze moved up and across the edge like a low, slow beast, hugging the ground, carrying smells and scents of heather and peat and deer and smoke.

Rotating my head to the east to the south then to the west, the sound of a dog accompanied the smell of smoke; both came from the south-west, along the breeze. It was obvious that they were to the south-west of me, they were therefore upwind of me so I would receive their noise and scents rather than them receiving mine. I was now happy that I had made such a big loop to get downwind of them so that my noise and scents went off over the hills behind and away from me. I guessed that they could be camped in amongst the scrub on the top edge of the shallow valley in front of me. There were gritstone tors and rocky outcrops that provided shelter in all conditions, whichever way the wind or rain blew, if I was the Dog Men that was where I would be. The rocks were not far away from me, I thought about it and reckoned that if I set off as soon as it started to get light that I could be there as the sun came up, which depending on where they were camped, might put the sun in their eyes when I attacked them. Deciding that an attack just as it was getting light was my best tactic; I turned and went to find shelter for the rest of the day and night.

In a narrow grassy valley that faced eastwards, I found a dry streambed, at this time of the year many of the small streams and rivers in this limestone area disappeared underground. I got out my fire kit and made a fire from the dry grasses and twigs that lay along the banks of the dry river, left there from when it had been flowing only a few weeks earlier. There were a few small sorrel plants growing on the banks so I gathered some. I cooked the deer meat very simply by skewering it on a stick and heating it on the fire, chewing it slowly because my mouth was dry and my thoughts were elsewhere, thinking about myself. Not in a self-pitying way, but in an awareness way, I was working through all my body, a kind of kit check just to make sure that I was working alright, I would need it tomorrow and I didn't want it to let me down. Starting with my feet, I felt into them, moving my toes, moving my ankles to work my feet from side to side, I noticed that the arch of my right foot felt bruised, I needed to keep an eye on that. Rocking gently on my haunches I checked out my shins, knees, thighs, arse, cock, belly, chest, back, shoulders, arms, hands, neck, face and head. To help me relax I imagined that I was back in the sweathouse, warm and comfortable with the sound of the drum in my ears, I let that image run for a while. Nibbling at the sorrel leaves my guts seemed full and I couldn't be arsed to eat any more, so I took a good swig from my water bladder then put the fire out and looked for a place for the night. Above me on the south facing slope, I noticed some layers of limestone that could offer me shelter so I made my way up toward them. They stuck straight out from the side of the valley so that they provided a good shelter from wind and rain; the rocks themselves were covered with rock brambles. Although they carried some fruit on their scrambling stems, I didn't bother to eat any. They were not as juicy as the blackberry bramble and they had a stone in the fruit. Tucking myself down beneath the layers of limestone, I noticed that the ground in front had been worn away in the past by some animal that had obviously sheltered here and now it was my turn. Two animals separated by time, both seeking shelter, both finding shelter. Me, a hunter, perhaps the animal that had once sheltered here was also a hunter, or it might have been the prey. Whatever it was, it had needed shelter. The animals might have changed but the rocks hadn't and they probably never would. I was scared and concerned about what might happen to me when I found these men, and who knows, the animal that had sheltered here before me might have been escaping from a hunt, a pack of wolves perhaps. Perhaps it was as scared and concerned as I was now, as it had sought the shelter of these rocks and crawled into their comfort. These rocks jutting out of the earth were the ribs of the mother, showing through the thin skin on which we all walked and lived. I nestled as close to the ribs as I could, as close to the breast of the mother as I could, so close, that I was sure that I could hear her heartbeat... the heartbeat of the earth.

Chapter 6.

Apart from a doze just before it went dark I hadn't slept well at the rockshelter, my mind was racing which kept me awake for ages, then a wild cat woke me up by attacking my feet. I nearly shit myself, lying there prone in the dark with this mental ball of fur going crazy with my bootlaces. The commotion had caused me to sit up quickly and bang my head on the rock, I wasn't going to get back to sleep after all that so I decided to make my way over to the men's camp while it was dark. It had been difficult with not much light; the clouds had covered the moon and I had to pick my way from memory, slowly across the heather and the peat, thankful that the peat here was dry and that I hadn't fallen into a bog.

Through the darkness I saw their camp, they were either not expecting any one to come after them or they were very confident in their abilities. They were as I had expected, camped at the nearest tor. Their fire lit up the many nooks and crannies of the strange pillars and it was somewhat alarming. The tall pillars gave the appearance of many men and I found it difficult to work out exactly how many were actually in the camp, five or as many as eight? Although the lad had told me that there had been five of them, there could be more here. Looking for cover, I noticed that a dense thicket of pine and birch, mostly small stuff, surrounded the tor. It began to spit with rain so I crawled into the dense cover, sat down and waited, making sure not to fall asleep. I couldn't see the girl anywhere amongst them; and as the night wore on I heard laughing, singing, farting and snoring.

As soon as it was light enough to distinguish between rocks, men and trees, I moved, stepping slowly and carefully, placing my whole foot flat to the ground at once.

There were five of them lying next to the fire; I had no fear of them now they were the same as me, fallible. What I feared was the dogs, they were fast, could smell me a way off, could hear me a way off, they were big and strong and had teeth. To make sure that my arrows were at their most effective I needed to be no further from a man than about 30 paces. At this range, the heavy arrow should still impact the body and pass into it with force. If I was further away I risked just wounding the man and he could either shout for help, fire back, or both and then I would have to use another arrow to shut him up. It made sense to get as close as possible and try to limit the number of arrows that I had to fire. Sitting in a clump of bilberries, I weighed up my options. I could work my way around the back of them using the scrub as cover then clamber up a gritstone pillar so that I had height. This would give me an advantage in that I could fire down on them from a protected position and the dogs were less likely to try to climb the pillar after me. The other option was to just nail the bastards where they lay, but that would give me a low angle of fire over the heather and would mean that I had to make every arrow count, and with the best will in the world that would be difficult. It would only take one arrow to miss my target and I would quickly be on the receiving end.

I didn't have to make a decision; while I was pondering and planning, the man nearest to me stirred, got up and walked straight towards me, closing fast. I was unsure whether he had seen me as he was unarmed, but what could I do? If he saw me, he would shout and I would quickly have them all after me.

My arrow hit him straight in the chest; I reckon it hit him right in the heart because he dropped like a stone. Unfortunately, it was a noisy stone and as he fell, he landed on a dry birch branch, which cracked loudly alerting a dog. I rolled away then crawled quickly, then ran bent over to stay low, down the slope until I was out of eyesight of the camp, then I legged it to the north so that I was downwind again. Behind me, I could hear dogs barking and men talking, which soon became shouting as they gathered their kit together. By now, I was flying through the pine and birch scrub, relying on my peripheral vision to make sure that I missed taking an eye out on any branches. The advantage of spending all my life in a woodland environment was demonstrated, as my excellent peripheral vision led me through the dense wood. You had to have good peripheral vision if you lived in a woodland otherwise you would scratch your eyes on branches, or get caught up on something and you would never see anything to kill, deer weren't stupid, you had to see them way before they saw you.

Behind me came the noise of crashing branches, wherever these men came from it wasn't wooded. Rushing through the woodland I got too confident, stupidly turning my head to see if they were following. Running straight into a tangle of honeysuckle, I twatted myself on the forehead on a stubby tree branch, so much for peripheral vision. Fighting my way out I gathered my bow which had fallen from my hand; fortunately it was alright, no damage to the bow or string, but my head throbbed and blood started to run into my right eye, forcing me to half close it. I slowed my pace and trotted on down to the stream then started to follow it up hill to the east, to its source; I knew that there was a boulder field with scrub woodland further up the stream, which would provide me with good cover. The flow of the stream was fast here and it ran over many small waterfalls, making it very noisy, the constant sound of rushing water would cover my footfall, hiding my noise from the sensitive ears of the dogs.

Pressing on until I was knackered, I finally sat down among some boulders, sinking low to the ground I gasped in air then did a thorough kit check. Boots were good, a bit wet but bearing up, trousers the same, shirt fine, camouflage on my hands was good. I reached into my pouch and took out a finger full of the greasepaint and applied it to my neck, face, ears and the back of my hands, I probably didn't need it but it meant that I was focussed on what I was doing here. Using a small piece of wet moss, I carefully dabbed the blood from my right eye, trying not to scratch the eye itself. That done, I checked the bleeding from my forehead, it seemed to have slowed down but I stuck a small piece of moss on the small hole in my forehead. The blood caused it to stick; it would work as temporary patch. Finally settling into the ground, I sighed and relaxed into the setting; turning my head very slowly, I didn't want to make any sudden moves; I needed to know what was happening to my left, my right, in front, behind, above, even below. I needed to be aware of everything that moved, crawled, flew, called out, breathed, farted, everything, if I wasn't alert then I would be dead, it was very simple. Similarly, I needed to blend into the landscape so that other animals and birds would not know that I was here and they would move in around me. They themselves would act unwittingly as my camouflage. If the dogs and men came near to me and scared a load of birds and animals, the men would assume that I wasn't there. They would think that if I had been sitting there, the birds and animals would have been scared away; at least that was my theory. A momentary feeling of panic arose from these thoughts; I took this feeling and channelled it into a positive. I gave myself a mental talking to; *Allow yourself to be scared so that you realise the seriousness of the situation, use that feeling to focus, to concentrate your mind, to focus your self, to channel your senses into protecting your world. This is **your** fucking space and if anyone comes into it, **they** are dead. Visualise the kill. Visualise the victory.* I repeated this to myself several times until I believed it.

Feeling calm and almost relaxed, I slowly moved my head round to check my bow and quiver, the bow was there but no quiver; I looked again just in case I was being stupid, I wasn't being stupid, I had lost it. "Shit!" It was the quietest curse ever, no quiver meant no arrows.

Chapter 7.

They were below me; not far away, I could hear the echoing of their barking dogs and the shouts of the men as they thought they had my trail, I was buggered. My mind was scrambling desperately for some idea of where I had dropped my quiver; it must have been when I was tangled up in that fucking honeysuckle. I could backtrack to that spot, but it meant that I would be walking towards the men, walking towards them with no arrows would not be a great idea, so I gave up on it. The fact that my quiver also contained my three lucky white swan feathers upset me even more so. I started looking around for somewhere to hide but I could see nothing. One option was to get down the slope and into the stream, then cross it and drop back past them, hoping that they would think I was still heading upstream on this side. The problem with that was that I would get wet and cold and if the dogs got my scent, I would be wet, cold and spotted. I was panicking and could think of nothing, I was going to get buggered sitting here with no weapon. Grabbing my antler deer head totem, I prayed to the Great Spirit.

Almost instantly, several red deer hinds burst out of the woodland down to my left, they had been disturbed by the dogs, they ran down through the boulders and into the gulley past the dogs and men. Of course, the dogs went berserk and chased off after them, all I could hear was, "Oy, come back, come back you bastards," followed by whistling, more cursing then more whistling. The voices began to fade away, off downstream; taking a deep breath I prayed to the Great Spirit once more, thanking her for saving me, and then set about working on a plan.

While the men were pissing about trying to get the dogs back, I got to work. Cautiously leaving the boulder field, constantly scanning about me in case someone was watching, I got into the dense scrub where it would be difficult for an arrow to hit me, just in case someone was around. Scouting about I was lucky to find a couple of guelder rose bushes, so I broke off several of the straightest stems, they were nice and stiff, ideal for my purposes. In the streambed, I could find nothing that would act as a single arrowhead, so using a flint blade from my pouch I simply shaved off thin slivers of wood until I had pointed the thicker bottom end of each guelder rose stem into a point. I then knapped off several small flint shards from the blade that I was using and set three of them in a line close to the point of these thicker bottom ends by sliding them backwards and forwards until they cut their own groove into the wood of the stem. Working some of my pine resin between my fingers until it had warmed and become tacky, I used it to stick the flint sliver in place. I had set the arrowheads at the thicker end of the stem because this is where the natural weight of the stem was, so the thinner lighter end would now hold the fletching.

While this type of sawing arrow was fine on a roe deer, I doubted its stopping power against a man who was wearing skin clothes and possibly a cape. I would have preferred my single-point arrowheads, but they were lying on the ground somewhere over on the far slope, and beggars can't be choosers. I reasoned that as long as I fired at close range to my target, the speed and force of the impact wouldn't do them any favours and I would just have to follow up fast after it.

At least now I had something that I could stab someone with, but to turn this stem with a few flint shards on it into a flying arrow, I needed to sort out the fletching. I am not the greatest arrow maker and people often comment on my crap fletching, my tribe are almost anally retentive about their fletching, whereas I couldn't be arsed. As long as it flew straight and where I intended that was all I was bothered about. I was great at creeping up on things, so as long as I had that quality, it put me into close contact with my prey; close contact meant a higher chance of a kill. I dare say that when I get old and stiff I might have to spend more time on my fletching because I will find it difficult to creep up on things when I am bent double and creaking. A wood pigeon carcass supplied me with the primary feathers from the wing, they were a bit short but would have to do, I was now ready to go to work. First job; turn these arrowhead-carrying stems into smooth shafts. Using a blade to scrape away the bark from the stems, I also planed out any knots or bumps until they were as clean and smooth as I could make them. Even though my hands were used to this kind of task, I was working with a sore left thumb, which made things more fiddly. This was a result of the bitten nail from a few days ago, I must have removed the nail right back to the quick and the unprotected skin on the end of my thumb had now split. It was red raw and throbbed away as I prepared the fletching. Cursing myself for being so stupid, I was annoyed at myself for damaging part of my natural tool kit.

I made sure that each shaft had three feathers for the fletching, and that each feather I used for a particular arrow came from the same wing. This maximised the stability of the arrow in flight as the feathers have a natural curve, which generates spin and drag. Using a sharp blade, I trimmed the feathers into oblongs as long as my forefinger then cut along the quill of the feather splitting it lengthways so that I had a base to hold against the arrow shaft. Holding the trimmed points of the quill against the shaft, I worked along the feathers, winding sinew through the feathers and around the shaft. Licking my fingers, I regularly ran them along the sinew before I made the next wind, when this damp sinew dried; it would tighten on the feathers, clamping them in place. I finished off by trapping the sinew underneath the previous loop three times. It was always a fiddly thing to do, even more so when you are expecting to be attacked by men and dogs at any moment, but I managed. Repeating this process with the remaining feathers and several more shafts, I stopped when I had made five arrows. The final thing was to brush each feather with my fingers so that they locked together as a feather should as it passed through the air. Despite it being a quick job, they looked alright, but I was not happy at the lack of arrowheads. Sure, a pointed stick with a few bits of flint on it flying at you is going to hurt you, but I wanted to maximise the stopping and killing power of my arrows. Deer didn't normally fire back or set their dogs on you, I was up against a quarry that would do both.

Then I remembered the sturgeon scale that I had found on the beach, taking it from my general odds and ends pouch I sat looking at it. It was hard and sharp. Scraping the pointed edge on a sandstone boulder until it was as sharp as I could get it without breaking it; I then cut a slit into the pointed base of the best arrow shaft and inserted the scale. After using another short piece of sinew to bind it tight to the shaft it was done; it was far from perfect but at least it looked like an arrow.

Chapter 8.

With my new arrows I looked for a kill site, we used kill sites all the time and we often made them. Every year we put a fast burning fire through areas of scrub woodland, this had four results; firstly, we used the regrowth of the thin withy branches of the scrub for basketry. Secondly, the grass or heather came back better for a few years until the scrub woodland got too thick again. Thirdly, deer and aurochs would graze the fresh growth of grass in these areas, and fourthly, we would kill them by firing from the cover of the remaining scrub woodland into these cleared areas in which they grazed. In a created glade the animals had no cover, they were unprotected and we had the advantage, it was our kill site and we killed them. I needed one now and I found one.

The valley at this point was only about 10 paces wide at the bottom with the stream running down the middle. This narrow corridor was the only way up the valley unless you scrambled around through the boulder field or the dense woodland on the other side, but those options were dodgy, after all I might be sitting in the boulder field or the dense woodland. It was unlikely that they would expect me to be lying out in the open, so that is exactly what I did.

I didn't see him, but I knew that he passed me only four or so paces away, he was good and he was quiet. I knew that he had passed me because I felt the length of honeysuckle move. I was lying with my back against a small rock and another larger one behind that for protection; I had strung a long piece of honeysuckle creeper across the ground and put it under my right knee. It was not there as a trip-line, it was as tight as possible but lay flat to the ground, so as soon as anything caught it or stood on it, it would pull my knee gently. I didn't move, I was covered in deer shit, soil and leaves, my face was plastered in mud, my hair was full of moss and leaves and my bow was by me with the five arrows lying next to it. My hands were in front of me pushed into the leaves. When I knew that he was in front of me, I opened my right eye very slowly, I was worried about his dog; if it smelled me, I was knackered. I was helped by the fact that when I had made my buckskin clothes I had smoked the skins using pieces of rotten birch; I was now lying amongst lots of rotting birch so my clothes already had that smell. I was also hoping that the deer shit that I had rubbed all over me would help to mask my own scent; I just hoped that the dog didn't like deer shit.

It passed by, nose up; there was lots of deer shit around so it wasn't interested in me. When the man was about six paces away from me, I lifted my head slightly, I let him walk on further, and at ten paces, I fired an arrow at his back, four arrows left. The plan was that he would spin round to face me and my scale arrow would already be flying at his heart. Good plan, wank first shot. I was so focussed on hitting him on the right side of his back that I hadn't counted on all of the honeysuckle hanging around. The first arrow must have touched several of the creepers just enough to send it off to the left, so instead of hitting him in the back it hit the ground. He didn't spin round to face me, instead he dropped to the ground rolled to the right and sat himself behind a rock, "Shit," I couldn't help my exclamation. Now for good measure the dog was roaring toward me like a wild thing. Grabbing an arrow that had flint slivers rather than the scale, fear gripped me and I focussed, aimed and hit the dog full on the chest. He went down howling in agony as the small blades sawed their way into him and his lungs collapsed, his howling subsided as blood coughed from his mouth only an arm length away. Three arrows left. The man was shouting to his mates, I had to stop him fast. I was up and firing an arrow at him to keep his head down, two arrows left. I moved three paces to my right, reloaded and fired, then moved three more, only one arrow left. My only advantage was my camouflage; I knew this because he was looking wildly and firing in the direction of the point of origin of the last arrow. Crouching among the undergrowth, out of the way of the arrows, I threw a rock well over to my left then moved forward two paces. He fired toward where the rock had fallen and shouted again exposing the left side of his head. As he did so, the world stopped. All that I could see, all that filled my vision, all that I was aware of, was that spot, I could almost see the scale arrow in his head before I had let it go. It was instinctive, almost as though now that I had imagined that it would happen, it would happen. I did not need to think... I saw, I was aware, I fired. The scale arrow hit him in the face with a loud smack, exactly where I had imagined that it would. He started screaming and shouting, holding his face. He was in no fit state to load his bow so I ran at him and jumped feet first at his head knocking him over onto his back, his kneeling legs crumpling beneath him.

Standing over his head, I could see that the arrow was sticking out of his left cheek, the shaft up between my legs. Pulling the arrow back out through his cheek I could see that the scale had made a right mess; he was struggling violently, lashing around with his left arm. I kicked down hard into his face with the heel of my right boot so that his head slammed back, then I pushed the arrow down into his left eye as far as it would go. As I pushed and wiggled the arrow shaft he screamed like that weird thing in the reedbed, then there was some cracking, loads of green and yellow snot flew out of his nose, then blood and he stopped screaming. I left the arrow in there, it was past re-use... he was still breathing and moaning quietly, not loud enough to attract his mates so I could have left him, but I wasn't happy about that. Despite the fact that this bastard had tried to kill me, I didn't like any living thing to suffer. So I made sure that he was dead by filling his mouth with soil and moss and pushed it into his throat as far as it would go... that stopped him. Then, grabbing his bow, quiver and pouches, I left him to rot into the woodland floor, like the piece of shit that he was.

Moving as quickly and as quietly as I could, I made sure that I was far enough downwind from the kill site so that my scent wouldn't carry to the dogs, I was breathing like a fish out of water, gasping for breath. It had been a long time since I was in a situation where someone was firing at me, so I was struggling to keep my emotions under control. I was happy... fucking delighted actually, that my plans had worked so far and I had now got rid of two of them, so I almost felt like laughing in relief. However, I was also scared of what might have happened. The first man that I had killed wasn't expecting anything, he was a standing target, whereas now the rest of them knew that I was here and I would find myself in increasingly dangerous situations, again I reminded myself that I needed to stay sharp, as sharp as a flint edge. This last kill had been a close thing and I had nearly fucked up, particularly with that first shot. I needed to focus and gather my thoughts. Despite his shouts, it appeared that his mates hadn't heard him, I heard no shouting and no barking so I believed that I was alone.

257

Dropping down to the stream, I gulped in water to rehydrate then let my left hand cool down in the stream before shaking off the excess water and placing it on the back of my neck. I did this several times, I was keen to cool down but I didn't want to wash the camouflage off my face. Looking into the clear cold water, remembering again that this river and all its water connected Golden Woman and me, it struck me that if I died on its surface and floated downstream, if I was lucky I might eventually wash up on the north bank of the Great North River, at her feet. Though it would be more likely that the scruffy shit bag would probably piss on me first.

When I felt a little calmer, I moved from the stream and headed up slowly back into the boulder field, finding a new spot in which to sit, just in case the other men had found my original hiding place and were waiting for me. Once I was happy that I was safe, I settled down into the landscape and decided that there would be no more killing today, at least by me. I would rest here and think about the remaining task, then do a kit check and try to get some sleep during the night. It looked as though after they had retrieved the dogs, the men had split up to cover a wider area. For the rest of the day I saw no one and heard nothing. This surprised me, I thought they may have stuck together when they came looking for me, it was to my advantage that they had split, I hoped that they would stay split. As the sun moved down behind the ridge and the darkness followed, I settled uneasily into my den, I would try to get some sleep during the night.

Chapter 9.

A blackbird woke me up; it was doing its aggravating alarm call. Normally I would tell it to shut up, the one that nested in the top of my house drove me to distraction, but here it meant trouble. Sure enough, one of the men was moving up through the boulder field, with a dog next to him. It was a long lanky looking bastard with big teeth and jowls that were slobbering. I didn't like the look of it and I made a very slow move to get my bow into firing position, though who I should fire at first was a problem, the man or the dog? He was a big man and he had a wolf skin cape over his shoulders, below him in the gulley I could hear another man shout that he had found a body, Wolf Cape looked about him, said something to the dog then both of them trekked off down to join the other in the gulley. Breathing a sigh of relief, I spent quite some time looking about me, checking that I was still alone among the boulders. When convinced I slipped out like a snake, crawling up through the boulder field, always checking and stopping regularly until I emerged at the top of the slope where I had good views of everything. This was a good position to be in, I knew that they were below me; I knew that they had to come out at some point, and if I could pick the best spot, I could catch them unawares. The man that I had killed in the gulley had eight arrows in his quiver, well made and tipped with single pieces of a mottled grey/white flint, a type I had not seen before. They were nothing fancy, just short pieces as long as my thumbnail, about as wide as my little finger, thin but strong and pointed. It looked as though he had nibbled at the cutting edges slightly, probably using an antler tine, to give the arrowhead a jagged almost toothed edge that would bite when it entered a body; it looked as though they could be very effective arrows, I hoped they were.

After some time where nothing was happening, I noticed that one of the men was moving rapidly up the opposite slope to me, on the south side of the stream, unfortunately the girl was walking just behind him. She was tied to a length of rope and every now and again, he would yank her toward him. The trouble was I still wasn't sure how many more men were left in the gulley, I had killed two and one was opposite me with the girl. At their camp, it seemed that there were five of them; if I was right then I had three more to kill at the most.

I got my answer as Wolf Cape and his mate emerged close together crouching low with bows in firing positions, two dogs by their side, all walking slowly towards me. They were over to my right, about 100 paces away. Suddenly, my spot was not such a good position, with these two together they would be a harder target to hit. Fire at one I might get lucky, but if his mate was next to him, I would most likely get an arrow straight back at me. Also, the fact that the girl and what I assumed was the head man were now on the other side of the gulley, meant that I had to go back down through the pissing boulder field, into the scrub, cross the stream then make my way up that slope and into a potential trap. How the fuck did I get into this?

I wondered why they were now coming my way; the only thing that I could think of was that they must have spotted my tracks. I didn't believe that they had just been lucky, perhaps the dogs were working my scent after all, whatever, I needed to do something, otherwise I would have arrows, fists, feet and dogs teeth to contend with. I had no option; I had to kill the dogs first. The men I could tackle, but not the dogs, they were big, powerful and used to hunting wolves; so they would show me no mercy. I didn't fancy being ripped apart by them while still alive, I wouldn't do that to another living creature, but I didn't feel good about killing them.

The time had come to act, moving down the slope quick and low, not wanting to give myself away but needing to make some headway, I stopped when I was about 30 paces from the scrub and stream at the bottom of the gulley. I stood, deliberately letting myself be seen. The result was immediate, the men pointed and shouted and the dogs set off. Over the rocks they charged, the rough terrain not bothering them at all and their long rangy legs ate up the ground; meanwhile the men picked their way through the boulder field after them. The men were still 90 or so paces away from me, much too far to shoot accurately and they would not want to waste any arrows either; there was no need when you had two big hungry dogs. They were closing on me fast, barking, growling, howling, I wasn't too happy about it and I was desperately trying to concentrate on where I put my feet, the last thing I wanted was to break my ankle and end up sitting here amongst the rocks waiting for the dogs and men to finish me off. The stump of an old ash tree stuck up through the boulders, it was about my height and was perfect as I climbed into it. The dogs were quickly at the base, going crazy at me, flashing a glance at the men I could see that they were now about 60 paces away, I needed to kill these two dogs now then bugger off sharpish. I couldn't let the men see where I was going, surprise was my only advantage. Loading the bow I fired straight into one of the dogs open mouths, it fell away writhing and yapping, it was no longer a threat. I tried the same with the other one and missed, the next arrow succeeded but I was now down to five arrows. Even though I knew that either of the dogs would have killed me it didn't console me, I didn't like to kill things that I wasn't going to eat. The men were a different proposition, I would kill them because they would kill me, kill or be killed was a simple enough problem to work out.

Checking where they were, I turned back to face the stream, jumped from the tree and legged it into the scrub.

Looking for the muddiest part of the stream bank I made for it and jumped across, digging my heels in on both the jump and landing sites to make the biggest most obvious track that I could. I ran up towards a decent sized badger track that went up the slope to the left, making some obvious signs that it was me, heel prints, broken branches, and bent some vegetation so that it pointed uphill. Then, jumping high and to the left as far as I could away from the track, I landed at least two paces down the slope away from the track, I then hopped from one leg to the other over the vegetation in as random a manner as I could back toward a small but noisy waterfall. If I had done it right, they would spot where I had crossed the stream, spot the tracks going to the badger track and the broken vegetation and in their haste would take off up the slope after me. Tucked in against the wet rocks, the noise of the waterfall masked my rustling and heavy breathing. One of the dogs was still whining and I felt real pity for it; it was only doing what it was trained for, still... I couldn't do much about it now.

Voices to my right, they were with the dogs, one of them cracked a rock down on the whining dog and ended its misery, I was thankful for that. I watched both men, now only about 30 paces away from me through the scrub. I would have no chance of hitting them because there were far too many branches, I had to be closer or they had to come toward me. They quickly found my crossing spot, I watched as they both hung around, sitting on their haunches with bows at the ready, staying low in the boulders in case I was waiting for them, they were planning.

Chapter 10.

A dipper started to walk up through the stream toward me, ducking under the water to feed. The thin sheen of water all over its head and back looked like a great bubble that was protecting it. As much as I liked to see them, I didn't want it to come too close because if it saw me it might fly off downstream calling its alarm, and they would know it had been scared off by something. This stream was so much cleaner than the one running from Wolf Edge; I could see small pebbles rolling along the bottom. I could also see the dipper as it moved beneath the water, the bird, it seemed, had become a fish. Right now, with these men so close to me, I needed to be like the dipper, I needed a protective bubble over and around me, particularly as they now split up and began to move.

The other man had dropped back downstream about ten paces, so he was now about 40 from me, while Wolf Cape man had walked toward me and was now only about seven paces away scaring the dipper away. My heart was thumping in my chest and I was breathing in short sharp bursts, trying as hard as I could to be quiet. A tiny black fly landed on my nose, which started to itch. There was no way that I could shift it so I put up with it, even though it was driving me crackers. Fortunately, it flew off and my concentration returned to the big man in the Wolf Cape, who was now moving to within five paces of me. Dry mouth, sweating, banging heart, short breath, I was not in control of the situation, waiting for him to either arrive in front of me or cross the stream. If he crossed the stream, I would gain control.

The man 40 paces away was first to jump the stream and he disappeared from my view, as Wolf Cape man brought his arms up and back as he started to jump, the cape lifted enough at the side to present me with a target, I shot him in the left side. He let out a cry, falling heavily into the stream, which was shallow and full of cobbles and boulders. Leaving my bow and quiver on the ground, I ran at him as fast as I could, not giving him chance to shout to his mate. I had no time to waste. As I splashed my way into the streambed, he had rolled on to his right side and was looking at the arrow in his left side just below his ribs, then up at me. He shifted onto his back and although he was half in the water and had an arrow in his side, he kicked up at me with his left foot. He was lucky, because as I was falling on top of him with my arms outstretched, his heel caught me solidly under the chin. The combination of my forward speed and his upper kick jarred my head back violently, cracking my neck. Falling on to my knees upstream of him, I experienced a moment of blackness, seeing stars and feeling faint. I had landed in a shallow pool and I struggled to get my head sorted. My vision came back but everything was still blurred and my head was pounding, blood in my mouth started dripping into the water, it was coming from the hole in my tongue, the result of the kick, my lower lip was already swelling. Then I was under the cold water as he pushed me forward and kneeled on me and punched me twice, hard in the back of my neck. I was out of it, head spinning, gagging for air, small stones flying around my face as my forehead hit the gravel and my nose crunched as it was pressed flat against the streambed, unable to breathe. Lungs burning, coughing the air from my lungs as the icy grip of the water made me gulp, I was about to drown and my stomach started to spasm, my teeth ground against a cobble, both my lips were punctured. I couldn't think of anything to do, other than just lie there in the gravel of the streambed getting punched and getting killed. My hands tried to push against the bed of the stream, trying to get me up for air but there was no way that I could lift both him and me. My left elbow ached as the tendon gave way and I dropped to the bed. Suddenly he stopped punching me… I could just make out his right hand scrambling next to my head for a round stone with which to finish me off. I was desperate; my lungs were bursting, my head was killing me, mouth full of blood, a broken front tooth, my brain freezing in the tumbling icy water, feeling as if it was being crushed. The noise of the rushing water filled my ears preventing any other sound, sand and grit was up my nostrils and in my eyes, something was sticking into my bollocks, and all this with a man kneeling on me holding me down in the water. I was about to die. Then, from nowhere, I reached back and up with my left hand, waving it wildly, and found what I was looking for. I yanked the arrow shaft from side to side, whatever way that I could and he fell back off me in pain. I was not prepared to die here, not here in this cold wet hole and so I pushed myself out of the water and though I could hardly stand, I turned to face him. He was on his knees in the pool, grimacing and holding his left side; it looked as though I had snapped the shaft from the arrow and widened the hole in his side at the same time. I needed to finish him now before he finished me but I didn't have the strength or energy and neither did he. We looked at each other, both gasping for air, pain on our faces, hearts banging in terror and anger, both of us bleeding into the water, saying nothing, both of us wondering how this would end… both of us wondering who was going to die.

It was important now not to show a weak side, not to show any vulnerability at all. If he saw weakness in my eyes, he would know that I feared death; he would know that I was scared. This worked both ways, if I saw any sign of fear in his eyes I would win. I knew it. Many years before, when I was a young man, we had been fighting in the camp fight; all the young men fought each other when they were old enough. I had made it to the final fight; we had both sat there exhausted, as now, facing each other. He had bitten my ear and broken my nose and I was bloodied and in pain. At that time, I had decided to be honest, to say to him that I was in pain, that I was scared, that the fight was pointless, and that we should stop and share the honour. He had listened impassively to my reasoning, but instead of seeing it as being an attempt at a mature way of solving something; he saw it as weakness, as vulnerability. He kicked my head in. Now, all these years later, it still made me feel weaker knowing that there was a man out there, somewhere, who had seen my fear, seen my weakness, knew of my vulnerability and even though we were both much older, he would still have that mental hold on me, wherever he was. Back to this moment, I needed to show this man no fear, no weakness, no vulnerability, instead I needed to find a reason to make me dislike him even more. To make him less of a man, to make him the only one here who was going to die.
This was the first time that we had been able to see each other face to face. Close up he was an ugly fucker, he had a short black beard and short black hair, and despite the fact that he had an arrow in his side, he seemed to have an arrogance that I disliked, he sat sneering at me, both hands on his thighs. He also had big ears that stuck out sideways, with ear lobes; I made use of them now as I moved at him and grabbed them, pulling as hard and as fast as I could. I forced his head forwards against my rising right knee and

smashed it into his sneering face. He dropped backwards onto his arse, but I lost my footing on the slippery round cobbles and fell to my left, back into the water, giving him the chance to sit upright. Managing to recover, I turned and lurched toward him again, this time I tried to punch him in the face with my right fist but it was a weak punch by a weak, wet, cold man and I missed. He simply leaned back and I fell onto him as I stumbled once more over the round cobbles of the stream. He grabbed my shoulders and nutted me on my right temple, it hurt like fuck, then he punched me in the left side of my face with his right hand, there was a crack as my upper tooth came out and I bit my cheek, he rolled me away with his left hand. I fell exhausted like a rotten tree, into a shallow riffle where I stayed on all fours facing the stones, like an old dog panting for air, waiting to die.

Of all the things that had happened in the short time that we had been fighting; the broken front tooth, the bleeding tongue, the loss of my upper left tooth, the bleeding cheek, the swollen lips, the near drowning and the throbbing temple, what pissed me off the most was that I had a lot of cold water down my neck. I really could not stand cold water down my neck and he was responsible for it. Pain burst through my knees as they crunched into the gravel as he resumed his attack, kicking down on my back, my wrists pushed forward into the gravel under the strain, my left elbow aching and sore. He was moving in for the kill and I needed to respond before he succeeded. He was bigger and stronger than I was and there was no way that I could beat him pound for pound, I needed to make a weapon. Kicking me again, I went down; catching the right side of my head on a big round cobble, next to this was an oval shaped yellow-brown rock about as big as a head. With what little strength I had remaining, I drew my knees under my chest, pushed up with my arms, and raised myself from the bed of the stream. I was now kneeling and bending forward. He moved in toward me as I picked up the oval shaped nugget firmly in both hands and struck it about a thumb knuckle length from its far end, against the far edge of the large round cobble. The far end of the oval nugget that I was holding immediately split away, to provide me with a perfectly fitting palm sized circular blade. Grabbing it, I held it in my right hand, the smooth oval exterior against the skin of my palm, exposing the circular cutting edge along the bottom of my hand. As he moved down toward me, I swung round and up to my left and with the last bit of power that I had left in my aching body, hit him across the neck in a slicing action. The circular blade made a neat cut and he dropped to his knees in shock, holding his hand against the point of contact. I had so much rage within me that I picked up the large end of the oval nugget and smashed it repeatedly into the left side of his head. Spitting my blood into his face with each exertion; gasping for air, wanting to shout at him and vent my anger, knowing that I couldn't for fear of bringing his mate here. Water and blood dripped from my bedraggled body, my left arm weak and in pain, my right arm cramping with a lack of energy as I cracked and crushed his bloodied skull before pushing him forward into the pool and sitting on him until he was full of water.

After taking time to catch my breath, I stood and stepped back from his body, then dragged myself to where I had left my bow and quiver in case his mate came back. I sat on the ground with my back to a large boulder, the roar of the water surrounding us. Only five paces away, the back of the man was out of the water, I saw steam rising from his neck and head, which were lifting and nodding in the flow. The steam rose into the air, or perhaps it was his spirit, rising from his body and returning to the Great Spirit. But that was unlikely, this man was not a decent man, and although he had done me a favour by getting rid of my bad tooth, his spirit would not go to the Great Spirit, his spirit and possibly my spirit for that matter, would bugger off to the land of monsters.

I thought about what had just happened, I had won because I had been lucky, a yellow-brown nugget of rock, solid, dense, unmoving, had provided me with what I had needed to kill him. He was a big man, bigger than I was, yet I had just beaten him. Dwelling on this, I had mixed feelings. On the one hand, I felt good that I had beaten him in a hand-to-hand fight, but on the other, I was concerned that if the remaining two were big men, they might eventually beat me. I would have to avoid these fistfights, if they were all big men it would take a lot out of me each time and I wasn't sure how much I had left to give. Then another thought popped in to my head, it was something that my father had said to me when I was young. "What matters is not the size of the dog that is fighting; it is the size of the fight in the dog." He was right.

As I sat there aching, hurting and shivering, the rage began to wear off and I began to feel ashamed of my actions. It occurred to me that the man in front of me lying face down in the stream would have someone out there who loved him. Yet no one would be able to tell them of his fate. Watching the steady red stream of blood wash away from him, I began to grieve that the pure waters of this stream would run into the river on which my tribe relied, and would take his blood all the way past the Nugget Family camp, into the waters of the Great North River and past the home of Golden Woman. That it would perhaps even wash up on the sand under her naked feet as she walked along the shoreline. This man's blood and my terrible actions here, tainting the skin of that beautiful Golden Woman all that distance away. I prayed to the Great Spirit, asking her to forgive me, praying that she would see that I had little choice here and asking that she would smile on me and look after me as I continued on this journey.

After I had taken his arrows and his wolf cape, I pushed him off downstream, watching his body wash up against the roots of an old ash tree, he lay there arms outstretched in a bloody tangled embrace. Above me, three ravens, possibly the ones that I had seen earlier with the eagles, were watching all my actions and looking at the fresh carcase. They flew into the topmost branches of the ash and began their planning, as I hobbled away to lick my wounds.

Chapter 11.

Back in the boulder field, I crawled into the shade of a gnarled hawthorn and drank as much water as I could manage. Eating some of the hawthorn leaves which were tough and not as tasty as in the spring and chewing on some of the berries, which were dry and pithy, perhaps because the tree was growing through the rocks and didn't have much water. The cuts that I had sustained stung and throbbed and I felt the worse for wear, in fact, I was knackered. My muscles ached and it seemed as though I had jarred my right elbow, perhaps when I was on my knees in the stream. Feeling around the elbow joint it was very tender, but I could still move my fingers, make a fist and grip, and that was the main thing, my left elbow ached like fuck, it felt useless. That fight had hurt me; my tongue was swelling and was painful where I had bit it, my cheek was raw, the broken tooth was aching, my lips were swollen and my left eye was sore. As for my head, it was pounding, as far as I could tell I hadn't broken my head, it just felt like I had, but as it slowly warmed up my brain started to work again. Removing some small pieces of grit from my nose and some crap from out of my right eye, I was a cold, sodden crumpled mess and I lay back exhausted on to the small patch of soft moss and though I tried hard not to, I fell asleep.

The heat woke me up, the sun was out and there were few clouds, so I was now fully exposed to the sun. My clothes had got a bit stiff after being in the water then in the sun, so I wriggled in them moving my shoulders, arms and legs so as to get the stretch back in them again, it didn't take much wriggling due to the smoking of the buckskin when I had made it.

Although I still ached in places, I felt better for the little sleep and started to focus my mind on the next task. It seemed as though the other man had followed the badger track quickly up the slope, in the direction that the man and the girl had taken. I guessed that when he and Wolf Cape were planning their action at the stream they had assumed that I had legged it up the slope after the man and girl. They had probably decided to split up and follow me up the slope while keeping their distance from each other so that if one of them surprised me I would run toward the other. If I was right then the other man was still climbing the slope toward the man and the girl. I felt as though I didn't have the energy to fight the remaining two men close up so I needed to be smarter. I knew the area better than they did so I should use that advantage, however, they were moving away from me so I had little choice in the matter, I would have to follow before they buggered off altogether. Filling my water bladder in the stream, I moved off up the slope 30 paces upstream of where I had killed Wolf Cape. I walked as slowly and as quietly as I could in a straight line up the slope, hoping that I was right and that the other man downstream was doing the same so that we were parallel to each other and wouldn't meet.

One of the problems of moving through a wood like this was that as I walked forward I would agitate birds as I entered their territories. The result of this was that they would make their alarm calls and fly off in front of me until they reached the edge of their territories at which point they would fly back around and behind me and continue to make their alarm calls until I had passed out of their territory. The trouble was that here several bird territories overlapped, so that try as I might to be quiet as I walked up the slope I was surrounded by alarm call after alarm call, with birds flying off in all directions. Another hunter would recognise this bird activity as indicating that a predator was around and if the other man was anywhere near, he would pick up on it. I just hoped that he was having the same trouble that I was.

I had reached the top of the slope as it was getting dark but I had sat in the edge of the scrub for a while, as I didn't want to go out onto the open heather moor. A few red deer were grazing and the birds in the wood had shut up for the night. I could see no sign of the other man; he was probably doing the same as me and lying up until dark, but I needed to press on after the man and the girl so I decided to make myself seen and draw him in. When it was dark I sat myself down on a flat outcrop of sandstone and got a fire going so that I was obvious, I then sat with my back to the direction that I expected him to come from, I was exposed and wasn't comfortable about that at all. However, my thinking was that he would expect to meet his mate at the top of the slope; his mate would be expecting him and might get a fire going, particularly if his mate had been successful in killing me. So I sat there waiting, with the wolf cape draped around me, hoping that he would just walk in thinking that I was his mate.

Shortly after I was thinking that he wasn't coming I heard rustling to my left, he said something to me then asked me a question. I knew that he was checking who I was but he was too far away for me to do anything; I had hidden my bow in case he recognised that it wasn't his mates, so I couldn't spin round and fire and for all I knew he might have an arrow trained on me right now. He moved nearer and asked me another question, I was reluctant to speak because I didn't know what his mate's voice sounded like, so I started to cough and pretend that I was choking. I had my water bladder in my left hand and pretended to take a hefty swig then pretended to choke again. "Hey mate, steady there or you will kill yourself choking," I put up my right thumb as a thank you for his advice and he moved closer. "Did you kill him?" he asked, I shook my head still choking, and gave an exaggerated shrug to suggest that I hadn't even seen him. I was now confident that he was thinking that I was his mate as he continued talking, "No... nor me, I lost him way back, I even backtracked to the stream and started again but I couldn't find him or his tracks." As he said this, I nearly crapped myself because if he had backtracked to the stream he might have seen the blood in the river and walked upstream to find his dead mate lying face down, hugging the roots of the ash tree. Perhaps he was toying with me, perhaps he had already found his dead mate and he was now standing behind me with an arrow about to go through my neck. "I think the bastard must have given us the slip, perhaps he has just gone on after the girl." He paused before carrying on, "I am fucking parched, have you any water left?" Throwing him my bladder without turning, he caught it, so I knew he wasn't about to fire an arrow. He took a swig then carried on talking, "And those fucking birds, all the way up through the fucking wood, cheep, cheep, fucking cheep for fuck's sake, what a fucking noise giving me away, fucking birds." I was about to make a move on him but was quickly glad that I hadn't. "Why didn't you crack on over to the one hill with the big rock face, I thought we were all supposed to be meeting up there?" I shrugged again and carried on choking,

"Do you know something, you are a miserable fucker, I can't get any words out of you at the best of times." He gave up talking to me and took another swig of water from the bladder; I glanced at him out of the very corner of my left eye. As he tilted his head back again to take another swig I stopped choking, stood up and twatted him around his head with a long heavy stick, the end of which I had been burning in the fire. He fell over backwards defenceless, so I pushed the burning stick down hard into his face setting fire to his beard and burning him badly. He couldn't scream out because I was now standing on his chest, pushing all the air from his lungs with my weight. When I was sure that I had buggered him up enough so that he wouldn't fight back, I moved the stick away from his face and used my right heel to kick his nose straight back into his head. My mind was in a dark place now, I was doing things that I had not experienced before and I was surprised at how easy this was now becoming for me. He was a problem and I was the solution; it was that simple. I also thought that the dark anger that I was now experiencing came from the fact that I was reluctant to be doing this in the first place. Although I had been on the wrong end of a bow and arrow years ago, I had escaped uninjured and I had never killed a man before, yet I had now killed four men in two days. I was so angry that I had been forced into this situation, angry that these men had created the situation in which I now found myself. Angry that instead of enjoying a new life with a beautiful person down on the coast, I was having a shit time in a dark place, on my own. Discovering a side of me that I never knew existed, experiencing things that I never thought would happen to me and doing things that I never thought I could. I wondered how I would live after this, if I didn't get killed. How would I go back to a normal existence knowing what I had done and seeing what I could do? My tribe, our elders, had drummed it into us that we did not kill other men, that when we had rages with other men, we walked away or we talked about it and always sought a peaceful way to deal with the rage. Yet here I was, killing four men with another man to go. What would that make me in the eyes of the tribe? How would my tribe treat me and what about Golden Woman, what would she make of me? If I did get back, I needed to seek advice from the elders on these questions so that I could go back to a normal life.

But for now, at this moment I was most angry at this piece of shit lying in front of me, I knew that he wouldn't have given a flying fuck about killing me, so right now I didn't give a flying fuck about him. Stealing his pouches, his belt, his bow and quiver, I dragged the unconscious heap onto the fire so that he could burn... I had run out of wood anyway.

I should have stayed awake in case the head man came after me, but I was totally knackered and couldn't give a toss, I felt so dirty by what I had done I almost welcomed death. Making sure that I was upwind of the stench of the flesh, I had fallen asleep under my new wolf cape, occasionally waking and drowsily listening to the sizzling, gurgling, popping sounds as he burnt.

Chapter 12.

When I woke, he had largely burnt away. The area stunk and I could taste his burnt flesh in my mouth and smell it in my nostrils. I felt like shit, I smelled of shit, and I was so tired that I could have collapsed right there. This tiredness was a fatigue, born of guilt, anger, lack of sleep and stress. Though I was a hunter, my prey didn't normally fight back and I was fucked, absolutely physically and mentally fucked. I had given up praying to the Great Spirit because I did not want to draw attention to myself. Kicking myself up the arse by muttering about focussing and finding them, I got myself going again.

I had decided that for this last bit of the journey I needed to travel as light as possible in order to catch up with the man and the girl, and to be as quick as I could over this open moorland. Taking a last big swig of water from my bladder, I spotted a hiding place for my kit. I found a nice wide nook at the base of a rowan tree, its branches were full of berries and it stood out on its own among the heather and bilberries, so it would be easy to spot when I came back this way. Opening up the wolf cape and laying it on the ground, I began to remove the things I didn't think I would need. I didn't look at what was in the stolen pouches, it didn't occur to me, I simply put them on the cape along with his belt, bow and quiver. On it went my wood bowl, food pouch, fire pouch, my fire bow, water bladder, camouflage pouch, blade pouch, odds and ends pouch, and that was that. All I had now was my buckskin trousers, buckskin shirt, rawhide belt, stiff boots, bow, quiver and arrows. Thinking about it for a moment, I took both spare bowstrings from the odds and ends pouch in case I needed them. Wrapping the kit in the wolf cape, I stuffed the bundle into the hole as best I could and set off onto the moorland carrying my bow in my left hand and my quiver in my right.

In places, the heather was as deep as my waist and was a ball ache to get through, yet in other places, it was taller but it had fallen over to create bare areas. Trying where possible to avoid these thick clumps in case the remaining man was sitting in there waiting for me, I still needed to leg it to get to the big rocks, hoping all along that he would be there and so would be the girl. Making my way by jogging where I could and walking when I had to, I made my way south-west toward the big rocks... sweating, panting, and knackered.

The final approach was up a long slope through tall heather and low scrub, this rough vegetation caught and snagged me as I walked, branches snatched my bow then my quiver from me and sent me into fits of rage and anger. I had to keep stopping to pick them up and orientate myself to the one hill with the big rock face; the place where I hoped this killing would end. The rest of the slope in front of me shimmered with webs; I was pleased that it was a good year for spiders because I could now see a clear track, it looked as though two large animals had walked through in single file, breaking them. The broken silks of the webs waved in the breeze highlighting the direction of the track, and I walked with confidence through them towards the summit.

It was true; there they were, on the top of the one hill with the big rock face, about 60 paces away from me. He was standing by the strangely shaped rocks right on the edge of the cliff face, the strong wind lifting his long grey hair. The girl was sitting down in the heather just to his right, her hands were bound, her legs were free, she wore a buckskin shirt and trousers, she looked ok, her hair was matted but she was intact. I waved to let her see me and held my hand to my mouth so that she would keep quiet, then ducked down again. I could see that he was holding a rock and was scraping it over the old pictures, randomly damaging them. I was surprised at his actions, it was not normal to do this, people didn't do that kind of thing, but then people didn't normally steal young women from other tribes and slice off a young man's face while he was still alive. I ran through a range of options, considering angles of attack, considering plans, wondering whether I should attack now, later, or tomorrow. It was only one man so part of me thought that I should just get on with it, but part of me also thought that I should relax and heal and sleep, reasoning that as I was now close to them I could stay near until the opportunity for action presented itself.

Sitting in the heather, I remembered the time when I had visited the deep caves a very long way to the south, it was hot down there; it had taken something like 4 or 5 cycles of the moon just to reach them. We had gone with others, travelling as a group, walking for four days and resting for two, we would walk as far as was comfortable in a day. To save time having to walk to narrow or shallow points when we got to rivers, my parents would trade for canoe rides where possible. My mother would play her bone flute and my father would sing; that seemed to be the going rate. However, where the rocks were soft and white there was a very wide river running east to west, so the adults clubbed together to trade for the crossing, they hired several skin on frame canoes and I can recall seeing the sea over to the right, to the west. I remember that when we did eventually get to the caves my parents seemed much moved by the images that were inside. These caves and rockshelters were along a winding river in a gorge, the paintings were already old when we had visited. That was why we didn't recognise some of the animals, but the keeper of the caves showed us round and explained that the big red animals with huge tusks were mammoths, they were impressive. There was a young woman working in one of the caves, she was touching up some of the paintings and adding others. I can remember that she was naked, had jet black hair, a lithe figure probably from all that reaching and stretching and had ochre all over her arms, face and tits where the paint kept dripping on her as she looked up, she was making a hand stencil of her left hand. What struck me most was that she was standing on a platform made from pine poles tied together with thick bands of willow cord. I think that I was a bit too young to appreciate all the pictures, but I did bring back a couple of pieces of antler that had a horse and a mammoth carved on them. We had once seen horses, far to the south of our lands when I was very young, some were black, some were brown and some were spotted, white skins with brown or grey spots, but we had never seen a mammoth. What happened to the carvings that I had bought back I had no idea; I must have lost them sometime when I was on the move. I had thought about returning to the caves but it was such a long walk, and it had taken us a year to get there and back, so that by the time we had returned many of my friends had gone off to other areas, so I was well pissed off. Also, someone from the south of my lands had told me that the flat land near to the white soft rocks with the big river running east to west, was now filling up with seawater. I didn't know whether to believe him but he seemed genuine. A few years later I had travelled to a nearer site, to the east of here, it had only taken about three or four days to walk there. The pictures were in caves in a little gorge overlooking a small river, but they were nothing like the ones far to the south. These nearer ones had been scratched into the walls of the cave and I could recognise some of the animals. There was a red deer stag and what looked to me to be a dodgy aurochs, it had a big hump on its back but it didn't look quite right somehow. Apart from a pretty well carved head of a curlew on the roof of the cave, there were some weird triangle shapes. But to be honest, I wasn't impressed and got the feeling that it was a poor version of the southern ones and that the man showing us the caves was trying to make a living from trading with people to look at them. It had cost me two arrows to get in; I felt it wasn't worth it. A while later I tried to engrave some antler myself, but it looked crap and the girl I made it for couldn't tell what it was supposed to be, she thought it was a salmon; it was the head of an elk for fucks sake.

He was shouting, probably asking where his mates were, it jerked me back to the situation in hand, he turned to the girl and said something, she shook her head. He laughed and started to undo his trousers, what was his plan? It was time to move. I began inching my way slowly forward because the heather was tough to move through without making a noise, I was also conscious that I could put up a meadow pipit or something. However, I had few options so on I went; fortunately, the wind was stiff enough to mask my noise so I was now within about 20 paces of him. I could see that he was taking a piss into the air, laughing as the wind splashed his piss across the ancient carvings; full of anger at this disrespect I knew that it was time to finish it. Taking an arrow from my quiver, I placed it to the receptive bowstring that seemed to be straining with the tension of the situation; I started to draw... then thought about this action. The strong wind could push the arrow to the right, if I got this wrong I could hit the girl instead and if I over compensated to the left I might miss him and forewarn him at the same time. I watched him, it was a long piss, but there was no cover for me to move into. I had no other option, I had to strike now and I did.

It was ironic that I had been sitting in the heather thinking of my method of attack, planning how I would execute my plans and so on, so I was expecting something a bit grander. Instead, it was simple. He was standing on the edge of the cliff pissing and laughing, so I ran up behind him, grabbed hold of the rocks to stop myself falling over and kicked him so hard up his arse that I thought I had broken my toes. With a surprised expression across his face, he was still holding his cock as he hit the rocks, way down below.

When I was sure that he wasn't going anywhere I dropped to the floor holding my right foot, "Bollocks, my fucking toes, shit, fuck." The girl was howling with laughter as she rolled from side to side, I sat looking at her. "What the fuck are you laughing at?" When she had finally calmed down, she started to talk. "That was great, what a kill, such a skilled hunt, you kicked him up his arse and he fell over the cliff, fantastic." I was too busy to reply; I had removed my right boot and was gently massaging my toes, grimacing as I did so. She sat there and carried on chuckling as I hobbled over and untied her, I changed the subject. "Are there any more of them, any of them hiding nearby, or waiting to meet up?" "No, just him and the other four bastards." "Hmm, I have met them already, so how are you then, did they treat you alright, did they do anything to you?" She looked solemn, "Like what?" "Did they"... pausing for a moment, I tried to think of how to phrase my question. "Did they, mess with you? Did they do things to you?" I was met with only blank looks as she sat there twiddling with some stalks of dry grass. She cocked her head to the left and frowned, "Mess with me?" I shuffled uneasily, embarrassed but impatient, "Yes, you are a woman now, not a girl anymore; a young woman and you are filling out and becoming attractive. You are ready to have children, which is prized and celebrated amongst most people, so... did they mess with you in that way?" Looking down at the floor for a moment she hid her face from me, causing me some concern and I waited for some disturbing news. "No, not at all, I think that they wanted to take me back to their tribal leader as an offering, to try to get back in with their tribe. I suppose that I would have been valuable to them. Me, deer and wolf skins, quite a gift for someone. No, they did not mess with me, you would not

278

mess with the main gift before you gave it to someone would you?" She was right. Smiling at her, I extended my right arm holding out my hand, taking it she allowed me to help her to her feet. "You know, when I was travelling through the Great Plain, I met a young woman similar to you." I told her about Ochre Girl and her skills with the skins, she listened intently as I talked of trading camps and travel. "Can you take me to the camp?" "Ask your family to take you; they owe you a treat after what you have gone through." "I will," she said.

Standing side by side at the top of the cliff, we looked at the smashed form of the headman lying on his back on the rocks below, moulded to the sandstone, his arms and legs at strange angles, a ring ouzel sat near to him chirping away at the unwanted visitor. Images of the other men, their injuries and bodies, now flashed through my mind. I looked at her and saw that she was crying. The wind was blowing her tears from her hazel eyes back toward her lobe-less ears, her long brown matted hair moving only slightly despite the stiff breeze. Putting my right arm around her shoulders, I led her away from the view. "I was planning to escape, but you did it for me." I suspected that there was a certain amount of show in her comment, nevertheless I asked her about her escape plan. "I was going to poison them; I was going to give it a while then start to offer to make the food. I had collected some death cap in the woods a few days ago when they let me have a wee… that was my plan." "Good plan, I can see that you probably didn't need me then." She shook her head, talking through the tears, "What and miss that arse kicking, no way."

We wandered back along the ridge I was absolutely wrecked. It had only been something like seven days since I had left the camp but I was exhausted from all the concentrating while I was tracking, stressed because I had kept on expecting to get an arrow in the back at any moment and I was buggered up from all the fighting. I had also become a very different man from the one who had set out and right now I didn't know what to make of it all. I hadn't wanted to become a killer of men yet it seemed as though I had found a skill at last. I didn't know whether to feel pleased about that or upset, I would ask the elders to help me to sort that out. On top of everything, I hadn't eaten properly for two days so I was starving. Perhaps Golden Woman was right about being sharper for not eating, I didn't know, and right now I didn't care.

We arrived back at the rowan where I drank and drank from the bladder before offering the girl any, I hadn't left her much but I reckoned that I needed it far more than she did. There was no need to retrace the huge loop that I had made when I was slowly tracking the men; now they were dead we could just bugger off home, travelling as normal across the moor and through the scrub woodland, instead of skulking around in the vegetation as I had been for the last seven days. We simply followed a small stream north then north-west across the wide gentle valley, this stream would get us onto our river and that would lead us back home.

As we walked we chatted about what had happened to both of us, it seemed that we were both keen to discuss the details with someone else, to get it off our chests, to get rid of it. I didn't really know her from camp, up till recently she had been a child but now she was clearly a young woman, she was alright. We managed to make it down the stream and joined the river where it ran south-west, I was still hobbling because the toes on my right foot were killing me and the bruising in the arch seemed worse. Deciding that as the sun was setting we would make camp at a good spot and get a fire going rather than walking through the night, we stopped amongst the trees close to the water. She borrowed my fire kit and I left her to it while I limped off to collect food and fill the water bladder.

Cupping my hands, I drank from the river, my river, our river, then splashed the water onto my face and arms to clean away the crap and camouflage, concerned that I might be drinking the blood of Wolf Cape man that would still be flowing down the river. Running my wet fingers through my hair, I looked into the clear swirling water and a sudden wave of emotions flowed from me. Breathing in deeply then sighing out slowly, I let all the bad energy that had built up within me over the last few days leave my body. I held off breathing in for as long as I could so that I didn't breathe the bad energy back in again. When my lungs were about to burst and I was happy that the bad energy had floated away on the breeze I breathed in slow and deep. Holding that new energy in my lungs, I started to weep. Fuck knows what I was weeping for, I am not a Shaman, but I think that it was relief; I was relieved that I was still alive, that the shit was over and that I could now bugger off back to the coast and stay out of trouble. Looking at the water flowing past me from right to left, I bellowed as loud as I could, getting rid of all the air. Filling my lungs, I bellowed repeatedly, as loud as I could, my body shaking with the shout, ears rattling, head hurting, till I had no strength left in me.

I don't know how long I had sat there bellowing but when I was exhausted, I splashed more cold water on my face to wash away the tears then got on with getting food. From the river edge amongst the rocks and hollows, I was able to get four crayfish; from an old stump I collected some yellow mushrooms, and from the floor, I found bilberries, cowberries and some leaves of cuckooflower and bistort in the wet areas, then some sorrel on the drier bank. On my way back to the fire, I gathered some hazelnuts. "Nice fire girl, I will cook, you relax." Throwing the crayfish into the ashes I watched them move a bit at first then they started to pop and hiss; I had an image of the man on the fire and shook my head to rid myself of it. Spreading out two of the bistort leaves as plates I then divided out the berries and the other leaves, I held the other two bistort leaves over the flames to wilt and add a smoky flavour to them. I prefer my hazelnuts to be roasted and warm; I assumed that she did too so I laid them in the ashes at the very edge of the fire. She threw some twigs of bog myrtle on to the fire, the scented leaves spat at first as the oil burnt but they produced a lovely smelling smoke that seemed to keep the midges away. Wrestling with my boots, they almost steamed as I released my feet into the fresh air; the stink was nearly as bad as Shitbags seal sick. I put the boots away from me downwind and pushed my feet into the cool damp leaves of the woodland floor, the cool tickling caused me to sigh in pleasure, easing the ache in my right arch and helping me to relax a bit more. When the crayfish were done I gave her two and I had two, then I rolled the nuts away from the ashes. Putting my ear close to them I could hear them gently sizzling from the heat, cracking them open I divided them between us their sweet smell was wonderful. The fire crackled, we ate and drank without speaking, we were both knackered and both of us had had a bad few days.

Chapter 13.

I awoke with a start, it was early and it was drizzling and quite cool. She had let me sleep under the wolf cape so I was warm and dry but she was sitting by the fire shivering and wet. She had been busy; the fire was hot, there was a hare on a spit over it, I could see that she had stuffed its gut with more leaves of bog myrtle. Water was being heated in my little wooden bowl in which pine needles were infusing. I stood, stretched and yawned, "Good morning, you have been busy, when did you do all this?" "What was that?" she asked. I stopped yawning, "I said… good morning, you have been busy, when did you do all this?" Mirroring my stretching she replied, "I couldn't sleep at all so I kept the fire in and borrowed one of your blades, I hope you don't mind. I collected some willow bast and made a snare, I set it on that track over by the hazel and I thought that we could have a warm drink. It was the least that I could do considering your efforts to save me." I thanked her and gave her my new wolf cape to keep her warm, then hobbled off for a crap; my foot was sore and still hurting.

Back at the fire, she gave me three white swan feathers, "Where did you get these from? Was there a quiver with them?" She shrugged, "No, no quiver, just three feathers, they were in a glade over there," she pointed into the distance.

The smoked meat of the hare tasted excellent, the myrtle leaves had infused it with a sweet taste and lovely scent, the pine needle tea cleaned the grease from my mouth, I had three new white lucky feathers from somewhere and I had enjoyed a proper solid crap, overall it was a decent start to the day.

What a contrast between the tracking days, even with my knackered toes we got back to camp well before the sun was at its highest. It seemed as though everyone was there to greet her as we walked in, whooping and cheering and hugging her, she was the centre of attention so I left her to it and slumped off to my house where I collapsed face down in a stinking pile on my bed.

The persistent knocking at the door eventually woke me up and I stared through the gloom as it was opened and in came Beautiful Eyes, she was crying. "You are such a brave man, she has told us of what you did and what you experienced, you must not feel bad about what you have done, the fact that the Great Spirit has brought you back to us safely must mean that she smiles on you and forgives you." I smiled at her, "Thanks, I hope so." She sat with me and made me a bowl of mint tea, talking to me all the while, frequently touching my right arm gently with her left hand, my friend, my good friend. After she had gone, I looked about me and realised that someone had changed my bedding for me, the house was neat and tidy, the roof was properly repaired, it was clear that they had expected me to return.

Another knock on the door, this time an elder came in; he was old with long white hair, the skin of his face was tough like rawhide, thick and red from the sun and wind, his features engrained with lines and life, his grey eyes looked into mine. "You will come with me now to the main campfire; the elders need to talk to you. He stretched out his right hand and shook mine, "You have done well son."

All five elders were sitting in the main house around the campfire; I was shitting myself. I was here to be talked to; as far as I knew, they might tell me that I was now an outcast because of what I had done. Though that wouldn't be very fair considering that it was they who had sent me in the first place. I was about to speak but the man with white hair held up his right hand to stop me. "It is alright, you have no explanation to make if you do not wish to, the girl told us everything, she may have made some things up like the arse kick over the cliff, but we believe most of it. As we understand it, there were five men and they had dogs, you killed them all, you spared none. It is wrong to kill other men, you know this and we have spent all your life telling you this… so how do you feel about killing them?" I was stunned really, I didn't know what to say, I sat on my arse on a log and stared at the softly glowing fire, I tried to speak. "I feel like I am a very different man from the one who went out from this camp… I feel that I am, so tired… so very tired and I do not know what to think or say." I shuffled uneasily and then one of the women spoke. "Perhaps I can help you…tell us son, tell us what you truly feel, we are all alone in here, no one else will know what is said in here, it is between you and us and this is your time to let go of the pain. It is your time to let the man who did those things go away, time to regain the man who you were, the man you are. Please tell us." Swallowing dryly, heavily, I began to let go, slowly at first, I told them my story while they listened patiently. "In the end I wanted death to come to me, I did things so brutally and with such anger that I did not recognise myself... I went into a dark place where it seemed as though I could do anything to them; it makes me ashamed to talk about it." She urged me to tell them exactly what had happened, every single gory detail, I felt dirty and foul as I described what had happened, becoming more and more ashamed of myself with everything that I revealed. Every now and again I would stop, only to be prompted by her into continuing, never once did I raise my eyes from the fire, I didn't want to see the disgust in their eyes. By the time I got to describing how I dragged the unconscious man onto the fire and slept as he burned next to me, I was openly sobbing, trembling, my words spitting out of my mouth as tears flooded down my face onto the dusty floor, wetting a woodlouse that was wandering past. My head dropped towards my lap as I let go of the pain, crying between the words. "How can I have done those things? How can I... how can I live now knowing what I did to those men... what will the Great Spirit make of me now... and how can I look my woman in the eyes and feel happy?"

A hand was placed very softly upon my right shoulder, it was the woman. "Cry as much as you want son, there are not enough tears in the world to cry for what you have done, but you must cry and you must let the pain go." Kneeling down next to me, she spoke softly, "Many years ago my man and I were out on the Great Plain hunting elk, we met a lone young hunter and he stayed with us for a few days, sharing skills and stories, he became a friend to us and we grew to like him. However, one day my man, who was much older than I was, was taken sick and he had to stay in the shelter to recover, the young hunter and I went off to collect roots from the marsh. When I was bending over, the hunter threw me to the ground face down and lay on top of me, forcing me down into the earth, trying to rape me. He was a strong man and he was holding me down with his weight as he sought to pull my skirt aside. I could not shout for help because my face was in the shallow water and I could not breathe… I knew then that he had no intention of me staying alive after this… he would be content for me to drown, he just wanted me for his pleasure and that was that. I thought of my poor man sitting alone and unwell in the shelter, unaware of what was happening to me, trusting this young hunter with my company. I thought of this young hunter, just leaving me dead in the water and my man wandering around in the marsh calling for me and receiving no reply. I thought of my man returning home to the tribe without me and having no explanation for why I was not with him. Worst of all, I thought of how the man that I loved with all my heart, would simply assume that I had run away with the young hunter, it would break my man's heart if he thought that I had left him and it broke my heart to think of this. Fortunately, the Great Spirit is a woman and she must have decided that this was not the fate for me; so she sent a small brown bird to help me, a water rail; it walked out behind him and called. Now the call of a water rail sounds like a young boar screaming in pain and it caused the man to lift himself off me and turn, surprised that there was a boar behind him. In my right hand was my sharp flint knife that I was using to cut roots and I kneeled then turned as fast as I was able and stuck it in his face as many times as I could. Then the Great Spirit sent me such strength, anger and rage that I stood in front of this kneeling man and stabbed and cut the main blood flow in his neck… I watched him as he died… kneeling there in front of me. To this day, I am ashamed to say it, but as he died, holding his neck with his left hand his blood running through his fingers and his face becoming as pale as a winter moon, I gave him no sympathy. I spat at him and swore at him in my rage telling him that the Great Spirit would fuck him off for what he had tried to do to me, that worms and leeches would eat him in this marsh and that no one would care. His young face looked up at me, pained, scared and sad, but I cared not and I watched as he slumped to his right and his spirit left him in a great sigh. I washed my hands and face in the water and sank to my knees to pray to the Great Spirit, begging for forgiveness for the terrible deed that I had just committed, wailing that this should have happened and feeling such guilt that I had taken this young man's life when he hadn't actually raped me… I can assure you that my grief was great. Suddenly through the marsh came my man and he ran toward me and joined me kneeling on the ground, I broke down utterly as I told him what had happened, he had come looking for me because he was concerned for my safety and had heard the wailing. Holding my head against his chest, he thought for a while before saying that if the man had not attacked me I would not have had to defend myself. He told me that the fact that I was still alive might show that the Great Spirit had already judged the situation and had found the young man guilty and me innocent, and that was why he was dead and that was why I was alive. I sat and thought about what my man had just said and I recognised that he was a wise man and I knew that I was a lucky woman to be with him. Even so, I was uncertain whether he was right because no one can speak on behalf of the Great Spirit and I knew that this was just his way of seeing things and trying to make me feel better. But, at the very moment that I thought of this, a beautiful pale butterfly with the tail of a swallow flew past us, we had never seen one before and I have never seen one since. I knew then that this was a message from the Great Spirit, telling us that it was all right and that sometimes we have to do things that we are not happy about and that sometimes others force us to act in ways that we would not normally act. My man died many years ago and my loss was... is great, but I believe in what he said and I believe that you should think on this. The reason that we the elders tell everyone that it is wrong to kill other men is because I know just how much it hurts in here... even if you know that you are right to do it." She was pointing to her heart as she finished. Despite her words, I was struggling with all of this, shaking my head, shaking the words away. "I hear what you are saying, I do... but it doesn't make me feel any better, not at all, not at all. I was killing as easily as I can snap my fingers; I was killing as though it was easy, as though it did not matter." She cut in, "You had," pausing, she was thinking of something to convince me. "If a bear attacked us, what would you do?" "What has that got to do with it?" "Just answer the question." "If a bear attacked us, I would attack the bear." She nodded, "Right, and would you kill it?" She was urgent, pushing me for an answer, "If I had to, of course." She jumped in, "Yes of course you would, if you had to, of course you would, so what is the difference? You would kill if you had to, yes?" Now I nodded, "Yes, if I had to." "Well... you had to, you had to, just like I had to all those years ago,

286

do you hear me, do you hear what I am saying? You had no choice in your actions, you saw what they did to one of the brothers and they left the other to die, these were not men to reason with, they would have killed you and left you in the same way that you killed them. Like me and the water rail, the deer saved you when you were in the boulder field, that I am sure was the work of the Great Spirit, she looked after you." Lifting my head with her right hand, she gestured to the rest of the elders who were all gently smiling at me. "We all think that the Great Spirit thinks highly of you. We have often thought that she favoured you; we have watched you grow and you have always been such a happy boy and man. It is of course difficult for us to imagine how the Great Spirit thinks, but we elders have lived for a long time and have had many experiences and together we carry within us the knowledge of our ancestors and all the stories of our world. We think that the fact that you were successful and returned with only a broken tooth means that the Great Spirit wants you to be with your woman and enjoy your life." Breaking off, she offered me a bowl of tea that one of the elders had been brewing, taking it I took a sip; not recognising the flavour at all. Then she rose from her knees and sat beside me on the log, I looked into her deep dark eyes, it seemed as though the entire world was within them. She whispered so that only I could hear, "Listen to me... even if you have heard nothing of what I have been saying so far. The men acted without a thought of the consequences, they killed one of our young men, they stole one of our young women, they had no thoughts of us and you treated them in the way that they treated us. They were wrong and they brought it upon themselves. The women who were away collecting tinder fungus have spoken to flint traders from the south-east, these traders told them that the men who stole our young woman were outcasts from a tribe about ten days walk to the east of here. The flint traders had met the men and had at first thought that they were alright, until they woke one morning to find that one of them had been murdered and robbed of a grey flint, probably the same flint that the men were using in their arrows, the arrows that you described. So these five men were outcasts as well as murderers and thieves, they would not have been cast out from their tribe unless they were bad men. You did a good deed for everyone, our tribe and the flint traders, so you should be proud of yourself." Pausing again, she could see that I was still not responding in the manner that she had hoped. "Listen, how you choose to live with it is up to you, but be sure that you know that everyone here loves you all the more for what you did and the tribe will never forget your deeds. We will talk about your strength and courage forever. Now, you can either forget about it, dwell on it, or accept that the Great Spirit gave you a challenge because you were the best person for the task and that the Great Spirit watched over you throughout your task. If I were you, I would thank the Great Spirit for her love and protection and accept that you were the right person. If your woman at the coast is a good woman she will care nothing for what you did, she will just be happy that you have returned. Remember, we are always here for you, you are never on your own, if you ever have dark thoughts just come to meet with us and we will tell you again of our great pride in you and our great love for you… you are a good man." I could see that she was looking for something to add, "We never know how long the Great Spirit will let us stay here among the living, and we never know how much time we have on earth. At times, we find things difficult, we find life difficult, we slog on trying our best to live. Making sure that we are safe for winter, making sure that we are ready for spring, making sure we are ready all the time. Yet every now and again, in between the slog of living, we get a glimpse of pure joy or pure love. The skill in living is to recognise when these lovely events happen and to make sure that you enjoy them to the full. Now… go and enjoy yourself."

Back in my house, I sat quietly on my own my, mind spinning, thinking of what she had said to me. Though the image of the gently smiling faces of the elders was comforting, I still felt tired to my soul and I was not happy about things. I felt as though I was in the dark and wanting to find the light of the door, but there was no doubt that I felt a damn sight better than I did earlier. Plus, I had finally found out what had made that awful noise that night in the reedbed.

I got some sleep, still in all my stinking shitty clothes and still with my pouches on my belt, face down, uncomfortable yet comfortable at the same time. The noise was still outside, people being active about something, I just kept dozing off, in and out of sleep. Beautiful Eyes woke me up by shaking my right leg and whispering, "Hey, hey, it's time to sort yourself out now, your bath is ready." Shaking myself awake, I sat up and faced her, looking at her through bleary eyes. Kneeling next to me, she suddenly launched herself at me, hugging me tight like a limpet to a rock, and I hugged her back. We held each other for some time, this woman, close together, the woman who I would be with if only we knew who her father was.

This time the sweathouse was being used as a bath. The depression in the ground was lined with two large skins that had been double stitched together and sealed with pine resin and beeswax along the stitches on the underside of the seam, the side to the cool ground. Into this large skin bowl had been poured almost as much water as it could hold and then hot rocks had been added to get it quite hot. Finally, crushed pine needles had been added to the water and a load of crushed chickweed was on the side ready for me to use as soap. The youngsters had been sorting the bath out while the parents were busy sorting out the feast; I could see them, dipping their elbows in the water to test how hot it was. Once I was in the water, they placed the dome over me so I was able to lie back and let the aches and pains of my body and mind be taken away. It felt wonderful, much nicer than a quick warm shower under a hide bag suspended from a tree. A hand came in through the flap with a bowl of hot valerian root tea, I thanked whoever it was and drank it slowly, it was sweetened with honey to help hide the earthy taste, I dozed off for ages.

A sudden rush of cold air woke me and I was surrounded by giggling children as they lifted the dome from me. Beautiful Eyes was standing amongst them looking down at me as I blinked in the sunlight, "Your meal is almost ready, you have been in the water for a long time and you are beginning to wrinkle... some parts more than others." Covering my wrinkled parts I clambered out of the bath, she had collected handfuls of dried moss and while she gently patted my back and buttocks dry, I patted my front. As she patted me dry, she picked the deer ticks from my back, pinching them out between her nails, being careful not to leave the head still stuck in my skin. She helped me to dress and then walked with me back to my house; three children had stripped off and were already making the most of the bath. Pausing before I went inside she got something off her chest. "I think that we both know that but for fate we would be together, the fact remains that we might be brother and sister, so we cannot be together just in case. But I want you to know that you are the man that I have always loved and will always love, and though it pains me to say it; I wish that you find love and happiness with your new partner." Tears were in her beautiful eyes as she turned her head down towards the earth. I needed to respond. Taking both her hands in mine, I did so; "We have loved each other ever since we knew what love was; you are with me whenever and wherever I go. If we are sister and brother then we are right to feel love for each other and we are right not to take that love further. If we are not sister and brother, then I have never felt such love for someone as I have for you and I cry that we couldn't take it further. I believe that the Great Spirit is not punishing us for something that our fathers may or may not have done; I believe that she is showing us that we can experience love in many forms. In my mind, I have a face for the Great Spirit; it makes it easier to pray to her if I can see a face upon her… I want you to know… that the face that I see, whenever I pray for safety, for comfort and for protection… is yours and yours alone." We hugged, and cried, and kissed each other on the cheek.

The party in the main campfire house had already started by the time that I had changed into clean clothes, well, cleaner clothes; I wandered over to join them. All the instruments were out; three flutes made from the hollow leg bone of a red deer, the holes had been drilled using a small flint tipped hand drill and beeswax had been used to stop up and shape the mouthpiece. A big rawhide drum an arm length across and stretched over and stitched to a hoop of rowan bark that had been peeled away in one piece, this was held in shape by an inner hoop of hazel. There were three smaller drum skins stretched over three wooden bowls of descending size. A wide bow that had several lengths of plied deer gut for strings and a sound box made of birch bark attached to the bow half way down. Even some of the kids were bashing away on a range of bones and logs in between clapping and stamping. While the rest of the kids danced awkwardly in the shadows, not under the influence of fermented drinks they were shy of their movements in front of the adults. In fact, it seemed as though everyone was singing and dancing. I was absolutely starving and as this party was being held in my honour, I had first choice of everything. Taking my time, I savoured the food on offer. Roast boar, not one of ours of course, basted in honey with thick crispy crackling and hot crabapple sauce. After I had filled up with meat and fat, I ate roast acorn and thyme flatbreads, with a side dish of roast hazelnuts, roast burdock root and heated mushrooms. A mix of various greens was followed by late season blackberries, bilberries and cowberries mixed with honey, as for the drinks; there was fermented crabapple juice which had been watered down but was still incredibly sour and potent. The youngsters were egging each other on to drink it. Their was also fermented elderberry juice which had been watered down and sweetened with honey and a fermented honey and water mix which was a bit thick but which always had excellent sleep inducing properties. For the kids, there were unfermented juices and water, though once the adults were all out of it on the alcoholic stuff, the kids started to experiment.

Sitting there amongst the din of the singing and the dancing and the music, I let it wash over me like a great wave of joy. Apart from getting up to go for a piss, I don't think I moved from my seat, I just sat there watching as people enjoyed each other's company. I hadn't experienced this sensation for a while because I had grown to associate the camp with negative thoughts, my partner had died in childbirth here so I didn't want to be here. But sitting here now, I realised that it wasn't the camp that was at fault, it was my attitude, there was nothing here that was negative, far from it in fact, it was a camp that was full of laughter, of love and life. Breathing deeply, I drew the smell of the camp into my lungs and into my self. Realising that I was surrounded by a safe familiarity, a familiarity of place, a familiarity of time and place. This is where my people were from, this is where I was from and no matter how far I travelled, this was my home, and the people here were my family. A huge smile spread across my face and I started to laugh at it all, a great sigh of relief, of love for... everything and everyone.

As the light of the fire grew against the dark of the night, I saw across the flames the young woman that I had rescued sitting next to the elder woman who had spoken to me so candidly earlier. They were smiling at me and both nodded at me as they clapped along to the songs, I had tears of joy in my eyes as I nodded back.

Much later, when the party had finished I was in my house enjoying the feeling of total relaxation. I could hear snoring, farting, burping and giggles as some of the kids watched others who had experimented with fermented alcoholic drinks, stagger around being sick.

The day dawned bright and warm, the swallows had gone for the winter to follow the sun and many of the leaves were turning from green to yellow and red, like the ochre colours on the inside of Golden Woman's house. Having no need to tidy up, because someone had already done that for me, I was happy that my house was ready for winter. It might be that I would be back soon, but it could be that I would spend the winter at the coast, so now everything was in order before I left. As I shut the door I half expected the mice and bats to be lining up to go back in. Looking around the camp, I could see that the elders were making the kids tidy up the mess from the party and clear up any sick, giving them all a bollocking as their parents slept off their excesses in their houses.

Down at the river I packed my few things into the canoe, it was still in good shape and I patted it in affection, it had brought me far and it would carry me further. I thought about the journey back and wondered if I could leg it past the Nugget camp at night so that I didn't have to see them again and end up talking about transoms and crap like that. My brother joined me, "So, you are off then?" I turned to meet him, "Yes brother, I am off," "To the coast?" "Yes, to the coast." He looked at the canoe, "Nice canoe, what is the skin?" "Seal," "Ah, seal, I have never seen a seal, what are they like?" "They are like... big men of the sea, they have faces like a dog and hands almost like ours and they sit in the water and watch us." He shook his head in amazement, "I would like to see a seal," "You will brother, if you come to visit me at the coast." We stood silently for a while listening to the water rippling against the canoe and the gravel. I broke the silence, "Can you remember when we fished this river as children; we would stay out all day, almost till dark, trying to catch more fish than each other. The elders blamed us for taking all the fish from the river, we would catch that many." He laughed, "Yes, of course I remember, good times." "Yes very good times… either I will return by the next moon or more likely in the spring, depending on what happens with the woman at the coast. Then we will go fishing, we will tell the women to go off to gather birch sap and take the kids with them and we will catch every fish in the river and get told off by the elders." Laughing again he said, "You are a confident man if you think that you can tell the women to go off and take the kids with them," this time I laughed, "Alright, we will ask them nicely." I needed to share something with him, something that I felt I had learned throughout my journey, "Brother, did you know that some people have ear lobes? Fleshy bits of skin, at the bottom of their ears, unlike us." He felt at the base of his ears, "Really?" I nodded in reply, "Yes really." "What are they for, do they help them to hear better?" I shook my head, "Fuck knows, but now I've noticed them I can't stop looking for them." We shook hands and embraced, patting each other on the back, then stood facing each other, both of us puffing out air through pursed lips, sad to be saying goodbye. "You know that what you did was remarkable, I am ashamed that I didn't come with you, but the elders were adamant that it should be you, I." I held up my hand to stop him, "It's done, it's done, they had their reasons, they had their justifications, they wanted me to go, I went, I was successful, I returned, therefore they must have been right, mustn't they?" "I suppose so, I suppose so." He cast his gaze around the river; I could see that he was upset. "Look, I am here, the girl is back, the only loss was the young lad who was killed by the men. In the great cycle of life it is but a small turn, we are here, and with the blessing of the Great Spirit we will always be here, our camp, in this place in the woods, by the river, always." He looked at me with tears in his blue eyes, "Be strong, be brave, be sensible," he said, "I will, and you," I replied as he smiled.

I stepped into the canoe and kissed it, kneeling into position I checked again that all my gear was with me and turned to face him. "Just in case I did want to visit, where are you staying?" "Just follow the rivers all the way down to the sea, we are on the north side of the very mouth of the Great North River, by a small river. You can't miss it, and anyway the Nugget Twins will direct you, you can be sure of that, if I am still there after the next moon come and visit us." "I might just do that… take care brother," I waved back, "Will do brother, and you," and with that, I felt into the canoe with my knees then used the paddle to push myself gently into the flow and I was off.

I knew that this was the right decision, I fancied a change of scenery over winter and the house by the shore was beautiful; it was full of life and resources. Besides, I needed to get away from the shit that I had just been through. The other thing was that she could teach me many things that I didn't know, all those coastal skills appealed to me and who knows, perhaps there were things that I could teach her, though on second thoughts, I shook my head realising that I couldn't teach her anything. The canoe building would be good, that would be good to learn and after all, I needed to get a skill seeing that I didn't have any. I guessed that with the flow of the river behind me I could easily be there in four days. I thought about my possible stopping points for the journey, the idea of being back in that camp with her was very appealing. Four days should be fine, four days, I would be with her, four days and I would be walking barefoot on the warm sand. My mind went back to that wonderful honeysuckle embrace that evening on the sand, when we held each other tight and realised our love for each other. Gliding over the gravel beds, I could see many salmon beneath me, some with lampreys attached to their sides. The salmon were charging around making redds and hurriedly spawning in a frenzy, the water was white in places with the milt from the males. They had completed their long journey upriver and were now fulfilling the purpose of that journey by frantically breeding. I thought about this for a moment, and then started to paddle quicker; I reckoned that if I paddled during all of the daylight, I could do it in three days.

Printed in Great Britain
by Amazon

42671417R00167